# Rhizome

# Rhizome

## A Novel 

James M. Wright

Metamorphic Press

To Susan T. Landry for more than can be reckoned, especially for the use of her poems, "The Invention of Poetry" and "The Sisters."

To the stalwart members of the Casco Bay Writers' Group, for listening to page after page while remaining generously alert.

To Sampsa, who stands with and within the forest.

# 1

# SEVERANCE

*Life has always seemed to me like a plant that lives on its rhizome. Its true life is invisible, hidden in the rhizome. The part that appears above ground lasts only a single summer. Then it withers away—an ephemeral apparition. When we think of the unending growth and decay of life and civilizations, we cannot escape the impression of absolute nullity. Yet I have never lost a sense of something that lives and endures underneath the eternal flux. What we see is the blossom, which passes. The rhizome remains.*
C. G. Jung, *Memories, Dreams, Reflections*

[1]

It happened when he was eight years old, up against the white ash tree. His uncle said it was the right thing to do. It was Owen's first time out in the woods hunting with a real gun and although his mother had her misgivings, the uncle said: "it's time he learned." And that was that. He had no father to agree or disagree and his ever-exhausted mother leaned on her brother's advice, thinking that he was a man and a man would know how to make a man out of a boy. He knew many things, the uncle did, but he didn't know that.

Uncle Caleb was a frequent visitor to the dilapidated home that Owen shared with his mother, Isadora Black. The only survivors of a mysterious family tragedy, Caleb and Isadora referred to their history with vague allusions but otherwise left it buried in silence. The name of his father was never mentioned, despite Owen's persistent questions, and Isadora deflected every conversational turn that required an inspection of the past. "Nothin' to be done about it," she said and changed the subject to dinner or the endless chores.

Isadora farmed a few acres tucked away in the woods of Downeast Maine, a region of convoluted coastline and dense forest. The farm was a legacy passed through several generations of Blacks. Not a prosperous venture, but it provided. Owen helped around the farm and did what his mother needed him to do. Whenever he could escape the chores, he ran into the woods, first to play, then to explore, and finally to learn. Inside the hollows of partly rotted trunks, he found the best places to hide. His wedged his wiry body into the duff-filled crevices, molding his form to the tree, pretending to be a knot within the grain. Motionless, he absorbed the sounds and vibrations in the wood as the wind swept through the branches, the creaks and groans of the resilient arbors, the skittering echoes of mammals racing over the bark. In exchange for these disclosures, he whispered back the secrets of his life.

Shy by nature, Owen kept to himself and was spurned by his peers. Uncle Caleb tried to coach him in a proper response to the cruelty of boys, summed up with drunken advice like "knock 'em down—they get up—knock 'em down again." Owen ignored the advice. Instead, he floated. He got light in the head and the world slipped away, no matter what was going on. It worked every time.

"Owen, you pay attention, now!" Caleb hissed at him, dropping to a crouch and creeping forward through the trees, waving at him to fall in behind. Apparently, there was something ahead. Owen sensed nothing. Several times earlier in the day Caleb had done the same thing, all the while slinking through the hardwood forest with a pretense at stalking, but with the snapping of twigs and undisguised rhythms of human motion, no animals had been seen and no shots fired. Owen wasn't sure what they were supposed to be hunting. Rabbits, maybe, or turkeys. He knew they were too noisy to sneak up on anything. Caleb was drunk, having taken more than a few drags off the pint stashed in his jacket pocket. He packed a .357 magnum revolver, which he claimed was "dead accurate" because he was such a good shot. Before leaving the truck this morning, Caleb had smiled in rapture as he loaded the gun, handling each bullet with ritual precision, sliding the gun into its holster and patting it with affection.

"This is a man's weapon, boy, you'll see."

Owen carried a .22 rifle that he had fired at a few targets but, for the most part, it scared him. He carried it gingerly, as if it might turn on him.

Caleb stopped, straightened, and took a drink. "Son of a fucking bitch!" Another false alarm. The swearing was getting more frequent. Owen didn't know what to think—his uncle was clearly in a bad mood. Maybe it was Owen's fault.

"Aw, fuck it." Caleb set off with resolve, striding through the trees without looking back. Owen was a dutiful boy and ran to keep up. He didn't like it when his uncle got in these moods, he was unpredictable and rough. Owen knew better than to make things worse than they were—there was no way he wanted to get hit or even yelled at. He didn't whine—he just followed.

They soon came to an opening in the woods. A white ash tree reigned over the clearing, broad and tall, neatly centered amidst the browning grasses of fall. It was an inviting spot, serene in a way unattainable within the darker woods. His uncle charged across the clearing and stopped at the trunk of the ash, stroking its furrowed bark, lost in thought.

"Owen, come over here and feel this." His tone was definitive, but his voice cracked. "Right here, boy, press yourself up against the trunk just like you're huggin' your mama. Go ahead, it won't bite." He stepped back and used his hands to urge Owen's body into greater contact, pushing him into the tree. It hurt a little, but he didn't resist.

"That's right, just like that, relax and melt into that hard, old tree. Feel that power, boy, soak up the strength in that wood. That's right, you've got it, don't worry now. Just give in to it, let it pull you in, it's the right thing to do, oh yes...."

Caleb's hands were too full of touch and Owen felt a twinge of panic, but he knew better than to disobey. He closed his eyes and floated his thoughts toward the tree. Maybe he could go inside, like his uncle said, see what rested within the mighty being, just leave his body and go right through the rough bark. Something stirred outside the normal range of consciousness. Something... deep. Owen pushed his thoughts beyond the flesh, reaching for the tree's mind, hoping he could sense it there within the arboreal indifference.

Owen drove his focus into the tree. When Uncle Caleb pulled down his pants, Owen neither flinched nor shivered as his bottom was exposed to the crisp air and the caresses of the man's gnarly hands. He didn't want to think about his uncle's probing. He wanted to merge with the ancient tree that beckoned to him. It offered a bridge to the freedom of the sun and sky and nothing was more important. As he leaned into the trunk, he heard a faint humming, a harmony in the deep tones of the earth, a music that played the tree like an instrument. The music called to him, he felt its draw, and as he flattened his ear against the bark, it surged into his head, taking him out of time and place, pulling his awareness into the shelter of the tree. Now he belonged. He didn't even hear the thump of his uncle's gun belt as it hit the ground.

[2]

In the years following Owen's first encounter with the ash tree, his uncle used him ruthlessly, spending his sharp pleasure into Owen's body, admonishing him never to tell anyone, least of all his mother, rewarding him with gifts as he kept silent. Owen honed the skills for leaving his body, sending his mind into other places while his uncle harried the flesh. His mother didn't know, or, if she did, she said nothing. When she wasn't distracted, she was sweet to Owen and lenient, but what he really wanted was her protection. Instead, the shame filled him with sickness. Owen thought everyone could read the taint on his face, but it seemed that no one did, and the violence continued.

As he aged, he spent less time hiding in the woods and learned to flee his circumstances in books. Reading was a reliable escape, giving him alternate worlds to inhabit, a place where he could dwell for hours at a time. In most of these worlds there were rules and punishments for transgressions, and even though dire events persisted, there were heroes who guarded the weak and avenged the wrongs. His mother approved of the reading, hoping that it would make him smart and successful, but she paid little attention to the library books that streamed in and out of the house. The fantastic narratives that appealed to Owen represented an impenetrable puzzle to his mother, whose notion of reading never left the province of magazines from the grocery store rack. She knew that he read books, grown-up books, and that was enough for her.

As Owen grew, working on the farm made his body hard. He became a large, sturdy boy strong enough to throw bales of hay or shovel for hours. His insecure postures and hesitant gestures were only contradicted by the glint in his eyes, blazing out beneath a mop of dark brown hair. He turned an awkward thirteen, trying to contain the jumble of his desires. Part of that project involved seeding dormant fields of anger. His uncle's predations grew less frequent, perhaps because he sensed that Owen was slipping beyond his control. But after another night of solitary drinking in their kitchen, long after his mother had taken her pills and gone to bed, his uncle crept into his room. Caleb tried for stealth, but his drunken breathing was loud, and his steps were heavy. This time Owen was ready. As Caleb lifted the covers, Owen grabbed his baseball bat and went at him, swinging wildly and screaming like a demon. Nightgown flapping, his mother raced in, snapping on the light to find her brother on the floor, bloody and crushed. Alive, but broken.

Uncle Caleb went to the hospital and never again visited the farmhouse. Life went on with Owen and his mother, just the two of them. Nothing was ever said about the incident. It was as if it never happened. Owen didn't want to bring it up out of fear that even a mention of his uncle's name would conjure his presence.

At first, he was relieved and thought that things would change. But they didn't, not in a way that brightened Owen's life. No matter how he tried, he couldn't contain his agitation. Even if the threat was gone, peace eluded him. Alert, constantly scanning the surroundings, he reacted to anything that put him on edge. Often, he over-reacted, yelling at people because they entered a room behind his back, occasionally throwing a punch before he knew what was happening. When he got going, he was hard to calm down. He had little control over himself and his life began to resemble a roller-coaster of despondency and out-burst. In high school, he obsessed over sex. He had no idea how to approach girls: he longed for them and desperately wanted to be touched, but he was too withdrawn and too anxious for so-cial success. He also felt aroused around boys and wondered if he was gay, but it was far too frightening a thought to entertain for long. So, he hid in his room at home and masturbated furiously, driving his lust into dark fantasies until he felt, once again, his mind slip from its bonds and drift away. As if perched on a dis-tant throne, he would watch his body pumping its way toward spasmodic release, a pathetic beast wearing its flesh down to the bone.

Things changed one day when his mother came into his room to find him naked on the bed, stroking himself with one hand while the other pulled a belt tight around his neck. She exploded in screams and cries and awkwardly tried to hold and hug him and gather him up like a baby, but he was too big for that. Failing a motherly embrace, she held his head between her hands and kissed his forehead repeatedly while bathing his face with tears.

Soon after this episode, he started seeing a psychotherapist in Machias, the only nearby town that offered such a service. There were few practitioners to choose from, but his mother selected Dr. Helen Chouinard, maybe because she found the old French name less threatening than the other options, all so clearly from away. Indeed, Dr. Chouinard had grown up in Lewiston, passed most of her adult years in New York City, and had recently moved back to Maine. In Machias she found a sleepy town, broken down with the burdens of the past. The residents were preoccupied with trying to scratch out an income from fishing, logging, or working the blueberry fields and didn't have a lot of time for reflection. This suited her purposes, because Dr. Chouinard was coming to the end of her working days, and the natural beauty and quiet of Downeast Maine was a balm for all the years of toil in the urban psyche. The town provided an extension of the state university and an adjunct position that gave the doctor all the financial stability she needed. Her weatherworn house sat on a quiet back street and had an extension that she converted into an office where she saw a few patients, just enough to keep her hand in the rhythms of a life's work.

Isadora Black had no background to evaluate the credentials, but Helen Chouinard was a doctor, she taught at the university, and that sounded respectable. Also, she had openings and could see Owen right away. Most importantly, she was a woman and Isadora didn't trust men, not anymore.

Owen balked at meeting Dr. Chouinard. He grumbled about the time wasted driving ten miles to town from their farm in the hills near Cutler, but his protests were half-hearted. Inside, he was more curious than resentful. A part of him craved an honest connection with another person, something he had foregone when he was forced to seal himself into the cave of his own thoughts in order to survive his uncle. But Owen wasn't sure what to expect from therapy. All he knew was what other kids talked about, those that had to go see a "shrink," who scoffed about how they lied and manipulated their therapists, recruiting them as allies against their parents, against the world. Owen had the impression that none of these kids got much out of their time. It seemed like a game that had to be played. He was anxious about joining these unconvincing peers in a futile pursuit, but he would play. Anyway, his mother hadn't given him a choice. He was so ashamed by her reaction to his masturbation that he felt obligated to follow her wishes.

When he entered Dr. Chouinard's office, he walked into a room of surrealistic novelties. It was a mosaic of colors and shapes, busy with complex imagery. Blankets, possibly Indian, softened the walls. He saw paintings of things he'd never imagined: bones, unreal animals, circles filled with lurid geometry, landscapes unseen on earth, and faceless figures stretched into thin and grotesque distortions of posture. Here and there were masks with exaggerated features, adorned with feathers and fur. And everywhere in between there were books. Shelves and shelves of books. It was a madhouse. But then, he thought, of course it was a madhouse.

Dr. Chouinard was a short, plump woman with gray hair and a round face that looked like the moon. She wore a loose robe of brown and black, draped with an indigo scarf. Her wrists were heavy with silver bracelets. On the inside of her left forearm he could see a tattoo of a circular maze. She beamed at him as she walked over, offering her hand. He shook it, limply, and did not know what to say.

"I'm Helen Chouinard. You can call me Dr. Chouinard, if you don't mind. If you do mind, well, we can discuss alternatives. What would you like me to call you?"

"Uhhh, Owen, I guess. That's my name." He barked a sharp, nervous laugh, then looked down and blushed.

Dr. Chouinard ignored his awkwardness and pointed at an enormous couch. "You're welcome to sit on the couch, but, really, you can sit anywhere you like, on the floor, even. I usually sit in this chair," she pointed at a plush leather office chair, "but you can sit in that if you prefer. Or, you know, if you want, you can stand. Or lie down. I don't have rules about things like that. Just make yourself comfortable. Or at least as comfortable as you can be, given that you've just walked into the office of someone you don't know and who is likely to ask you things you don't want to answer." She shared a mischievous smile as she waited for Owen to choose a spot, then flopped on her chair when he gingerly eased himself on to the couch. Clearly Dr. Chouinard was nuts, thought Owen, and he liked that about her.

[3]

Dr. Chouinard sat with a solid calm that was unknown to Owen. Relaxed and quiet in her body, she radiated strength that defied her stillness. Owen wanted to crawl up on her lap and lay his head on her breasts. He stared at her even though he worried that she could read his thoughts, then he squirmed around on the couch and wondered what would happen next.

"Owen, do you have any questions for me? You can ask anything you like; I don't mind. I can't promise to answer everything, but I'll always explain why."

"Uh, no, no, I don't think so. Well, yes, actually. The sign on your door says 'Jungian analyst.' What does that mean?" Owen was careful to pronounce the "J" as a consonant.

"Ha, excellent question! You know, people walk through that door and you'd be surprised how many don't ask. Well done, Owen." Her voice reminded him of the sound of a brook in the woods and he wanted more. "Look, I'll give you the short answer for now, but later, if you're interested, there is a long answer. One of the early psychologists was a Swiss fellow named Carl Jung. It's a Germanic name, so the 'j' is spoken like a 'y.' Jung thought that humans were connected to each other and to the world on a level that we aren't aware of most of the time. We do know that level contains the stuff of myths, dreams, and creativity. Jung called it the unconscious and worked to bring it into awareness, into the light of day. And that's what I do. I help open the doors to the unconscious."

"Wow. Sounds heavy."

"It can be. But it's amazing work. Think of it like surfing the tides of the imagination, catching the waves as they roll out of the deepest, dark corners of the psyche." Dr. Chouinard moved from her chair with graceful speed, bracelets clinking, and spread her arms and legs to assume a wave-riding pose. Owen thought of one of his favorite comic book characters, the Silver Surfer.

"Psyche?"

"Ah, yes, that's a word we use to cover all the complex layers of mind. It's an old Greek word that means *soul*. There's also a myth... Are you interested in myths, Owen?"

"You mean like King Arthur and stuff? I don't know much about it."

"Exactly like King Arthur. But myths are everywhere. Humans can't stop making myths. Comic book characters are mythic, like Batman or Spiderman or even Wile E. Coyote – they embody personalities that are larger than life. Real people act out myths, too, using life as a theater for the psyche. Sports figures and entertainers, people like LeBron James or Beyoncé—these folks get caught up in their myths. The thing is—they don't really know it—it's as if the myth is acting through them. There's a power in that, but it's not always a good thing."

Owen, intrigued by what she was saying, blurted out, "You know, Dr. Chouinard, it's funny you say that because a minute ago I had a flash that *you* were the Silver Surfer! A comic book character... in case you don't know." As soon as he said this, he blushed, thinking he should have kept his mouth shut.

Dr. Chouinard beamed at him. "Oh, I know the Silver Surfer. A very, very interesting character, an embodiment of Hermes, one of the most important myths ever told. Owen, I'm taking that as a major compliment! Wouldn't you just love to be able to glide through the universe like that? What an image! Thank you."

Owen felt so much warmth emanating from the doctor that he wanted to melt into her. He'd only been in her office for half an hour, but he was already enamored. He hadn't felt this good in a long time.

"So, Owen, let me explain what I do not do. I do not spend our valuable time together teaching you tricks to control your breathing, or tricks to control your thoughts, or tricks to help you get your emotions under control. I'm not against such things and if you're interested in them, I can give you stuff to read on your own to learn those tricks. They are simple and easy to teach yourself; you don't need me for that. I also don't spend time interrogating you about your past or your problems. We all have pasts and problems and most of them aren't pretty. I assume yours aren't, either. If you want to tell me about these things, I welcome your words and I'll listen for as long as you need, but I will not probe."

"Then what are we going to do?"

"We're going to explore the dark realms of the psyche, Owen. The places no one wants to go, the places where demons dwell. I'll be your guide so that you don't get lost down there. We'll invite the demons out into the light of day, we'll tease out their myths, and we'll learn what wisdom they have to teach us."

Owen thought this was a weird thing to say. It gave him instant chills and he felt the hairs on his neck stand up. He didn't understand what was happening and he felt an urge to panic, but as he looked into Dr. Chouinard's eyes, he saw reassurance. From under his tumbled thoughts emerged a spark of hope.

The doctor looked at him with concern. "You look like you've seen a ghost."

Owen shook his head and came back to the present. "I don't know what to say about your thing. It sounds a little crazy, you know."

Dr. Chouinard laughed, and for no reason he could identify he thought about the sound of wind in the pines. "That's exactly what it is, Owen. Crazy. But I think you'll be alright. You might even like it."

"Okay. I'll give it a try, though I'm still not sure what we'll do."

"Well, we're nearly out of time today so I can't show you much. We'll do different things, but nothing without your consent, so please don't worry that I'll make you do something you don't want to do. That will never happen. If you can accept a little suspense, let's leave it at that for now. I do have a thought about how you might get started on your own, though. Do you read for fun, Owen?"

"Yeah, sure. Quite a bit, actually."

"What kinds of things do you read?"

"Mostly science fiction and fantasy."

"Perfect. Do you have any favorites? I'm a big Harry Potter fan. An old myth, really old, in completely new trappings."

"Yeah, I read those. They were pretty good."

"How about *Lord of the Rings*? I love that book. It's a straight mythic salad, not even dressed up or modernized, just served up as pure as ancient light."

"Well, I saw the movies. And I played the video game."

"Ah, of course there's a video game. You might try reading the book sometime. Hard to imagine that you wouldn't like it. But for now, I'm going to give you a book to take with you. You don't have to bring it back until you're done with it. It might be a little tough reading in places. But what I would like you to do is thumb through it, look at the pictures, read any text you wish. Don't get bogged down and don't plow through it. At least not on my account. Just sample it, back and forth, let it trickle into your head in whatever way feels right to you. You could take notes on how it affects you, if you want. When you come back next week, we can go over any reactions you wish to share. But no expectations. This isn't a school assignment, there's nothing to complete. Do as little or as much as you wish. Are you game?"

"Sure. Thanks, Dr. Chouinard. I...." but Owen didn't have the confidence to put his thoughts into words and he settled for saying "I'm glad I came here."

"I am, too, Owen."

Dr. Chouinard handed Owen a large hardbound book. It was tan in color, without a dustjacket, and imprinted on the cover was a golden impression of a design like the one he saw tattooed on the doctor's arm. He looked at the spine: *Man and his Symbols* by Carl G. Jung. The book was heavy and felt serious in his hand. He pointed at the image on the cover and asked, "What's this?"

"That is a labyrinth, a symbol for the path to the unconscious. More metaphor than map. Sort of magical, don't you think?"

"Yes. Like your tattoo."

"Not exactly. But yes, the same idea." and she held out her arm to display the design, turning it back and forth under their gaze. "This is the classic labyrinth, the symbolic form that's been passed on for thousands of years. Kind of looks like a thumbprint, doesn't it? I keep it on my skin as a constant reminder of the path of life and where it leads."

"What do you mean? Where does it lead?"

"To death, Owen, to death." She studied his grave expression with one of her own, then suddenly, like a meteor flashing across the sky, she winked. "But before then, vast riches!"

[4]

On the way home from the first meeting with Dr. Chouinard, his mother asked about the session and he bristled against her curiosity. Deflecting her interrogation with one-word responses, he finally exploded, yelling that he didn't want to talk about it. Chastised, Isadora dropped her queries. For Owen there was something pure about what happened in that room and he wanted to keep it that way. So, he put a wall around it.

When he got home, he went to his room, closed the door, and opened the book with the labyrinth on the cover. Following Dr. Chouinard's recommendation, he flipped through the pages, looked at the plentiful pictures, read some captions, and skipped around the book with no direction. His head swam with the imagery. It was strange material, ancient and modern, religious and explicit, a dizzying assembly of cultural fragments. He stopped on one page and stared for half an hour at the array of pictures: a naked woman betraying Samson; a boxer and his trainer in a corner of the ring; prisoners of war in Stalingrad; a painting of a centaur from a Greek vase; and Superman flying off with a prim Lois Lane in his arms. All were supposed to illustrate a point he didn't understand about heroes. The images were frequently disturbing, but he couldn't stop looking at them. If he turned his own head inside out and dumped everything on the floor in a crazy tangle, it would look like that, he supposed. He returned to the beginning, seeking an order to the riot. What he saw was a full-page photo of the entrance to the tomb of Rameses III. Decorated walls retreated from the camera eye through deepening shadow into total darkness. He couldn't stop staring at the blackness in the center of the picture. "Approaching the unconscious," it said on the facing page. He felt a wave of vertigo and snapped the book shut.

True to her word, Dr. Chouinard did not pry into Owen's history nor did she offer a panacea for his problems. Instead, they listened to music or talked while he made artwork under the doctor's gentle coaching: ink and pencil drawings, paintings, plaster masks, free-form constructions, whatever crossed her mind or drew his curiosity. These exercises started shortly after he walked in the door for the second session.

"Owen," she said, with a smile that made him feel weak, "would you be willing to draw a picture for me?"

"Sure, I guess. I don't know how to draw. Stick figures, that's about it," and Owen started to fret.

"Stick figures are best, I think. No worries about proportion or anything so fussy. I'm not asking you to draw me down the moon. Very few of us are skilled artists, but all of us can doodle. I just want to start you working with the images sleeping inside you. Speaking of images, what did you think of the book?" Dr. Chouinard handed him a tablet of drawing paper and a small box of colored pencils.

"Weird. Really weird. But I kinda like it. I didn't bring it back, sorry. I forgot."

"That's okay. Like I said last week, I think you should keep it for as long as you wish. In fact, you don't have to bring it back at all. As long as you're getting something out of it."

"Great, thanks." Owen fiddled with the colored pencils. "What should I draw?"

"Well, what kind of mood are you in today?"

"Mood?"

"Yes, happy, sad, mad, afraid, nervous... that kind of thing."

"Umm, I dunno. Sad, I guess."

"So, draw me a sad picture."

Owen stared at the blank paper as if waiting for it to create its own art. He chewed his lip and fidgeted. Tentatively, he started to draw. He had been reading a fantasy novel by Robert E. Howard, one of the Conan series, and he was captivated by the lusty violence of the main character, an untidy hero whose ambivalent motivations reflected his own. Despite that, Conan had raw physical power and a determination that was a beacon to Owen. He drew a large stick figure with an enormous sword. The sword was beheading two stick figures on their knees. The heads were shown flying off, leaving a spray of droplets colored red. He looked at the drawing and thought it was childish and disturbed, but he handed it to Dr. Chouinard.

"Okay," she said, "this is truly sad. Such violence is tragic, both for the victim and the perpetrator. But there is also power here, and maybe some anger." She pointed to the crude expression on the swordsman's face, which did, indeed, look angry.

"Yeah. Sorry, it's dumb. I don't know how to do it." He felt mortified at the depth of attention the doctor gave to his scribble.

"No, please don't say that. I asked you to do something a little uncomfortable and you did it. I respect your effort. And, sure, this won't make it to the art museum any time soon, but it's a meaningful image of something inside of you."

"It is?"

"Yes. Do you know the story of Orestes? No? Then let me tell you a bit," and Dr. Chouinard settled into a rhapsody of storytelling. The tale of Orestes was intense, and Owen felt the blood drain from his face when she came to the part where Orestes beheaded his own mother out of rage for the death of his father. By the time Dr. Chouinard drew her summary to a close, Owen had plunged into a realm somewhere between the adventures of Conan and the ancient deeds of the Greeks. He looked up at Dr. Chouinard, into her eyes, and she regarded him with a look of compassion. He soaked up her gaze and realized that something was happening to him, something for which he had no reference.

As they continued to meet and weeks turned into months, Dr. Chouinard regaled him with many mythic tales, an activity that delighted them both. She was a story machine, seemingly knowing every plot ever devised. He didn't always get her point in telling a story, but he listened and let himself float away on the tides of language.

Within and around all the myths and art, they also talked about Owen's life. His shyness dissipated and he talked to Dr. Chouinard with experimental honesty. He didn't know that there were so many words inside him waiting to crawl out. Dr. Chouinard encouraged all of it, his talking, his fumbling artwork, and his youthful attempts to understand her complex way of seeing the world. He wrote down his dreams and brought them to her. No matter how embarrassing they were, whether silly, depraved, or frightening, she did not make Owen feel guilty about them. She welcomed everything without judgment. For Owen, this was enough to make it valuable.

Owen ventured down the path of healing. By the time he graduated from high school he had grown taller, thinned out enough to define his well-worked muscles and the sharp features of his face. His ears were too big, but he had a classic nose and many thought him a handsome young man, especially when they looked into his green eyes. It had been two years since he started working with the doctor. He still slept poorly, his appetite was erratic, he was nervous most of the time, and he startled like a rabbit in the bush. But no longer did he lash out in sudden fury or sit by himself in a moody sulk. He learned to recognize the currents of mythology running through his life, from the transgressions of Eros to the fury of Orestes. Naming these passions gave him a chance to influence them, or at least to recognize their appearance in his daily moods and look for ways to let them speak to him without trying to shove them back into the closet of his untidy mind. This was where the endless sketching came in handy: so much better to draw himself as Orestes, lopping off the heads of relatives, rather than descend into a dark passion that shredded the kind intentions of everyone in reach.

Dr. Chouinard planted a seed within him that grew into a thicket of mythology. After high school, he enrolled in the local university branch, using literature studies as a framework for his explorations of myth. This allowed him to stay on the farm and do most of the chores, work that was becoming more difficult for his ageing mother. She was happy to watch Owen develop some enthusiasms, and she was pleased that he stayed with her because she felt very tired. She was damaged, exhausted by the Sisyphean task of reconciling family circumstances. When she learned that cancer had invaded her flesh, she chose not to fight but welcomed the chance to pass out of this world. She didn't tell Owen about the sickness because she didn't want him insisting on treatment. She didn't want treatment; she wanted to die.

His mother's deterioration was gradual and escaped his notice. He saw that she wasn't as vigorous as before, but he believed her complaints about old age, and even though she wasn't that old, Owen didn't inquire too closely. A notion lurked under the surface that there might be something he didn't want to know. Besides, he was distracted by his school assignments, the farm work, and the pursuit of his private researches into the murky worlds opening to him through his work with Dr. Chouinard.

He met a girl in one of his classes and they went on a few dates. Owen found the experience confusing. He thought Jennifer was attractive, and he wove her into his fantasies, but he had little sense of how to spark a romance beyond holding hands. She finally lost her patience with his hesitations and kissed him in the truck one night. His arousal was intense, but it was flooded with the smell of his uncle and after the kissing and fondling left no doubt about what they were doing, he started crying and could not be consoled. Jennifer was sympathetic and cuddled him softly, but she wondered what was wrong with her, or if it was him, and what would happen next. Owen was unable to explain anything; the ugliness inside him left him mute.

They tried another time with no better results. The girlfriend thought he might be gay and she felt sorry for him, but her interests required a less awkward relationship and they drifted apart. Owen was too discouraged to try again with anyone else and though he made friends with female classmates, he dodged further opportunities for intimacy and buried himself in his studies.

He earned a degree and stayed on the farm, enrolling in a graduate program in anthropology at the state university in Orono. Once a week he drove there for classes; he could do everything else via computer and the internet. His mother grew feeble and it was no longer possible to disguise her condition. She told Owen she was dying and after a flood of tears he handled it by avoiding further mention of the subject. Isadora was content with this. He talked with Dr. Chouinard and she urged him to excavate the myths rotting away in his world. He dug and dug and though he found some crumbling nodes, he ignored the piles of matter heaped between himself and his mother.

Isadora Black died just before Owen completed his master's degree. He plunged into a doctoral program in comparative religion, shielding himself from pain with the details of his obsession. The farm was now his and he kept working it because it was a reliable refuge from the world. He had no idea what he was going to do with a doctorate degree. He would be a master of mythology, but that wasn't a job, not in the backwoods of Maine, perhaps not anywhere. Regardless, it held the meaning of his life.

And then Dr. Chouinard, no longer robust, began a steady decline and closed her practice. She sold her home and moved into an extended-care facility. Although Owen was no longer her patient, she was fond of him and asked him to visit her whenever he could. He came to the facility several times a week and they continued the conversation started years ago. But Dr. Chouinard soon started losing her edge, her memory slipped, she lost track of what they were saying, and Owen had to let go of his desire for their exchange of ideas. His role became supportive, and sometimes they only played cards and listened to music. Owen couldn't stem the rising panic. He was losing his guide into the unconscious and he would have to navigate that dark realm on his own. In desperation, he went to the tattoo parlor and had her labyrinth design inked onto the inside of his left forearm, hoping that it would serve as a talisman to hold the forces of the world at bay.

Owen's moods occupied the foreground of his thoughts and he lost the focus on his studies. In time, it was obvious that he couldn't continue, and he withdrew to the silence of the farm. On a sunny day in October, after he harvested the last of the garden vegetables, Dr. Chouinard died, and Owen was alone.

[5]

One night after the funeral, Owen took a razor blade and traced the outlines of his tattoo, slicing lightly into the flesh, drawing just enough blood to mark the lines of the design. It was painful but he was in a reckless state of mind and his head was choked with images of mythic sacrifice. At this point, there seemed little to care about, least of all himself. The full measure of Dr. Chouinard's importance to him had been revealed. He had loved her, no, he had worshipped her. All through the years he had known her, he wanted to bury himself in her soft, ample flesh as well as her enfolding mind. He didn't mean that in a sexual way, not exactly, though Owen was so confused about sex that he had trouble distinguishing the limits of desire. What Owen desperately wanted was a safe, warm place to nurture his body, a place where he would be protected.

As he continued to cut into his skin, the pain dulled. So, it was true, what he read, that the body could make its own opiates. Balm for the pains of the flesh and good enough to ease his troubled thoughts. His breathing slowed down and he was able to think again. He stared at the bloody labyrinth on his arm and turned it back and forth like the doctor did when she first showed it to him. The path to death, she had said, or the unconscious, or both. He had followed it down into the darkness, avoiding the subject of death, looking for answers. He had found many things, but had he found any actual answers? "Well, Owen," he could imagine Dr. Chouinard saying, "first you have to have questions." It was true that he had been reluctant to ask questions. He was afraid of the answers.

The tattoo reminded him of the myth of Ariadne, who possessed the key to the original labyrinth. Out of love she had given the secret of its solution to Theseus so he could kill the vicious Minotaur, the beast that consumed sacrifices at the word of Ariadne's father, the king of Crete. Her secret was a ball of golden thread that could be tied to the threshold and unwound as Theseus probed into the darkness of its winding passages. With that thread, he could retrace his steps and find the way back from the duel at the labyrinth's center. Or so he hoped. All Ariadne asked in return was that he take her with him, away from the decadence of Crete and her father's domination. The well-prepared Theseus killed the Minotaur. And thus Ariadne sailed away in the arms of a Greek hero. But Theseus was a scoundrel, like many heroes, and off-loaded Ariadne on the island of Naxos in order to avoid awkward explanations of her presence in Athens, a kingdom in thrall to Crete. Ariadne was heart-broken from the abandonment. After Naxos, the story branched into a variety of endings, some convoluted, but the one that had always captivated Owen was the one where Ariadne was driven down with grief. No longer able to tolerate life, she hung herself from a tree overlooking the sea.

Owen wrestled with this story, still stunned that someone who held the secret of labyrinth navigation was driven to suicide. Was Dr. Chouinard deluded in offering him the labyrinth as a symbol for life and healing? Had she considered the implications of Ariadne's fate? Why had she exalted such a confounded icon? Did she point to a similar end? He should have interrogated her more thoroughly, should have demanded concrete answers instead of accepting the vague chestnuts of psychology. He lashed himself with regrets. Alone with his ruminations, he avoided the rational and selected the whirlpool of panic and self-pity. The lesson he was left to consider was that all the mucking about in the corners of the labyrinth had done no good. It still only offered death.

Well, then, death it would be. Poorly equipped for solo excavations of the underworld, he craved peace. He gained new appreciation for his mother's end and her embrace of the final rest. Fatigue, after all, was the true condition of life. It seemed time to put all the suffering behind him. He had endeavored to make meaning out of it, but if there was meaning to be found, it eluded him.

He would go back to the tree where it all started, the white ash tree in the woods. He couldn't stop thinking about Ariadne. Her story played through his mind like an endless tape. He imagined her on the beach of Naxos, curled in the sand, naked and sobbing yet still beautiful, a testament to the lack of justice in the world. He thought of nothing else. It carried the stench of inevitability, the whole episode. And it would end, for him, as it did for Ariadne, on a tree.

The garden on his farm was done for the year, but he still had a few animals: some chickens and a few goats. He sold them all to the neighbor down the road at a bargain price. He went through the house and shut it down, draining pipes, turning off the utilities, and preparing it for someone who might come after. He didn't know who that might be. There was no one to whom he imagined leaving the farm or anything he owned. It wasn't his problem. No reason to waste a good house, though, and he left it so that it could be started up again. It was rare that anyone came to the farm, but he left a note on the kitchen table, just in case. Not a final note, just a statement that he had gone away for a while. Cryptic, which seemed right. Let them figure it out.

He made a final trip to town and stopped at the hardware store where he purchased thirty feet of 6mm yellow kernmantle rope. It was a beautiful coil of rope and he liked the feel of it in his hands. When he returned home, he stood in the living room and stared out the big window, absently coiling and uncoiling the rope. This would serve as Ariadne's golden thread. He wondered if he had lost his mind. Surely, the compulsion to stage his own version of an ancient myth would be exhibit A. But he didn't feel crazy. He was clear-headed, more focused than he'd been in years. He had an action plan that would resolve all the problems of his life. What else did he need?

He rolled up the rope into a neat ball and threw it into a rucksack, along with a bottle of water. He told himself that it didn't make sense to die of thirst before he got to the tree, a thought that provoked a harsh cackle in his throat. He and his uncle had driven on back roads into the woods when they went hunting, but Owen didn't want to leave his truck parked along a road where it would, eventually, draw attention. It was about five miles on old paths to the tree so he would walk, which seemed more in line with his mood, anyway. It would be a procession of one.

The next morning, another crisp, sunny autumn day, he ate a light breakfast, grabbed his pack, and locked the house. He held his palm on the front door for one last feel of the place, then turned and walked away. The farm was tidy and neat, an empty page waiting for a new artist. As he walked, his determination was firm. Reflections of his life accompanied a swift pace, clicking through a slide show of frozen moments: Dr. Chouinard, his mother, his brief almost-girlfriend, his books, the farm, and always, his uncle, his vile, disgusting uncle. Molten anger sloshed over the lip of a crucible deep within Owen. The cruelty of humans was senseless. We have fucked up each other and the earth as well, he thought. What a miserable mess, this world, so full of promise and yet so bitter in the end. He would be glad to leave it.

His route linked footpaths and dirt roads, taking him inland, deeper into the woods. The vast stretches of woodland here were seldom visited. Deer hunting season was the height of human activity and it was still a couple of weeks away. There might be someone out bear hunting, but Owen knew they never strayed from the roads. He saw no one during his grim march, just a rabbit spooked by the crunch of a twig. By mid-day he was standing at the edge of the clearing that belonged to the white ash tree.

It was exactly as he remembered it, a quiet, solemn place. The thought crossed his mind that his uncle might be lurking in the shadows on the far side of the meadow or hiding behind the tree, and his pulse quickened. Reason told him that his uncle was long gone, maybe even dead, at least everywhere except in Owen's memories, where he still reigned over secret torments. Owen reminded himself that he was there to kill the shadow of his uncle and there was nobody left to stop him. His breaths came slower and he stepped into the meadow.

The stately ash tree stood in the middle of the clearing—a hundred feet tall with branches nearly as wide. It wore the golden mantle of autumn, although a few leaves had fallen, revealing some of the structure of its branches. The trunk was three feet in diameter, a big tree for these woods. Its form was balanced and symmetrical and the lowest branches were within reach. As Owen approached the tree, the deep furrows in the bark reminded him of the scratches left on his face when his uncle pushed him against the trunk and raped him. Such a horrid thing

– did the tree know that it had been used for such a purpose? Owen stood underneath and tipped back his head to look up into the canopy, admiring the streaming kaleidoscope of light. A beautiful being, this tree, a noble being.

Owen heard the voice of Dr. Chouinard, or maybe it was just a memory, but it seemed to emanate from the air around him like a shivering of leaves. "Owen, do you know about the great ash tree?" He hadn't, but she had taught him, and that knowledge flooded back as he reveled in the presence of the tree. She'd told him the Norse myth of Yggdrasil, the ash tree at the center of the universe, its roots buried in different worlds, its every particle a host for powerful beings and deep, mystical power. Odin had given one of his eyes for the privilege of drinking from a spring under the roots, a spring that contained wisdom and understanding. Her voice came again with the chime of silver bracelets, "And the runes, Owen. Don't forget the runes..."

How could he have forgotten the story of the runes? In his obsession with Ariadne and her death, he had been blind to other mythic tales of hanging—such as the one that happened on the Norse world tree. To quench his thirst for knowledge, Odin returned to that tree and hung himself from one of its branches, dying the death of a god, which is to say, not dying at all, but going through the darkest of passages before finding his way back to resurrection. With this act, he was given an understanding of the runes and their considerable power, a gift from the world tree.

Owen took off his pack and sat down against the tree, placing the ball of yellow rope in his lap and drinking the last of the water. He was confused. It had seemed so clear to him, his planned repudiation of the merry-go-round in his head, a dramatic act to terminate the churning labyrinth, an escape from an existence that never felt quite right. He had identified the myth beneath the surface and sought to carry it through to its conclusion. With Ariadne's thread, he would leave the labyrinth, once and for all. But was his interpretation wrong? In his fixation on Ariadne's abandonment, he had not considered that there might be other possibilities. Not surprising, perhaps, given that he had scant patience for Nordic myths. He blamed the Nazis. And why not? They deserved it. They had ransacked cultures for symbols to prop up their totalitarian fantasies, none more so than the Norse. Myths were icons of social power, but what the Nazis did, as they appropriated many wondrous things for the purpose of evil, was horrific.

Aside from that, he thought the Nordic myths provided simplistic narratives of dominant heroes, a tiresome lot of brutes. Owen wanted nothing more to do with brutes. He found more resonance in the Greek and Welsh traditions, more appealing to him with their ambiguous psychologies. The Greeks had heroes, too, but they were complicated characters riddled with tragic flaws; they seemed to stumble through life rather than dominate it. The Welsh had no heroes at all, no central, organized system, just a panorama of shapeshifters, tricksters, and mysterious women fey with power. Yet this Norse story of the runes was something that Dr. Chouinard considered important. He trusted her insight and tried to focus.

He cleared his mind and started over. It didn't seem to matter how he wanted to interpret the myth. Quibbling over details didn't change anything. All roads led to a hanging. Whether Ariadne, Odin, or even Christ, once it happened, he would be dead, or become as a god, or whatever. The option of walking back to the farmhouse and resuming his life held no call for him. Might as well get on with it, then.

He put the rope back in the pack and pulled himself up to the lowest branch. From there he reached the next big branch and scrambled up the trunk so he could straddle the crotch, his back to the tree. The branch was a foot in diameter and nearly horizontal, projecting into free space fifteen feet above the ground. He took out the ball of rope and dropped the pack to the base of the tree. Fashioning a noose-like slip knot in one end of the rope, he placed it over his head, pulling it snug against his neck. He would squirm out on the branch as far as he could go, tie the rope to the limb, leaving a couple of feet slack, then roll off. He was sure the fall would snap his neck so there would be no desperate attempt to escape the agony of a slow strangulation.

He lay prone on the branch. All his preparations were complete. He stared out at the quiet beauty of the woods and tried to summon the image of Dr. Chouinard, to ask her forgiveness, to thank her for everything, to hear her voice one more time. But the world was silent. He pressed his ear against the branch and detected a faint humming that sounded like it came from the tree. Owen was reminded of the time with his uncle and how he had sensed a mind within this tree. He had reached for that mind then, extending himself in a trance, and it seemed as if the tree sang to him. He wondered if he might hear the singing again, but he knew that his patience with this drama was played out. Time to go. He rolled off the branch and felt the lurch of the rope as it cinched tight.

The fall did not kill him and he hung in strangled confusion. The branch had shown more spring than he anticipated, perhaps cushioning the drop. Or his neck muscles were too strong. Regardless, the rope cut into his throat with a devastating grip; a few moments of dangling and he would suffocate. Gravity pulled at the weight of his body. Suddenly the force dissipated, he floated in space and began to move. Opening his eyes, he saw that some of the branches on the tree flexed around him and he was held by hundreds of terminal twigs, like fingers, grasping and pulling him toward the trunk of the tree. Other tree fingers tore the rope from his throat, breaking it as if it were thread. The tree pressed him to its trunk, and slowly the bark parted, unpeeling itself and flowing apart, separating into folds of flesh-like cellulose, a human-sized arboreal vulva that sucked him in. He was stunned. What the hell, he thought, the tree plucked him off the branch like a ripe fruit and was consuming him. Or maybe he was already dead, and this was an hallucination on the road to rebirth. The tree sealed shut and he blacked out.

2 |

# THRESHOLD

*We have had traitors to race, country, religion, but we have not yet bred any real traitors*, traitors to the human race, *which is what we need.*

Henry Miller, "Peace! It's Wonderful!" from *The Cosmological Eye*

[6]

Owen woke up in a forest of giants. Naked, laying on a bed of moss, his eyes climbed a broad trunk that soared into a maze of boughs. If there was a sky beyond the canopy, he couldn't see it. Even the lowest branches were so high that he couldn't make out the shape of the leaves. Needles, maybe, like a conifer. A faint breeze tickled his skin, but the air was warm.

Curled up on his abdomen was a furry mammal of some sort, asleep and snoring. Or maybe there was more than one, it was hard to tell. He raised his head to get a better look. Simultaneously, three heads lifted from the mass of gray fur and gazed back at him with eyes of obsidian. A chill rippled down Owen's spine. The three creatures unraveled from the fur pile and sat up on their haunches, maneuvering carefully to keep their paws fixed on his skin. After rearranging themselves, they stared at him. Each was about the size of a ground squirrel. The bare skin humanoid faces, large, tufted ears, and long tails reminded him of the marmosets he had seen on a childhood trip to the zoo. But the faces weren't right for marmosets – they resembled humanoid faces. He studied the creatures as intently as they studied him, realizing that, as far as he could tell, they were identical in shape, size, and color. That was odd, he thought. Clones came to mind.

The one on the right wrinkled its nose and said, "Hello, dear. Back to life, are we?" It had the voice of Dr. Chouinard.

Owen readied himself for the rush of tension and panic that always came with weird situations, but aside from some twitching in his guts, his muscles stayed loose. He had no idea why he wasn't reactive. At this point, he should be jumping out of his skin. Instead, he was mostly curious, although hearing the voice of his former therapist coming from the creature was more than a little creepy. He took a breath and found his voice. "Where am I and how did I get here? Who are you? And why the fuck do you sound like Dr. Chouinard?"

The middle creature, an expression of triumph on its face, looked at the one who had already spoken and barked out a sharp laugh. "We said not to do that! His system is fully maxed and this is an unnecessary complication!" It also used the voice of Chouinard.

The first speaker turned to its critic. "The voice of his mentor was selected for its familiarity, thus allaying some of the psychic shock of reanimation. We all know that."

The middle one sneered. "Worked well, didn't it? In the rush to be all warm and fuzzy a few things might have been over-looked."

The third creature, so far silent, watched the exchange between its companions, then peered into the distance and intoned, "Advice was given/Advice was scorned/Thus was a heart/Tweaked and torn."

Owen winced to hear Chouinard's voice from this creature as well.

"Okay, okay. Point made." The first one, still speaking like Dr. Chouinard, turned to Owen. "Would you prefer a different voice, then? One less personal?"

"Yes, please. By all means."

"How is this?" The creature now sounded like one of those soothing digital voices that had become ubiquitous. Still unnerving, but more tolerable than the sound of Owen's beloved ghost.

He nodded in acceptance. "Whatever. I can live with that."

"That's good, because we definitely wish you to live," replied the first creature. "As to your questions... well, they are very good questions. Very good, indeed! The answers, we are embarrassed to admit, are not short. Some patience would be of benefit right about now—" It turned to glare at its companions, then started muttering. "We probably don't need these anymore—"

Owen's attention was drawn to the creature's forelegs, long primate-like limbs that ended in agile-looking hands. The fingers of those hands appeared to be inserted into Owen's chest. He watched in astonishment as the creature steadily withdrew one long finger after another from his flesh. A slight popping sound accompanied each extraction, followed by a swift, fluid movement of his tissue to seal the hole. He didn't understand the flex or the lack of sensation. He wondered why he felt no pain or distress during this bizarre experience. The creature wiped its fingers on its fur, then looked at the others, who repeated the procedure, one after another, withdrawing their own digits from Owen's torso.

When the extraction was complete, the three sat back on Owen's abdomen and continued to clean their fingers by licking and rubbing them on each other. The first one spoke. "Sorry about that. Kind of gross, in a way. Necessary for the treatment, though."

Owen didn't know what to say. He opened his mouth to speak but what emerged was a laugh, a clean laugh of joy. Everything was strange. Probably he should be screaming, but he didn't feel like screaming. He was alive – an amazing thing—and he felt good. In fact, he was sure that he had never in his life felt this good. Maybe he was high or having one of those magnificent lucid dreams where everything seems real. Digging his hands into the moss underneath, he scooted up until he could prop his head against a projecting root. The creatures clung to him while he shifted.

"Comfy? Okay, I guess we could start with where you are..." began the first creature.

Owen interrupted. "You could. But you just said 'treatment.' What did you mean?"

The third creature, who had spoken in poetry, stood tall, put its hands behind its back, and declaimed, "He wants to know the Why/And much more/To untangle the Where/And then What For."

Owen snorted. The last thing he remembered before waking up in this Neverland was the attempt to hang himself. He recalled the intense, crazed panic of suffocation as he swung from the branch of the ash tree. For months, he had been in a hellish torment of depression and despair; finally, he decided that death was the only release. As the noose had tightened, he lost consciousness. There was no memory of anything else, yet clearly he had not died, but was somehow transported elsewhere, into an improbable cartoon idyll, and instead of waking to hopelessness, he was stifling giggles and listening to a marmoset recite doggerel. Was this related to the "treatment?" His mood shift was too drastic to be his own invention. He never took drugs, but he suspected that even a psychedelic trip wasn't this weird. And if this was a dream, it was a doozy. Perhaps he had died, after all, and traveled to a surrealistic afterlife like the *bardo* stages of the Tibetans. He had spent hours poring over *The Tibetan Book of the Dead* in his mythological studies but there was nothing remotely like this. Well, he would play along. Did he have a choice?

The middle creature yanked on the poet's tail, throwing it off balance. Owen's stomach muscles clenched in anticipation of the landing, but the creature was feather light. Ignoring this, the middle one cleared its throat. "Ahem. We are your assigned treatment team. We created an interface with your physical structure," the creature lifted its hand and wiggled the fingers to demonstrate, "then, we used that linkage as a platform to stage a system recalibration. Not as complicated as it sounds, really. Starts with one cell: a diagnostic, an intervention, then moves on, cell by cell until the whole system is refurbished. Tip-top."

The poet glanced warily at the middle one and as soon as it paused, yelled out. "Not only to be new/But make a better you!"

The first two creatures turned their heads and frowned at the poet, who looked away and pulled its ears. The original speaker reclaimed the podium that was Owen's belly. "We know that you've suffered and suffered dearly. Our assessment procedure uploaded a comprehensive overview of your memories and knowledge. But not to worry—no, no. We were oh-so-gentle as we sifted through. Have no fear. Nothing was removed or blocked. That would hardly be therapeutic, anyway. Carefully, very carefully, we re-tooled your biosystem to function cleanly, free of destabilizing feedback loops that, well, undermine your rational thinking."

The middle one looked at the speaker. "Bet you anything he doesn't know about destabilizing feedback loops."

"Goodness," said the first one. "Is that true?" It looked at Owen with concern.

Owen studied the three creatures, feeling both befuddled and amused. It was like trying to have a conversation with the Marx Brothers, only these creatures were as identical as the Marx Brothers were different. If they switched places, he wouldn't be able to keep them straight. At least not until they started talking, because their personalities appeared to be distinct, if not downright incompatible. "You know, gang, I appreciate that you're trying to answer my questions and get me up to speed or whatever, but you're also driving me crazy. You keep interrupting one another and either use obscure jargon or speak in even more obscure rhyme. And then this dead ringer presentation is baffling.

How am I supposed to tell you apart? And... I can't tell you how creepy this is... why do you kinda look like me?"

The first one looked puzzled. "Tell us apart? Why ever would you want to do such a thing?"

The middle one groaned. "Because he has a unitary mind, dummy. He, like all humans, has little to no understanding of or appreciation for collective consciousness. To them, everything is singular, individualized, fragmented. It permeates every aspect of their existence, including their pathetic attempts at society. In sum, he thinks we're separate. He can't see us any other way. He even thinks our discourse involves interruption because he can't recognize the natural progression of thought."

"Wait a minute." Owen said. "You mean you aren't separate creatures?"

"Nope!" They said in unison.

The middle one lifted a paw and inspected its digits. "Nor are we separate from you."

Owen lifted his hands, brought them to his face and rubbed his eyes. He suddenly felt tired. "What? How can that be? Wait. There're so many questions, I can't prioritize them." He took a breath. "Okay. So then, what are you? I think I asked that before."

The poet answered with, "Questions left alone/Draw dust to the bone."

"Gah!" The middle one barked. "That doesn't even make sense."

The poet started to cry. The first speaker reached around to stroke the poet's head while staring angrily at the middle one.

"That was uncalled for. What kind of example are we setting for our dear, disoriented fellow?"

The three of them formed a tight huddle, wrapping their arms and tails around each other as they hugged. Owen used this opportunity to push himself further up on the root, resting his shoulders against the wood while the three creatures settled further into his lap. So far, the conversation had been bewildering but, on the other hand, he couldn't remember the last time he had been this diverted from the gloom of his own moods.

The creatures hummed in their cluster, creating a sound that reminded him of the forest breeze. In unison, they fell silent, and as they parted, they changed colors. One became solid red, one black, and the other white. He wasn't sure which was which because their faces remained identical, although the features no longer resembled Owen's. Instead they looked like androgynous versions of Albert Einstein—frizzy hair but no mustache.

The red one spoke. "Dear heart, we're so sorry to confuse you. Please accept our heartfelt apologies. We don't do this sort of thing often, and when we do, it's always different, the requirements and parameters, you can't imagine! Anyway, we've adopted a color scheme to simplify your perceptions. And we pulled this visage from your cultural memories; it seems to evoke a favorable emotional response. Will that make you feel better?" Owen guessed this was the same one who had first spoken, the "therapist."

"Thank you. You're very kind. But it would also help if you could tell me your name, or names, or what I should call you."

"Names?" The black one arched a hairy eyebrow. It then turned to the red one. "Do we have names? And if so, why haven't we been told?"

The white one adopted a pose that promised a recitation, which it swiftly delivered. "Oh dear, for the lack of a name/ Who or what deserves the blame?/We haven't been told– what a shame!"

Disdain animated the black one's face. "What an idiot."

Before the three came to blows, Owen interrupted. "Okay, okay. So, you don't have names, need names, want names, or something. It was just a question. Personally, I like names. They help sort things out."

The red one eased away from its fellows. "Names are so problematic. We know you have one, as humans usually do," and here it released a prolonged sigh, "but we don't endorse such distortions of reality, not if we can help it. Names create divisions and disguise relationships. They imply that the elements of a system are separate fragments and more important than the connections between them. We understand that human language is based on nouns and names and labels but you must accept that these are not significant aspects of the communications within our systems."

"Okay, maybe I get it. Or maybe I don't. But, as you say, that's not the way I think. For my own sanity, I'm going to want to call you something. I guess it could be *Red*, *Black*, and *White*. Seems a bit bland, though. Forget it, just go ahead with answering my other questions. Please."

The three creatures shuffled from paw to paw, reminding Owen of admonished children. The red one said, "Very well. Important feedback, that. We'll make more of an effort to stay on track." After looking at its companions with a silent plea, it continued. "Part of the challenge is that your questions overlap. To answer any one of them requires answering all the others. For no reason other than a priority of place, we've decided to explain where you are and go from there. Okay?" Without waiting for a response from Owen, the red one nodded to the black one. "Give him the whole nine yards, then: string theory, multiverse, quantum mechanics, go for it."

The black one stood up by putting its hands on the shoulders of the other two and pushing. "Ahem. The physics is quite complex—too complex for you, in all probability. But, in sum: the universe is not a single continuous space. It is, in fact, a multiverse, an infinite compendium of quantum possibilities manifesting in parallel universes, each separated from the others by membranes. For amusement, the separations are sometimes called 'branes,' not to be confused with a place of cognition. Anyway, the unending parallel universes are like a series of theatrical stages placed side by side and providing all the possible enactments of energy and matter. Universes can feature different numbers of spatial dimensions, different natural laws, and different manifestations of form. They can be radically variant or virtually similar. For example, there are quite likely many universes where you exist, or some version of you, playing out a different role in each universe. No being can grasp the full extent of this nature because it requires a comprehension of infinity."

As the black one paused for breath, the white one chanted softly. "Babble and babble about the brane/Drive us all completely insane."

The black one clapped a hand over the white one's mouth and continued. "You, Owen the human, are not in the same universe where you were born. All because the tree where you chose to terminate your existence is linked into a brane."

The white one struggled out from the grip of the black one and yelled, "Brane, brane/Crazy insane!" The black one snarled, gave a shove, and pushed the white one off Owen's lap.

"Hey!" Owen said, and he collected the sniffling white one in his hand and brought it to his chest to pat and stroke the soft fur. "That was just mean."

The red one scowled at the black but said nothing. The black one increased the volume of its lecture. "Continuing on, forests are a complex micro-universe in themselves, an ecological system of subtle relationships. Forest systems are poorly understood by your human science, which has always been better at deconstructive analysis than systemic overviews. We hesitate to admit it, but even poets come closer to the truth."

The black one paused and offered a conciliatory bow to the white one. "Anyway, one of the fundamental characteristics of forests may surprise you. It is not a collection of entities living in discrete biological shells – no, the entire forest is an enmeshed life system. It's connected underground in a complicated web of roots and fungal strands that link all the flora into a vast exchange of molecular nutrients. These webs, or mycorrhizal networks, have many interesting properties, but one of them is their ability to penetrate branes and extend into parallel universes. Thus, forests can link across universes to form a kind of consistent multiverse forest."

Despite his dislike of the pompous black creature, Owen was fascinated by the content of its monologue. "Incredible. I see where this is going. So, I'm in an alternate universe, a parallel world? That's right out of science fiction. Or mythology. It's an ancient concept, not only the existence of alternate worlds, but travel between them. Yet it usually involves magic, which I'm guessing is probably not what brought me here."

The black one looked at Owen and offered a thin smile. "No. Magic is an extraneous delusion. The universe is wonderful enough as it is. In this case, your bio-signature was recognized by the ash tree and a decision was made to stop the termination event. The network biosystem that includes the ash tree activated a recalibration of elementary particles, focusing quantum variance waves throughout the tree, and allowing it to boost the plastic potential within its cells. Thus, the tree stretched beyond its usual form. It flexed branches to hold you, pulling your flesh into contact with its own modified structure. Proximity enabled certain quantum possibilities within your cells to flow and join the mycorrhizal network. You dissembled into components, then trickled through the brane and were reconstituted in this world. So, you are still on the Earth, as you call it, it's just another Earth."

Owen cuddled the white one and it purred in contentment. He looked at the red and black creatures standing in his lap. "But why? 'A decision was made' you said. What decision? By whom? And, I ask again, why?"

The black one and the red one exchanged glances and the black one sat down. The red one looked at Owen and winked. "A mind is a funny thing, dear, is it not? What is it, anyway?

Switches, links, and energy pressed into a ball of matter stuffed within a skull? Mmm. Doesn't really seem sensible, does it—thought begins and ends there? No, minds are many things, but above all, they are assemblages that create consciousness. The material specifics are variable. They can be tiny, even cellular, or they can be vast. Like a forest."

"Oh yeah...," Owen muttered.

"What's that?" said the red one.

"I was just remembering a novel I read. The author imagined something called a 'Vast Active Living Intelligence System.' Actually, he was talking about God, or a god, or some kind of a divine presence."

The red one opened its mouth to reply but the black one was faster. "That's good. Vast Active Living Intelligence System. Yes. That describes the forest, though divinity has nothing to do with it. It's a mind, pure and... well, definitely not simple. You could compare the mycorrhizal nodes to neurons; they have similar functions. A forest doesn't just mindlessly shuttle nutrients around, it acts as a communion of consciousness. It's an assembly of elements and associations, processes and relationships, all woven into a labyrinth of fungus, rhizomes, and ancillary matter. Many things work together to form this system. It's not the same as your limited human notion of consciousness, isolated within a single body. Consciousness is not an awareness of separation from other things; it's the exact opposite."

Owen shook his head. "Okay, okay already. The forest is a mind, I get it."

Suddenly a voice sang out from the white one in Owen's hand. "Vast is the past/Wide the divide/All space and time/Combine in mind."

Black and red looked away and the rhymes lingered in the air unchallenged. Owen smiled down at the white creature curled up on his chest. "So..." he said, "back to treatment. The whys and what-fors...."

The red one glanced at the black, who waved its arm, deferring the answer. The red one combed its fingers through its fur and looked pleased. "Well then, you already know that your body is a cell-based biological system. What you may not know is that balance within any biosystem is maintained through interactive processes, namely the relationships between components. These relationships are governed by feedback loops. Feedback, by the way, can be physical, mental, you know..., whatever. Negative feedback influences the action of the component. For example, if you eat junk, you turn into junk, which makes you want more junk. Addiction works on a feedback loop. Or in an argument, anger feeds anger, creating a chain reaction of hostility. Before you went to the tree to end your life, your system was far out of balance, driven by a spiraling negativity of mood. Which is another way of saying that your mind got caught in a loop of despair and convinced your body to self-destruct. We will never blame you for that action; we empathize with your misery. We, too, know suffering."

"You do?"

"Yes, we do, indeed. And we will show you."

"Later, though," interjected the black one. "Later."

The white one wriggled out from Owen's clutch and rejoined its fellows in his lap, then delivered another verse. "From every root to every leaf/Our truest name is Pain and Grief."

Owen was startled: all three began to sob. They threw themselves into another huddle and cried loudly for a moment, subsiding to a whimper before peeling apart.

The red one wiped its eyes, cleared its throat, and resumed the explanation. "The tree where you sought to resolve your suffering is part of a life system that did not want you to die, at least not yet. Not before your time. There's a reason for that, but we'll get to it later. Anyway, once you crossed over to this place, we inserted our awareness into your biosystem and tinkered a bit at the cellular level, as we've said. So now, instead of relentless anxiety and spikes of agony you will experience a fundamental calm. You still have to carry the burden of your memories and you will feel stress, but it won't be debilitating. A full make-over, to be sure."

"Gee," Owen replied, "I should thank you, then. I did wonder why I wasn't melting down into nuclear anxiety what with talking animals, parallel universes, and all that. So, thank you! But I still don't get why you would do this. Why save me? I am, after all, just another dumb human, as you've pointed out more than once."

The three creatures looked back and forth at each other nervously, waiting for someone to field a response. The red one sighed. "No, no, Owen, please don't get the wrong impression. We may be critical of your species, and there are reasons for that, but we want you to be here and to be happy. Well, as happy as anyone can be in these times of duress."

"Duress? I thought I was the one who tried to kill himself."

"Suicide is possible for any form of consciousness, don't you think?"

"What are you implying—that the forest mind is suicidal?"

"Our duress will be explained in time, dear, along with the cause and recourses. But for now, let's return to your query about why you were saved and treated. As we said, the forest network around that ash tree remembered you from your childhood and the travesty that happened there. Emotions are at the core of what defines mind and consciousness, and the suffering experienced by you as a child was absorbed into the forest. It lodged in that same area, translating the pain into a rhizome memory map. When you returned to the tree to put an end to your conscious existence, those old, painful memories left in the rhizome were inflamed, and the map began to burn anew. The forest system was compelled to act, not only out of kindness and care, but out of a wish to avoid pain for itself. Compassion and self-interest have the same goal at a systemic level."

"Hmm. Well, thanks again for saving my life and fixing me up. I'm guessing you can't bill my health insurance, so I'm in your debt."

The black one quickly replied. "I'm sure we can find something for you to do in return...."

The red one elbowed the black one in the ribs and they exchanged glances. A curious interaction, Owen thought, until a sudden inspiration distracted him. "Hey, look, whether you guys like names or want them, really, you should have them. Just humor me here. I know, I know, I heard everything about divisions and connections, and I dispute none of that. But names for you are already taking shape in my mind – I can't help it and, look,

I really need something other than 'red,' 'black,' or 'hey, you.' I promise not to tell anyone else and blow your anonymous cover."

The black one snarled in disgust, the red one struggled to maintain a neutral expression, and the white one jumped up and down, clapping its hands and chanting, "We shall have immortal fame/When lowly god dubs a name!"

The red and black one collapsed in spasms of laughter while the white one, triumphant, continued the chant. Owen smiled at the outburst of silliness and harmony between his benefactors; their passion was contagious.

After the white one settled down and the other two stopped snickering, Owen sat upright, careful to maintain enough lap for the creatures. "Okay, then, I'm going to take that as permission to proceed. So... summoning my lore in forest mythology, I'll name you all after the hawthorn tree, a tree of cultural importance, and a favorite of mine. Thus, you'll still be together in name yet distinct enough for my feeble comprehension." He pointed at each one in turn, "In light of the nonexistent powers conferred upon me, I dub thee Redthorn, Blackthorn, and Whitethorn. This calls for a ceremonial feast!"

"A feast? Really?" questioned Redthorn.

"Hunger is a sign of the full return to the body," explained a bored-looking Blackthorn.

Owen looked at Whitethorn. Predictably, it tried to sum things up. "We may not have your usual feast/But food there is to feed the beast."

"Good," said Owen. "I'm so hungry I could eat a tree."

The three Thorns gazed back at him. Smiles played at their lips, making Owen a little uncomfortable.

[7]

One by one, Owen removed the Thorns from his lap, placing them on a root. He stood up slowly, stretched his arms overhead, leaned to one side, then the other, and tried twisting his torso. Muscles and joints were stiff, but he relished the sensation of life in his muscles.

"God, how long have I been laying there? Feels like it's been a while."

"A week, you would say," answered Redthorn.

"A week! Does that mean the same thing here as it did... where I came from?" Owen felt a sharp wave of vertigo as he considered how far he was from home.

"Yes, dear, time is the same, or at least it moves at the same pace. The seasons, however, are reversed, so your winter is our summer. Or vice versa, as you wish."

Without warning, the three Thorns leapt into the air, somersaulting, and landed on Owen's shoulders. Redthorn took the left while Blackthorn and Whitethorn fought for vantage on the right. Owen plucked Whitethorn from the tussle and placed it on top of his head. The pads of their fingers were rough but gave them good purchase on his skin without much discomfort for him. He was glad they didn't have claws.

Blackthorn cleared its throat, a sign Owen guessed signaled another lecture. "Up there, somewhere through the treetops, is the sun. The Earth goes around the sun and the moon goes around the Earth. Just like in your universe. There are significant differences between here and there, but not on the cosmic scale, at least nothing bigger than planetary position and such. Biology, now, that's a different story."

Whitethorn peeked down over Owen's forehead. "If you have time/To hear our rhyme/'Twill be sublime/And right on time." After delivering the verse, it popped back out of sight.

"We were discussing a feast of some sort, I believe," reminded Owen. A growl escaped his stomach. Idly, he scratched a bug bite on his arm and as he scraped it, he noticed that he had many welts. Suddenly feeling the itches, he scratched with vigor. The Thorns watched him without comment, adjusting their positions to maintain balance as he reached for the awkward places.

"Does it bother you, the insect feedings?" Redthorn asked while stroking a bite on Owen's shoulder.

"Hmm, yes, you bet. Definitely. I mean, being from Maine I'm used to it. As much as one ever gets used to it."

"Our apologies. We were certain you could spare the blood."

Blackthorn provided another educational segment: "The need for nutrients is universal. Energy is the fuel of life. Which was certainly the motivation of the mosquitoes and ants that shared in the bounty of your flesh. You will find that here, as in your world, all life-forms ingest nutrients. Fauna like yourself require energy to be consumed through the mouth, stomach, intestines, and so on. Flora are different, we tap into vegetable pathways and absorb nutrients directly from roots and mycorrhizal networks." Blackthorn stuck a hand in front of Owen's face and, as he watched, he saw writhing clusters of thin tendrils extend from under the nails of each finger.

"Good grief. That's what you had inside me?"

"Yes. Very useful for a variety of bio-linkages." When Owen cringed at the wiggling extensions, Blackthorn withdrew tendrils and hand.

Redthorn pointed through the forest. "Anyway... there is a stream not far from here and some fungal items you might devour. That's the main fare on the forest floor, at least for mammals. Quite nutritious."

From the voice on his head, Owen heard, "Yes yes you will see/You are going/to eat a tree." This was followed by giggling.

Owen walked in the direction of the stream, tentatively at first, easing his way back into kinetic familiarity with his muscles. Despite the dense overstory, at ground level the trees were large and widely spaced, with moss, duff, and grass scattered underneath. Occasional tree seedlings, bushes, and young forest growth claimed the odd spaces, and it reminded Owen of an untended park.

Light filtered through the trees, diffused by the vast canopy, creating an ambiance of stained glass and cathedrals. An occasional butterfly or moth fluttered through the shafts of light. It was silent, except for the sound of Owen's passage. The ground yielded under his bare feet and he enjoyed the textures of dirt and moss curling around his toes as he pressed down on each foot. His movements came easier and with more grace than he remembered. The mere act of sauntering naked through the woods filled him with delight. Things had changed for him—that was clear.

Every now and then, Owen stopped, unsure of the direction, and without a sound, Redthorn would lift an arm and point. Owen was reluctant to break the silence, but his curiosity yearned for answers. "So, tell me this: how do you know so much about what happens on my world? I'm guessing you don't get it from the newspapers."

Blackthorn snorted so loudly Owen jumped and his passengers scrambled to keep their footing. "Ha ha, newspapers, very funny. Love the dark humor. They're made from trees, remember, not necessarily an activity we approve of. But we don't need them, anyway, the newspapers."

"Please don't cut us, begged the trees/But ne'er mind the useless pleas/They were chopped right at the knees!" Whitethorn clapped, pleased with its verse.

Owen was less convinced. "Wait a minute, Whitethorn. You say 'chopped at the knees' but most trees are cut as close to the ground as possible, so wouldn't it make more sense to say 'chopped to the feet?' Of course, that doesn't rhyme with trees."

Blackthorn rushed to object. "We're wondering if you're really paying attention. A major portion of the tree is below ground, as we did point out. If we want to criticize the poetry, which is probably a good idea, it would be to go the other way. 'Waist' makes more sense than 'knee.' Or even 'armpit.'"

"Really, the ratio is that dramatic?"

Whitethorn, emboldened by the discussion of its craft, offered more fodder. "You think the tree is what you see/But the truth will be underneath."

Redthorn groaned and Blackthorn's tone was sharp. "We're really pushing the envelope here, aren't we?"

Owen couldn't see what Whitethorn was doing, but it felt like it was scratching his head, which felt good and he hoped it would continue. He tried to steer the discussion back to his question. "Was there an answer in there, somewhere?"

Blackthorn resumed its lofty tone. "Not so as you'd notice."

"The poetry function is very important to the system," interjected Redthorn. "It drives a creative synthesis often overlooked by analytical functions." Here it craned around Owen's face to glare at Blackthorn. "But creativity is always a gamble. Sometimes it's only possible to arrive at a beautiful synthesis after a series of false starts."

"Anyhoo," said Blackthorn, unfazed, "Remember that the mycorrhizal network spans the branes from our world to yours. And beyond, to other worlds as well. Information, such as the molecular structure of your body, travels across the branes via this network – which is how it can be reconstituted here. But information of all sorts comes through. So, no, we don't need your newspapers, we get information directly from the trees themselves. The forests of your world are more intelligent than you know, and the collective mind of those forests not only learns from input but also is a repository of data about everything in nature, including human culture."

Blackthorn paused for a breath and Owen slowed down his walking pace, not wanting to disrupt Whitethorn's thorough scratching of every square inch of Owen's scalp.

"Understand that the leaves of trees don't simply act as receptors for light energy; they can receive and transfer any sort of energy, including electromagnetic energy, sound energy, heat energy, you name it. Many lichens also have this capacity. The whole atmosphere is a reverberating ocean of data that's absorbed by trees. And through the linkage provided by your digital internet system, all it takes is one root wrapped around a buried cable to tap into the entire world network of human information exchange. Which is then fed back into the forest mind, digested, evaluated, collated, and stored. When you walk through the woods, here in this world, on your world, on any world where there is forest, you are walking through a cosmic library. The information is there—if you know how to read it."

Blackthorn leaned forward to put its head in front of Owen's face, clinging to his ear, and flashed him a broad smile that may have been intended as warm but was ghastly, featuring rows of sharp little teeth, completely undermining the absent-minded professor look. Owen stumbled and fell forward, catching himself with his hands before he slammed into the earth. Leaping in all directions, the Thorns abandoned Owen for the surrounding moss. His reflexes surprised him. Laughing, Owen relaxed to the ground and rolled over on his back. He was giddy with the new strength of his body.

Whitethorn crawled onto the open palm of Owen's left hand. It stared at the labyrinth tattoo on the inside of his forearm. There was a halo of scar tissue around the periphery from the repeated efforts to cut himself open and dull the shame. Redthorn bounced over to Owen's arm, touched the scars, and gently ran the tip of one finger along the trail of marred flesh. Owen felt a slight tingle. Tendrils emerged from under Redthorn's nail and slithered along his skin. Three circuits were stroked and when Redthorn was done, the skin around the tattoo was fresh and unblemished. Owen stared in awe.

Redthorn patted the tattoo. "This design permeates your memories. It seems to be both an echo and a beacon. We don't fully understand its function, but perhaps that needs a singular perspective."

Owen rolled onto his side, leaving his left arm where it was so he wouldn't disturb the two Thorns as they continued to study the tattoo. Curious, Blackthorn jumped onto his hip so it could see. Owen traced the pattern of the tattoo with his right forefinger. "The labyrinth is an ancient culture symbol in human societies. Means different things to different people, depending on time and place. It can be a simple sign for a maze, like the maze of the mythic hero Theseus, if such a thing can ever be labelled 'simple.' Or it can signify one of the most complex of human ideas—the collective unconscious. One scholar, name of Jung, considered labyrinths as archetypes: symbolic distillations of the inner essence of life. I think when I got this tattoo, I wished that it would be a catalyst of hope and mastery—a beacon, like you said. But labyrinths can spiral into a vortex as well as out into the world. As I've learned."

In a whisper, Whitethorn offered its own summary. "Without a doubt/The drain goes down/Just find your way/On past the spout."

"Hmm," Owen replied. "I guess I splashed down here, in a new labyrinth. Thanks again for hauling my ass out of the old one."

"You're welcome," they said simultaneously.

"Speaking of Jung, he once compared the unconscious to a rhizome. He said that the unconscious was underground, hidden from sight while our restless attention stays focused on the above-ground blossom of life. But the real business is in the roots. Almost sounds like Jung was talking to you all and your forest buddies."

"He probably was," asserted Blackthorn.

"What's that supposed to mean?"

"Oh, you know, stuff has a way of sticking around. Conservation of energy and all that."

Owen wanted to question Blackthorn about its cryptic reply, but he fell into the tangled memories of his conversations with Dr. Chouinard about Jung's ideas. She would have loved this discourse and she especially would have loved the three Thorns and their talk of systems and mycorrhizal networks. As he thought of her, a spark ran along his spine. He imagined her sitting under one of these giant trees, humming to herself and making something with clay, a magical clay that could be worked into life. The image was vivid, like a dream that seems real even after waking. Abruptly, he sat up and looked around, half expecting to see her. The woods were silent, and nothing moved except for the Thorns, who jumped away in a start.

"You okay?" asked Redthorn.

"Yes, yes. I just had this sudden image of Dr. Chouinard, as if she were here."

"In a way, Owen, she is. Wherever you go, she is with you. We thought you knew that."

"I'm a slow learner. Plus, you know, sometimes the things you guys say are just too weird. Hey, enough philosophy. I'm starving. Where is this food you mentioned?"

Owen scrambled to his feet and the Thorns leaped back to their riding perches. Redthorn pointed through the woods again and they resumed the walk, winding around the enormous trees and the occasional boulder parked in solitary meditation. Soon Owen heard the gurgle of a brook and a few more meanders brought them to the edge of a stream. The water was clear and unrippled. Carpets of thick moss and liverworts lined the shores and a few small flowers bloomed in delicate pastels. The stream was only two feet wide and Owen straddled it, dropping a knee on each bank and bending forward to open his mouth and suck in gulps of flowing water. The Thorns scattered to watch the acrobatics, and at least two of them chuckled when Owen dipped too far and had to snort the overflow out of his nose. When he sat back on the bank next to the Thorns, Owen had the look of a satisfied child.

"That was refreshing. Now, what about food?"

"Ah, the single-minded mammal. It may not look like your usual lunch, but those fungi are tasty and nutritious." Redthorn waved at a large branch, presumably fallen from the tree overhead. The branch was covered in yellow mushrooms that resembled cauliflower. Owen crawled to the branch and sniffed the fungus, which gave off the odor of strong cheese. He pinched off a hunk and peered at the firmer-than-expected texture before taking a bite. Although it had the consistency of cheddar, the actual taste was closer to musty tofu. As he chewed, a surprising hint of pepper worked its way around his mouth. Strange, but not unpalatable. He took another bite and sat next to the branch.

While he dined on the fungus, the Thorns hopped over and climbed up his back. Owen was chewing through the third bite when he felt a needle stab in his penis. He jumped up suddenly and his passengers toppled off. Looking down, he saw a mosquito-like creature hovering around his mid-section. "What the hell? These things drive me crazy!" and he pointed an accusing finger at the insect while turning to his guides.

"Ah yes, presumptuous little things, aren't they?" Blackthorn snickered.

"Do you need them on this world? One could hope there would be one place in the universe without them."

"Well, they have their part to play in the system. They tend to stay close to water and have a short season. But there are times and places where they proliferate. You've been to such places on your world and you know what it's like."

"All too well."

"Just swat it away. There's more what that came from."

"You know, if there are going to be such things, I might need some kind of clothing. I'm not keen to have my flesh drained at will by miniaturized vampires. I don't have lovely fur like your-selves." Owen scratched his bug bites again.

Whitethorn made note of it. "For life in the air/Fur's better than bare."

Blackthorn sneered. "And some of us don't care."

Whitethorn clapped its hands. "Ooh, ooh! A random rhyme/ From the merchant of gloom./'Tis well past time/To crawl outta your tomb."

Blackthorn coughed out a glob of phlegm which landed near Whitethorn's hind paws. "Don't push it."

Redthorn, the default mediator, changed the subject. "There's no clothing anywhere near here, at least not in your size. But we can obtain a type of fabric, then you could fashion your own covering. If you know how. Probably a good idea. And while you're at it, you could make a bag to carry supplies, because we need to take a journey."

Owen looked at Redthorn. He had the impression that something important had just been revealed. "A journey?"

"Oh yes. You don't think we brought you here just to see the sights?"

[8]

Owen felt pin pricks of anxiety as he realized that he was at the mercy of his hosts and there was nothing he could do about it. "Okay, I get it. This where you tell me what's really going on."

"He wants the truth/Don't tell a lie/Let him catch it/Then we'll cry."

Owen shook his head, not understanding the lyric. Blackthorn snorted in derision. "Do we have any quality control over this material? No need to answer – it's a rhetorical question."

Redthorn pointed at a small white object descending through the trees, wafting one way, then another, falling in the haphazard manner of a dry leaf. "See that? Here comes your answer."

"What is it? It looks like a snowflake."

"It's not. As the poem said, see if you can catch it."

Owen positioned his outstretched palms under the flake as it fell, but it danced past him to lodge on the moss underfoot. He bent for a closer look. It was flat, thin, bone-white, and about the size of his thumbnail. Although it had straight edges like a crystal, it had the shape of an irregular polygon. The flat surface had incised marks of some sort. Gently, he picked it up between thumb and forefinger and placed it on the back of his hand. A closer scrutiny revealed no recognizable geometry on the surface, merely an intricate chaos etched into the flake.

"What the hell is this?"

The Thorns were silent. Owen glanced up from his inspection of the flake and was surprised to see tears on the faces of all three. Blackthorn wiped its cheeks with its fists and looked gravely at Owen.

"It's a fragment of the forest, a holon of sorts."

"Holon? I don't suppose you're going to tell me what that is?"

"Of course, you don't know, do you? It's a systems concept, where a fragment reflects the whole. In this case, best understood metabolically rather than intellectually. Put it on your tongue and let it dissolve."

Owen frowned and continued to stare at the flake.

"Go on, it's okay. There's no... danger."

Owen thought that something wasn't right, but he might as well do what they suggested; he was in no position to challenge his guides. The flake vanished on his tongue. First came a faint taste of pitch, then his entire body exploded in pain so intense that it screamed through his bones like an electric shock. Before he could gasp, the pain vanished. He glared at Blackthorn.

"What the fuck! What was that about?"

"That was a concentrated remnant of the forest, the very one that surrounds us. But it comes from a place where the life system is being tortured, traumatized, and killed. These flakes detach from the trees as they die. They are picked up by the wind and carried around, terminal messages of pain loosed into the ecosystem as warnings of destruction. They carry a microcosm of trauma, a last testament of life."

Whitethorn stopped sniffling and offered another summation. "The tincture of a tree/Knows what it means to be."

Redthorn put its arms around its companions and pulled them close. "As you might imagine, there is much more to tell. Right now, it's important for you to know that your presence is relevant to the trauma of the forest. There may be something you could do for us, dear. And not to put too much of a point on it, your participation could prevent a suicide. That would make for a nice balance, don't you think? But please, hold your questions. In time, they will be answered. Sometimes it's best to take things in portions rather than one gulp. So, let's attend to your request for clothing. That requires a brief errand into the canopy, but you'll be fine here."

"What? Do you all have to go?"

Blackthorn shook its head and looked frustrated. "He still thinks we're separate beings. Are you sure this guy can handle everything?"

Redthorn patted Blackthorn on the head. "He can learn. And he will learn, we have faith."

"He will learn/Or we will burn."

The three creatures jumped to the bark of the nearest tree and raced up the trunk. About forty feet up, Redthorn turned around and called down to Owen. "Meanwhile, if you're still hungry, you may eat more of the coral mushroom while you wait. Or, if you want something different, try the orange polypore growing on that venerable elder down the stream. Better than it looks." Redthorn waved at the bole of an ancient tree that was large even for these woods.

"Be right back," it blew a kiss to Owen and scampered up the trunk to join its fellows. He watched them climb, following their ascent until they were lost in the maze of branches that began about two hundred feet off the ground.

As soon as he was alone, Owen felt rattled. The stillness of the woods emphasized his dependency on the little creatures and their good will. Despite his new emotional strength, he sensed the old well of panic just below the surface. Pointless or even rude though it may be, he wanted to call out for help. Agitated, he turned around, scanning the landscape. When his eyes came back to the big tree down the creek, he thought he saw someone sitting at the base. It looked like Dr. Chouinard. She was working with her hands as if kneading clay. Excited, Owen set off at a trot. He called out to the doctor, but she didn't lift her head, just continued to work. Half-way to the tree the image dissolved. Keenly disappointed, Owen stifled the urge to cry. He slowed to a shuffle and continued to the tree but there was nothing to suggest the image had been anything other than a trick of light or desire.

The fungi on the tree were real enough, though—a vibrant array of orange conk mushrooms projecting from the bark. These must be the polypores, he thought.

The trunk was at least thirty feet in diameter. The orange clusters grew in tight, shelf-like arrays arcing around the curved wall of bark like a modern art display. Owen's anxiety faded as he admired these wonders. He reached out to touch one of the projecting shelves and found it stiff and unyielding. Grasping a small one, he snapped it off at the trunk. It was thin like a cracker.

There wasn't much of an odor beyond a savory hint. He bit down. Tough going for food, almost at the limits of his ability to chew, but as his saliva worked on it, it softened enough to swallow. It tasted like a Ritz cracker, a familiar comfort.

He had just finished off two polypore segments and was reaching for a third when he heard a noise above his head. Looking up, he saw the three Thorns racing down the trunk at full speed. He wondered how they had followed him, then understood that the canopy must provide an overlapping network of branches. Further musing was cut short when Redthorn yelled at him, "Get out of the way! Back from the trunk!"

Owen stood transfixed for a second, then saw something in Redthorn's expression that called for action. He turned and ran, barely noticing as Redthorn leaped from the tree and landed on his back, quickly followed by the others. They clutched his neck and scrambled for purchase against his back, jostling around like necklaces. Redthorn's breath was loud in his ear, "Faster!"

Owen was at full stride when Blackthorn called out, "That should do it."

Owen stopped, panting, and turned his head to Redthorn, now back to its usual shoulder perch. "What the hell?"

Blackthorn took the other shoulder while Whitethorn reclaimed the top of Owen's head. Redthorn indicated the tree they had fled, and Owen watched as a bundle the size of a duffle bag fell two hundred feet from the lowest branches and thumped into the soil. "Your costume, dear," it announced.

Owen looked at Redthorn from the corner of his eye. "Was all that really necessary?"

Redthorn kissed his cheek. "Probably not. But kind of fun, don't you think?"

They walked over to the bundle. As Owen bent to inspect it, the Thorns jumped off and took up stations where they could watch. The bundle consisted of large swatches of coarse brown fabric folded up and tied together with a sturdy cord. As Owen unwrapped the package, a smaller packet fell out. Fashioned like a Native American parfleche, the packet was a wallet decorated with colored geometric designs. He opened it and found a skein of thin twine and a needle made of bone or hardwood. Also, in the packet was a well-crafted knife wrapped in leather. It had a wooden haft lashed to a black stone blade. As he ran his finger along the blade it sliced into his skin. "Wow," he exclaimed, "is this obsidian?"

"Yes, be careful. The edge is one molecule thick and will cut between the cells of your flesh."

Whitethorn lay back on a square of fabric and put its forepaws behind its head, a remarkably human posture, Owen thought. "You think your flesh is married together/But cells slice apart when you're so clever." This verse went unacknowledged.

"Okay," Owen said, "where did this stuff come from? Manna from heaven?"

Redthorn grinned, briefly revealing its set of pointed teeth. "No, no, nothing so mysterious, though your mythological yearning would like that, wouldn't it? Still, the reality may be even more wonderful."

Blackthorn stared at Owen and offered another lecture segment. "Most of the ambulatory life-forms in this forest live in the upper canopy, much the same as in the old forests of your world.

Above us, in this area, there's a primate civilization. They're tool makers with a sophisticated culture, and are quite clever, as our poet implied. Only rarely do they descend to the ground, which they find too gloomy, being sun-lovers in body and spirit. In order to accumulate water, they peel bark from certain trees, shred and mash it into a fabric, which is virtually waterproof, and sew it into large tarps. These are strung from branches to collect rain that pools neatly in the center of the tarps, then is drained and stored in hollow branches. For handy use they refill pouches which can be worn on the back while traveling in the trees."

Redthorn raised its voice. "You know, they were supposed to put one of those pouches somewhere in the bundle."

When Owen fished out a pouch, Redthorn looked pleased. "Anyway, there should be enough fabric for you to make a simple outfit as well as a satchel to carry supplies. We have a few days of walking to do and if you can bring your own nourishment then you won't have to forage. Plus, as you'll see, there isn't much of that where we're going. So, if you want to start crafting right away, we can talk about our mission while you work."

Owen didn't know much about sewing other than what he had picked up from standing alongside his mother when she worked on her machine. Being a frugal New Englander, she had made many of their clothes and kept them in repair. Sometimes she let Owen pull a few stitches by hand, but often, no matter how unobtrusive he tried to be, his presence seemed to bother her, and she would shoo him away. Once, as he left the room, he turned back at the door and saw her remove a bottle from the drawer, a bottle he recognized. After that, he never intruded again.

Some knowledge of the craft must have lodged in his brain, though, because after laying out his materials and recruiting the Thorns to take a few measurements with string, he started cutting the fabric and matching it along the edges to make seams. A simple outfit would do, he decided, a sleeveless tunic and a pair of short pants, both size baggy. He could cinch up the pants with cord and, if necessary, there was enough extra material to wrap his feet for protection, though he preferred to keep them bare. He relished the contact with the earth. Making his own clothes was an ancient activity, he realized, one with indigenous and mythic significance. He liked that.

When the sewing project was lined out and the stitching begun, his attention returned to the greater concern. "You've dropped some hints, mentioned a journey, a mission, and systemic suicide. I tasted the pain of a dying forest. Before my eager imagination fills in too many more blanks with rabid speculation, perhaps you can just give it to me straight." He looked quickly at Redthorn, who was sitting on its haunches next to him with one of its rear paws tucked behind its head in a yoga pose.

"Better be straight/'Fore it's too late," came from Whitethorn, immersed in scratching Blackthorn's back, much to Owen's surprise.

"Fair enough." Redthorn looked pointedly at Blackthorn. The black creature responded with a pained expression, shrugged off Whitethorn's massage and stood up to face Owen. It clasped its hands behind its back and focused on a spot just over Owen's head. Another lecture appeared imminent.

"The problem starts in your world. Because of the links through branes, we're sensitive to what goes on across the divide. Anything that affects the mycorrhizal network in your world has the potential to cross the brane and affect us as well. This fluid enmeshment has been mutually beneficial for ages. Unfortunately, in recent centuries humans have invented and applied aggressive technologies of influence within their ecosystem. As a result, there've been some spectacular catastrophes and a general degradation of systemic functioning. No doubt you've heard the rumors. Some of this damage is leaking out of your world and into ours. The impact here so far has been confined to small areas, but in your world the dysfunction is accelerating at an alarming pace and few places are unaffected. We assume that will be our fate as well."

Owen's cheeks flushed with shame, and he raised his head from the sewing to be caught in Blackthorn's stare. "Your kind has generated awareness of the problem; we know that you know. We've been forced to study *homo sapiens* as an evolutionary factor. It may be that our own survival depends on it. Although we recognize that there is constructive potential in human beings, in the present situation we're required to focus on what is destructive. We can no longer observe and learn. It's now time to act."

Owen tore his eyes away from Blackthorn's accusing stare and focused on the work in his hands. What could he say? He was ambivalent, at best. He loved the creativity of his kind, but he did not love their behaviors, the selfish cruelty that was commonplace. He remained silent and waited.

Whitethorn marched up and down, swinging its arms stiffly in a military cadence, chanting. "Too late for tact/And that's a fact/It's time to act!"

Despite the seriousness of the discussion, Owen laughed at the sight of the little poet stomping back and forth behind Blackthorn, who whirled around in a rage and spit.

Redthorn abandoned the yoga and leaped between the other two, raising its paws to hold them apart. The conflict evaporated and Redthorn gave a human-like shrug before turning back to Owen as if nothing had happened. "The question is, how to act? We have no heart to engage in warfare against your species, even if we could."

Blackthorn continued. "The brane boundaries allow transfer of substance and energy, but we're certain that there are limits to accurate reconstitution. Your passage through the brane is an example of an innovative trend for the system. It may be a further development of the same mechanics that allow toxins to pass the brane boundary. At this point we don't comprehend all the implications. Understanding an ecosystem requires a mind at least as complex as the ecosystem being studied. Knowledge is infinite, but mind is not."

Redthorn eased in front of Blackthorn and took over. "And that's just the physics, dear. More perplexing is the philosophy. Justice is always a complicated endeavor, never mind one that tries to span species, ecologies, and worlds. Is it within our ethical domain to activate changes in your world, or is that a presumption? Or even worse, the violation of a fundamental paradigm? Or did the ethical violation originate with the mycorrhizal explorations across the branes? We don't know. These concerns seem less relevant if your species is a participant in the action. Then we could cultivate a shared ethos."

Redthorn again combed its fingers through its hair, a gesture Owen had observed in women as they preened. "Look, in order to act in your world, we need an agent, someone brave enough to be an ally. That agent would need to understand the problem and agree to work on it. We believe that most humans are far too complacent to work for radical change. But radical change is required. It seemed important to recruit someone who has suffered at the hands of other humans because such a person may be able to step back far enough to see things as they are and wish for change. Someone with something to prove, perhaps.

"When you brought yourself to the ash tree to die, we, the multiverse forest, sensed that you might be a candidate for change, someone who carried pain inflicted by humans, someone who could understand that there is a sickness in the genes that must be dealt with. You were brought here to be nurtured and rebuilt, to hear our plea, and perhaps to act."

Owen had stopped sewing and stared openmouthed at Redthorn. "You're shitting me. First you tell me that the forest rescued me to avoid additional suffering or some such goopy crap. Now you're saying that there was another motive altogether! You want me to be some kind of multiverse revolutionary? To act against my own species?"

Blackthorn nodded its head vigorously but let Redthorn continue. "Yes, exactly. Though it's more accurate to say that we would like you to do something *for* your own species, because if something doesn't change soon, you'll probably extinguish yourselves. Keep in mind that reducing your personal suffering, the suffering your suicide would have caused the forest, and reducing the suffering being spread across the multiverse are not entirely different motives. They just happened to come together in a focus: you. So, yes, you could be a revolutionary. A revolutionary hero. You can frame your own myth around it—that should appeal to you."

"I don't know what to say. I'm not really the hero type. I can be a great victim; I've got lots of experience with that. I think you've got the wrong guy." Owen shook his head and bent back to the sewing, seeking distraction from a swirl of troubling thoughts.

The three Thorns stood together facing him, arms around each other as Redthorn adopted an encouraging tone. "No, we don't think so. We've taken some of your measure since you've been here. We're pretty sure you're the perfect guy. We think you're one of those with something to prove."

"Something to prove/Means time to move/Sooo.../Get in your groove!"

[9]

Owen recognized that the recruitment pitch played to his guilt and aspirations. Awareness of that didn't make it less effective, though, and he sat in confusion, ashamed of his people yet intrigued with the tease of savior mythology. He longed for noble achievements, from his earliest escapes into the world of fantasy where he craved the swagger of Conan the Conqueror to later, more nuanced identifications with Greek and Celtic heroes who, despite their shortcomings, managed to get things done. Important things, whereas Owen's life was full of failures. Although he had accepted his history of suffering, an accomplishment which Dr. Chouinard had reminded him was more than nothing, his primary response to stress had been to flee and hide. Sure, he had accumulated a store of knowledge, but it was mostly useless, like a dragon's horde. In the end, he was unremarkable. Now he was urged to save the multiverse, a summons, really, from a collective mind so far beyond his comprehension that it had to present itself in the form of cute animals so he wouldn't freak out. The situation was ludicrous. Perhaps he had crossed over a threshold, not into another world, but into lunacy. Or, recalling a previous notion, he was dead, and this was all a barrage of Tibetan *bardo* theater, testing him until he passed into the Great Liberation or was reborn to slog through another unfortunate existence. Whatever it was, he had no template for action. As this thought rose out of his old despair, his hands flew through the sewing. When his left arm turned again to pull the stitch, he noticed the tattooed labyrinth. There was a template. One he had used for the last decade and which had, as Redthorn said, served as a beacon in the darkness. Not likely that he had exhausted the depths of meaning in that symbol. He stared at the tattoo, following the circular lines as they wound around each other. When his eyes got to the center, he remembered what he had done when he was thirteen. Tired of his uncle's abusive terror, he had taken a baseball bat and crushed him, left him on the floor of his bedroom, bloody and broken. He hadn't regretted it then or at any time since. The fucker deserved it. And it stopped the abuse. Thinking about the intensity of that moment, the whirlwind of fear and anger that had spun around him, he felt warmth in his blood. Maybe he wasn't as hapless as he thought. Maybe, when it really counted, he did know something about action.

The Thorns watched without a word, letting him wander within his thoughts. Owen's spiral meditation led him around to what he knew best: the myths. He remembered the story that took him to the tree. It seemed so long ago, something out of the mists. "Once upon a time," he muttered under his breath. Yes, at that point he had embraced a sense of kindred with Ariadne, an obsessive identification that led him to his own noose, but he knew that he'd deliberately ignored the other narratives of Ariadne's fate, the ones that contradicted his blazing will to die. His allegiance to Ariadne's suicide had been a compulsion; he saw that now. However, the story offered several variations, not all of them grim, some downright triumphant. Take your pick. He had picked despair. In a different ending, after Theseus abandoned Ariadne on Naxos, she "invoked the whole universe for vengeance," as Robert Graves had written. Her plea was favorably received by Zeus, who caused Theseus' father to throw himself to death from the top of the Acropolis. Ariadne was plucked from the Naxos beach by the god Dionysos, accompanied by a train of satyrs and maenads, and crowned as his wife. She led a long, fruitful life as the queen of a god. In that version, Ariadne, rather than remaining the victim of a ruthless man, rose up in anger and struck. Owen had also lashed back at a ruthless man—even though there had been no god to stand behind him. His desperate act had eventually led to Dr. Chouinard. She may not have been divine, but she cast a holy light into Owen's life. And she had shown him the labyrinth and helped him unwind some of its secrets. As he stared at the tattoo in a daze, his choice seemed clear.

He looked at the Thorns, appreciating their patience. "So, what do we have to do? I'm not saying yes, but I'm thinking about it."

"We could tell. You were sewing so fast it seems you are almost done with the project."

Owen looked down and saw that Redthorn was right. A few more stitches and he would have a shirt and pants.

"His itches for stitches/Have led to new britches," intoned Whitethorn. Blackthorn made strangled noises, fell to its knees, and began to tear at the fur on its head. Owen couldn't tell if it was choking or laughing.

Redthorn ignored the histrionics. "If you're satisfied with the clothes, we should start the journey. We can talk as we go."

"Are we in that much of a hurry?"

Redthorn scratched its nose with the back of a hand. "Depends on how you measure time, dear, in little chunks or big ones. Rather than get into the technical stuff, though, let's just go with *yes*."

"In other words, it's all relative..." Owen was surprised to see Blackthorn, having collected itself from the ground, flash a thumbs up gesture. Before it could start on a lecture about relativity, Owen stood and slipped into the pants and the tunic. He turned this way and that in front of the Thorns, mimicking a runway model. The clothes were loose and ridiculous, but they covered his torso. Insects would no longer have uninhibited access to his tender parts. The fabric was more comfortable than he anticipated. It was supple enough not to scratch or irritate his skin. He lashed some cord around his waist to hold up the pants and added the last touches to a bag he could carry over his shoulder on a strap. He put the parfleche and remaining fabric scraps into the bag, then walked over to the stream to fill the water pouch.

While he did that, all three Thorns ran up the polypore-laden tree and broke off several of the projecting shelves, dropping them to the ground for Owen to collect. As Owen filled the remaining space in the bag with the crispy fungus, he thought of a new question. "Hey, do you guys eat this stuff?"

Redthorn, still clinging to the tree bark, scurried around to face Owen and wrinkled its nose. "Sort of. But not like you think. We know you see the Thorn things as separate beings, but we're not. We aren't even animal. A Thorn is another sort of holon, a manifestation of this region of the forest mind, grown on a tree like a fruiting body, then expelled to move about on its own, a kind of emissary of the forest, a mobile node of contact. Eating, as you think of it, is not necessary for us. We live like the forest because we are the forest. Or a part of it, anyway."

"So... you're a tree... thing?"

Whitethorn ran down the trunk, launched from twenty feet up and landed on Owen's shoulder. The impact barely shifted his posture. Whitethorn nuzzled into Owen's ear, kissed his cheek until it tickled, and began to croon. "What about a reckless fling/Guaranteed to make you sing/With a tree collective thing!"

Owen plucked Whitethorn off his shoulder, cuddled it in his palm and brought it to his face for a kiss. "Aren't you just the sweetest thing?"

Whitethorn giggled. The other Thorns jumped from the tree to Owen's shoulders and he placed Whitethorn on top of his head. Redthorn pointed upstream and Owen set off through the woods.

"So, do you require nourishment at all? And if so, how do you get it?"

From his right shoulder, Redthorn stroked Owen's cheek. "We approve of your curiosity—a crucial trait for heroes."

On the other shoulder, Blackthorn clutched Owen's ear and talked as fast it could. "Perhaps you, like most humans, are unaware that trees feed each other through the mycorrhizal networks. The underground links are for commerce as well as communication. This is true here and it's true in your world. Nutrients are passed back and forth between points of consumption, distributed from areas of excess to areas of need. Individuals in the network don't exist in isolated nutrient economies; all resources are shared and redistributed. The Thorn manifestations are not separate beings but are part of this continuum and thus participate in the nutrient flow. As manifestations, the Thorns need minimal nourishment because they are time-limited units. If necessary, they can use finger tendrils to sink into the soil and tap the mycorrhizal network, but in most cases, there's no need for that. The unit contains enough stored nutrients for the anticipated span of existence."

"Hold on. Time-limited unit? What are you saying? Are you guys going to die? How long until this happens?" Owen's voice was shrill, and he could feel the incipient panic. Abandonment warnings clamored in the back of his mind. He peered at Redthorn from the corner of his eye, then plucked the creature from his shoulder and held it in his palm where he could see it better.

"Oh goodness. You're crying," Redthorn observed. Whitethorn leaned over Owen's forehead, balancing itself with a hand on his nose, and watched a tear trickle down his cheek. It wiped up the tear with a finger, then brought the finger to its mouth. Smacking its lips three times, it declaimed, "Never fear the tear/A sign of what's dear."

The simple lyric triggered Owen's vulnerability. He stopped and coughed up torso-shaking sobs. Redthorn scrambled up Owen's arm and back to the shoulder, placing the palm of its forehand on his right temple. Blackthorn palmed the other temple. It wasn't long before Owen felt a tingling run through his body, as if each cell received an electric charge. Within seconds, both his mind and body found equilibrium. He was no less sad, but the sadness carried power. Like a sponge, he absorbed the vitality of the forest, blending his sadness into the life around him, shaping it into an organic communion. Energy crackled in his bones. He was connected to everything. It was all there. He wasn't separate; he was a part of the web of life.

"Wow! What the fuck did you do?"

"Aw, go on, you did it yourself. You have these powers. True, they've been dormant, unavailable behind the contorted screen of your suffering. We've merely reconnected you to your potential." Redthorn, with a satisfied expression, combed its fingers through the fur on its head, then looked at Owen expectantly. He took the hint and resumed walking. "We're touched by the depth of your caring for the Thorns. Really, this confirms the wisdom in bringing you here and asking for your help. We honor the attachment you've made to a mere node of the forest; it indicates the willingness of your love."

Blackthorn butted in, pedantic as ever. "Ahem. It is absolutely essential for you to accept that the Thorns are a medium, not the mind. The Thorns are like a pinecone that carries the seeds of the tree. Those seeds are the genetic legacy. The cone expresses those seeds into the world, spreading the wisdom of the tree and thus of the forest itself. But the cone then falls to the ground and is digested back into the network. The fungal mycelia slip into its decaying matter, extracting the substance of the cone and returning it to its original state. The matter is never lost, only the current form. This is true for all life, you know, including yours."

"Okay, I get it. You guys are just pine cones that dropped onto my head and I shouldn't get bogged down with the cone and think it's gonna last, even if I happen to like it and want to take it home and put it on the shelf forever."

"A cone on the head/Is better than dead."

Redthorn had a different take. "You have to find your way to the mind. The cone, the Thorns, these are signifiers chosen by the mind to convey meaning. But they are not the mind."

"Come on down/You will find/Lots of room/In our mind," sang Whitethorn.

Blackthorn showed its impatience by jumping up and down, hanging on to Owen's ear for balance, "Balderdash, all of it. We're going to a place where you'll experience a direct neural interface with the mind. Our mind. Trying to explain it within the limits of your language is a waste, let us repeat, a waste of time. Not to belabor the obvious, but the faster we go, the sooner we get there."

"Yes, sir!" Owen saluted smartly with his left hand, which took Blackthorn by surprise, forcing it to cling to Owen's neck as they resumed walking.

Owen moved gracefully between the trees, keeping the water course in sight. Judging from the incline ahead, he guessed they were leaving the flat ground. "So, if you guys are a time-limited phenomenon, how much time are we talking about? I need to know. I don't like people leaving me, which is what always happens. At least, that's the way it's been so far."

"We have plenty of time," Redthorn stated.

"You're not going to tell me, are you?"

"Nope," the three said in unison.

Owen sighed. "Okay then, can you at least tell me something about where we're going and what we're doing? If you're my guides and shit, then I damn well want the full tour. With all the footnotes."

In the silence, Owen figured that the three of them were consulting, though he didn't know how since there was no additional movement beyond the usual clinging and swaying as he walked. Finally, Redthorn spoke. "We follow the stream in reverse, up the hill, on beyond its source. Eventually, we top out on a ridge. The rest of the journey tracks along the crest of that ridge. As we ascend, the ecology remains forest-based, but the scale is less lofty. However, what upland forest loses in the way of height is made up for in density. Despite the differences, the biostructure in that zone is another manifestation of our extended being, another diverse mask in the multiplicity of our world's personae."

"Personae? You mean like Jung's idea?" Owen broke in.

Blackthorn barked and took over. "Not really. We don't have a persona in the sense of something other than what we are, like an artificial mask; our masks are accurate expressions of being. But the forest mind is not a unified totality, either. It's a complex web of nodes. These nodes are not organized into a coordinated hierarchy; it's an anarchistic assemblage. Each node cultivates its own personality and in congress with the other nodes forms a diverse multiplicity. Not the best comparison at all, to use these convoluted metaphors of Jung. But, whatever... if it helps you understand something complex."

"No, no, I love it! Dr. Chouinard would be tickled pink. Stuff like this confirms everything she believed in."

Redthorn rubbed the furry side of its head against Owen's ear. "We are pleased to see how you honor this teacher. It does you credit...."

Blackthorn wasn't ready to yield the lectern. "Anyway, as we were about to say, the upland forest where we're going has a strong brane connection to your world; there's an extensive cluster of linkages through the mycorrhizal network. And that's where things are dying—trees, everything. Trees die anyway, of course, as part of the cycle of life, but when all life-forms within a section of forest die simultaneously, it suggests that something is killing them."

As they trekked, Owen worked his way around the trees, circumnavigating the gigantic trunks with their extended root buttresses, always returning to the brook to stay on course. Except for the change in slope, the forest looked the same in all directions and he imagined it would be easy to get lost.

Blackthorn was eager to continue its lesson. "We're sure you haven't, but for the sake of form, we ask if you've ever heard of the hemlock wooly adelgid?"

A puzzling question, Owen thought. Almost nonsensical. "No, can't say I have."

"Not surprising, not surprising at all. It's a tiny insect in your world that breeds in hemlock trees. It weaves fuzzy webs for its eggs along the tips of branches. They hatch in great numbers and start devouring the leaves, or needles as you call them, in order to make more eggs. Eventually the tree is stripped and dies. In the commercial forests of your world the land managers have decided to fight back against the adelgid. Capital resources are being affected – an unacceptable outcome for profit margins."

The voice of Whitethorn hovered over Owen's head. "Now who would think/A little bug/From neighbor world/Has pulled the rug."

Blackthorn made choking sounds. "Isn't it past time to rethink our commitment to poetry? If we can even call this stuff poetry."

Redthorn was haughty. "Tsk tsk. Of course not. There's no point in asking."

"Gah. Anyway, as we were saying.... Human biologists developed an invasive method of attacking the adelgid. They're using a syringe and inoculating trees with chemicals to kill the pest. Managers want to believe that these chemicals don't harm the trees. Generally, this has been true, and the trees are still alive. But that's also true of the adelgid. So, they've escalated the conflict by introducing a new chemical. When this chemical leaks through the brane, as they all do in time, it goes through a quantum mutation that changes it into a lethal toxin. It's killing things in our world—rapidly. We considered severing the brane links, but those links are ancient and represent a valuable extension of our open life system. Cutting the linkage would be like amputating your finger or a hand. Sure, better than the loss of the whole system, but a last resort. We're not there, yet."

Owen said nothing. He didn't know where to start. Should he apologize for his species? What was the point of that? Wasn't his own shame enough? Did he also have to carry the burden of humanity?

Redthorn, as if sensing Owen's discomfort, patted his head. "We understand this is a lot to absorb. It's probably blowing your mind off. Is that the expression? But really, to use another of your phrases, you ain't seen nothing yet. We're going to show you the dead zone, splice you into the rhizome mind, reveal everything you might need in order to understand the situation. Then, we want you to go back to your people and do something about it."

"Hmm. No small task, I'm sure."

"No, indeed."

"I'm willing to try to help, but I have no method, no expertise at this. There's a lot of science involved. Maybe you need a forester. Or a chemist."

"No, we don't need a so-called expert. We need someone with a heart. And don't worry about coming up with a method, dear. We'll give you that."

[10]

The way through the woods steepened and Owen stopped to catch his breath. Splashing loudly along a series of cascades, the stream leaped over rocks and ledges with no hint of the lazy brook it would become on the flats below. He looked around, taking in the soft light slicing horizontally through the forest. Tree trunks glowed with a beauty that brought an ache to Owen's heart. As the sun set, it threw out a blaze of gold before it merged with the earth.

"How much longer do you want to push on?" He asked the Thorns.

"We can stop here. The ground gets even steeper ahead," Redthorn obliged.

Whitethorn, however, in a squeaky voice, offered something else. "Would you go deeper/If it got steeper/Or be a reaper/A downright creeper/So says the sleeper!"

Out of the corner of his eye, Owen saw Blackthorn throw its arms over its head as if beseeching the heavens. "Good grief!"

"I don't really get it, either," Owen admitted. "But I'm going to assume the use of the word 'sleeper' is a cue." Redthorn chuckled while Blackthorn continued to grumble.

In the fading light, Owen scanned the slope and spotted a level space on the uphill side of a tree. He walked to it and slipped off the satchel, careful not to dislodge the Thorns. One by one, they jumped to the trunk of the tree and clung there for a moment before exploding into a wild chase up, down, and around the trunk. Owen sat and watched, enjoying the acrobatics. Hungry, he chewed a mushroom without enthusiasm. In a synchronized sequence, the three Thorns scampered off the tree and parked next to him in a row.

Between mouthfuls, Owen announced: "I'm tired. It feels like we've been walking for days. I may have slept for a week while you did your doctor thing, but if that counts as rest it's worn off. I don't suppose you guys need sleep."

"Not really. But you should make yourself comfortable and rest. It'll be too dark for us to find our way," suggested Redthorn.

"You know I want to ask about this method, the one that's going to change the world."

"We know."

"But I'm not going to ask, because I've a hunch you won't tell me."

"Correct. It's not a secret, but learning is a sequence and we aren't there yet."

"When will we get there?"

"Soon enough. Be patient, dear," advised Redthorn. "Learning makes the most sense when it's lodged in the landscape. You'll see."

Owen wanted to say more, but he was too drowsy. The persistent flow of information was exhausting. Overloaded with mind-expanding data, he struggled to recalibrate after each new bit. He walked behind a bush to relieve himself and came back to the nook at the base of the tree. The Thorns were gone. He might well have been anxious, but he was too tired to care. He settled into the moss. There was enough of a breeze to discourage the occasional mosquito. He sighed in contentment. Putting his satchel under his head, he fell asleep as the last light drained from the sky.

He dreamed that he lay in a forest more tangled and somber than the Thorn world. It was dawn. His head was in Dr. Chouinard's lap and she stroked his hair with one hand while the other cradled his neck. Every nerve in his body tingled with life. Blood thickened his penis. He blinked and then a female sat across his hips. She had a human shape but was covered in luxurious moss and the details of her features were cloaked under the greenery. This apparition seemed the most beautiful creature Owen had ever seen. He looked up at Dr. Chouinard, whose eyes were shut. She seemed to be in a trance, still stroking his head. The moss-woman lifted slightly and put his penis inside her, sliding down over his erection. She rocked her hips as he thrust into her and they fell into a rhythm. The conjunction eclipsed all thought with waves of sensation. His cells were pure electricity. In a rush of blinding light, he uncoiled his energy into the critical mass of orgasm.

He awoke to the gray light of the real dawn, continuing to ride the exhilaration of the dream until it trickled away and he was alone. There was a sticky wetness on his abdomen. Embarrassed, he looked around, but the Thorns were nowhere to be seen. He sighed, yanked off his pants, and walked over to the stream. There was a rock for scrubbing and a bush to hang his garment to dry. It was odd that he didn't feel a gnawing shame, the usual accompaniment to his sexual experiences. He felt a little sheepish, but at heart he was glad for the dream. Even the simplest sex was never easy for Owen, and the dream, though weird, provided an uncomplicated ecstasy.

The sun poked its way into the woods as it breached the horizon. Owen wondered what happened to his guides. Maybe he should break the silence, despite his reluctance to intrude on the sacramental sounds of falling water. "Redthorn?" His first call was tentative and barely above a whisper. He felt silly. "Thorns!" He bellowed.

There was movement on an exposed root of the tree where he had slept. It was a gray, shapeless mass which he had taken for a lichen, but it raised itself off the trunk, unfolding and separating into the shapes of his three companions. "Are you done?" demanded Blackthorn.

"Done? Uh, yeah, sure. I'm ready to resume our journey, if that's what you mean. Well, as soon as my pants dry."

Redthorn looked at Owen and wrinkled its nose. "Ecological systems rely on an array of drives and mechanisms for maintenance and integrity. Pleasure is part of it."

Owen did not reply. It was not a conversation he wanted to pursue.

Whitethorn pursed its lips, scrunching its face, then spit out its own summation. "If you can't fornicate/Go ahead and masturbate!"

Owen smiled thinly. Redthorn stared into the woods, apparently lost in thought, while Blackthorn glared. Pleased with itself, Whitethorn flipped over backwards, landing on its feet and grinning at Owen. Obligingly, he reached down and gave it a pat on the head.

For breakfast, there was fungi and water. The lack of novelty was tiresome, but he didn't feel hungry or undernourished. Whatever was in the food would keep him alive, it seemed. His pants dried faster than he expected, and he was soon ready to travel.

"Okay, commanders. Up the stream?"

Redthorn winced at the title but nodded. "For now, yes."

Owen scooped up a handful of water from the cascade. Refreshing, it tasted like rock. He'd only been in this forest a short time, but already felt a reverence for it. Beauty was expressed in the patterns of growth and woven into a harmonic whole. When he inhaled, he absorbed a feeling of balance, like this was the way things were supposed to be. Romantic nonsense, he thought, but the feeling was there.

The Thorns leaped back to their accustomed positions on Owen as he set off. The angle of the slope continued to increase, as did the prevalence of outcrops and massive boulders. Soon the hike required the use of hands and his gait slowed to the step-pause-step motion of ascending stairs. This movement was tiring but also satisfying. Owen felt the strength in his muscles and the grace of his bones as he climbed. The Thorns sat on top like captains at the helm, adjusting postures with every pitch and yaw.

After scrambling over a small outcrop, they came to the source of the stream. Under a cliff was a basin scooped out of solid rock and filled with water. It overflowed the lip and poured down the outcrop at the lower end, forming the first of the long chain of cascades. At the back of the pool was a granite wall cleaved by a narrow seam. The water bubbled out of that seam from somewhere within the earth. Owen wanted to linger and daydream while soaking his feet.

"What now?" He asked hopefully.

Redthorn was gentle. "A precious place, to be sure. But we're nearing our first objective, so let's push on. Go around the pool and its headwall to the left. Once we get a little higher, you'll see to the top of the ridge. Our path takes us there, then along the crest. Such a sublime area, it's a shame this will all be dead shortly."

"We're that close to the toxic zone?"

"Not as close as you might imagine," Blackthorn interrupted. "But the efficiency of the mycorrhizal networks in linking the forest means that toxins can migrate through them at a disconcerting pace. We haven't figured out how to slow this process... short of amputation."

"What's that, you say/All cut away?/Shut up and pray/Just... shut up and pray." Whitethorn slapped out the rhythm on Owen's skull until he reached up to stay its hands.

Owen drank in the beauty of the pool with a final glance before climbing around the headwall. Above the rock, he paused for a moment, savoring the declining angle ahead. As promised, the trees were smaller, there was more sun making its way to the ground, and the horizon of the ridge top didn't seem far. The trees, tiny compared to the giants in the flats, were less than a foot in diameter and perhaps only fifty feet high. They grew close together, with few branches on the lower trunks, and thrust the broadleaf clusters of their crowns into the sun. Swaying back and forth in the wind, they seemed to Owen like a cheerful crowd, happy in their element. The scale of this forest was easier to comprehend, although walking became tricky as the stems increased in density. Proceeding in a straight line was impossible. Sometimes the distance between trees was almost as narrow as his shoulders and he had to forge a twisting path through the arbors.

Soon they were on the ridge top, and a few sunbeams found a way to Owen's face through the dancing leaves of the canopy. Like the sun of his world, it felt warm, a comforting familiarity. They walked along the ridge, which had some ups and downs but was mostly level. Owen appreciated the ease of movement and glimpses of sky after days of living underneath a vast overstory. Ahead of them, he saw a bright clearing.

They came to the edge of the forest and stopped. Beyond was a sight that raised the hackles on Owen's spine. Everything in the clearing was dead. All the trees and bushy stems were bleached a glossy white, like a surrealist boneyard. There were no leaves on the trees, no grasses, no flowers or shrubs. The unfiltered sun glared on the clearing and the light was reflected by the sheen of each exposed surface. As he stepped into the zone, Owen squinted. He lifted his right hand to shade his eyes and Redthorn clambered around to claim space on his left shoulder with Blackthorn. They pushed and grappled until they found a balance.

"Oh, sorry. I wasn't thinking."

Blackthorn grumbled, "No problem. We adapt. But we haven't figured out how to adapt to this."

Redthorn waved a forearm to encompass the devastation. "There is so much sorrow here. It reeks with threat. Can you feel it?"

"I've never seen anything like it. It's worse than a clear cut. It *looks* poisoned. Reminds me of the bleaching of coral reefs. That's when the water gets too warm and the reefs die. Instead of the colorful mix of sea life they turn a uniform white. I've seen pictures... eerie, very disturbing. This is like that. I heard that with climate change all the reefs on Earth are supposed to die soon. Do you know about all that? I don't even know if you have oceans on this world."

"We have oceans," Blackthorn answered. "And cooperative corals that can link to our forest rhizomes in the substrate. Hard to comprehend the agony of a massive die-off of those ancient networks. Corals built some of our oldest life systems."

"Yeah. This is awful. It's like the myth of the wasteland, where a blight on the land causes it to wither and die. Usually as a result of the misdeeds of the king... or the people."

"When we think about your people from our collective perspective, we see human culture as a sort of group mind itself. More than a little ironic to consider that myths and parables of that mind provide lessons about the dangers of misbehavior and its impact on the land. We don't understand why that culture mind continues to make your homeland into a wasteland, acting contrary to your own knowledge. Such behavior offers little promise for evolutionary success." Blackthorn shook its head in dejection.

"Yes, it doesn't add up, does it?" Owen remembered one of his research topics: the junction of myth and morality. "Part of the problem is the value attached to the misbehavior. In mythology, the wasteland isn't a consequence of poor stewardship or political opportunism. It's usually caused by a transgression of taboos. For example, in the myths of several religions the cities of Sodom and Gomorrah are destroyed because the inhabitants engaged in forbidden intercourse. And in the Grail legend of the Fisher King, the lands turn to waste because the king's wound causes him to be impotent, possibly as a result of infidelity or homosexuality. The wastelands are retribution for moral failure, typically failure of a sexual nature. And we're not talking about criminal behavior, usually just something considered deviant. Regardless, it always seems to come down to some kind of transgression against a moral code. These myths reinforce the idea of punishment more than they provide a cautionary lesson about how to live on the land."

Whitethorn craned its neck far enough forward to lean over and stare straight back into Owen's eyes, upside down. It licked Owen's nose with a wet, rough tongue.

Blackthorn started to laugh but covered it with a cough. "Anyway, we're coming to a point of applying our own judgment and, in a way, our own retribution. Out of necessity, not in response to taboos. The transgressions that caused this wasteland were done in the name of greed. And it's not the only place like this. Toxins from your world are filtering through the network and spreading pollution into our world and other worlds. We have been patient, but the pace is accelerating. Soon it may become a matter of survival. And though acting on a broad ecological scale like we're considering raises ethical questions, even your own scientists acknowledge that the fundamental principle of biological value is survival. This is true of all life-forms. We're no different."

"Okay, I get it. I'm on board. So, what do you want me to do?"

Redthorn patted Owen's ear. "Let's continue, straight along the ridge. There is something else to show you."

[11]

As they moved through the bleached remains, Owen's spine wilted at the absence of life. More than a zone of death, it was a zone of nothingness, the nullification of being. Malaise settled over him and even the Thorns held a glum silence as Owen shuffled forward.

Underfoot, the soil was crunchy and sharp, poking his soles, forcing him to step lightly. He thought about wrapping his feet with the leftover fabric he had saved, but he realized that he didn't want to shield himself from the pain. Some of the old masochism lingered on—not a surprise, really. He imagined that the pain in his feet was a compensation he owed the land, the least he could do. Time to step up and be responsible for the deeds of his kind. Humans are so fucked-up, he mused. Even if this zone was an accidental consequence, how many times have humans created a disaster out of reckless action? How much slack do we deserve? He was enraged and shamed at the same time. Rape of the land – there needed to be an accounting. Rapists must pay, he had no doubt about that. Yes, he could be the one to avenge this transgression; after all, he had done it before.

A quarter mile of walking brought them to the far boundary of the dead zone. Everyone relaxed when they moved out of the clearing into the living woods. Owen inspected the bottoms of his feet, abraded and bloody. Wiping them on a carpet of soft moss, he wondered what the Thorns thought about this evidence of self-abuse, but nothing was said except for a quiet rhyme from Whitethorn, "A little bit of blood/Dissolving in the crud."

For a while, they walked in reverie, relishing the forest's embrace, soaking up the soft breeze, the tinkling of leaves, and the play of light, a few of the many signs of life. It wasn't long before Owen noticed that the ground started to angle away, and the ridge faded into a slope. As they descended through the trees, Owen saw that a broad saddle interrupted the ridge.

Redthorn broke the silence. "When we get to the low point of the saddle, there'll be a small clearing off to the left. You'll know where to turn because there's a formation of stones set in the ground in the shape of a spiral."

"A formation? Who did that?"

Familiar throat-clearing noises from his shoulder warned Owen that Blackthorn was seizing the stage. "It's been there for a long time. A hundred thousand years, perhaps. We're not sure who did it. Previous inhabitants with sentience and culture, no doubt. They must have been mobile and capable of moving large rocks, but how or why remains a mystery. We can't assume that they were fauna, because there are floral forms that move around and are certainly large enough to shove boulders. Within our networked minds we can access memories for many thousands of years, but the age of this construction is beyond existing memory."

"I've been so caught up in the here and now that I haven't given much thought to the idea that this world has an entire history, pre-history, archaeology, and geology, just like ours. Sometime, perhaps, I could learn more."

"Perhaps. For now, dear, we have more pressing matters" said Redthorn.

Owen sighed. "I knew you would say that."

At the low point of the saddle, Owen had no trouble finding the stone works. Gray rocks the size of hay bales lay in a spiral line that unwound from a central pillar in a few turns and faded away in diminishing sizes. Embedded deeply in moss, the tops and sides of the stones were covered with orange and black lichen.

Owen stopped to touch one of the stones, feeling the rugosity of the rock under the lichen colonies.

The tail of the spiral functioned as a pointer and Owen followed the direction. Minutes later, they came to a meadow featuring seven tall menhirs set in a circle. Each menhir was at least eight feet high and equally spaced from its neighbors; the resulting circle was about twenty feet in diameter. The rock looked to be the same material as the spiral construction and was also covered with lichen. Owen felt a force emanating from the circle, like a powerful wind or current, offering a wall of resistance against further advance. Waves of energy rolled from the center and played tricks with his vision, wrinkling his sight like a mirage. He had no idea what was happening in that circle; he only knew it represented power, something mysterious and terrifying.

Blackthorn started explaining before Owen could move, breaking the spell. "Impressive, eh? We know you feel it. As do we. We don't understand everything that goes on here, but we do understand a few things. The circle is a nexus of brane connections and provides a junction for at least a dozen universes. Gravity is one of the few physical forces that readily permeates brane boundaries and this spot acts as a funnel, blending together a diversity of gravitational energies. That's the primary power that you feel."

"Hunker down and cling to the gunwale/When you're sucked through gravity's funnel."

"Ha, that's a good one, Whitethorn."

"For a change," grumbled Blackthorn.

"Holy shit," Owen said, "It's strong! Standing here, I can feel the pulses, like waves stacked so tightly there's no respite."

Blackthorn continued, "We don't know if the nexus was always there or if the configuration of stones brought it into being. Either is possible. The ancients must have had an awareness of what they were doing, or so we think. But that's speculation. What's important for us, right now, is what's under the ground. Beneath this meadow we find one of the most interesting mycorrhizal networks in the world. It's linked through the nexus to all these other worlds, at least the ones that have soil and forests, which most do. About eight thousand years ago, a seed fell into the circle, a seed from a tree akin to the white ash of your world. Despite the unusual forces in the circle, or because of them, the seed took root and grew. It grew to a full span. It must have been a remarkable sight, such a tree framed by the stones. In time the tree reached the end of its normal life. It gradually weakened and was finally broken apart in a windstorm, leaving a stub."

"Another ash tree? I'm going to have to dig into Norse mythology."

"Anyway, that ash tree – well, it's not really an ash tree, but *quite* similar – that tree helped to weave together a rhizome network of unprecedented complexity. Its disintegration was a loss to our collective being. So, we didn't let it die."

"What? How does that work?"

"The tree in the stones/Left really good bones," came the almost predictable verse.

Blackthorn grabbed Owen's ear and leaned out as far as it could. "Even though the part of the tree above ground was disintegrating, the root system functioned, and it was still linked to the mycorrhizal network. The stump couldn't gather photosynthesized materials and bring them underground, but it could receive nutrients from the subterranean network. This allowed us to feed it and keep it alive. There was too much value, too much memory, in that node of the forest to let it perish. Although there's not much to see, the tree is alive. Underground the tree embodies its fundamental being, anyway; we've explained that."

"Yes. Hard to accept for those of us who can only see the majesty of the above-ground parts. What's in the dirt seems inconsequential. But I get it. It's not."

Redthorn jumped in. "No indeed, that's where the mind does most of its work. But right now, what we need to do is to get you linked to that tree. So, if you're ready, we're going to walk over to the circle and lay down right smack in the middle."

"Good grief. Can we really get closer? Without being crushed or torn apart?"

"Oh yes, dear. In some ways it gets easier."

"Okay, commanders. You haven't steered me wrong yet."

Owen, with Thorns attached, entered the clearing, planting one foot in front of the other as he crossed to the standing stones. It was like walking underwater. At first, he felt his stomach lurch from the roiling gravity, but as Redthorn predicted, he adjusted and by the time they reached the circle, the only effect he noticed was sluggishness.

"You feel the gravity, no?" Blackthorn peered around Owen's cheek.

"Shit, yes. Interesting."

Owen stepped between two menhirs and saw the decaying stump in the center. It must have been a big tree at one time, but now it was a subtle rise covered with moss.

"Just lay there. Put your head on what's left of the stump," Redthorn directed.

The Thorns hopped to the ground and Owen stretched out, tucking the satchel under his head. Redthorn provided further instructions. "Okay, this is going to be weird again. Please lift your shirt and expose your belly. Then we're going to do as we did before: burrow, ever so carefully, into your nervous system. Close your eyes if you like. It won't hurt, though you'll feel a tingle or two. We'll work in sync, penetrating you with one hand while the other goes into the earth and connects to the rhizome. When that happens, prepare for a jolt. Big time. It won't be painful. It might not even be disorienting, but it will be intense. Just let us know when you're ready."

Owen lifted his shirt. He decided to watch everything. At this point, why the hell not?

The Thorns climbed onto his abdomen and arranged themselves in a cluster, facing out. Each bent and placed a hand splayed against Owen's skin while the other hand hovered over the ground. Owen watched their fingers curl slightly and, in unison, slip into the flesh of his midriff. It was a bizarre sensation: he felt the tingling without pain or discomfort, yet he could see the fingers stuck in his body. His mind told him he should freak, but curiosity prevailed. Then they pushed their fingers into the dirt and paused.

In a rush, his brain flooded with razor-sharp awareness. He felt everything around him with detailed precision. It wasn't that his senses were keener, it was as if he developed new senses altogether. He saw the Thorns perched on his stomach and the menhirs looming overhead; he felt the grass and the sun, but he also sensed things beyond the norm. The local rhizome network filled and expanded his awareness, each nook and cranny and all the tangle of connections in between until it receded from his perception into a distant blur. Ego dissolved as his essence drained away from the physical body toward the nether regions of the network. There was no effort in this, Owen let go of everything and became everything at the same time. He experienced himself as a labyrinth of complexity, devoid of boundary between his brain and the rhizome. There was no difference. Energy radiated through the whole linked consciousness, powering intimacy within the network of life. He was in the web, but it was also in him. There remained only the contradictions of perception. He was one with all yet still, somehow, himself. He sacrificed nothing in this union; ego was gone but the self was intact. Within that self, there coursed a vitality that swept away the trivia, bringing a sense of emptiness, not as a void, but as a clarity of understanding lifted on a clean wind.

He would have said that it was like an acid trip, but he had never dared to take an acid trip. His hold on reality had been tenuous enough. But he knew that this was no acid trip. It was a different order of experience, without a doubt. This was the stuff the Tibetans talked about. This was the liberation of being.

And then it was over. The Thorns withdrew their fingers, cleaned themselves, formed a line on Owen's belly, and looked at him.

"Well?" Redthorn queried.

"Mother of god. That was amazing! I was everywhere and everything, all at once."

"And that's exactly what happened. You merged with the consciousness of the forest mind." Redthorn studied each of its fingers one by one. Then it looked straight into Owen's eyes. "And you will do the same for your people. You're going to take that experience and you're going to give it to them and we're all going to hope that's enough to change the world."

"But that's been tried before. By Buddha, by others, there've been no end to attempts to offer enlightenment to the masses."

Blackthorn looked at Owen with eyes narrowed. "Yes, well, you're not exactly going to offer it. You're going to enforce it."

Whitethorn saluted everyone in turn and chirped, "It's time to make a choice/Speak up or lose your voice."

[12]

Owen groaned. "I figured there was a catch."

Redthorn climbed down from Owen's abdomen and motioned the others to follow. "Don't be dismayed. We must be practical. But let's leave this distracting vortex. Better to sit over in the woods at the spiral and you may eat and drink while we talk. It's time to fill in the blanks regarding the path ahead."

Owen nodded, rolled to the side, and grunted to his feet. He was woozy, and as the Thorns climbed back on board, he staggered out of the circle. After some labored steps, they entered the shelter of the forest. Owen relaxed; it was easier to breathe away from the gravity nexus. Sagging to the ground, he leaned against the comforting stability of a rock in the spiral. As he retrieved the water pouch, the Thorns crawled off and stretched out on the rock behind his head. Redthorn gave a soft pat and stroked the brambles of Owen's hair.

"Your hair is growing faster than normal, it seems."

"How can you tell? I haven't been here that long." Owen reached up to touch his hair. "God, it's a mess of knots, anyway."

"We gauge that it's growing twice as fast as it should, at least according to your normal genetics. Likely an emergent effect of our alterations." Redthorn worked on Owen's hair, combing and grooming. He kept his head still because he didn't want it to stop.

"When you say *emergent* I hope you don't mean *emergency*."

Blackthorn lay on its side, arm bent, head propped on its palm. Owen saw it from the corner of his eye, and he thought the posture looked too casual for the anticipated pronouncements. "No, no, not like that," it commented. "Emergence is a critical aspect of systems philosophy. It refers to new properties that derive from the workings of the whole. As we mentioned before, systems are much more than the sum of their parts. In fact, the relationships between the parts are more important than the parts themselves, at least in understanding the system. When you start tinkering with complex networks, changing the elements or the relationships, then the system can develop fresh properties, what I referred to as emergent. These are sometimes predictable, sometimes not. To a certain extent, this can be engineered, but there are almost always surprises. Your hair growth is a surprise."

Owen was silent for a moment. "The hair is okay. It's not a bad trade-off for the improved neurochemistry. But should I wonder if there are unpleasant surprises ahead?"

Blackthorn yawned and Owen heard Redthorn's reply from behind. "It's not impossible. Unlikely, according to our rather comprehensive metabolic survey. But not out of the question, dear. Bioengineering is tricky business. We didn't anticipate the hair. Sorry if that bothers you."

"Well, since I had given up on life altogether, I'm not complaining about the uncertainties of a new one, even if it is hairy. Life seems to come with a steady barrage of uncertainties, anyway."

Whitethorn flipped into Owen's lap with a somersault, then sang out. "He doesn't give a care/'Bout the weird new hair.../Neither here nor there!"

Blackthorn stuck out its tongue and made a raspberry noise. Redthorn clambered over the top of Owen's head and down his chest to stand next to Whitethorn. "We're pleased to hear your acceptance of the uncertainty factor. Systemic health and evolutionary stability consist of adaptation to change. Nothing stays the same – nor should it. Which brings us to the point. Our hope is that an enlightenment experience—very much like what you felt at the stump—will change the behavior of humans. Do you think that's possible?"

Owen looked at the two Thorns in his lap and scratched his nose. "I hate to sound skeptical, but I don't see how it would. For as long as history or pre-history indicates, humans have been exposed to the possibilities of enlightenment. After a pertinent experience, like going to church or a session with a guru or a therapist, the best outcome is a short-term alignment with what was learned. Then as time goes by, we typically regress into whatever bad habits and sloppy thinking we had there in the first place. It's sort of like New Year's resolutions: it sounds good at first, but we turn out to be devious beasts who excel at fooling ourselves. Admittedly, many of these experiences probably weren't as intense as what I just went through, though I'm in no position to judge."

"You do seem to have the measure of your kind," Blackthorn agreed. Now it was picking its teeth with a twig. "Which is precisely why we're thinking of a more comprehensive intervention. Instead of an incidental exposure to enlightenment, we're proposing a constant immersion in it. As a way to sever bad habits, mind you."

"And how would you do that?"

Blackthorn sat up on its haunches. Both arms swept out, like a conductor priming the symphony. "Here's the program: we'll encode your DNA with a new virus for you to carry back to your world. This virus will have little effect on you, but it'll have a major effect on the forests." Blackthorn's arms swung a broad arc of inclusion. " It's a blood-borne virus, so by implanting a small amount of your blood into the forest network, tree by tree, it will be absorbed and spread rapidly." Blackthorn aimed at trees and mimed shooting them with its finger. "And you—you'll be the prime vector." Blackthorn pointed at Owen and smirked. The display was distracting, but not enough to quell Owen's dismay at the words.

"The virus goes to work in the forest by catalyzing the manufacture and release of a novel kind of pheromone. This chemical is expired by the leaves of the trees and permeates the air within a large range. Neurochemical responses in humans are activated by the pheromone, responses that produce an identical effect to the connection experience you had at the stump. Small quantities of a similar chemical already exist in your trees, which is why humans often seek meditation and peace in the forest. But this virus incites a mutation and acceleration of the pheromone, rendering it vastly more potent." Blackthorn studied the tips of its fingers, blowing on them before rubbing them on its chest fur.

Owen shook his head. "You all—and by that, I mean the whole damn extended family of Thorns, Hawthorns and Thornicles—are crazy."

Blackthorn shook its head. "Doubtful. Our mind, because of its collective nature, doesn't develop aberrations of thinking like the individual human mind. Strength in numbers, if you wish. Not to say that collective deviance isn't possible... but that's another subject. Anyway, as the virus spreads through the forests of your world, the atmosphere will become saturated with pheromones of enlightenment. Humans will be breathing it – all the time. A significant change to consciousness is unavoidable. For the better, we think."

"But... I don't even know where to begin. I was blown away over there. How are humans even going to function? We'll be stoned out of our gourds all the time."

Redthorn pulled Owen's shirt to get his attention. "Please don't exaggerate. Surely you noticed the ability within yourself to adapt to that state. It doesn't terminate basic ego operations or anything like that. Admittedly, it takes a little getting used to. But before long, it becomes another background set, like your awareness of your body, for example. There's a calming and compassionate quality to this pheromone experience. It'll change behavior; we're pretty sure of that."

Whitethorn stood on its head, wiggled its legs and chanted. "Don't say/You don't wanna/Give your folks/True nirvana!"

Blackthorn made a gagging noise and when Owen turned to look, it resumed its lecture. "Our estimation is that it will decrease aggression and self-centered thinking. It's going to be hard for humans to manipulate others for gain when the blow-back from negative deeds is fully internalized. There will be no rationalization that can override the reciprocity of those feelings. Conversely, the good feelings from cooperation and mutual aid will be reinforced with pleasurable sensations."

"I suppose. So, we'll be drugging the entire population of the planet. Like the old notion of spraying tranquilizers through the hospital ward to calm the rowdy patients. All for the greater good."

"Overstated melodrama. We understand that acting for the good of a group can be difficult for a self-identified consciousness, especially if the action seems to undermine the idea of autonomy. But your species is on the brink of an evolutionary cliff. You can learn how to climb down it together, or you can plunge off one after another. There is nothing sacred about the self; it's just a node in the network, you know."

"After everything you've shown me, I guess I should know that. Still, I'm already on your side and yet I have a hard time swallowing all this."

Redthorn answered, forcing Owen to swivel his head. "Of course. What we're asking isn't simple or easy; we realize that. But the situation is beyond a solution from afar, at least an ethical one."

Blackthorn coughed and when Owen turned back, it was scratching its chin and looking thoughtful. "It might be possible to pump toxins into your world and kill all the humans – that would be a solution. At least for the short term. If it would even work; things have a way of changing when they go through the brane."

Redthorn tugged again at Owen's shirt. "Yes, yes. Anyway, such an act would throw tremendous imbalance into the multiverse, both physically and ethically. We would like to enlighten your species, dear, not destroy them."

"I still don't see why you need me. Seems simpler to do it yourselves—just pump the virus back through the rhizome connections in the brane. It works or it doesn't, but if it does, your problem is solved."

Redthorn rushed to answer before Blackthorn. "Sure, we could try that. However, the connections with your world are limited. It would take too long, even if the virus made it through intact. Encoded in the DNA will be more reliable, we think. A mobile agent who can carry the virus through the brane and then disseminate it gives us the best chance for success. And—this is important—we want someone to represent your species in all this."

Owen nodded as the implications sunk in. "Sure, I get it. You want to turn me into something like yourself: an agent of the forest, a lackey to do the work of the collective mind."

Redthorn's shoulders slumped and its expression was imploring. "Is the prospect of this mission really so dreadful?"

Whitethorn, having abandoned the headstand, lay on Owen's thighs, hands behind its head and knees up, with one leg crossed over the other. "You can feel the dread/In the middle of your head/But isn't that better/Than ending up dead?"

Despite the jocular tone, Owen felt a chill at the rhyme. He was offered a choice, but was it really a choice?

Redthorn patted Whitethorn on the knee and looked into Owen's eyes. "We're simply providing an enhanced vision of reality to a confused humanity. It's not a drug that distorts the world. It just emphasizes what's already there: the interrelatedness of all beings. It'll be like developing a sixth sense. And your role is more that of a prophet than a lackey. Regardless, you're free to choose to be involved or not. We wish to persuade you, not force you."

Owen looked away, ashamed of his harsh words. He scratched his head and thought before responding. "No, I'm sorry, I think I'm finding this all a bit much to take in. But sure, I guess this enlightenment you describe isn't much different than some found in human cultures. There are plenty of beliefs that honor connection to the world. The third eye of the Tibetans. Or *Mitakuye Oyasin*, as the Lakota say, which means: all my relations. That's a mantra to acknowledge the links in the life-web. Though it doesn't seem to stop them from fighting."

Blackthorn made throat-clearing noises and Owen rolled his eyes before turning his head. "The pheromone provides more than a belief. It not only gives an awareness of the web, it produces a constant link to the web. More than a philosophy of connectedness, it makes it impossible to think only in terms of a self, a family, a group, tribe, or nation. Benefit is determined by the functioning of the life system, in the broadest possible terms, across races, species, and all forms of sentience. But competition and conflict remain in ecosystems, regardless. This is a problem only when competition becomes the dominant paradigm and cooperation is relegated to niche zones. Mutualism and symbiosis are the fundamental mechanics of healthy ecosystems, but there is always competition."

"Yeah, makes sense." Owen agreed, unable to resist his excitement as he recalled his college research. "Many anthropologists believe that tribal warfare served as a titrated struggle – a mechanism to release social pressure. Rarely lethal to entire groups, more of an outlet for aggression that sharpened the group. Not sure if I agree entirely. I guess there's a logic to it. My own sense of the world as a rational, nurturing place was trashed when I was a kid. The only way I could stop being a victim was to fight back. So, if a world includes predators, then knowing how to fight has a purpose, whether you're battling cancer or a rapist. Which sounds like it's still mostly about survival of the fittest, despite your mutualism." Owen's thoughts reeled him back toward the horror of the past, but instead of losing balance and falling into the chasm, he wrestled down his panic. With a shudder, he turned away from the consuming gravity of his trauma.

Owen looked up to find Redthorn and Whitethorn staring at him. Whitethorn wiped a tear from its cheek. Redthorn placed its hand on Owen's chest, over his heart. "You've been through so much. It's a dreadful burden, what you carry. But is the childhood travesty against your body so different than what we're fighting here? And yes, we're fighting back, if that's the language you want to use. Though we're opposing violence with compassion and wisdom, which we believe is more effective in the long run. If there were a way to cure the man who violated you, to take away his violence, his cruelty, his brutal domination, wouldn't that be preferable to destroying him?"

"Of course." Owen petted Redthorn's fuzzy head. "And if your grand scheme doesn't work?"

"We'll find out. Even with a deep understanding of complex systems, it's impossible to foresee all contingencies. For now, this seems to be the best plan."

"And have you factored in the patterns of potential emergence?"

"Very good, such a pertinent question!"

Whitethorn clapped its hands, giggled, then sang, "When the blind man came to the elephant/He asked only questions that were relevant."

Blackthorn growled. "Of course, we have to consider emergence. We've plotted as many variables as we can compute. The genetics have been engineered to minimize random outcomes. We think this will do exactly what we anticipate: propagate an atmospheric constant of pheromones boosting cooperative behaviors in humans. No more; no less. With no harm to anyone, you least of all."

Redthorn hugged Whitethorn, then turned back to Owen. "We've grown fond of you; we hope you know that."

Owen looked away from Redthorn's earnest face. He stared into the trees for a while, watching the play of light and wind in the canopy. "Okay, group leaders. How does this work, exactly?"

"We thought you'd never ask." Blackthorn crawled closer and spoke softly in Owen's ear. "When you return through the brane portal, you won't be able to bring any objects with you. On the other side of the boundary, your reincorporated body will be the same as it is now except for some genetic modifications that include the virus. You'll retain the metabolic enhancements we've provided. Like we said, the virus is blood-borne. It can be transmitted to the forest by inserting your blood into the cellular matter of any plant connected to the mycorrhizal network, preferably trees since they have the most extensive linkage. Only a few drops are needed. Just make a hole through the bark and dribble in some blood. Then it'll take its own course. Your task will be to move to another area and repeat the process. The faster you disperse your blood through the rhizome, the sooner we'll see the results."

Owen's mouth opened in disbelief. "Sounds fucking religious, pardon me. Are you washed in the blood of the lamb and all that shit."

Redthorn looked puzzled. "Are you referencing mythology?"

Owen snorted. "You don't know the half of it. Mythology is full of notions of blood sacrifice – offering the blood of some hapless creature to appeal to divine forces. Mostly for favors. Heal me, save me, make me wealthy beyond dreams – that kind of thing. The sanguine road to salvation. I'm not a fan."

"Are you saying there's a problem with the method?"

"You tell me, commanders, it's your show." Owen took a breath, shaking his head. "I don't know—maybe not. I find it a bit ironic, though. Since I was a kid, I craved the glorious life of a mythic figure, a hero and all that. So here we go, and I get to be the lamb."

Blackthorn flipped off the rock, turned a somersault and landed on Owen's lap next to the other two. Whitethorn jumped up and the three of them scuffled until they established a new equilibrium. Redthorn spoke as if nothing happened. "You'll find a noble frame for this role; we have no doubt."

"You can be a big hero/Or you can be the zero." Whitethorn tried a gleeful caper, but Blackthorn grabbed a leg and flipped it off Owen's lap.

Whitethorn curled into a ball and whimpered until Owen cradled it in his palm, at which point it started making a deep, vibrating hum. Owen scowled at Blackthorn. "You guys are worse than kids." He placed Whitethorn back on his lap, next to the others. "Anyway, this plan is pretty weird, I don't mind saying. Takes getting used to. But Dr. Chouinard said we can't all be eagles and wolves: some of us need to be rabbits and there's just as much honor in that." Owen scratched Whitethorn behind the ears, and it resumed purring. "You know, although I have a little money left from my mother's inheritance, it's nowhere near enough to jaunt around the world bleeding into trees. This project is going to take more capital than I have at hand. Not to mention the time factor. I assume your vast network mind has calculated the rate of dispersion of the virus, so what are we talking about here?"

Blackthorn ignored the favor shown to Whitethorn and launched into further explanation. "Very hard to estimate. Our best calculations, based on one inoculation of your blood into one tree, suggest that with no other inoculations the pheromone levels should reach the desired atmospheric threshold in around two hundred years."

"Well, *that* sounds practical. A lot of poison will cross the brane before then."

"Indeed. One inoculation is clearly insufficient, but it does provide a baseline for estimation. With two and three inoculations, the speed of dispersion increases geometrically. Geographic spread of inoculation sites will also increase the rate of dispersion. However, it won't be necessary to inoculate all the trees in your world in order to produce enough pheromones. Atmospheric concentrations will be uneven at first, but the desired consistency can be achieved in time. At a minimum we'd like to have a thousand inoculations."

"Is that all? A thousand? Presumably you'd like to see results within my lifetime. Hell, I'd like to see results within my lifetime."

"Yes. Remember, this is a blood-borne virus: you can transfer it to other humans and they will become additional vectors. A simple blood transfusion is all that is required."

"Simple? How simple? I'm wondering if I can manufacture blood fast enough for this enterprise."

"Again, a drop or two of your blood entering another human's bloodstream will be enough to make them carriers. It is a robust virus."

"Great. I'll be the notorious un-vampire, forcing others to drink my blood instead of the other way around. Really, it sounds like we need a cult for this job."

Redthorn took over. "Yes, it's best if you recruit other humans to the task. If you think that will happen better under the guise of a cult, that's your decision."

"I don't know. How am I supposed to know? And what about blood-borne pathogens? Humans are scared to death of them; many won't go near anyone else's blood for fear of potential contamination. And if I'm transferring blood to others, how do I avoid contamination from people carrying disease?"

Blackthorn jumped back in. "The virus will keep you healthy. It provides a mutational boost to your immune system, establishing a resilient antibody barrier against infections of all sorts. There should be no problem with pathogens."

"So you say." Owen shook his head, trying to digest all the information. "I was kidding about the cult. But that's the way people will see it. It's not like I can say, 'Hey, wanna do a good deed for the multiverse? First, suck my blood. Then pour yours into as many trees as you can. It's all good.' Do you have any idea how that's going to sound? I can guarantee that it's a swift road to the psych ward."

Redthorn looked concerned. "Well, these are your people. Do you have suggestions?"

Owen scratched his hair and new beard, trying to summon an idea that didn't sound ridiculous. "Good grief. I can only think of one thing that might work. That's to bring folks here, across the brane boundary, so they can see for themselves. Humans are like that: 'Show me.' Skeptical and ornery, that's us. Until you beat us over the head with reality. Of course, that doesn't always work, either."

"How could you think/There was a gain/To bring your friends/Across the brane?" Whitethorn put a finger on top of its head and spun around after the rhyme. But Redthorn and Blackthorn remained silent, lapsed in thought, or more likely, it occurred to Owen, they'd reached into the greater forest mind.

"Okay," Redthorn finally said. "We'd prefer to minimize the crossings, but if it's necessary for the project, it can be done. We'll provide you with a means of activating passage from your side."

"Wow, really? Cool. I can start selling vacations. Humans are so crazy to go to exotic places that we'll be able to marshal an army in no time." Owen saw the alarm on their faces. "Kidding again, sorry. I wouldn't bring anyone here if it didn't seem necessary. As I ponder on this nutty idea, the notion of starting a cult actually makes some sense. Humans will do very strange things in the name of mysticism. It's a dedicated hobby for many. The whole procedure can be packaged as a ritual, sort of an outgrowth of the blood-brothers idea. They don't even have to know what they're really doing because we don't have to say word one about science. All mystical, all metaphoric. 'Commune with the trees in a sacred bond... mingling life essences to form a union of spirits....' Stuff like that. Damn. I'm scaring myself."

"Why do you say that?"

"I didn't know I could be such a conniving schemer."

[13]

Whitethorn swayed in rhythm and added a chant. "You can be a schemer/You can be a dreamer/But whatever you do/Just don't break a femur!"

Blackthorn wrinkled its nose and peered with skepticism at Redthorn, which Redthorn ignored and instead turned to Owen. "Many sacrifices will be required to achieve the balance we're seeking between our worlds. We can only proceed with the belief that it's worthwhile. We don't wish you to compromise your integrity; what you do and how you do it will be your choice. Of course," and here it smiled thinly, "we hope you choose to implement our plan."

Owen patted each Thorn in turn, gathered them together in his hands, and placed them gently on the ground. He stood and looked around the woods that enclosed the ancient stone spiral. He felt the tug of the place, knowing that he'd leave and possibly never see it again.

"Okay, bosses, where to next?"

Redthorn jumped to the rock, then to Owen's shoulder, followed by the other two, all reclaiming their riding spots. "Are you ready to return to your world, dear? If there are more questions, now's the time to ask them."

"Already?" Owen sighed. "Is there anything else I need to know?"

"Just how to use the tree portal through the brane boundary. But we can go over that when we get there."

"Okay, let's do it."

Redthorn pointed down the slope. The forest below was dense and dark. "We'll go this way. It'll be a short walk to a suitable tree."

"So, we don't have to go back to the same tree I came through?"

"No, there's flexibility in routing passage. Everything in the rhizome is connected to everything else, so it's possible to start anywhere."

As they hiked down from the saddle, the angle of slope lessened. Before long, they were back on flat ground amidst the forest of giants. Owen drank in the beauty of the megaflora, then slowed to a stop as a question occurred to him. "Hey. If I emerge on the other side at the same tree I entered, the one, you know, where I tried to...." he struggled to name the deed.

Redthorn stroked Owen's cheek. "That was a long time ago. You're different now."

"Yes, I know. So different, perhaps, it's hard to understand who I was when I tried to... do away with myself. Thank you for the help to make that difference."

"You're welcome." Together, the three Thorns patted and stroked Owen's head.

Owen brushed away a tear. "Anyway... if I come out at the same tree, naked, it will be a long walk back to my house. There wasn't snow on the ground when I left, at least not yet, but that could have changed. All I'm saying is that I don't want to freeze to death before I get to shelter. Plus, how long was I unconscious after I came through?"

Redthorn answered. "We predict that you'll be able to reorient quickly following the second passage. And no, we don't want you to perish before you get to shelter. Do you know of any mature ash trees close to your dwelling? Ash trees make the best portals."

"Um, yes. There's one across the clearing behind the house, just inside the margin of woods. When I was a kid, I had a tarp there for a hideout. The ash tree was one of the anchors. I spent a lot of time under that tarp, reading and creating my own magical world."

"Perfect. From magic to reality. That will be the portal in your world." Redthorn pointed ahead to a large tree with furrowed bark. "And here we are at the exit from this one." Before Owen could absorb the implications of what was happening, they stood next to the tree.

"Time to go, but we still need to construct the virus within your cells. It won't take long."

"Oh, right. That. What should I do?"

"Just lay down and lift your shirt. It'll be like before." Owen followed Redthorn's instructions and lay down. The Thorns crawled up on Owen's belly and slipped their tendrils into his skin. He felt a tingle radiate through his body, followed by an overpowering urge to sleep. The next thing he noticed was Redthorn's wet tongue on his nose.

"So, that was it? And now we're done? Just like that? Good-bye and write if you get work?" Owen regretted the sarcasm, a default mode to mask the grief that separation set in motion.

"It's as good a time and place as any to end this stage," Redthorn said. "You'll always be part of this rhizome. Your cells have mingled with the network and will never be forgotten."

"Look. Everything in life that has meant anything to me has been taken away. I know that I'll go on, but I've grown to really like you—each one of you. I understand you're just a manifestation of the forest and not separate beings, blah blah blah. To me you're interesting and funny and I... I don't want to say good-bye. If I come back to this world, will we be able to see each other again?"

"No, probably not this exact formulation. Once you leave, the immediate use for the form will have ended and it'll be re-absorbed. Try to remember you've been communicating with the whole forest. Should you return, the forest will still be here and will welcome you. Assuming, that is, that you're successful in your mission and we survive."

Owen didn't bother to stop the tears. The Thorns stood in a line, watching him cry. He picked each one off the ground and gave it a hug and a quick kiss on the head before returning it to its place.

Redthorn used a soothing tone. "We honor you and the depth of your feeling. Please, take that profound connection and use it to sway your people."

Owen sniffed. "Yes, Commanders Three, reporting for duty. I'll do my best, sirs or madams or whatever."

Blackthorn offered final instructions. "Lean into the tree. Hug it tight and let it gain awareness of you. It'll adjust and open to pull you in. You'll lose consciousness inside the tree but should regain it quickly once you're pushed out on the other side. The tree will retain a deep cleft in the trunk after you emerge. To return, or to have someone else come through, snug yourself into the cleft and push some of your skin into contact with the open wood. Then wait. The tree will respond, and you'll meld into its cells for transport. Any questions?"

"You forest thinkers certainly get into this liquid cell thing."

"Life *is* fluid."

"Now you sound like Dr. Chouinard."

"We'll take that as a compliment."

Owen embraced the tree. This was the same posture he had assumed at his uncle's command, just before the first rape, but he experienced no flashback to the suffering. Despite the parallel, he felt no desire to dissociate or run away. He wasn't afraid. Although a visitor in this world for just a short time, he had learned to trust. As the transformation started, his skin itched.

The Thorns jumped on the tree and ran to a stance above his head.

Redthorn and Blackthorn spoke in unison. "Goodbye and good luck."

"Goodbye, Thorns three, and thank you."

Owen was pulled into the tree, like being absorbed by vertical quicksand. Before he disappeared into the blackness, he heard one last thing: "All the best and very good luck/We sure hope that you don't get stuck."

# 3

# PLATEAU

*We call a 'plateau' any multiplicity connected to other multi-plicities by superficial underground stems in such a way as to form or extend a rhizome.*

Gilles Deleuze and Felix Guattari, *A Thousand Plateaus: Capitalism and Schizophrenia*

[14]

Owen regained consciousness while being pushed headfirst out of a tree. The wood, now pliant, stretched to accommodate his emerging torso, and as his back scraped across the frozen ground, he saw the sky of his home world. Pain and cold brought him fully alert. He observed the rest of his body, coated in thin mucus, reborn from the tree. The process was fascinating yet repulsive. After his toes were free, the lignin cells flowed back to their original state as hardened wood, leaving a deep, wide furrow in the trunk. Shaky, he stood up, trying to ignore the cold on his skin and extended a hand to touch the center of the furrow. His arm tingled and the wood of the tree flexed and oozed around his fingers. There was a distinct tug. Quickly he drew his hand back and the bark regained its former shape. It looked like the trunk of a typical ash tree—not the portal to another world.

He walked around the tree and saw his house, just past the edge of the woods and a hundred yards across a grassy field. There was no snow on the ground, but it was frozen hard, and the air was crisp enough to snap his breath. No place to linger for a naked man. After the vaulted canopies of the Thorn world, the sky seemed close and it bore down on him with a wintery chill. He took a few tentative steps, then broke into a trot, ignoring the pain on his soles from the ragged turf.

Despite his eagerness to get inside, as he approached the house, he couldn't help but notice the flaking white paint and cracked clapboards. Had it always been this run-down? Or had he just been too depressed to notice? It was past time to do some renovation. But then, he remembered, he already had a project.

He reached behind one of the shutters on the kitchen window and felt for the extra key. For many years he and his mother had simply thrown it under a brick next to the front steps, that is, when they bothered to lock it at all. But in recent times, as opioid addiction had swept through the county, it was no longer safe to leave a home open to the world. What a mess humans have made, Owen thought. Is it possible to change for the better? Do we even want to? Well, some of us do, he acknowledged as he inserted the key.

After stumbling through the entrance, Owen was gratified to see that everything was the way he had left it. The house was brutally cold, though, and he raced up the stairs to his bedroom, toweled off the remaining lubricant, threw on layers of clothes and stepped into old boots. He clomped back down to the dining room where the wood stove stood in front of the fireplace. He opened the stove door to find it full of perfectly laid kindling. He had prepared his demise with admirable detail, leaving his life in order. Had he even considered that he might come back? No matter, here he was. He lit a match and the sticks caught fire with a satisfying roar. Next to the stove was a stack of split wood. He took a few small pieces and set them on the fire. Next, he went into the pantry and opened the electrical box, flipping on the switches to the machinery of household living, remembering that he had left the power service connected. Why? He couldn't say, exactly; maybe he needed to leave an option. Just in case he lost his nerve. After a descent into the basement to turn on the water pump, he ran back up and stoked the fire. Cranking the thermostat for the baseboard electrics, there was nothing left to do but pull a chair over to the crackling stove and wait for the warmth.

Heat radiated from the fire but not enough, so he went to the kitchen and put a pot of water on the range. In the cupboard he found a box of ginger teabags – a legacy from Dr. Chouinard. She had served him this tea one day during a session, steaming hot with two spoons of sugar, and it had slipped down his throat like an elixir. He drank it ever since; after all, it was a sacrament from the doctor. Tea in hand, he returned to the chair in front of the stove. Sipping the tea reminded him that he should calm down and focus. This wasn't the time to let his unbelievable experiences over charge his brain. To his surprise, he realized that he was calm. Excited and a little disoriented, yes, but a far cry from agitated or fearful. He was alive, he was home, and he felt pretty good. Sitting back, he took a deep breath, and absorbed the warmth of the cup in his hands.

"There and back again." Shortly after they started therapy, Dr. Chouinard had convinced him to read the works of Tolkien and that phrase from *The Hobbit* stayed with him. It was the condensed version of any adventure. No matter what happened in between the beginning and the end, the framing story was always the same: to go there, away from the familiarities of home, experience the unexpected, and come back again. This was the primal structure of the initiatory myth. Coming back represented a kind of success because it meant that you'd survived the liminal phase of the quest, the threshold where one's life was turned inside out and put back together again. Then, after the ordeals, you came home. To... what? That was the question, the challenge, the proof of having been somewhere. What did you bring back: a treasure, a gift, a blessing for your people? Owen knew very well what he brought back: a virus.

He walked to the bathroom to drain his bladder and remembered that he hadn't opened the water valve at the toilet. When the reservoir started filling, he decided to go pee outside instead of waiting. As he moved past the mirror over the sink, he stopped and looked at himself. Who was this character? His black hair hung well past his ears in tangled disarray and his beard was thick and scruffy. He looked like a wild man of the woods, which was perhaps not far from the truth. More than that, what arrested his attention was the look in his eyes. They were still green, but there was steel in them, too—the eyes of someone with a mission. Was this really him? Interesting question, and worth more study in the mirror, but he needed to pee, so he left the reflection and walked out the kitchen door to the back yard.

Gazing across the field, he considered his situation: here was a man with a troubled past standing in the place that contained the history, and he was pissing on it. The past wouldn't dissolve, though, he knew that. No matter what his biochemical alterations, it would always be part of his story. He looked around at the farm as the afternoon light angled toward darkness. Things looked the same on the surface, but he knew he would never see them that way again. It was impossible to ignore what was underneath his feet, the roots of the rhizome, and even now, in the quiet of the day, he knew the grasses sang in the earth. If he silenced his thoughts, he could hear them. Yes, he was fashioning new symbols for his life, a life entangled with others. He wasn't alone. The Thorns had predicted that he would create a frame to justify who he was and what he had to do. As a child, he had been thrust into the role of the tragic victim. Now it was time to come to terms with a different role: that of a catalyst to rectify the sins of his people.

When he stepped back into the kitchen the house was warmer, so he shed a layer. He was hungry. He almost reached for the satchel with the mushrooms, but with a snort he realized that it was sitting in another world—if they hadn't already recycled it. His pantry was stocked with shelves of canned goods, some from the garden, some from the store, and between them he could eat. He grabbed a jar of homegrown tomatoes, a can of commercial meatballs, and a box of noodles. Simple enough.

As the tomatoes and meatballs simmered, he waited for the pasta water to boil, then decided not to hover over the pot and wandered into the dining room to shove a bigger chunk of wood into the stove. The dining room had always been his favorite part of the house. It was the only room with a large, single-pane window, installed by his mother when she started worrying that he was going to go blind from reading in dim light. Or that's what she said; maybe she just wanted to have a clear view of the long dirt driveway. In the country it can be important to know who's coming.

The table was piled with books, journals, and papers, and a laptop computer parked at one end. Opposite the computer there was enough clear space for a plate. An easy chair sat next to the window, more to facilitate staring across the field at the woods than to provide reading comfort. Before he had left, his life in the house had been a rhythm of movement from kitchen to dining room and back, with forays to the bathroom and a single journey each evening up the stairs to his bedroom. Otherwise the remaining rooms in the house were closed. Unheated and full of unwanted memories. This sad, old dwelling was a suitable heritage for the family.

He rushed back to the kitchen when he heard the water boiling. In a few minutes, he had a meal, which he took to the table with a glass of water. Within the house, the solitude was acute. At least he could see the trees and know that he was within a community. Still, he missed the lively company of the Thorns. And Dr. Chouinard. And, in a way difficult to admit, his mother. He had learned to live outside of society but that wasn't going to be enough anymore. He needed to populate the social void. Before sitting down to his meal, he walked over to the shelf with the sound system. He had a collection of discs, perfect for filling the blank spaces. After scanning some titles, he picked out an album of West African kora music. The sounds occupied the room with sweet company.

He ate the pasta dish, thinking that it needed mushrooms. Maybe his new metabolism was addicted to fungus. He wouldn't be surprised, now that he was an agent of the rhizome. The image of himself in trench coat and fedora, lurking behind the trunk of a tree, made him laugh and he almost choked. In the past, this kind of hilarity would have mutated into hysteria, then anxiety, before cascading to panic. But he felt solid. He could let himself be a bit giddy, a bit self-deprecating, and he knew that these emotions were not going to tear him apart.

The food was boring, and he'd only eaten half of it. "Fuck this crap," he said to the plate and carried it to the kitchen where he scraped it into the trash. Tomorrow he would go to town and buy some better food. Fresh vegetables, nuts, yogurt, and yes, mushrooms—that kind of thing. He'd go to the health food store instead of the supermarket. He'd buy organic, which he had never done because he was frugal, like his mother. He wondered how much money was left in the account. Aside from the farm, that was his only inheritance. God knows how she had squirreled it away, but New Englanders were good at that. What they weren't good at was having fun. He sighed and wished that the Thorns were here to scamper around and jump on the furniture while arguing, lecturing, and reciting atrocious poetry. He missed them, even the pompous Blackthorn.

But money would be a problem. What was it his mother often said? "If wishes were horses, beggars could ride." A dour reminder: wealth of the imagination would not enhance his bank account. The saying never failed to annoy him, implying that money was more important than vision. He remained unconvinced, though he couldn't argue with the logic. It was hard to get things done without dough. For example, was he really going to travel around the world, giving his blood to the forests? He couldn't possibly afford that. Despite his mother's admonishments, money had not been a compelling subject for Owen. A year ago, he figured he would just spend the inheritance until it was gone, then waste away like a hermit. Had he really been that melodramatic? He thought about the obsessions he had constructed around the myth of Ariadne and he had his answer. Yes, definitely a flair for the drama.

He headed for the computer to check his account balance. As he waited for it to warm up, he danced with the kora music and made his way back to the stove to cram in more wood. The room was toasty, so Owen stripped down to the last layer. Then he realized that he had canceled the internet service when he closed the house. Or had he? He wasn't sure. Though his preparations seemed meticulous at the time, he might have missed that. Or, the thought was inescapable, he had planned to come back all along. Hard to tell—that whole frame of mind was remote and fuzzy now.

The icon on his computer displayed an active internet connection. Well, well. Another crumb of evidence. Other than getting rid of his animals, he had done nothing final. His life waited for him like a coat on a hook. He did a double take on the date provided in his software toolbar. He had only been gone ten days. It felt like ten years.

When he logged into his bank account, it showed fifteen thousand in savings. Not a lot, though nothing was owed on the farm and the taxes were minimal. Utilities and food were his primary expenses and he could go for a while on what he had. But travel would be different. He didn't even know what that might cost. He searched sample airfares to Germany, where there were a lot of forests, or so he had heard. The dark forests of the Grimm Brothers—he had wanted to see them, anyway. What he found was daunting. A thousand dollars. Good grief. Then there would be expenses overseas. His money wouldn't last long. He checked the cost of a trip to the Pacific Northwest. Cheaper than Europe, but not by much. How the hell was this going to work? He sat back from the computer and let the music soothe some of the tension. He'd just have to figure it out, that's all. Be clever and all that. Surely not impossible for someone who sallied across the multiverse and has his own portal for return trips. He would start locally and wait for inspiration. For now, he was going to take a long, hot shower and go to bed. Tomorrow he'd start saving the world.

[15]

Owen fell on his bed, exhausted, and woke up three hours later. A carousel of ruminations cranked around his head, marginally amusing at first, but after an hour, tedious and out of control. Sleep took on a desperate allure. He decided to try an old trick that Dr. Chouinard had taught him, an exercise from a bodywork practice that she prescribed every time he complained about insomnia. At first, he had resisted, but when he gave in and tried it, he found that it worked, even though he didn't believe in it.

He settled into a supine alignment, closed his eyes, and folded his hands together so that his left thumb was tucked in the fingers of the right hand while his right forefinger was tucked into the fingers of the left. He could hear the doctor's voice assuring him that the resulting energy circle would reinforce the link between both sides of his body. He focused on his breathing and drifted slowly back to sleep. Two hours later he woke again, and after another period of runaway thoughts, he used the same technique.

This time he dreamed. In the usual way of dreams, a figure appeared out of nowhere. Since it was Dr. Chouinard, he was overjoyed. She danced for him, her full body swaying gracefully within her robes, bracelets tinkling like water music. Owen was entranced and aroused. Awareness shifted to his penis and he realized that the doctor held him in a firm grip. It seemed wrong, but he didn't want her to stop. He was hungry to be touched. His eyes snapped open and filled with the light of dawn.

He lay on the bed, still tangled in dream. Stretching his arms, he tried to dispel the shame of the unconscious drama. Unquestionably, there was a lingering fondness for Dr. Chouinard, but sexual thoughts were an example of therapeutic transference, the projection of deep feelings, and not to be taken on the surface. Or so she had said many times. Whatever else was going on, he also believed that, on some level, this was a manifestation of his love for her. He hadn't wanted to have sex with her, not that. Yet intimacy thrived on touch and touch was always so confusing. The Thorns had triggered similar desires in him, at first with the usual tenderness he shared with animals, then deepening into a bond of mind and matter. As the embodied representatives of the forest, they remained the totems of that connection. Now the forest was inside him, ingrained, and he was an extension of that collective mind, a node in a matrix. In fact, Owen wasn't even sure who "he" was anymore, not as an individual. His life was in tune with those trees, that moss, the rocks, and the thrum underground of the rhizome network. Was that not love, the deepest possible link between beings? Or maybe it was something else altogether—he was hardly an expert on love.

Owen threw off the covers and reached for his pants. The house was warm; he had forgotten to turn down the thermostat. No need to scramble into layers of clothes, instead he could relish the feel of warm floorboards on his bare feet. It was too soon to go into town and shop. The supermarket opened early for workers heading off to the woods or the docks, but he was determined to avoid it and its numbing aisles of gaudy packages. The natural foods market kept casual hours and wouldn't open until mid-morning. He had time to do some research, not that he ever needed an excuse for that.

As soon as the kettle boiled, he made ginger tea, noting that at this rate he should put it at the top of his shopping list. Sipping the brew, he parked in front of the computer and typed in the search term "rhizome." Jung had compared the life of the soul to a rhizome because of their subterranean natures, an insight revealed in the prologue to his memoir. It was an intriguing metaphor, one that stayed with Owen. What else was out there, he wondered? Had others mulled over the ramifications of roots and systems?

Skipping over the botanical references, which he decided to save for later, he chose the first entry for "rhizome (philosophy)". There he encountered a sentence he read several times to make sure of what it said: "*Rhizome* is the first chapter of *A Thousand Plateaus: Capitalism and Schizophrenia* by Gilles Deleuze and Felix Guattari." The combination of terms was perplexing: rhizome-plateau-capitalism-schizophrenia. It barely seemed like English. Several items on the list referred to Deleuze and Guattari, as well as the Italian Umberto Eco. These names were new to him, though he thought he might have heard of Eco somewhere. A bestseller, perhaps? He swigged the cooling tea and clicked forward into the internet morass.

What he found excited him. Deleuze and Guattari were controversial French philosophers who commentators either loved or hated. Samples of their writing showed a style dense yet playful. Right at the beginning, they claimed that *A Thousand Plateaus* was a not a book; it was a rhizome. In the excerpts that Owen read online he could barely follow the assembly of intellectual flight lines, as if their rhizome was a major airport. He gathered that their investment in multiplicity was so thorough that they sought to embody it in every way. If so, they succeeded. Owen had to read every sentence several times, each time peeling off another layer of meaning without believing he quite had the full measure of it. But as he read, he realized that he was gaining a vocabulary relevant to his experience in the Thorn world.

When he extricated himself from the wilderness of Deleuze and Guattari, he plunged into the work of Umberto Eco, who was, indeed, a popular novelist when he wasn't being a philosopher. His specialty was the weird field of semiotics where he analyzed the complications of meaning in signs and symbols, sifting through everything from pop culture to medieval texts. He was enamored of labyrinths. According to Eco, there were three basic types, which he placed in oddly named categories: unicursal, wandering, and network. The unicursal was a labyrinth constructed from a single line and could be unrolled. Eco unrolled the classic labyrinth design of Knossos to reveal Ariadne's thread, which caught Owen's attention. He was stunned. So, Ariadne's thread wasn't just the key to the labyrinth, it *was* the labyrinth. The implications were crucial to Owen's understanding of himself and the role of symbols in his actions. He looked down at the tattoo on his arm and wondered how much Dr. Chouinard had not taught him, or how much she didn't know. Meanwhile he pushed through the material in front of him. Eco compared the wandering, or maze, style of labyrinth to a flowchart and made the curious observation that if it were unrolled, it would be a tree. At first, these statements sounded daft, but as he let them sink in, Owen became excited. The man saw right through the skin of reality.

Trying to drink tea while peering around the upturned cup, he spilled on his shirt as he came to the section on network labyrinths. He set the cup aside and ignored the wet spot. Eco said that the network labyrinth could not be unrolled at all because it had no inside or outside. In fact, every point was connected to all the others, the structure was fluid and in constant change, and this type of labyrinth was best summed up as a rhizome, deliberately plucking the term from Deleuze and Guattari. The text went on to say that "...a multidimensional network of trees, open in all directions, creates rhizomes..." Owen repeated the phrase aloud. "A multidimensional network of trees..." He wondered if Eco had any idea how close he was to the truth of the multiverse.

Three hours of skimming texts and skipping around links left Owen in a daze. His head was stuffed with noisy ideas, unleashing energy and enthusiasm. These philosophy fuckers didn't know the half of what they were on to, he mused.

Needing a break, he stood up and reached to the ceiling, just touching the cheap panels that concealed the original beams. Once white, the ceiling paint was well on its way to ash gray, a side effect of the wood stove. He had an urge to rip down the ceiling and expose the beams. It would be good to see the bones of the house, he thought. Let's get it all out in the open. He filed it away with the other improvements.

Before going to town, he decided it was time to get started on his real work. He walked through the breezeway into the barn. A nook contained a variety of tools, most of which he had learned to use out of rural necessity. As he picked up the brace and a three-quarter-inch bit, he remembered the first time he had used that tool, under the tutelage of his uncle, who clamped a piece of thick lumber on the work bench and set him to work drilling holes in it. He must have been six years old, still innocent, full of the importance of being given a grown-up task. He adored his uncle then, despite the moody spells and volatile temper. Owen didn't know any better; he thought that was the way it was with grown men. Memories lived in that brace and he could feel them in its heft. Even as a child, while he drilled happily in the lumber, his uncle stroked his back and praised him for being a big boy. The set-up was in the works, he knew that now. As Dr.

Chouinard had called it: grooming. He wanted to hurl the brace across the barn. Instead he allowed himself to feel sadness as he held it; yes, it was just a tool. A tool that he could use to change the world.

He walked out of the barn and across the field to the woods, making a direct line for the ash tree that was his portal to the Thorn world. He couldn't resist touching the furrow, and like before, it yielded to the contact, lignin flowing around his fingertips. Pulling out with a slight pop, he was reassured that the portal was real and not a dream or delusion. He circled to the other side of the tree. This seemed like a logical place to start, right where there was a link. He wondered if drilling into the tree would hurt it and it made him queasy to think about the pain. This was the plan, though, developed by the trees for the trees. Rhizome, he corrected himself. It's all about the rhizome; the trees are merely expressions of a greater being.

He drilled through the bark and into the sapwood. Putting the brace on the ground, he took out his pocketknife. It was razor sharp, like always. His uncle taught him that, too, the bastard. He made an incision in his little finger, squeezed it until a drop of blood formed, then he stuffed the finger into the hole. He let it bleed for a moment and withdrew. Blood oozed from the cut on his finger. He should have brought a bandage. Add it to the list for town, he thought; purchase a thousand Band-Aids.

Back at the house, he threw an extra log in the stove and damped it down before heading out to his truck. An old Toyota, it started right up like always. Although he had been driving since he was sixteen, the motions of shifting and steering felt odd, as though he had never done them before. And the sensation of hurtling along the road, even though he was barely at the speed limit, felt completely unnatural. Not that he had ever loved driving. He preferred to walk. However, that wasn't much of an option in Maine, not if you wanted to play any part in society. Owen wondered what might happen to the fossil fuel industry and its parasites after the forest enlightenment covered the Earth. Would we walk or go back to riding horses? Would horses even let us on their backs?

He turned on the truck radio for distraction. Scrolling across the bandwidth, he paused in succession on sports chatter, trite rock and roll and country music, soporific public radio mumble, and evangelical hysteria before turning it off again. Human culture was not bearing up well to the scrutiny of his new perspective. How much of this bullshit was necessary? None, he thought. None.

He cruised into Machias, a small city like many others along the coast: a combination of decaying historical landmarks, Victorian houses, trailers, tree-lined residential streets with crumbling sidewalks, and shacks surrounded by lobster traps stacked to the eaves. The center of town was a mix of empty store-fronts and ventures that found enough of a niche to cling to solvency. One of these was the natural food market. He knew that it relied on the university, catering to vegan students and the organic-inclined faculty. He'd never shopped there, although when he was a student on campus, he'd overheard peers raving about one obscure item or another.

Inside he found a casual lay-out, warmer and more comforting than the sanitation of the supermarket. He took a basket and wandered around, throwing in things that caught his eye. He had little idea what to get and the glimpses he caught of the prices suggested that he could spend a lot of money and not get very much. It didn't matter; he would learn. It seemed important to eat well; the Thorns had urged him to attend to his health, which made sense. How else would he be able to churn out blood cells?

He walked out with two bags of groceries for a hundred dollars. It was shocking, but maybe it was worth it. As he left the store, a poster in the window caught his eye. "RALLY TO SAVE THE TREES – DON'T CUT THE CUTLER PRESERVE! – STOP THEM NOW." He read the poster twice. He couldn't believe someone was going to log the Cutler Preserve. It was a swath of state-owned land, not far from his farm, and one of the most beautiful places around. Despite being of modest size, the tract of land included an old forest perched along hundred-foot high cliffs overlooking the Atlantic Ocean. Many times, Owen had gone there to sit on the moss under giant pines and gaze over the water, watching for whales and eagles. The land had been set aside for conservation, but the current governor had made it a priority to undo as much of that as possible. Now it had come to this: logging another old growth forest.

The date for the rally was today. People were urged to come to the trailhead parking lot, the only access to the preserve. He needed to go. He could drop off the groceries at his place and continue to the preserve, just a few miles further down the road. It seemed clear that the campaign to save these trees was part of what he had to do. Besides, he could use some allies.

[16]

The parking area at the Cutler Reserve was occupied by the over-sized machinery of logging: a skidder with six-foot tires, a bulldozer, a log-loading crane, and one of those insectoid mobile harvesters. Owen had seen a harvester at work; he remembered watching in awe as the hydraulic arms grabbed a trunk, severed it, waved it around like a matchstick, then fed it through its claws, delimbing the entire length. The presence of these machines chilled Owen; they resembled armaments in the war against the forest.

On the other side of the lot, a group of bundled-up people stood, perhaps a hundred in all, holding signs proclaiming sentiments like "HANDS OFF OUR TREES" and "THIS FOREST BELONGS TO YOU AND ME." They chanted and stomped, probably as much to stay warm as to make a statement. Separating the protestors and the machinery was a wall of police, primarily from the county sheriff's department, but augmented by state troopers and several forest rangers in dark green jackets and trapper hats. Owen drove slowly past the lot and pulled over at the end of a line of cars parked along the shoulder.

He walked back to the confrontation. The anger was inescapable, on both sides. It rolled over him in waves as he approached. In the past he would have hidden from such a turbulent swell of emotion. He might be stronger now, but this slammed into him like a gut punch. He walked in measured steps, dragging his reluctance as he went. He used to filter these things out with dissociation and distraction, but those defenses were no longer an option; his awareness had been torn open, not to be closed again. That seemed to be a good thing when he was with the Thorns in the forest. Now he could see the disadvantages. Human pain was sharp and noisy and often narcissistic. Were these people here to make themselves feel good or did they really care about the trees? Was this kind of thing the best way to preserve the forest? Judgments swept through him, leaving a bad taste. Who was he, lord of the realm? Shouldn't he be more generous? These folks, the protestors, anyway, could be his allies. Their hearts were right—at least they cared enough about trees to do something. In contrast to the anarchy of the protestors, the police formed a line, just in front of the machines, tight-lipped and anxious, no doubt worried that the crowd would become a mob. A few faces in the line of enforcers showed smirks that caused Owen to think they would welcome a chance to beat down a few tree-huggers.

Owen slipped to the edge of the protest group and was welcomed with smiles. He saw some familiar faces from the university, though no one seemed to recognize him. He guessed that his new beard and shaggy hair provided a disguise of sorts. He eavesdropped on a nearby conversation, audible between cheers and chants, and learned that the logging was scheduled to start tomorrow morning. People were swearing and ranting about the governor's legal loophole for this project. In the end, despite all the protective legislation, he only had to downgrade the status of the preserve, reclassify it as open resource land, and order the harvest. There had been no public review. This move baffled everyone since the forest, though old, offered nothing out of the ordinary in merchantable timber. Some folks suspected the governor wanted to show yet another tough side to his personality and simply ruin a favorite recreation spot. He had never held back his contempt for nature lovers and soft types who didn't meet his criteria for a justified existence.

The protestors milled around the parking lot. They glared at the police from time to time, but mostly faced inward. Chants and sign-waving increased in tempo, then subsided. No one seemed to know what to do. Journalists were absent, a situation that concerned many of the protestors. Owen heard some people claim they had notified the press and couldn't understand why they weren't here.

The police had a clearer mission: protect the logging gear. However, none of the protestors made any moves toward the machines or even talked about sabotage. Owen guessed that some of them knew the loggers that owned the equipment and were reluctant to attack the livelihood of folks in the community. They wanted to save trees; they didn't want to destroy things, even the machines of destruction.

Owen stood around the group for about an hour, nodding and listening without knowing how to act. He'd never been to a protest and he wondered what would happen next. Excitement sparked through the crowd when a van with Oregon license plates pulled into the lot and squeezed alongside the clustered protestors. A few people cheered. The van looked as if it had seen many miles of road. Paint covered the exterior in an array of psychedelic colors and shapes, executed with more enthusiasm than skill. Across the side of the van, in large black and red letters, Owen read "FOREST RESCUE CREW" and under it, in smaller letters, "FIRST AID FOR TREE FRIENDS." The side panel slid open, and two burly men jumped out, grinning and waving at the protestors. The Oregonians were young, hairy, and dressed in expensive outdoor clothes. Behind them, in the van, Owen saw mounds of coiled ropes, slings, harnesses, and climbing hardware. The young man with the longest beard, a bush that covered the upper half of his chest, lifted his arm in a clenched fist.

"Hello, righteous ones. My name's River. This here—" and he waved at his partner, also bearded and with a thicket of wiry hair, who stood grinning like he couldn't imagine there could be anything more fun than what he was doing at the moment, "—this is my solid brother in the trees, the Gnarly Garth. Mostly we just call him Gnarth." The crowd laughed and hooted while Garth clasped his hands and waved them overhead in victory. Owen couldn't stop looking at the hands. They belonged on Paul Bunyan or a grizzly bear.

River motioned for people to come closer. "Okay, folks. We heard about this malicious project; we track these things. No shortage of that kind of mischief, but this one seemed really fucked up, if you know what I mean. So, we drove non-stop cross country to join your protest. That's what we do. And, if you're of a mind, we can take it to the next level. Literally."

Garth's broad smile settled into a smirk. He pointed dramatically into the tree-tops. "When he says up another level, he means it. We're gonna climb these trees, ones marked for cutting, and camp there as guardians. They won't dare cut them down; they'd never live down the publicity and lawsuits. We've done this before, and I can tell you that it works. I can *testify*!" Garth raised his arm and shook his fist. The crowd cheered.

"However," said River, "we need your support. So if this is something you want, you can do a lot of good right here on the ground. We'll need folks just like today, taking a stand. We're also gonna need some brothers and sisters willing to bring us food and water and someone to be a communications link. No telling how long we'll have to stay. But we've got the gear, so have no fear, just keep us stocked in goodies and beer!" Laughter and applause erupted from the protestors. Owen clapped hard, blinking back a tear of nostalgia for Whitethorn.

Climbing the trees—what a brave and foolish thing to do, Owen thought. He looked around to see if the police were paying attention to these boasts. He couldn't imagine they would stand by and let these fellows ascend a single trunk. Once established in the canopy, they would be hell to remove. But the police, perhaps tired of holding a line against an unthreatening crowd, had fallen back to the machines. Some leaned against the giant tires and tracks, chatting with each other, apparently unconcerned. A few studied the van with obvious amusement. Owen noticed that the van had been cleverly parked to obscure its contents from the eyes of the authorities. Perhaps they weren't so foolish, after all.

Owen turned back to Garth to hear him say that they had enough equipment to set up an additional tree-sit if anyone wanted to join them. People looked at each other, intrigued by the idea, but no one stepped forward. Owen took two breaths and raised his hand.

River signaled Owen to come forward. The crowd parted like the Red Sea, leaving a clear alley between Owen and the two tree climbers. What had he gotten himself into? Whatever it was, it was the way forward, so he took the steps. When he offered a handshake to River, it was converted into a hippie-style clutch. Garth did the same thing.

"Done this kind of thing before?" Asked River as he stared directly into Owen's eyes. The stare penetrated into Owen's nerves and he fidgeted.

"Kind of, but not really." Owen remembered that his only tree-climbing experience was when he scrambled up into the white ash to hang himself.

"Well, it's hard core stuff, man. Mass work-out, top to bottom. Nothing easy about it. And it's gonna be colder than a witch's tit up there."

River's eyes continued to bore into him like searchlights. Owen looked away and saw that the exchange was followed by the quiet and attentive crowd. Owen was not the type who liked to be a center of attention and he started to regret his impulse. He looked beyond the array of faces, expanded his focus and saw the trees of the forest, silent witnesses to the assembly. They had a palpable presence, an energy in their roots, which wove throughout the landscape, even under the gravel of the parking lot. The Thorns were right – it was like he had grown an extra sense, for he could feel those roots underfoot. The rhizome was there; he heard it or felt it or something, but he was connected. He drew himself up and looked at River.

"I've done worse," Owen said.

Garth burst out laughing. "Oh man, don't take him so seriously, man. That River is seriously insane, dude. He just wants to see if you're gonna stick it out. Once you get up there, man, we don't want you gettin' all sketchy and remembering that your mama needs you home for dinner. No posers allowed, you know?"

"I understand. I won't let you down. I'm not like that. I... have a thing about trees. Nothing's more important."

"Cool, man. You've got heart, I'll give you that. And you look like a sturdy guy." River clapped him on the shoulder. Owen understood that he had been dubbed a fellow and was now one of the Forest Rescue Crew.

River turned to the crowd. "Hey folks, here's the thing. No offense, but this protest you got going here right now isn't doing much. Tomorrow morning is when the shit's gonna hit. We need to be set up in the trees before then, but there's no way that's gonna be possible as long as the cops are here. And the cops are gonna stay here as long as there's a crowd. So why don't we all *vamos* and let the cops do the same? The three of us will come back later this afternoon and get situated in the tree-tops. You all need to be here at the crack of dawn tomorrow morning and whoop it up. Bring your neighbors. And, for fuck's sake, somebody get a reporter here." There were nods and murmurs of assent throughout the protestors. "And anyone who wants to help us once we're up there, please check in before you go. We'll give you a list of things to bring, and when." Ragged cheers rose from the group and people started to move. A few came forward to take copies of River and Garth's printed list for how to support a tree-sitter.

Garth looked at Owen. "We assume the cops will leave. You know any different?"

"No, makes sense to me. It's still early in the day. Too cold to stand around if you don't have to. Hot coffee and doughnuts can be quite persuasive."

Garth laughed again, an open, hearty guffaw that seemed to uncoil from his feet. He turned to River. "I like this dude!"

Owen was warming to these characters. They seemed larger than life, almost mythic. "Hey," he ventured, "I've got a place just a couple miles from here. We can go hang out there for a while till things settle down. I'll cook you a meal, we can warm up and plan the next step."

River looked at Owen and nodded. Garth slapped his thigh and said it again: "I like this dude!"

[17]

Owen described his truck to River and Garth and said he would wait for them at a crossroads about a mile back toward town. He left the parking lot in the stream of protestors eager to gain the warmth of their vehicles. The air temperature was brisk and blunt. He guessed it was in the upper 20s with that sharp blue sky so common to late fall. It would get colder tonight and the following nights if it stayed clear. Clouds probably meant snow. He had ignored this reality when he chose to take up residence in a tree. He would need every piece of winter clothing he could find.

Maybe he still fit into the snowmobile suit his mother had given him for Christmas one year when she thought he was reading too many books and needed to get out in the world. Two days after the gift, she had talked him into joining the neighbors on a ride with their snow machines. It was perhaps no coincidence that the neighbor's daughter was home from college. Of course, she would accompany her father and Owen for a tour through the white-mantled woods. Owen didn't want to go but felt obligated to humor his mother.

The outing was not to his taste in any way. Riding around on the machines was incredibly stupid: they were loud, stinky, and dangerous. A couple of times he almost tipped over, which left him afraid to open the throttle. After an hour of torment, they stopped for a break and the dad extracted a pint of sherry from inside his snow suit. Owen was surprised to see him casually hand it to his daughter, who took a long swig, then passed it to Owen. He didn't drink, still bitter with the aftertaste of his uncle's drunken ways. Owen muttered something about his stomach and returned the bottle to the father. The father and daughter handed it back and forth until it was gone, all the while chattering about football. If his mother thought there were grounds for romance, they didn't materialize.

Owen pulled his truck over at the crossroads. He watched the protestors' cars pass in an erratic stream. A few police vehicles were in the mix, showing that they weren't going to hang around a minute longer than necessary. River and Garth's remarkable van was now visible, so he didn't wait, just pulled out in front of them, waving his hand out the window. He led them to a side road, then to a gravel road, and finally they pulled on to a narrow dirt channel through dense forest. At the last turn-off was a battered piece of wood nailed on a tree. "BLACK," it said in fading letters, proclaiming the family domain.

The house was still warm, but Owen went straight to the stove and threw in more wood. They were all chilled from standing around the parking lot at the presere. "Make yourselves at home," he said and swept his hand around the room in what he hoped was a hospitable gesture. "You hungry? I just bought groceries; I'll make us some food." Then it occurred to Owen that they might have dietary quirks, as seemed to be the case with so many of his peers. "Depending, that is, on what you prefer."

River loomed over the stove, soaking up its heat in a stupor. He did not respond. Garth had made a beeline for the shelves full of books to scrutinize the titles. "Man, you've got some serious reading here! What are you, like smart or something?" He looked at Owen intently, then grinned. "Don't mind me, man, I'm yanking your chain. Hey, River, look, this guy's got Culross Peattie!" Garth took the volume of Peattie's *A Natural History of Eastern Trees* and waved it over his head. "Duuude."

The appearance of Peattie roused River from his trance. He nodded in approval at Garth, then turned to Owen. "Man, let us cook for you. It's the least we can do. We've got a ton of food. Came prepared. Might as well start using it, then we can talk logistics over some grub."

Owen had no objections, so River and Garth went to the van for supplies. Minutes later they returned, River with a box of food, and Garth with an enormous bag of climbing gear, which he dropped in the dining room. It landed on the floor with a clanking thud.

River pulled a pot and a pan off the kitchen wall. He peered into his food box and said to Owen, almost as an afterthought, "So... what's your deal, man?"

"What's... what's my deal?"

"Yeah, you know. What gets you stoked? And why?"

Owen regained his composure. "Not sure how to answer that. Let me think."

"Fair enough." River pulled out a several clear plastic bags. The largest was stuffed with grain-like pellets while the others contained an assortment of wrinkled, unidentifiable items that reminded Owen of the mushrooms he ate in the Thorn world. River displayed the different bags proudly. "Homegrown from the Pac Northwest. Dried and packaged with loving care by yours truly. Tomatoes, zucchini, carrots, onions, mushrooms. We'll be hauling this stuff with us into the canopy. Grub for weeks."

While River set about cooking a hippie stew, Owen tried to answer the question. "I grew up right here. It wasn't what you'd call an ideal childhood. I spent a lot of time running away from reality, reading, and following academic pursuits. Along the way I learned a lot about mythology and anthropology, not that I could say there's much to show for it. Recently, though, something happened to me, something very strange. Changed my life."

River looked over his shoulder. "Oh?"

Owen considered his words carefully. "You can see what it's like around here: pretty much all forest. As a kid, I spent a lot of time in these woods; it was a sanctuary. But I never really thought much about what went on in there, other than the kind of knowledge you get from living and working on a farm surrounded by trees. But a couple of weeks ago I had an experience, a kind of enlightenment, you could say. For the first time I perceived the forest as a living being, and even more remarkable, I could touch and feel all the connections within that being. I understood that we're just parts of a greater system and everything is linked. Everything."

River had stopped fiddling with the stew and stared intently at Owen. He reached out and put both of his hands on Owen's shoulders. "Dude. You're one of us, aren't you?"

"One of you?"

"A tree-friend." River's tones were solemn and reverent.

"Sure. I guess so. I love the forest, if that's what you mean." When he said the word "love," an image of the Thorns and the beauty of their world filled Owen and swept away his hesitation about speaking his thoughts. "So I've decided to dedicate myself to the web of life, especially anything I can do to sustain and preserve the forests, not just the trees, but the underground rhizome network as well. The whole thing."

River looked puzzled. "Rhizome network?"

"Yes. One of the things I learned is that most of the life in the forest is underground, in the symbiotic mix of flora and fungus. In truth, if there's such a thing as a forest mind, and I think there is, it will be found under the soil."

"You sound like those one of those crunchy forest scientists up in BC, man."

"Crunchy?"

"You know, cool. I guess you're not from the West Coast."

"Never been there. Though I hope to go. I need to sit with those trees."

"Oh yeah, man, they're totally sick. Like nothing else."

"So, what's *your* story?" Owen thought that he had said enough, for now.

"Oh, that. Well, I didn't go to college. Grew up in eastern Oregon, started working with my dad in his construction business. That was right after my mom died. Cancer, you know. I was pretty young, still in middle school, actually. Dad worked all the time, so I started skipping school and working with him; he didn't seem to mind that much about the school. I had more money in my pocket than most kids, which probably wasn't such a good thing. Started getting in trouble and would have ended up in a bad way. But then I discovered rock climbing. That changed everything." The smell of burning vegetables brought them back to reality. "Shit, man, I need to tend to this. To be continued, okay?" River turned back to the stove and Owen wandered out into the dining room to see what was going on with the clanks and thunks he had heard.

As Owen left the kitchen, River called out, "Garth, man. This dude's got it going on."

Garth looked up at Owen and beamed. "Hey, I knew that!" He pointed at three duffels made of sturdy-looking material. They were tube-shaped with draw-string tops and carrying loops. "These are our haul bags. We each get one. We'll be living out of them, so whatever you think you'll need up there should go in now. Put in some food for yourself, but we'll share meals and hot drinks. We've done this half a dozen times already, so we're dialed in and gnarly, man. We'll pick three trees close to-gether, climb each one, then rig hanging belay stations with ropes for descent or hauling supplies. And, dig this, ropes to stretch across horizontally between the belays. That way we'll be able to send stuff back and forth without having to go down. River likes to do the cooking, he's like that. At each belay station we'll set up these rad portaledges. Ever seen one?" Owen shook his head, but Garth was already rattling out the answer. "Rock climbers use them for vertical bivvies—it's a little tent with a built-in platform. The whole show hangs from a single point. Actually, pretty comfortable, though space is a little on the sketchy side. Usually we spend the days sitting around on branches and stuff, enjoying the view, but with this weather we may have to be in the bivvy most of the time, hunkered into a sleeping bag. We've never done a tree-sit in this kind of cold. Should be interesting!" Owen could tell from the look on Garth's face that he was eager for the challenge. He liked these guys. They seemed childlike at times—if it was childlike to have ideals and enthusiasm—but there was more to them than the appearance of hairy freaks. Besides, at the rate his hair was growing, Owen would soon look like them.

"Anyway," Garth continued, "we'll pull up our ascent ropes after we're in the canopy, only dropping them for friends to bring stuff, pass notes, etc. We usually have a phone with a few extra batteries and let ground support keep them charged. Essentially, we'll be on our own up there. But never fear, we'll be stylin'!"

River announced that the food was ready, and Owen moved to the table, pushing aside piles of books and journals to clear enough space for the three of them. He set the table with mismatched utensils and bowls. River served a large crock full of the cooked grain and reconstituted vegetables, steaming with aromatic vapors. They were all hungry and scooped out heaping ladles to fill their bowls.

"What is this grain?" Owen had never eaten anything quite like it. "It's kind of like rice, but heartier."

"Oh, that's quinoa, man. Best grain on earth. Comes from the Andes." River spooned out another dollop, pointing at the pellets with his free hand. "Protein central, man."

They ate until the crock was empty, then Garth used his finger to wipe out the last traces, which he then sucked up with smacking lips. Owen smiled, appreciating the gusto.

Silence filled the room for a few moments, then River cleared his throat. "Okay, time to finish packing. Owen, you should gather your personal gear. Book, flashlight or headlamp if you have it, extra batteries, warmest sleeping bag you've got, warm clothes... what've you got for cold weather clothes?"

"Snowmobile suit, heavy mitts, that kind of thing."

"Oh, good, yeah, that should work. I guess you're probably used to it around here. Still, there'll be no way to get warm once we're up in the trees, except eating and staying huddled in gear. No alcohol, by the way. No way. Not on our watch – causes too many problems. You'll need every one of your wits about you. Can't have you taking a ground fall from a hundred feet."

"No problem here. At this point, I'm enthusiastic about continuing to live."

They both laughed. River continued, "Good man. This is pretty safe, really, but only if you stay in the zone, dude. You have questions; just ask. We appreciate you doing this. You may be a gumby but you're not a poser, I'm convinced. The more of us up in the trees, the harder it is for the loggers to get going. Plus, it looks righteous on the news. We'll fix all the lines for you, no worries there. You just have to climb up and down the ropes and tough it out. We'll show you what you need to know. Gonna be an adventure, brah. Alright. We should think about getting on the road. Got a few things to do before dark, eh?" River looked at Garth and they slapped a high five. Owen laughed; he felt like he was part of the team.

[18]

They loaded the gear in Owen's pickup, deciding to leave the florid Forest Rescue van at the house for discretion. It was early afternoon, but the autumn dusk wouldn't be long. When they arrived at the parking lot of the Cutler Reserve, it was empty. River and Garth leaped out of the truck and stalked around the periphery of the woods, identifying the most promising trees for climbing. Satisfied with the options, River sent a phone text to one of the protestors who had agreed to be a contact, notifying her that the tree-sit was on.

Owen's excitement mounted as he watched. He wasn't sure that he was advancing the multiverse agenda with this protest, but he had made two hardy friends, clearly allies, and he was doing something. He had no way of knowing how this would play out or if it would benefit his mission. He decided not to worry about it. Whatever was going to happen was bound to be interesting.

While Owen carried the haul bags and miscellaneous gear from the truck to the bases of the trees, both River and Garth strapped climbing spikes on their boots. They buckled into waist harnesses, to which each clipped a short, heavy loop of rope in front and a long mountaineering rope in back.

Garth looked at Owen with a sly grin. "Watch this, man." He exchanged looks with River and the two of them leaped like overgrown squirrels on to the trunks of adjacent trees, big old hemlocks, using the spikes to hold themselves on the bark. Garth passed his front rope around the trunk and clipped the free end into the other side of his harness. River did the same, working in near synchronization. Each climber leaned back against the front loop like a lineman, held in place by the tension between the rope and the boot spikes. Garth waved to Owen, River nodded, and the two charged up the trees, flipping the rope up after ascending two or three vertical steps. Owen stared in astonishment. It looked arduous, but River and Garth powered up the trees in a vertical ballet. Within minutes they were in the lower branches. Shortly after that he could only follow their movements by the bouncing of the trailing ropes.

While the climbers fixed the rigging for the belay stations, Owen had nothing to do. He gazed into the woods, thinking that it wouldn't be long until the first snow. The forest seemed sleepy and peaceful, but Owen knew better. By tuning out the visual stimuli, he sensed the activities of the rhizome reverberating from the ground, through his boots, reaching into his nervous system. He let his focus drop completely out of the body and into the network below. Some of the thoughts and feelings emanating from the underground system were recognizable. Not human emotion, but still perceptible as distress. The forest knew that it was going to be attacked and the trees marked for death were the oldest and most vigorous. What remained would be compromised, integrity amputated, and the survivors would be vulnerable to the predations of disease and bugs. The rhizome distress was both an outcry and a eulogy for the impending loss. It coalesced in Owen's mind as a mosaic of sound, a chorus of low tones woven into an expression of suffering. Despite the grief inherent in the strange music, it was beautiful and carried the air of a celebration, like the death chant of a Lakota warrior on the eve of battle.

Tears were running down Owen's cheeks when he heard River yelling from above. "Owen! Hey man, listen up! Hook the bags!"

Owen tore his attention out of the rhizome and ran over to River's tree. He clipped the haul bag into a loop at the end of a dangling rope. Cupping his hands around his mouth, he yelled towards the canopy. "All set! Haul away!" As the bag started its ascent, he went to the other tree and did the same thing for Garth. He wished that he could do more.

While waiting for them to complete the set-up, he realized that he could work on his mission and distribute the virus. It might be too late for many of these trees to manufacture pheromones, but some would be left standing, and the rhizome would continue its underground existence, spreading the virus through its network. He walked to a small birch tree that was unmarked and outside of the flagged logging zone. Using his knife to carve a notch through the bark into the sapwood, he then sliced his fingertip and pressed it to the notch. He had forgotten the Band-Aids, of course. He removed his finger from the blood-smeared bark and put it in his mouth. It was a curious sensation, tasting his own blood.

By the time he got back to the triad of trees that would be their new dwelling, Garth had rappelled down his main line and was scrambling up the third tree, the one for Owen. Garth looked down briefly at him, flashing a huge grin. "This is *so* gnarl, dude!" Then he was back to the ascent. Before long he called for the third haul bag.

The sun was settling into the tops of the trees when Garth slid back down to the ground and motioned Owen over. "Okay, man, this is it! You stoked? Of course, you are! Everything is ready for you. All you have to do is use these ascenders to climb the rope. It's a workout, man, don't get me wrong. You'll be glad to get to the top. But you can do it, just keep at it, remember to breathe, one step at a time. When you get to the portaledge station, holler down. Stay put, though, don't try to unclip. You can sit back in your harness. I'll come up and show you the set-up. River's over at his station, already cooking some grub, so we'll share that around when we get you all settled in."

Garth helped Owen put on his waist harness, bantering the whole time. "Oh, you're married to this baby, now, my friend. This'll keep your ass safe and sound! You'll sleep in it, eat in it, shit in it, it's your Honey! Just don't try to kiss the bride or you may throw your back out! Seriously, man, don't take off your harness, not till you're back on the ground. It's your means of staying clipped to the lines we've got set up. And, man, I assure you that you do not want to be unclipped. Being unclipped is one sneeze away from being dead. You feel me, brah?"

"Loud and clear, yes. I feel you." Garth laughed at Owen's formal response to the slang, then he gave him a hefty slap between the shoulders. Using carabiners, Owen attached to the ascenders and followed Garth's instructions as he started to climb straight up the rope. Each ascender had a sling for his foot. Owen took a vertical step as he slid the ascender up the rope, then repeated the motion with the other foot. Ten feet off the ground he was exhausted. He glanced back down at Garth, who watched him closely and laughed.

"Go on, man, you've got it. Step to it, find the rhythm, you can do it!" Garth's enthusiasm was irrepressible. Owen wondered what it would be like to live like that, to embrace life with constant gusto. His own temperament was subdued by comparison. Garth was a singular character. Such people were precious conduits for positive life energy. Dr. Chouinard had been like that, in her own way.

Owen found a rhythm of ascent and burned through the outrage of his muscles. Around a hundred feet up he came to the portaledge. It was a platform tent with a pyramid-shaped nylon roof. Suspended at the peak from a sturdy branch, he noticed that there were back-up and stabilizing lines linked to nearby branches. These guys didn't take any chances. The main climbing line continued up a few more feet, where it ended. From there, he saw that a horizontal rope stretched a hundred feet over to the next big tree and another portaledge. A different line continued to the third tree where he saw River, sitting on a branch in front of a makeshift shelf, presumably cooking. River looked up at Owen and waved his hand in sweeping arcs. Owen waved back in kind.

He called down the tree that he was ready before sitting back in the harness and waiting for Garth. These guys built a civilization in the treetops in no time. Owen was impressed. It reminded him of the hominids that lived in the forest canopy in the Thorn world, the ones who had provided the fabric for clothes. He was sorry that he hadn't been able to climb up and see them. What a way to live – Owen envied them their perch and perspective on the world. Perhaps it was essential to the primate genes, he wondered, this enthusiasm for climbing trees.

Owen watched Garth's bushy head rise through the branches. He stopped at the portaledge and beckoned Owen to descend.

Garth showed him how to open and close the tent and demonstrated the challenges of entry and exit. It was awkward, like getting in and out of a kayak, and required an athletic flair. Garth insisted that Owen try it under his supervision. He pointed out how a short length of rope could be used to stay clipped to the lines on the tree, even when sleeping in the portaledge.

"These anchors here are bomb-proof. Never, ever unclip from them unless you're descending from the tree. With your leash system, you can scramble up to the high point, sit on a branch, catch a few z's, whatever, and you're in no risk of ground fall. You got any questions, you just holler, okay? I'm only one tree away. Hmmm. Sun's going down. Incredible view up here, eh? Tomorrow we'll see the sunrise over the ocean. Fuckin' A – never see that on the West Coast; I can't wait! All right dude, good to have you aloft. Food delivery should be along shortly."

Garth extended his hand for a hippie handshake and Owen responded in kind. "Thank you. This is incredible. I'm really blown away."

"Well, if the wind comes up... don't be!" Garth guffawed and scrambled onto the horizontal rope. He attached a pulley to it and clipped his harness to the pulley, then slid off from Owen's tree over to his own, hanging beneath the line and pulling hand over hand. He made it look effortless.

Once Garth settled into his station, Owen saw River traverse from his tree to Garth's. He pulled a flask out of his daypack and handed it to Garth, exchanged a few words, then slid over to Owen.

"Hey, man. How's it hangin'?" Owen was treated to one of River's rare laughs, a kind of spastic chuckle that sounded like choking. "So what do you think? Pretty righteous up here, eh?"

"No doubt about it. I'm impressed. Hey, how long have you guys been doing this kind of thing?"

"A while. Like I was telling you before, I started climbing in high school, first rocks, then alpine stuff, then somewhere along the way I got my eyes opened to the state of the earth, man. I had already climbed a few trees for kicks, you know, when I read about that woman that did the redwood sit down in California. You know the one—Butterfly? She was in this giant redwood for over 2 years, dude. Two fucking years!"

"What? Two years? You're shitting me. And... butterfly?"

"Oh yeah, that's her name, man. She wrote a book and every-thing. Anyway, I figured if she pulled that off, what was stopping me? So, I protested every time I heard about old growth getting cut. Did a bunch of tree-sits; the longest was three months. I met Garth during a protest in southern Oregon and we hit if off im-mediately: true soul brothers, you know. He's a trip, huh? Good man, he's got your back to the bitter end. Saved my life one time when the loggers started cutting the tree right from under me. Fuck! He rapped out of his tree when the ruckus started, ran over to the logger and yanked the saw right out of his hands, swung it by the blade against the trunk and smashed the powerhead. He's a feisty son of a bitch at times. He got jumped by the whole log-ging crew and they beat the hell out of him. Gave me enough time to get out of the tree, though. They were determined to bring it down and they had their way that day, once they got rid of us. But a tree sit usually stops 'em in their tracks. It's too much commitment for them; they don't know what to do. Ever since then, though, we've rigged up these horizontal lines in the treetops. Escape route, you dig?"

Owen wanted to listen to such stories forever. They were mythic and represented a human spirit that he admired: tales of dedication to the world for its own sake and not for reward. This spirit was an astonishing power; why did it not distinguish the human condition? Owen had no answer.

"Anyway, man, here's some grub for ya. If you use a little drinking water to rinse out the bottle, you can swap it for more tomorrow. You're on your own the rest of the day, but we like to share one meal. Keeps the communion going." River handed Owen a quart plastic water bottle. It was warm and comfortable in the hand.

"Thank you so much. I'm humbled by what you guys are doing and how you do it. If there's such a thing as beauty in human action, you two shine with it. It's an honor to be here."

River looked at Owen with curiosity. "You're an eloquent dude. But thanks, yeah. I'm pleased that you're with us. Strength in numbers, eh? Anyway, have a cozy night. Should be pretty damn crisp, so hunker down solid, now. See you in the AM."

Owen received another hippie handshake and then he was alone in the tree. Or, he thought, as alone as one could be while perched in the upper reaches of a mind linked from sky to earth, on through the whole forest and across the boundaries of alternate universes.

[19]

It was a frigid night, but Owen's sleeping bag kept him warm. He woke up to a noisy dawn of rumbling diesel ignitions followed by the chants of a crowd. Somebody had brought a drum and pounded a rhythm. Owen peeked out of the tent door. Hundreds of protestors stood in lines, arms linked, facing a line of police. The protestors stomped feet in the cadence of their chant: "WHEN THE TREES WE LOVE ARE UNDER ATTACK, WHAT DO WE DO? STAND UP, FIGHT BACK! WHAT DO WE DO? STAND UP, FIGHT BACK!"

Through the branches, he watched River and Garth unfurl a large banner stretched between their trees. It said: RESPECT YOUR ELDERS. Garth noticed Owen's head protruding from the tent and waved at him. Owen waved back, then ducked into the tent to slide out of his bag and dress for the day. It was early, but clearly the show was on.

The police stood in front of the heavy equipment and the loggers huddled behind the police. Several loggers were pointing up toward the tree-sitters. They did not look pleased. Owen pulled out a plastic bag of gorp from the supplies and a water bottle he had kept warm in the bottom of his sleeping bag. Ginger slices in the bottle provided a passable version of a brew, good for several refills. Owen didn't mind that it was lukewarm. He nibbled the gorp, picking out the raisins, and sipped tea while sitting on the branch above the portaledge, observing the scene in the parking lot. The loggers huddled in a knot and had an animated discussion. He guessed they talked about how to proceed with their work, if possible. The protestors, no doubt inspired by the confusion, elevated the volume and intensity of the chants. The drum got louder and more insistent. On the refrain of "STAND UP, FIGHT BACK!" the protestors stomped in determined unison, raising dust from the gravel. The fierce energy sent chills up Owen's spine as he watched from above.

He tucked away the food and drink and leaned close to the tree, wrapping his arms around it. It was a venerable hemlock, maybe two hundred years old, judging from the girth. What a magnificent creature it was. He pressed his ear against the rough bark and blocked out the sounds from below, focusing all his attention into the tree. A sound came through the wood, like water rushing in pipes and Owen understood that he was hearing the flow of the rhizome traffic passing up and down the tree. Yesterday, when he tuned in to the rhizome, he had heard the music of a dirge. It rose again, but this time blended with a martial theme. It sounded noble and reminded him of virtue and solidarity. Was all that in the music or was he making it up, projecting his own emotions into the abstract chorus? He tried to listen, just listen, without thought, without interpretation, and open himself to the full message. It came through: the rhizome wove a song about humans and plants, a reinforcement of connection, an auditory embrace of fellowship.

Owen pulled his attention away from the tree and looked across at his friends to see if they could feel it, too. Garth stood on his haul bag, clipped to the tree and leaning forward as if he was on the prow of a ship. He pounded his chest and yelled to the sky. River sat at his stance in a lotus posture, wiping his cheeks. Down below, the drum was deafening, and the protestors chanted in unison, stomping their feet, arms linked in a tribal dance. The trees themselves seemed to sway in time to the rhythms, and the forest shook with the energy of an earthquake.

Owen shivered with a rush of ecstasy. It wasn't just him, everyone felt it. Even the police deferred to the energy by slowly backing away from the protestors. Loggers started shutting down the machines and Owen saw a couple of them shaking their heads and gesturing to the police. He watched them retreat to their pickup trucks, pile in, and drive away. The protestors cheered and danced. It looked as if they had won.

The intensity of the protest dwindled after the loggers left. The music stopped and the protestors chatted, invigorated by the victory. The police looked bored and, after a brief conference with a few of the protestors, they drove away, leaving the victors to congratulate each other before trickling back to their cars. It was too cold to stand around for long; Owen couldn't blame them for seeking warmth. Many of the protestors waved and blew kisses to the tree-sitters and there were a lot of thumbs-up. A few stuck around, yelling words of support into the treetops, but by mid-day it was just the three of them and the forest. The world settled into stillness. Owen welcomed the calm after the tension of the morning. He tried to stay warm by scrambling up and down the tree to the extent allowed by his leash. He read his book for a while, but he couldn't focus. He just wanted to breathe in the beauty of the woods and revel in the connection to the labyrinth that couldn't be unrolled, the network of every-thing.

That evening River and Garth slid over on the horizontal ropes and they had dinner in Owen's tree. Curiosity compelled him to ask, "What did you guys feel this morning during the protest? Could you sense something out of the ordinary?"

"Out of the ordinary, he says!" Garth burst in. "Fuck yeah, brah! The tree spirit was moving oh so righteously!"

River chuckled at Garth's exuberance. "Yes, indeed, Owen. It was... deep. Stronger than I've ever felt it before. It was as if the earth itself wanted to be heard, right here, right now. That was some holy, holy shit, man."

Owen beamed at them. Love filled his heart in a way that was beyond words, so he said nothing, just grinned and ate the food that embodied their communion. Handshakes were held longer than usual before they parted. Owen sensed that a bond was being forged in the tops of the trees; it helped him to appreciate how River and Garth became friends. What an amazing thing they were doing. As he crawled into his sleeping bag for the night, the excitement of the day lingered. Sleep came slowly, working its way around his thoughts, eroding them like the ebb and flow of waves on the beach. Just before he drowsed off, Owen wondered if *he* had played a part in catalyzing the unusual energies.

The next morning brought another clear day. It was too cold to abandon the cocoon. He stuck his head out the tent door and saw another crowd of protestors assembling in the parking lot. The protesters were subdued, talking in small groups, with a few looking up at the trees. A couple of young women saw Owen's face and jumped up and down, waving and acting enthusiastic. It made Owen feel shy, but he savored the warmth of connection. A single police car arrived, escorting a crew cab truck. They pulled into the lot but didn't even get out of their cars. Owen witnessed a brief conference between the open windows of the rigs, then they turned in a slow arc and left. Owen guessed there would be no logging today.

The protestors figured the same thing and a hearty cheer echoed through the woods. Owen saw that River sat at his perch and talked on the phone. Garth was just emerging from his tent, shaking his head like a newly roused bear, but he grinned and waved to the folks below, blowing kisses to the two women who greeted him with the same enthusiasm they had shared with Owen. An older woman walked up to the base of River's tree carrying a pack while she talked on the phone. River tossed down his primary line and the woman clipped on a canvas shopping bag. The bag soared into the tree as River hauled it up hand over hand. He bellowed a loud "THANK YOU!" and waved to the crowd. They roared back, "THANK *YOU!*"

Within an hour the protestors returned to their cars and left. It was quiet in the winter woods. When the wind was right, Owen heard the ocean crash against the cliffs, even though it was a mile away. He read a little here and there, munched his gorp, and tried to stay warm. Pull-ups on the branches were a diversion, as was climbing up and down, still limited by his leash, but it was enough to get the blood flowing. He listened to the tree, which today sang very softly, a contented background hum that made Owen sleepy.

Twice a state patrol SUV pulled into the lot and idled. Owen could see the window go down and a glint of light reflected from binoculars pointed at the treetops. Well, there was no place to hide. No doubt they were being photographed. It wouldn't be long before their images were fed into a data base. He noticed that River and Garth turned their backs. Perhaps they preferred not to be identified. Owen wondered if they had criminal records, not unlikely given their history of involvement with protests and environmental action. Although to Owen, they were warm, dear-hearted people, he could imagine that some wouldn't see it that way.

In the mid-afternoon they convened again in Owen's tree for an early dinner. River was happy. "Fresh veggies, man, bounty of the land, all from the good folks on the ground. Dig in!"

After they wolfed down a tasty stew, they munched on carrots and apples. River looked serious. "Hey, Owen, what do you know about the Legion of Odin?"

"Oh god. Talk about the dark side: they're awful. What about them?"

"I got a text from my contact this afternoon. Seems that the Legion of Odin may be paying us a visit."

Owen frowned. "They are extremely bad news. For years they've lurked around the rural parts of the state, a kind of pagan biker-type outfit. So it seems. They look and act like bikers, although they don't resemble a motorcycle club so much as a paramilitary cult. Lots of talk about bringing back the old Norse gods and the Viking way, whatever that means. They like to think of themselves as berserkers. When I studied mythology at school, one of the other students, a very weird fellow, talked about the Legion – I think he was a member, but he was coy about it. He might have been trying to recruit me. I gave him a spiel about authoritarianism lurking in the Nordic mythos. Which, interestingly, he didn't try to refute.

"Anyway, I thought it was just one of those wacky fringe groups until a few months ago. The governor, in his zeal for law and order, has outsourced some police activity to contractors, including the Legion of Odin. He claimed that the state forces were stretched too thin trying to wrangle immigrants, drug dealers, and deadbeats. Rather than expand the state forces at taxpayer cost, it was time to involve more private industry—the usual bullshit. I didn't know it was possible to consider a paramilitary group a private industry, but the governor has never let rational thinking slow him down. Back in September there was a large, extended sit-in at the capitol in Augusta protesting the governor's refusal to spend federal money on food stamps, even though the feds already gave the money to the state. He said it encouraged welfare scams and cheats and the funds would be released over his dead body. A few thousand people shut down the capitol by occupying all the doorways, halls, and offices of state buildings. That is, until the governor called in the Legion of Odin. They showed up, the police looked the other way, and a squad of berserk goons beat heads, dragged people off, and broke the sit-in. I heard it was a horror show. A lot of people got hurt. It was brutal, like the early days in the labor movement. There was a huge outcry, but the governor basically said that's the way it's going to be, folks. Don't break the law and you won't get hurt. And, somehow, he got away with it. The outcry died down and people forgot about it. If the Legion is coming here, we're in serious trouble. Do we know when?"

"Not sure. Maybe as early as tomorrow."

"Fuck."

Garth broke in, "Yeah, but what are they gonna do, really? Hard to believe they'd drag their fat asses off the ground. This is our turf! We're the kings of the canopy!"

River scratched his beard. "I don't like it. Listen to Owen, man, these guys sound extreme. We've seen severe reactions before, but we've never seen this kind of thing. Not this ruthless. And backed by the state. We're not the only ones that know how to climb trees. Some will cut them down, no matter what, as you well know."

"Yeah, I guess." Garth was reluctant to concede. "Well, we've made it this far. I don't feel like slinking away in the middle of the night. If they want to bring it, let 'em bring it!"

Everyone agreed that it was important to stay with the tree-sit. The people and the trees needed them to be strong. River and Garth had faced adversity before and didn't want to back down. But they agreed that if things got truly dangerous, they would retreat from the trees.

The next dawned warmer; snowflakes drifted down from a dull gray sky. It was early for activity in the parking lot, but a few cars pulled up with protestors, who got out and wandered over under the occupied trees. Many of them held steaming mugs and Owen felt a twinge of envy. He was extricating himself from the portaledge when three black SUVs and a van pulled into the lot. The doors opened and about twenty men emerged, dressed in camo and flak vests. A few of them wore motorcycle club patches. Oh shit, Owen thought, Odin's goddamned Legion. And there were no police anywhere to be seen.

Despite their shiny vehicles and coordinated attire, it was a scruffy group. Owen saw beards and long hair, bulging bellies, sunglasses, and arrogance: their swagger was visible from the tree-tops. With no warning, they jumped on the protestors, grabbing them by the collars and pushing, slapping, and herding them away from the trees toward the road. Echoes of screaming and swearing rebounded through the forest. Owen saw one protestor resist; he was knocked down without a word, then dragged off, limp and unresponsive. It happened so fast that the protestors couldn't organize or react defensively. In less than five minutes the Legion had cleared the lot.

By this time River and Garth were out of the shelters, watching the events. River spoke into his phone; Owen could see the tension in his body. A bullhorn voice came up through the trees: "You fuckin' hippie faggot treehuggers are done. We're not even gonna give you a chance to come down, we're gonna come up and throw you down!" The voice sounded familiar to Owen, but he couldn't identify it.

A big Legionnaire approached Garth's tree with a duffel. He dropped the bag and pulled out climbing gear, confirming one of Owen's fears. Some of these backwoods characters knew plenty about working in the woods and logging techniques, including tree climbing. Within minutes the guy attached to the tree and started the ascent, climbing rapidly. The handle of a short sword protruded from a scabbard lashed across his back. Of course, The Legion of Odin would have swords; they lived in a medieval fantasy. He was surprised they didn't have Thor's hammer and battle axes. But maybe they did, along with the assault rifles and handguns on display.

Owen watched Garth brace himself, checking his lines. Garth looked up and grinned at him, stuck his thumb in the air, then turned to River and shrugged. Owen didn't know what to do. River gestured wildly and continued talking into the phone. As the Legionnaire arrived below the perch, Garth yelled. "You get the fuck down, you son of a bitch! Get the fuck outta my tree!" Garth could have attacked the man's head as he climbed, but he held back, waiting. Then the Legionnaire was at the stance. Without a word, he leaped at Garth and they grappled for control. Like a wrestling match, they locked, muscles clenched as each sought to gain the purchase. Owen held his breath.

Suddenly, the Legionnaire dropped his shoulders and slipped under Garth's hold. From a crouch, he sprang to a full extension of his body, knocking Garth off balance while securing a grip on a branch. As Garth waved his arms, the Legionnaire drew his sword and in two sweeps sliced through the taut belay line and slammed the hilt into Garth's forehead. Stunned, Garth teetered backward and fell off the branch, away from the trunk, untethered from the tree. He crashed into the next branch and Owen watched him flail for a hold, but there was too much momentum. He bounced from branch to branch, finally clearing them all as he plunged a hundred feet to the ground. Owen's stomach lurched at the thud.

River unleashed a loud, moaning growl from his tree. Owen was shocked. The Legionnaire stood at Garth's station and pointed his sword at Owen, screaming like a valkyrie: "You're next, you fuck!" River looked up from Garth's body, a silent, unmoving lump on the forest floor, and quickly gestured to Owen to descend. Owen didn't need to be told twice; he grabbed his rappel brake, dropped the main line and set up for descent. By the time he was ready to go, he saw that River had already started down.

The bullhorn voice blared up at them. "That's right, you chicken shits, you get your asses down here where you belong!"

Half a dozen Legionnaires clustered around the base of the tree as Owen approached the ground. They peered at him with eager, cruel faces, but what could he do except surrender? He had no desire to be chucked out of the tree-top, an unceremonious sacrifice. Garth was dead, he assumed. It happened so fast that it didn't seem real. Had he really witnessed his great spirit snuffed by a psycho? What the hell was going on? Owen's eyes clouded with tears as he landed. Two Legionnaires held him against the tree while another sliced off his harness with a Bowie knife, then he was tossed aside. The Legionnaires swarmed around him and he felt the blows of their boots as they kicked and stomped. He didn't resist, despite the pain. He wouldn't know where to start—in truth, he was no hero. He curled up as best he could and tried to protect his head.

The blows continued to fall until a commanding voice took over. "Alright, men, that's enough. Let's see what we've got left here."

The circle of tormentors opened and Owen saw an older, beefy man step forward. He had stringy gray hair and a beard that failed to conceal the pock-marked skin of his cheeks. Owen knew him. It was his uncle.

[20]

"Well, fuck me sideways. It's little Owen, all grown up and turned into a faggot tree lover. Son of a bitch." And Caleb Black spit in Owen's face.

"You know this asshole?" asked one of the Legionnaires.

"Oh yeah, it's my wimpy nephew. I tried to make a man out of him, but you see what we got. Little cowardly cunt. Disgusting. What about the other faggot that tried to make a break for it? Not the one that jumped—all he wants is a body bag."

Owen started to protest that Garth didn't jump but the words died in his throat. What was the point? If there was a messenger of evil in Owen's life, it now loomed over him. Once again, he was in his uncle's power. A wave of nausea clenched his gut and he wanted to vomit. Instead, he looked straight in his uncle's face, finding the will to keep his eyes open and unblinking. He was in a precarious situation; this was no time to lose it.

A couple of the goons dragged River over and dumped him next to Owen. River's nose and mouth oozed blood and one eye was swollen nearly shut. They exchanged looks but said nothing.

Caleb looked down at the two of them and smirked. "Your lucky day, boys. I'm feeling generous, what with the touching family reunion and all. I think you'd have to agree that this protest is officially done. Mission accomplished. So, you two: git. Now."

River protested, "My friend... call an ambulance."

"We'll take care of that, seein' as how we're the legal representatives of the state hereabouts." There were snickers from the surrounding Legionnaires. "I'm sure the coroner will want to see the body before he declares it an accident. Surely you know how dangerous it is up in those trees. Not a place for girlies. It's really a shame you ladies banged into branches and fell on the ground in your hurry to get down and check on your faggot boyfriend, but that's the way it goes. No one can blame you for that. Our job is to clean up the trash around these parts before it gets any worse. So, you can get your asses outta here right now, or you can be part of the trash. It's only out of the deep feeling I have for my own blood that you bitches even get a choice." When Caleb made this last statement, he grabbed his crotch and smirked. Owen felt sick again. If there was a chance to get out alive, he wanted it, no matter what.

River struggled to accept the inevitable. "But... our gear. The ropes and hardware..."

"Tough break, sonny. Part of the trash left by a bunch of faggot litterbugs. My patience is done, by the way. Now would be a good time to drag your carcasses down the road. Oh, and don't bother trying to cook up some kind of bullshit lie for the cops. It won't fly."

Owen had heard enough. He staggered to his feet and offered a hand to River, who accepted it and pulled himself slowly upright. They hobbled away from the Legionnaires, who watched them go with laughter and catcalls. "Bye bye, faggots!"

They drove back to Owen's house in ghastly silence. As soon as they stumbled through the front door, River collapsed to his knees, covering his face with battered and bruised hands. Owen knelt beside him and put an arm around River's shoulders. He had little experience of comforting others and wondered if he was doing it correctly. But then, Owen too started to sob. Doubts fell away as they clung to each other.

Owen finally pulled back. "Let me get a fire going. I'll make us some tea and then let's figure out what the hell we can do." River remained kneeling and limp, slowly bringing his eyes up to meet Owen's, and nodded.

As the house warmed, the two men sat at the table and stared out the big window. The snow drifted down in small flakes with an aching grace. It wouldn't amount to much, Owen thought, just the first blanket of the season. But it certainly looked like winter.

"Those motherfuckers. And that was a relative of yours?" River spoke in a cold, dead voice.

"Yeah. My uncle. A real son of a bitch. Worse than that, actually. He was a terror to me as a child. The reason for ten years of therapy."

"What?"

"Yeah. He was vile, nasty... the worst." Owen did not feel like dredging up the details. Not now.

"Sorry, man. I'm sorry to hear that. He seems capable of anything. We should call the cops. Despite what he said."

"Agreed. Though I suspect he's right; it won't do any good. But only one way to find out. And if we don't, we'll keep thinking we should have...."

Owen had long ago yanked out the landline phone in a fit of despair, so he used River's cell to call the county sheriff's department. They took his statement and said someone would "look into it." They said he could come by the station if he wanted to talk to someone. Though if he did, there might be charges relating to the illegal protest, if he was involved. There was no sense of urgency in the voice at the other end. No sympathy and no interest. Owen hung up, emptied out of all feeling.

"Jesus, that was worse than I expected. At least we tried. I guess it'll be our word against theirs and we'll be the distraught friends, already discredited due to our involvement in the protest. We'll be smeared as a homosexual love triangle or some shit. Not directly, of course, just hints and innuendoes. Just like my uncle said, it'll be ruled an accident."

"Really? That's fucking outrageous! So much for justice."

"Yeah. Lot of that kind of justice going around."

They took long, blasting hot showers before sitting at the table with cups of tea. Finally, River cooked a batch of quinoa. They picked at it with little enthusiasm. When they looked at each other, they couldn't stop the tears. Conversation seemed pointless. After they gave up on the meal, Owen opened the long-closed door to the living room, letting the warmth of the house rush in and revive the space. The sofa unfolded to a bed. Owen stacked sheets, pillows and blankets and started up the stairs to his own bed. He stopped, turned around, came back, and gave River a long embrace. River stood, impassive, and Owen left him that way as he climbed to his room.

Sleep came with reluctance. When Owen got up at dawn and stumbled downstairs, he glanced in the living room and saw River wrapped in blankets. Owen's night had been full of the image of Garth falling from the tree. He watched it replay over and over like a movie beyond control. He wondered if this was what the character in *A Clockwork Orange* felt like, forced to watch violent deeds until he was sick. He put on a pot of water, slipped into a jacket and stepped out the back door. It had stopped snowing in the night, leaving only a thin coat on the ground. It would have been beautiful in the clear light, but the sky was still gun metal gray.

Owen stood behind the house and looked across the field at the wall of trees. What did they think, he wondered? A crow offered a single, harsh declaration, followed by a penetrating silence. Owen sensed the rhizome below his feet. His awareness dropped into the complex network and established a link to the woods. The forest grieved. Not only for the human loss, but for the elder trees that were falling in the logging operation several miles away. Each tree, as it was cut down, shrieked into the rhizome. Owen heard the dissonant pain and clamor of death punctuating the dirge that he had heard before, woven together in sounds of beautiful grief. This nobility of consciousness in the face of disaster startled him. No matter how dire the situation, it was time to get on with his work. If he needed more incentive, he had certainly received it. Fuck those devolved savages, he thought.

By the time he made it back into the house, River was up and cradled a cup in his hands.

"One ready for you," and he nodded toward the counter.

Owen stopped pouring the water when he heard a vehicle door slam. He stepped into the living room and looked out the window to see an over-sized pick-up. His uncle stood next to the cab, staring at the house with an unreadable expression.

"Damn that motherfucker, what's he doing here?" Owen raced to the front door and out to the yard. River followed.

"You're not welcome here! Leave now, you piece of shit! And don't come back!"

Caleb pulled an automatic pistol out of his pants and waved it casually at Owen. "Kinda thought you might see it that way. But you're gonna hear me out whether you like it or not."

Owen stopped his advance on Caleb and looked at the gun. What now? He was too angry to back down, but he didn't want to get shot, either. He looked at Caleb, narrowing his eyes. "Look at you. Big man with a gun. Like always. Bully and crush, hurt and destroy. Such a big man. You're beneath contempt. So what's next? You gonna shoot me?"

"Don't make me. You know, you were such a sweet boy. I thought we had a good thing going. Too bad you fucked it up. But what the hell, you were gettin' a bit long in the tooth, anyway. I like my meat fresh." He sneered at Owen. "Besides, I can see you got yourself a boyfriend. Not really my type but there's no accountin' for taste. You do what you gotta do. Hey, you learned from the best, eh?"

Owen couldn't believe what he was hearing. The man's sickness spilled out of him like black oil. It was evil, but pathetic. There was nothing for Owen in the taunting and narcissistic preening of his uncle. He drew himself up and stuffed his fear.

"Look, you scum, I'm glad you're pleased with yourself. You're so strong that you have to point a gun just to be heard. If you have more to say: say it. Then go. For once, just once, why not be a real man?"

Owen could see that his words stung. Caleb lifted the gun and pointed it straight at him, sighted along the barrel, and pulled the trigger. It was locked. Caleb snickered. "Don't be cute, boy. Not when you're facing a gun. I came here to do you a favor. I don't know what kind of faggot bullshit you've got yourself wrapped up in, and, frankly, I don't care. But seein' as how you're my sister's child, well, out of respect for her memory, I'm tellin' you to be real fucking careful. You get in the way of the Legion of Odin again and there'll be no free pass. You done used it up, boy. We don't mess around."

Owen laughed at Caleb. "Ah, the Legion of Odin. Like you idiots even know anything about Odin. You want the power of the runes, then do what Odin did. Go hang yourself from a tree! But you don't have the guts for that, do you? Not enough integrity to lay it all on the line, eh? Well, I did. I did what Odin did, and now I know. I know that you and your buddies are nothing more than fucked-up worthless shit. You know nothing. Nothing." Owen cut off his speech and the ground started to tremble as if waves rippled just under the surface. Caleb looked around wildly.

"What the fuck?"

Suddenly roots erupted from the dirt and laced themselves across the toes of Caleb's boots. In a panic, he unlocked the pistol and fired three rounds into the ground at his feet. The roots retracted slightly. Caleb looked at Owen, mouth open and fear in his face. It was the same expression Owen saw when, at the age of thirteen, he had hit him with a baseball bat again and again.

"You... you... demon!" Caleb screamed and wrenched his boots from the grasp of the roots, jumped into the truck, then sprayed gravel as he reversed down the driveway.

[21]

When the truck could no longer be heard, Owen turned back to the house. River stood on the porch, eyes narrowed and face tight. "I'm really hoping you can explain what just happened."

Owen shrugged off River's demanding gaze and looked around the clearing, a small island of open grass in a sea of trees. "I guess you mean the earth tremors and the roots and all that?"

"Yeah. Let's start there."

"Sure. I can tell you a few things, but I don't entirely understand it myself. Remember when we talked before about the rhizome, the mycorrhizal network, and that stuff about the underground links in the forest? You said it sounded... 'crunchy,' or something."

"Very crunchy. Yeah, I remember."

"Maybe you already know some or all of this, but here's what I've learned. The forest isn't a collection of separate trees, it's a linked being, like an assembly of parts, including other life-forms besides trees—fungi, lichens, insects, animals, even bacteria – the working assembly constitutes the ecology of the forest. All that—and this is the amazing thing—is a type of mind. Not a mind like you or I think of as a distinct personality in a world of separate entities. The forest mind is a multiple consciousness, so even though it's a thing-in-itself, it's not really a unity. No, it's more like a big, rowdy family all meshed together. Something like that – this is one of the things I don't entirely comprehend."

"Okay, I can dig that."

"So, I've developed a peculiar sensitivity to the forest mind. By focusing, like in meditation, I can sense the currents of communication within the rhizome. I know this sounds far-fetched, but I can tap into and hear the mind itself. Not sure how that works, there seems to be some kind of energy flow between my body and the underground network. Thing is, I feel like I hear it but I'm not sure that it's exactly audible. Anyway, I can sense the feelings and thoughts in the mind and the mind can sense my own feelings and thoughts. You could even say that it recognizes me. I think what happened was that it picked up my distress with my uncle and intervened. Frankly, I'm glad that it did or who knows what would have happened next."

Owen expected to see disbelief, but River's face glowed with admiration. "What, are you like some kind of magic dude or something? I mean, what the fuck?"

"No, no, nothing like that. I know it sounds crazy, but it's science, man. Admittedly, science unknown to a lot of people. Don't ask me to explain the technical stuff. I learned it by doing it, you know? Like driving a car; I have no clue how that works. But you could learn it, too, I think."

"Really? Hell, man, teach me! That is some awesome shit! And you know I'm down with the trees, I know you damn well know that."

"Yeah, I know that. Sure, it's a good idea for you to learn. No guarantees, mind you, I've never taught this before and it's still new to me. Not really sure how to go about it, but we can try."

In the following days, Owen worked to teach River the skill of tuning in to the forest mind. It was a welcome distraction from the grief of Garth's death and River was an eager student. The daily snowfalls threw a cloak over the sky and the land. It was graceful weather, quietly dropping a few inches here and there to encircle the farmhouse with a white coverlet. Bare ground remained under the trees where they could sit and conduct their meditations until the cold chased them inside. Owen brought River to the ash tree and made him stand next to it in bare feet, hoping that proximity to the portal would stimulate his sensitivity. River's toes turned blue and they had to dash for the house and the warmth of the woodstove.

Through all these fumbling attempts to share his knowledge, Owen was reluctant to reveal the alternate-universe connection. It seemed too much to swallow, even for a free spirit like River, and he worried that a hint about such things would drive him off. At this point a friend was too precious to gamble away. So, he held back many details; a choice that probably didn't help the project.

During the meditations, River achieved deep trances. He strived to bend himself into contact with the rhizome mind, and every now and then he would say things like "Oh yeah, I think I'm getting it, yeah, yeah." But it was obvious to Owen that he wasn't. Perhaps it was a skill that couldn't be taught with words. Owen had learned it from the Thorns' biochemical surgery when they created a physical and neural bridge into the rhizome. Finally, Owen decided to disclose at least part of the truth.

"Look, River, I can see that you want this and you're trying really hard. But it seems like there's still a barrier. There might be a way through that barrier if you're willing to try something a little more extreme, something, well, frankly, a little weird."

"I can do weird. And you're right, I do want it."

"I haven't told you everything about myself, so let's start there. I was trying to figure out how to tell you without you thinking I was off my rocker. You still may think that, I suppose. Takes some trust. Anyway, here's the deal. My genes are tweaked. They're encoded with a very strange virus, a virus that catalyzes a new kind of plant-human interaction. As far as I know, I'm the only human with this condition. The virus has one known effect: when brought into contact with tree cells, it spreads through the tree and out into the forest, ultimately causing the trees to release pheromones into the air. Get this—the pheromones change human consciousness when inhaled. Not like a psychedelic drug, not at all—what it does is link human consciousness with ecosystem consciousness."

"Far fucking out, man."

"Very. Yeah, so I think if enough of this virus gets into the ecosystem, humans won't be able to avoid sensing and feeling what it's like for other beings in the web of life. It'll counteract the selfishness we usually display, which I think will make the world a better place. We might even be able to live in harmony."

"Damn, this is some wild ass shit!"

"Indeed, it is. I had the same reaction at first. Anyway, I don't know this for sure, but I think this virus contributes to my sensitivity to the rhizome mind. So, if you want to try a different approach, it's a simple matter to pass the virus on to you, the same way I can pass it to the trees. It's a blood-borne virus, so sharing a few drops will be enough. I know most folks are reluctant to touch blood. I get it, but it's the only way to share the virus. There don't seem to be negative side effects to carrying it, so you won't get sick or anything. Hey, we could become blood brothers, you know?" Owen paused and considered what he was saying, wondering if he was trying to convince River or himself. Regardless, it wasn't like he knew what he was doing. Everything at this point was experimental.

"I thought I'd heard some wacked out gnarly shit in my time, man, but this is massive! Part of me thinks you are truly trippin', but I know you're not like that. You're a serious dude, so I figure there must be something to this. What, I have no idea. I mean, how did you even find out about this virus? And where did you get it?"

"Yes, well, the details get even weirder. See... I sort of ran into these guys, radical biochemists, I guess you could say, who know one hell of a lot about forest ecology. These fellows needed someone to run some experiments on. They had isolated this virus from a rare fungus and figured out what it was, what it did, and what it could do. Not sure how they got there, but they did. They wanted to spread it around to everyone. Save the world from human stupidity and such. But they really weren't sure how it would work, exactly, and there are laws against experiments on humans. They knew they were right, though, and needed someone willing to work underground. When I met these guys, I didn't have much going for me. Kind of depressed and at a dead end. So, I volunteered to be the guinea pig. Why not save the world? I didn't have anything to live for and didn't give a damn about the risks. Seemed crazy, and still does when I say it out loud, but I knew they were right. Humanity's at a crossroads; it's time to take some risks to make things better. I don't know if spreading the virus will do exactly what they thought, but meanwhile it's given me this ability to connect to the forest, and that's enough for me." Owen didn't feel great about lying to River, but it wasn't entirely a lie, just a distortion that omitted the mention of alternate universes and their inhabitants.

River stepped closer to Owen and gave him a bear hug. "Awww, man, I didn't know you'd been so depressed. Don't be down on yourself, man, you're a good dude."

Owen was tempted to melt into River's embrace, but at the back of this urge he sensed a complicated desire. He wanted no part of that. Of course, it might be exactly what he wanted—how would he know? Despite his neurological tune-up, he was confused about sex, and hearing his uncle's taunts didn't help.

He pulled out of the hug and gripped River's shoulder. "Thanks, man. You're a true friend. That stuff was in the past. Now, I'm on a quest, like the knights of old. What do you think – you want to be a part of it?"

"Hell, yeah. You got my curiosity stoked, dude. How could I say no?"

A ceremony was contrived, somewhat mythological but mostly a remembrance from old movies they had seen. They sliced into the heel of each right palm and clasped hands with vigor, pressing their blood together. Grinning through shyness, they held the grip for a long time. The ritual seemed right, and they hugged afterward, smearing blood on their shirts.

The next day Owen asked River if he would share his carpentry skills and help with some home improvements. Yes, he would, and in fact he was pleased to have a project. He'd had enough of lounging on the couch trying to make sense out of *The White Goddess*. They started by moving the dining necessities into the living room, now River's room, and covered everything left behind with drop cloths except for the wood stove. With wrecking bars and hammers, they tore down the ceiling in the dining room. Underneath the particle board panels and shabby trim they found 4x10 oak beams that spanned the room and served as joists for the thick fir planks of the upstairs floor. The change in the ceiling was dramatic. In one action, the room was transformed from a dingy monastic cell into a cathedral.

River whooped with joy each time they revealed another beam. He couldn't take his eyes off the rich brown wood. "Look at these things! Man! You never see wood like this in the West. Never. Who knew these beauties were hiding under that crummy particle crap? I can't wait to get this all cleaned up so we can use this room again. Come on, Owen, let's do this!"

River's enthusiasm inspired Owen, and they worked long days until the job was done. Instead of rest breaks they walked into the woods to continue River's meditation lessons, even though the snow piled up. On a day without snowfall, they carried a ladder and a broom to the ash tree. River climbed to one of the lower branches, a big, lateral growth on the opposite side of the trunk from the portal scar. After sweeping it clear of snow, he sat on the branch and wrapped his arms around the trunk. Owen stood on the ladder and pressed his palms against the bark. With deep, even breaths, Owen closed his eyes and heard the rhizome song pulsing through the wood. He lowered his consciousness into the forest network as if he were easing into a hot bath. Gradually he sensed something else in the rhizome, something human. It was a manifestation of River, a holon, as perceived and absorbed by the tree. Owen reached toward him through the rhizome, sliding his own awareness along the network. He halted in front of River's holon, which appeared as a golden node, pulsing in a heartbeat rhythm. Owen's consciousness formed its own node, he knew, and he moved it gently into proximity with River's. The rhythm in the golden node immediately spiked and the next thing Owen knew was that River was yelling and pounding his shoulder.

"Oh my god, oh man, that was it, that was... that was you! Wasn't it?"

"Yes, that was me. You were in the rhizome. You did it!"

"How fucking cool is that? Fuck!"

"Isn't it? Well done, my man! Okay, try it again. I'm going to stay out. I want you to reach through the network and into the ground, see how far you get."

"Oh yes! Man!"

River showed aptitude for the work. As soon as they finished the carpentry job, he spent hours bundled up in the woods, tapped into the network. Owen wondered if that much contact was a good idea, but River was so ecstatic with his new skill that Owen didn't have the heart to advise him against excess. Besides, he didn't really know if it was excess. The collective mind of the forest helped to dissolve River's grief, transforming it into a life song.

They drove down the coast to a stretch of woods near the logging project, wincing as they passed the slash-choked clearing where a few lonely trees stood as evidence of a selective harvest. Along an old spur road Owen showed River how to share his blood with the trees. Now there were two vectors for the virus and the potential dispersion rate had doubled. After the transfusion, they leaned against the tree and listened to the local rhizome, sinking into the cadence of the network's music. Trees falling in the clear cut echoed through the network, each one piercing the mosaic of sound with its death song. Fighting the urge to sever the painful connection, Owen leaned into the suffering in order to honor the life-forms as they perished. Paying attention, he picked up on something else. Something familiar.

He retreated from the network and tapped River on the shoulder. "River, follow me into the rhizome. I found something."

"What, man?"

"Not sure. Just follow."

Owen and River projected tandem awareness into the underground network, sliding along the labyrinth of linked pathways, probing through the forest. River followed Owen's node with little effort. Eventually they came to a singularity, a slow pulsing mass that didn't fit with the well-worn tangle of fungal hyphae and roots. As they contemplated the mass, they came to realize that it represented the decomposing remains of Garth. Stunned by the revelation, they lost focus and bounced out of the network.

River's face twisted into a mask of grief or rage—Owen wasn't sure which. Owen pulled him into a hug, and they clutched with desperate sorrow. Finally, Owen spoke. "That fucked-up piece of shit that claims to be my uncle didn't take the body to the coroner. He threw it into a hole in the ground and walked away. Probably lied to the cops that there were only two of us, or the other guy ran away, or whatever. No doubt our report to the police met a similar fate. Who the fuck knows?"

"Oh man, this is so messed up. I don't even know what to do." Tears ran down River's face; he didn't bother to wipe it.

"This may sound weird, but, you know, at least he's in the trees now. His essence is breaking down and becoming one with the forest. I don't know what that'll mean, but at least we can sense his spirit within the system, part of something bigger than any of us. I think he would have liked that."

"Yeah, you're right. He would have. He would have thought it was awesome."

A few nights later they stood in the field behind the house, burning debris from the ceiling project. Absorbing the heat of the bonfire, they watched trails of sparks leaping into the clear winter sky. In silence, they listened to the crackle of the wood, understanding that these scraps were once sentient trees connected to the web of life. Owen sensed River's restlessness. He hadn't been the same since they encountered Garth's remains in the forest. When River wasn't tapped into the rhizome, which was most of the time, he was agitated and unfocused. Owen couldn't blame him, though. It was a lot to contain.

"Hey, Owen."

"Yeah, 's up?" A few more weeks and Owen figured that River's vocabulary would be a permanent fixture in his speech.

"I'm thinking about heading out west, man. Back to Oregon."

"Oh?" Owen tried to hide his disappointment. He was fond of River and enjoyed his company, but more importantly, they were linked through the rhizome in a way far beyond the norms of human relationship. And they were blood brothers. Owen's heart sank at the loss of another being close to him.

"Yeah, man. You should come with me. You can see those big trees. Dude, I can't wait to tune in to one of those mothers! But mostly I feel homesick, you know? I used to have a girlfriend out there I wouldn't mind looking up. I dunno. It's cool here and all that, but I'm feeling the itch. Now there's no avoiding the scratch, if you know what I mean."

Owen looked at River and saw that his thoughts were far away, already back in his homeland. As much as he wanted to cling to their relationship, Owen understood that the journey was inevitable. He sighed. "I get it. But I don't think I'll come along. Although it's a tempting offer, there's still stuff I need to do around here, you know? I want to focus on what's going on in this region, at least for now. And there's definitely unfinished business with my uncle."

"Fuck him, man! He's not worth your trouble. He's an evil fucking snake and he's straight up dangerous, if you ask me."

"I hear you. The thing is, after what happened over at the reserve, not only with Garth's death but with the death of all those trees, I can't just let it go."

"Yeah, me too. But I really need to step away from it. Anyway, I was thinking of coming back."

"You were?"

"Yeah, despite everything that happened, there's something good here. You're a big part of that, Owen. I don't pretend to understand even a half of what you've shown me about the forest network, but it's amazing stuff. Life changing. I'm guessing there's a lot more to learn and I want to learn it. But, for now, I need to check in with my own roots, you know? I was thinking, too, I can probably round up a few folks and bring 'em back with me. Could be the start of your own gnarly rhizome army, brah. If you don't mind recruits a little fuzzy around the edges?"

Owen put his arm around River's shoulders. "You're too much, man. The rhizome army?! Sort of a contradiction in terms, but I know what you mean. So, sure, come back when you can. You're always welcome here. You and your tribe. But think about this. When you head west, you should stop as often as you can and give blood to the trees along the way. That would truly speed up the pace of this experiment. And if you feel like sharing your blood with other folks who can spread the virus, I say go for it."

"Oh yeah, man, righteous call! And I can take a different way when I come back east, hitting a whole 'nother latitude. I'll be like Johnny Appleseed, dude! Well, kind of."

Owen laughed at River's enthusiasm. "Johnny only planted apple trees. You'll be planting cosmic peace, man." River grinned and they slapped a high five.


[22]

Owen helped River pack the van, re-stocking it for a continental drive. They parted with formulaic vows to stay in touch, see each other soon, and similar promises that were heartfelt but uncertain. Neither one saw the future with assurance. Their shared experiences had taken them through tragedy and across a threshold into a new way of being, a union of animal and plant consciousness. Life-changing, certainly, but what were they supposed to do with it? Owen's belief in the virus campaign was based on his faith in the Thorns, while River's belief was based on Owen. Beyond that, the rhizome echoed with reverberations of mystery. Tentative, they hugged, and River drove away.

Owen wondered if he would ever get used to the losses. Five minutes after River's van disappeared through the trees, he stood in front of the bathroom mirror, staring at himself. He didn't recognize the face. His hair had grown faster than normal, as the Thorns predicted, and now it almost touched his shoulders. With the full bush of a beard, he looked like a backwoods redneck. Or a hippie. That seemed to work for River, but it wasn't right, it didn't feel like him. Impulsively, he grabbed a pair of scissors and started hacking off the beard. He kept at it until it was a rough stubble. Now he looked like one of those European actors. Running his fingers through the hair, he pushed one side behind an ear. Maybe a scarf, he thought. But that would require rummaging around the house, and he didn't have the heart to excavate his mother's old clothes, which was the only place he'd be likely to find one. They were probably musty, anyway.

What else? He knew he was channeling his despair into restless distractions, but it helped to keep his mind off the loss. Still, reality lurked in the back of his thoughts. Alone in a house in the woods, he was a target for predators, his uncle among them. Owen had scared him away but how long would that last? He knew his uncle would seek retaliation; somewhere, sometime. The rhizome had come to his defense before, but was that something to count on? He doubted it.

Owen looked down from the mirror and noticed his bare arms. They were muscular and hardened from the years of farm work. He let his eyes linger on the labyrinth tattooed on the inside of his left arm and he followed the curves unwinding from the center to the exit. His attention leaped to the other arm, a blank canvas. Dr. Chouinard's labyrinth had brought him this far but was it enough to take him farther? Yes, that was it, time to carve another tattoo into his flesh, another symbol to organize his world. He already knew what he wanted: something to reflect his connection to the rhizome. His understanding of labyrinths had developed beyond the classic spiral; he knew that the true labyrinth was a vast network, the rhizome of philosophers as well as a map to the web of life. It needed a symbol of complexity.

He went into the dining room with its shelves and piles of books and burrowed into research. He thought that there would be abundant possibilities for a graphic that fit his idea, but as he thumbed through the pages of images and symbols, nothing came close. Then he pulled down a well-worn book of illustrations from the Irish *Book of Kells*. As soon as he riffed through a few pages, he found what he was looking for. The complicated knots and vegetation themes were a perfect representation of the rhizome: a vast, interlocking, graceful network, linked, yet open-ended with suggestions of infinity. He studied each page, flipping back and forth, comparing designs, and finally settled on one. It didn't portray the entire rhizome, of course, just a node, or cluster of nodes—a holon. The design captured the multiplicity of the connections, the beauty of woven patterns, and the possibilities of systems within systems. And it would look good.

The next morning, he drove into Machias, to the same artist who had done his first tattoo. When Owen showed the artist the design he wanted and told him that he'd like it as a cylinder wrapped around the upper part of his forearm, the artist grunted and said, "Cool. You got all day?" Owen nodded and the artist pointed to the chair.

The initial pain of the needle put Owen on edge, but soon a numbness crept over him and he drifted into a trance. He recalled the past balms of self-mutilation, no longer necessary to get through the hard days. He was thankful for that. Many hours later, the artist put aside his tools and nodded in satisfaction. Owen held up his arm and admired the result. The tattoo resembled medieval armor for the forearm: a vambrace. Protection, not only for the flesh, but more importantly, for his psyche. He was pleased; he only wished that he could show it to Dr. Chouinard.

As stepped out of the tattoo parlor and glanced down the street, he thought that he caught a flash of the doctor, or someone like her, ducking into a café. The woman he saw wore a heavy red cloak like the doctor's, an unusual garment for these parts. He rushed to the café and peered in the window but saw nothing of interest. A trick of mind and eye, no doubt, another apparition. As much as he might want it, the doctor was not coming back.

Driving home, the idea of a regional road tour seemed appealing: a circuit of New England, inoculating trees with the virus along the way and seeing the country. Even if it was winter, it would be lovely in the snow. Plus, it offered a chance to do something constructive. The image of himself moping around the cabin was depressing. Now he understood why River had been so eager to get away. Garth's death had tainted the place, a contamination that he, too, needed distance from. He had no interest in the likely conflict that would accompany the return of his uncle. It wasn't the same as running away, really; just changing the perspective. He resolved to leave at dawn.

Back at the house, he spent the evening packing and devising an itinerary. In town he had purchased a five-pound bag of quinoa. River's influence, he knew, and in honor of his friend he cooked some for dinner. He spooned in globs from a bowl in his lap as he surfed on the computer, researching some of the areas he might visit. A link for the town of Keene, New Hampshire brought up a connection to Antioch University. The school advertised an intriguing philosophy and the courses fascinated Owen, especially the studies in whole systems design and ecopsychology. As he read about the Ecopsychology program, he learned that there would be a conference on that topic in a few days' time. The presentations sounded relevant to his interests, but one grabbed his attention. It featured an odd title: "Forestry as a Labyrinthine Pursuit." He mused over the possible interpretations, recognizing that while it spoke to him on an intuitive level, it also didn't quite make sense. The presenter was a woman named Dana Onnen but the photo provided of her was a picture of a tree. When he read her capsule biography, he started to understand. *Forestry as a Labyrinthine Pursuit* was the title of her most recent book of poetry. Previous collections included *With the Grain* and *Discarded Branches*. He liked the titles, but he especially liked the picture of the tree.

Exploring the wilderness of data available on the internet, Owen discovered some details about Dana Onnen, including a few photographs. She was thirty years old, a couple of years older than Owen, with a beaming face and an intricate tangle of hair that evoked tactile fantasies in his imagination. Her resume included poetry and activism, and descriptions of her contributions veered between respect and notoriety. She had participated in several environmental protests, at least two of which resulted in arrest. Literary critics considered her to be a key figure in what was called the school of radical nature poetry, which could mean a lot of things, Owen figured. Originally from California, Dana Onnen did not seem to live anywhere in particular; he liked another reference he came across that describe her as a nomadic voice. Curious, he decided that he would attend the Antioch conference and see Dana for himself.

It was snowing hard when he arrived in Keene after a long day of driving. Even though he had directions, the Antioch campus eluded him in a maze of snow-plastered signs and unplowed streets. At a gas station, he was given directions to Keene State College instead. There he asked a group of drunken students for guidance and they stopped their snowball fight long enough to point in contradictory directions. He averaged the results and drove slowly. Finally, he located Antioch in a cluster of modern office buildings that looked nothing like a university. Pulling his truck into the snow-filled parking lot he was thankful once again for four-wheel drive. He would deal with lodging later; if he was going to be on time for the presentation he needed to hurry. Inside the building he registered for the conference and found an adjacent table where he purchased a copy of *Forestry as a Labyrinthine Pursuit*. Book in hand, he rushed down the hall to the classroom where she would speak.

Student chairs, the kind with retractable desktops, occupied the room in haphazard rows. Owen slid into one near the back. Dana Onnen hadn't arrived, so Owen looked around the classroom, checking out the attendees, who were sneaking glances at him. There were plenty of empty seats. People elected to stay home, he assumed, hunkered down in the warmth of their shelters. Not an unreasonable decision on a stormy winter afternoon. The classroom was overheated, and Owen peeled off his coat and sweater. He caught a couple of people staring at his tattoos. He didn't mind. He was never quite sure about the etiquette of tattoos in public, anyway. They seemed to be there for the show if they could be seen at all. Then he realized he was sitting in a presentation about labyrinths and there he was, Labyrinth Man.

Owen's musing stopped when a tall woman strode into the room, waving absently. She stumbled over a cord on the floor, glared at it, laughed, and then turned to the group and announced, "Good grief, what an entrance! Anyway, hi, I'm Dana Onnen and clumsy I may be, but I'm your guide for the next hour. Watch your step." There was applause and laughter, which she met with an exaggerated bow.

Her appearance mesmerized Owen. Despite calling herself clumsy, she looked graceful enough, rangy yet athletic. Her black hair, such a wild mass in the online portraits, was cut short the same way his had been when his mother dragged him protesting all the way to the barber shop every three weeks. She wore a silver bracelet that spiraled, snake-like, around her left wrist. While she took a moment to settle into the space at the front of the group, she fidgeted with the bracelet, first turning it one way, then the other. She scanned the audience and Owen followed her dark eyes. The elfin haircut disappointed him at first, but he decided that he liked her air of androgyny. What impressed him most, though, was an indefinable quality of kinetic energy, barely contained, as if she might at any moment break into dance or a full-throated aria.

"Well, thank you all for coming out in this weather. I do appreciate it. As we burn through a few words, I hope that kindles enough warmth to get you through the night." She paused to take a drink from a water bottle. "First I'm going to talk prose at you before getting to the poems. Words will provide our method of roaming around in the devious labyrinth of the forest. At least the forest as I see it. And when I say *forest,* I mean the great mythic forest, the whole tangled wilderness of ecology and culture, not just a stand of trees separate from the human psyche. My psyche or yours, although since I'm doing the talking, let's face it, I mean mostly mine." She made a quick, wry smile and plunged ahead. "In fact, I've become increasingly critical of language that cleaves humans and nature into different categories. These days I'm hearing too many declarations that we need to be closer to nature or that we need to develop better relations with nature. We already embody our own nature and are never divided from it in any way. Even all our crazy artifices—the construction of vast highway networks, oil rigs, shopping malls, and thousand-acre wheat farms—all that is a manifestation of our nature and therefore part of nature, just as much as a termite mound, a coral reef, or the bear shit in the woods." Dana punctuated her speech with spirited gestures that seemed like a private sign language. Owen studied every movement, fascinated by her physical presence and excited by her words. She spoke a truth that he understood.

After another swig of water, Dana continued. "The philosopher Donna Haraway uses the term *natureculture* to refer to the interwoven tapestry of nature and culture. They aren't separate; they're a seamless continuity. So, along that line here is a poem about an important development in the history of human *naturecultures*... It's called 'The Invention of Poetry:'"

She closed her eyes and took slow breaths, standing upright as if fixed to the floor. Owen saw no hint of the almost awkward woman who stumbled into the room only minutes before. As she spoke, she began to sway gently back and forth. Owen recalled her conference photo and thought she really did look like a tree.

*"The Invention of Poetry*

*They asked me to herd the animals up the mountain.*
*But I stopped to gather mushrooms*
*and a lamb was lost.*
*They asked me to go to the river to catch the fat fish.*
*But I dropped the net when*
*storm fires crackled in the sky.*
*They asked me to pick the corn quickly,*
*ripe and tall in the field.*
*But I stayed idle, watching the geese fly south,*
*dark streaks across the sun.*

*Girl, they said. Enough.*
*You are worth nothing. Just stay out of the way.*

*I found a piece of coal and a strip of bark, and I wandered to*
*my hiding place deep in the wood.*

*I drew a map and marked the slope*
*thick with clover blossoms.*
*I added the rippling currents of the river;*
*And the wide, sun-baked meadow*
*where the corn silk sparkled.*
*I drew tiny triangles to show my grove of scented trees.*

*Each day I walked the thin lines I'd scratched in coal,*
*and added more.*
*I made secret signs that told of all the beauty in my world:*
*The day the bees came to gather pollen.*
*The day the swollen salmon tumbled upstream.*
*The day the soil thawed, soft and rich, ready for the seed.*
*The cool days, when the geese rose in flocks and*
*pine cones littered the forest floor.*

*You, they said. What is that you've done?*
*And they looked at my bark and they drew back in wonder.*
*They talked among themselves. The elders huddled with curved*
*spines;*
*the young men smoked; the women kneaded,*
*shaping corn cakes as they whispered.*

*At last, the chatter stopped, and the old one pushed her way to*
*me.*
*Girl, she said, you are our light.*
*You are our memory.*
*You are our music."*

When the poem ended, the room was silent. Dana stood motionless, as if all her energy had gone to ground. Owen looked at her, a blend of joy and wonder in his heart. When she looked up their eyes met and linked. He didn't know much about this Dana Onnen but he did recognize kindred.

[23]

Owen listened carefully to the hour-long presentation, reluctant to move on from certain words and phrases. Dana recited more poems, many of which cut straight into Owen's soul. Along with the poems, she quoted Haraway and other female scholars Owen knew nothing about. He made mental notes for research, later, when he had the time. As Dana spun compelling webs of prose and verse, he scrutinized her, trying to memorize her image and how she moved. When she recited a long poem about her quest for *the reliable root of the heart*, Owen had a mad impulse to run up and volunteer for the position of reliable root. Instead, when the presentation ended, he settled for falling in at the back of the line to have his book signed.

His turn finally came. Dana looked at him and smiled. She took his book without breaking eye contact and he grinned nervously. She arched an eyebrow and asked, "Who should I make this out to?"

"Owen." He wanted to say more, but he couldn't think of what it would be.

"Okay, Owen. Such a fluid name—a good Welsh name." She bent to inscribe the book when she saw his tattoos and froze. "Oh. Those are interesting. May I?"

Owen nodded and held out his arms for inspection. Dana leaned forward to study the designs. This close, she seemed absurdly beautiful. He felt the blood rush to his face as he looked at the shape of her head, how it extended from her shoulders on a long neck, and how the shoulders curved into her torso and along all the contours of her body. It had certainly been worth every painstaking minute of having those tattoos carved into his skin, just to have this moment of electric proximity.

"This one I know," Dana said, pointing to his left arm, careful not to touch. "The classic labyrinth, the construction of Daedalus, the bane of many Greek youths lost to the hunger of the Minotaur. You know the tale?"

Owen nodded again, still dumb, feeling like a dolt.

"But this," she continued, pointing to the knotwork design on Owen's right arm as he turned it for her, "this is new to me. It looks Celtic. Does it have significance? Do you mind me asking?"

Owen gulped and found his voice, thankful to have a familiar topic. "No, not at all. I don't mind, I mean. You're right, it's Celtic. From the *Book of Kells*, actually. I chose it to represent the... the rhizome labyrinth."

Dana inhaled sharply. "The rhizome labyrinth? Now that's something. I've heard of the rhizome of the philosophers and sure, it makes sense to think of that as a labyrinth, but what does it mean to link those terms?"

"Eco did that. Umberto Eco. His third type of labyrinth, the one that represents the true state of knowledge. Where everything is connected." Owen abruptly stopped talking, certain that he was making a fool of himself.

Dana said nothing for a moment, lost in thought, then she peered into his eyes with an unnerving intensity. Owen had the impression that he was being appraised. "Say, are you in a hurry? Do you have a few minutes?"

"No, Ms. Onnen, not in a hurry, not at all."

"Just call me Dana." She smiled again and Owen wondered at how such a simple gesture could make him so weak. The smile faded from her face and she looked down at her boots while rubbing the top of her head, ruffling her short hair into disarray as she appeared to be wrestling with a thought. Suddenly she looked up, the smile came back, and she spoke in a rush of words. "I'd like to talk more about this rhizome labyrinth, where everything's connected. I'd say let's sit here and chat, but I think they want this room pretty soon; and I don't know about you, but I find this building uncomfortably sterile; I'm ready to leave. How about going somewhere for a cup of coffee or tea?"

"Oh yeah, sure, definitely!" Owen couldn't believe his luck. Exhilaration and fear tumbled through his brain as he tried to anticipate what he was supposed to do. "I don't know this town, though. I'm from Maine."

"Maine? Never made it that far, although I keep meaning to. Heard it was a wondrous place. Anyway, I don't know Keene, either, but I do know somewhere close by that'll work."

Dana bent back to the podium to finally sign his book and while she completed that task Owen wanted to laugh in delight. Did she just say *wondrous*?

Dana handed the closed book back to Owen and noticed the amused look on his face. "What?"

Owen grinned. "Oh, you said *wondrous*. Not that common in conversation."

"True. Sometimes I talk like an old goofball. Stick around and you'll hear some weird shit—that I promise."

Owen smiled and said, perhaps too enthusiastically, "I will." Dana looked at him with a curious expression. While she gathered her coat and bag, Owen took a peek at the inscription in the book. Written in sloppy handwriting, it said "For Owen. We all need a friend in the labyrinth. Dana."

They walked out of the Antioch building to find the snow descending in large, slow-moving flakes. At least a foot lay on the ground already. Despite the early darkening of the day, Owen was too excited to give much thought to where he would spend the night; that was a bridge to cross later. Surely he could find a motel.

"This way." Dana pointed across the parking lot and they waded through the snow, crystals glistening in the streetlight. Owen followed her trail, wondering what was going on, exactly. He had just met this intriguing woman and now they were going somewhere for conversation and coffee, almost like a date. Is this how it happened, then? When you met someone? He tried to tamp down his anxiety about romance. Sometimes you just meet and exchange ideas and then you have a nice friendship. But she was magnetic, and he was unable to suffocate a hope for more. He almost walked into Dana's back when she halted at the rear of a Ford Transit van. It was one of the large models, tall and long. He read a Nevada vanity plate proclaiming the word "BARD" while Dana fumbled in her bag for keys.

"Nice van." Owen said because he thought he should say something.

"Yes, well, this is home, actually. My fully-paid-for, ambulatory shelter. Home, hearth, and horse, so to speak."

"You know, if you want to go somewhere, it might be easier to take my four-wheel drive truck. It's just over there." Owen pointed off through the storm.

"God! Where are the fucking keys?" At this point Dana had been rummaging around in her bag for several minutes. Then, she turned to Owen with a sheepish smile and reached into her coat pocket. "Pocket, of course."

She unlocked the back door of the van and climbed in, turning on a light and beckoning to Owen. "No reason to go anywhere. Got everything we need right inside. If you don't mind leaving your shoes on the mat...." She kicked off her boots and stepped out of the way as Owen scrambled in and closed the door behind him. The van had a high ceiling, with just enough room to stand up. Custom renovations had transformed it into a dwelling, with wooden shelves, counters, drawers, and a complicated array of nomadic living features. Everything appeared as if it could unfold into something else. Most of the wood looked like red cedar. Dana motioned to a small bench and Owen sat while she flipped over a hinged slab of wood to serve as a table, thus revealing a propane burner for cooking. Below the stove was a heating element at floor level, also propane, which she turned on.

"This'll heat up in a jiffy. Doesn't take much for such a small space. So... I have a gazillion different kinds of tea. Please don't ask me to rattle off the inventory, it's more than I can remember.

I'm going to have some chai, but if you want something different, just ask for it. It's probably here, somewhere."

"Chai? Don't think I've had that before."

"Another fad, it seems. Ten years ago, nobody drank it in this country, now you can get it everywhere. Originally from India, so they say. Cinnamon, nutmeg, pepper, sweet, milky. Liquid candy. Little bit of a caffeine kick to it, not much."

"Sounds good. You had me at liquid candy, thanks."

Owen continued his inspection of the interior. A door-sized slab of wood fixed to the opposite wall appeared to be a fold-down bed. There was a sink with a water jug next to it, and under the counter Owen noticed an icebox. A shelf of books ran the length of the van just below the ceiling. The only windows were in the back doors and those were covered with curtains made from an African fabric. A large curtain of the same material separated the cab from the living area. Efficiency determined every inch of space.

"This is amazing! The craftsmanship is incredible. And all this beautiful old cedar! We don't find that out here."

"Thank you. I love it. But it's not cedar; it's redwood. My favorite tree, my favorite wood. I dream better when I'm surrounded with redwood. Best to sleep in a living grove, of course, but this isn't a bad substitute. Been living in this contraption for about two years now. It suits me. I'm not a super-organized person, so the tight quarters force me to work at it. A place for everything, if I can only remember where. Sometimes I do my own labyrinth dance in here, rummaging around for lost threads."

Dana laughed at her own joke and handed Owen a cup of tea. He held the steam under his nose and inhaled the spicy aroma. "Wait. Did you build this yourself?"

"That I did."

"Wow. Impressive. Surprising. I mean... not that you couldn't have built it... I mean... Oh hell, I don't know what I mean. I'm sorry, I sound like an idiot."

"Don't fret about it. I learned long ago that most men are surprised when women know how to do stuff. For a few years I lived near Reno with a boyfriend who was an expert woodworker. He was a jerk, but he taught me how to build things. One night I got so mad at him that I stormed off to a casino and took it out on the roulette table. The gods were with me: I won big! I took it as a sign, simmered down, bought this van, and spent a year working in his shop, making all these installations. When it was done, I left him. He was pissed, but then he was always pissed. I couldn't tell you why I was attracted to him in the first place. A mistake, I guess we can call it. Not the first one, I'm sorry to say. Sometimes I can be pretty impulsive....

"Anyway, I never looked back, just wandered around, writing poetry, seeing the world... well, just the West, for the most part. Soon after leaving Reno, I lucked out and ended up at a conference at UC Santa Cruz – that's where I met Donna Haraway. She took a liking to me, said she thought I was doing good work, although I'm not sure I ever truly understood what that work was in her eyes. Anyway, she seems to know everyone in the eco-psycho-culture scene, so she helped me get started doing readings and lectures and I've been roaming around from gig to gig ever since, taking time off in between to explore the wilds and do more writing. I owe a lot to her. She's a trip, brilliant but a little odd. But those are always the best people, I think. So... I don't need much, it turns out. Living in the van and being on the road has changed my life in a lot of ways. For one thing, I learned how to be alone. Lot of people never seem to figure that out."

Dana folded down the bed and sat on it, stretching out her feet and wiggling her toes inside the socks. "The only thing it doesn't have is a bathroom. But that's what they made chamber pots for, right?"

They both laughed. "You know, I admire what you're doing. Like it says on your license plate, you're living the bardic life. I like hearing that you have a solid connection with your teacher. Mentors can really make a difference – I know that I'd be nowhere if I hadn't met someone like that. Hell, I'd probably be dead." Owen pulled the hair back from his face and tucked it behind his ears, momentarily wondering if the increasing length of his mane looked as silly as it sometimes felt. "But I do envy you the freedom and self-sufficiency. You're a gypsy. I feel anchored to the land, myself...." Owen trailed off, musing that his ancestral connection to the farm and his commitment to the forest mind of another world made him rooted in a way that would be incomprehensible to most people, especially to this vagabond spirit.

Dana stared down at her bracelet, turning it absently. Owen took advantage of this distraction to study her features. He saw beauty in the strong, lean form where he supposed many men would see a daunting Amazon. When he was still a teen, he had developed an obsession with the myth of the Amazons. Dr. Chouinard, pushing and probing as always, had urged him to pursue it deeper. "What's underneath your fascination, Owen? What draws you to the image of a powerful woman?" With the doctor's guidance, he dug into his messy unconscious and found the anima, his feminine soul, stretching out to take a shape in the conscious world. It was interesting how many elements of that image were echoed in the presence of the woman sitting a few feet away.

Dana glanced up and caught him looking at her. Owen blushed but she looked back at him with warmth. "Hey, I'm glad you like my bard-mobile. I don't get to play hostess very often—I hope you feel welcome. I have good radar for interesting people, and I could tell right away that you were one. I think there's a lot more than meets the eye with you. So, tell me something, Owen. Tell me about the rhizome labyrinth."

Owen explained what he had learned from his research, focusing on the semiotic analysis of Umberto Eco. Dana listened carefully, responding with mobile eyebrows. Their dancing independence charmed Owen and he worked to avoid staring at her face. Still lecturing, he took a gulp of his tea, forgetting that it was hot. Dana winced when he recoiled from his cup, and then responded: "Okay, clearly you're a studious person. I respect that. I learned some things from what you said. But what I really want to know is what does it mean to you, this rhizome labyrinth that you've marked in your flesh?"

He sipped cautiously, trying to figure out how best to answer her question. Just as he had discovered with River, it was hard to explain anything without explaining everything. "It's about the forest; I feel a kinship. Not so much to specific trees, but the forest as a whole system. Like you pointed out in your talk, under the ground is a mycorrhizal network that links all the trees. I have a peculiar sensitivity to that network." Owen paused to drink, hiding behind his tea. He would be mortified if Dana thought he was a nut or a new age space cadet. He wanted to impress her, yet his lack of familiarity with where she stood on so many things made him hesitate: he didn't know what to include in his story and what to leave out. So, he told her about his years of mythology studies, and he relied on that vocabulary to convey the main points, thinking that a poet would surely be receptive to a mythic way of looking at the world. Finally, he couldn't think of any other way to talk around his secrets. "I guess you could say that I'm tangled up in the myths and systems of the forest, or the rhizome, as I call it." He wondered if he sounded as lame as he thought he did.

Dana sat quietly and stared at him. "Hmm. I'm not sure I understand exactly what you're trying to say. Or not say. But we seem to share a connection to the forest. A connection most people don't think about, at least not much. The land, especially the forest, fills up all the space in my poems; it grows a wilderness in my soul. For me, it is a sanctuary. The ultimate safe space, where no one can hurt me. When I need to go there, nothing else will do. I suppose we all need such a space in our lives."

Owen looked at her with compassion, seeing pain worn into her features, wondering who or what could possibly have hurt her. He said softly, "Yes, we do."

They sat in silence for a while, sipping the tea and warming each other with their eyes. Owen was content. No longer did he think he had to impress this woman. With a few words they had achieved enough understanding and acceptance to feel safe together.

Dana broke the silence. "Just come over here, would you?" She patted the bed next to her.

Owen, eager to comply but mindful of the need to be suave, tried to mask his excitement with studied movements. His maneuver around the table lacked grace, however, and as he slid out from the bench, he bumped a corner, stumbled, and flopped face down onto the bed. Dana laughed and hit him across the shoulders with a pillow.

"God, you're as bad as I am," she said as she fluffed the pillow and set it against the van wall as a backrest for him. He grinned at her and levered himself upright, sagging back onto the pillow. Acutely conscious of the mere inches that separated their shoulders, he didn't know what to do with his hands. Dana smiled and he wondered if it would ever be possible to crawl out of those eyes. Her hand lay on the bed next to her leg, palm up, and in a moment of unprecedented boldness he placed his own hand over hers.

"Do you mind?" He asked, but her fingers had already curled to grip, giving the answer he needed. Her smile broadened and he wanted to kiss her. He wanted it but it didn't seem quite right, not yet. He thought she might expect it of him, but he wasn't sure about that, either. He really didn't know what he was doing.

Owen tried to stop thinking and just enjoy the sureness in their hands. "Touch hasn't always been very easy for me."

Dana nodded. "Yeah. Usually when someone touches me, I jump through the ceiling or scream. But there's something different about you. You're not like other guys. You're not even like other people. There's a cleanness in your spirit, something deep and not quite human, perhaps. Something that reminds me of the smell of the forest. I like that."

"You think I'm not quite human?"

Dana squeezed his hand. "Oh, don't take that the wrong way. I mean it as a compliment. I'm a bit of a misanthrope, anyway. Not entirely fond of people much of the time. We humans are a mess. We stomp on each other and all the other critters. As a species, we're the grim reapers. I don't know what will change that – maybe we need new genes."

A chill ran up Owen's spine. Did she really say that? Maybe he *could* tell her the whole story. But later. They hardly knew each other, he told himself, although in his heart he felt otherwise.

"I couldn't agree more. People can be cruel, ruthless, brutal, and for what? It makes no sense to me."

Dana studied his face as if searching for something. "May I ask a personal question?"

Owen held his breath for a moment. "Okay..."

"You don't have to answer. But when you spoke of cruelty, there was real passion in your voice. Has someone been cruel to you?"

"Yeah. When I was a kid. I'm better now, but for a while it nearly ruined my life."

Dana curled toward him, laying her free hand on top of his as if enclosing something fragile. "Aww shit, I'm sorry to hear that. So then, we've both been damaged by others. For me, it was rape." She paused and Owen noticed that her eyes seemed to focus on a distant point. "One of my mother's junkie boyfriends, a decade after she left my father, who I don't remember. It went on for many months, then she caught him in my bed. I was eleven. At least she had the sense to throw him out. Too late for me, though. Can't say I've ever had an easy way with relationships. I'm telling you this, Owen, because I like you. I know we've just met, but I feel safe enough, which tells me something. Cause I never feel safe with a man."

"Not you, too! No one deserves such abuse, no one, but a child...? What kind of a twisted shit does that to a child? It's downright evil." A tear trickled from Owen's eye; he wiped it away and held back the flood that wasn't far behind. "Thank you for telling me; I'm glad you feel safe enough to do so. And, yeah, I too, I was... raped. By an uncle. Started when I was eight and went on for a long time. There was fallout from that, even after it stopped, as you might imagine. It got so bad I tried to kill myself. Then, well, things took a surprising turn. I found healing in the forest, I guess you could say. Profound healing." Owen felt the tug of memory before he shook it off to stay in the present. "But, you know, I'm still pretty naïve when it comes to people, especially, well, women."

Dana snuggled against Owen and put her head on his shoulder. "That's okay; I can do naïve. I really would like to get to know you better. If you're open to that sort of thing." He was open, but he couldn't find the words to speak his thoughts. With a mind of its own, his free hand moved up to her head, stroking the hair behind her ears. She flinched at first, then relaxed and deepened her snuggle.

"So, hey, just wondering... where are you staying? Do you need to get going anytime soon?"

"I don't have anything set up. Figured I'd go find a motel or something. But I'm in no hurry. Honestly, it feels really good to be here with you."

"I feel the same. Why not stay here with me tonight? If you don't mind. Don't get me wrong, I don't mean to have sex—I'm not ready for that. I just want to hold you, and have you hold me. Is that a weird thing to ask?"

"I don't know, I'm hardly the best judge of whether it's weird or not. But, sure, I'd like that. Very much, thank you."

They cuddled together on the bed and talked as the falling snow muffled the sounds of the outside world. Eventually they slid under the covers, spooning around each other to enter a dreamless sleep inside the redwood hull.


[24]

During the night, it stopped snowing. They slept late, then Dana made a breakfast of boiled eggs and toast to go with the morning tea. While shuffling pans and utensils, she hummed and danced in place, a performance that Owen openly admired. He wondered if she was like this when she was alone and decided that she probably was.

She handed Owen a plate and announced, "I had a stellar night of sleep!"

"Stellar?"

"Yes, dummy, of the stars. Heavenly."

Owen enjoyed the way she called him "dummy." It suggested a welcome familiarity. They dawdled over breakfast, chatting and laughing, stretching out the moment as long as possible. When they finally talked about plans, Dana said that she had committed to several more stops on a book and lecture tour of the Northeast. Her final engagement was at the College of the Atlantic in Bar Harbor. After that, she suggested that she might continue along the coast to Owen's place, if he wouldn't mind. Of course, he wouldn't mind. He offered to come along with her on the tour, but she said it was something she needed to do on her own. She hoped he'd understand about that. He started to plead his case, caught himself, and realized that he was being childish, so he nodded and resolved not to sulk about it.

They exchanged email addresses and promised to write. Dana had a cell phone for emergencies but preferred not to use it otherwise. Writing would suffice, they agreed. Dana gave Owen one of her purple silk scarves, wrapping it around his neck with sure hands, patting his chest. They kissed, a last concession to touch, before Owen stepped out of the van, trying to compress nonchalance into every reluctant movement.

His gait lightened as the crisp air cleared his head. Floating across the newly plowed parking lot, he stopped to recollect where he left the truck. The toot of a horn made him turn and Dana waved at him as she drove away. He watched the van ease through the lot and out to the street, tracking it until it was out of sight. The sky was a translucent blue and the snow-draped world gleamed in the reflection of Owen's happiness.

Crawling into the cab of his truck, he twisted the mirror so he could see what he looked like with the scarf. It seemed like every time he surprised himself in a mirror, he was someone different. Damn if it doesn't look good, he thought, I'm never taking it off.

From Keene, he drove south into Massachusetts, stopping every hour to drain blood into a tree. His method was efficient:

he used the awl on a pocket multi-tool to bore a hole through the bark, then punctured the tip of his little finger with the knife point, just enough to squeeze out a few drops of blood. On days like this, when he did multiple blood draws, he kept a bandage over the wound until the next stop, then he'd peel it off and re-open the puncture. Fairly mechanical, the whole procedure, but he never went ahead with it before he leaned into the tree, listening to its rhythms. He always asked permission for what he was about to do. And everywhere the forest responded to him, asking for help, reaching toward him through a veil of sadness.

He worked his way eastward on Route 2, then continued through the slow crawl of traffic to central Boston where he walked around first at the Arboretum and then the venerable Common, sowing his fluid into the city's greenbelt. He stopped for a sandwich and headed north, following the coastal route with frequent stops in the nearby woodlands. Along the way he daydreamed. Dana had given him copies of her other books and as he sat in a motel bed at night, he read them closely, savoring the words, trying to plumb the depth of the woman within her work. Pulling the covers over his head when he could read no more, he longed for her embrace. One night it was hard to sleep, and he flailed for hours. When he finally found slumber, he dreamed of reciting Dana's poems aloud in a maple grove, surrounded by songbirds, jays, and crows. As the words flowed from his mouth, he was aroused and tingling with sex. On and on he proclaimed, while the trees swayed and rattled in the wind, until her words and his flesh wove themselves into a knot of sinew, feathers, and wood.

By the time he got back home he recognized a ragged anxiety at the edge of his moods. The intense longing was wearing him down. Of course, the big question was whether she would really come to see him. Distance and time enhanced his pessimism and made it seem less probable. He recognized the patterns of instability within himself and understood that in the past he would already be doing something stupid to mask his insecurity. At least he was no longer so vulnerable. Instead, he identified a worthwhile pursuit and threw himself into it: cleaning, re-organizing, and re-arranging. He knew enough about women to understand the value of a tidy house. Even if she claimed to be disorganized, the condition of her van suggested otherwise. Anyway, his place needed it after he and River had allowed their grief to clutter every corner.

He broke off the never-ending cleaning project at every opportunity and checked his email. Half a dozen messages from Dana had greeted him on his arrival home, and they continued to pop in unpredictably. He read them over and over. She wrote with a relaxed style, full of mischievous word-play. In contrast, he labored over his responses, relishing the connection but striving to make each note perfect. It got easier as they went back and forth, and Owen stopped worrying that he was blowing it. Their exchanges were convivial, yet intellectual and bold. Clearly, they were having fun as they dazzled each other with curiosity and enthusiasm.

The length of these messages varied from one line to hundreds. An early note from Dana said, in its condensed entirety: "Best Welsh source myth?" His reply was equally laconic: "*Mabinogion*, Sioned Davies trans." Two days later he received a reply that would have been cryptic to anyone else: "Owen = Owain." To him it meant that she had read "The Lady of the Well" in the Davies translation. Her response delighted him.

The emails formed a chronological jumble as they threw notes at each other, creating a delightful confusion. Missed queries and provocative comments lead to teasing and further tangents, but they didn't mind. If a conversation was dropped, another one would be along shortly, usually within hours. Owen noted that they were building their own rhizome labyrinth. He appended links to relevant works so she could appreciate the reference. In return, he received a quote from a work by an anthropologist who studied wild mushroom foragers and who threw out the question: "Might we think of mutualisms as a form of love?" "Yes!" he wrote back to Dana. "Yes!"

Between the thrill of these exchanges, he continued to work on the house, repairing minor damage, sorting out the seldom seen corners of the kitchen shelves, and tending to the myriad of household details that were usually put off till later. It was the right activity for his frame of mind: he was never far from the computer and the possibility of another email.

While knocking icicles off the eaves one day, he heard a vehicle coming down the driveway. He hoped for Dana, but it turned out to be a journalist in a rental car, claiming to be researching a piece for *The New Yorker* magazine. Owen asked to see credentials, which looked genuine, and as he handed them back, he inspected the journalist. A middle-aged man with a trimmed beard and wearing sunglasses. John Bixler, he said his name was – "but call me 'Bix'" – a freelancer on assignment and just wanting to ask a few questions about that recent logging protest. Bixler had been given Owen's name and directions to his place by the folks down at the local Forest Action office, although he was quick to point out that calling it an office might be an ambitious label for a closet-sized room tucked away at the back of the natural foods store. He didn't crack a smile, despite the sarcasm, and lit a cigarette as he leaned against the car, trying to look casual even though he was shivering in his windbreaker.

Owen was amused by the banter and invited him in out of the cold, offering a cup of tea, which Bixler declined. "No thanks. I wouldn't say no to coffee, though, if you've got it. Just black is fine."

"Mmm, probably not. Might be some old instant crystals of my mother's in the back of the cupboard, but since she's been dead for four years I can't swear to their potency."

"Jesus," Bixler muttered, "you are roughing it, aren't you?"

As they sat in the living room settling for tumblers of tap water, Owen learned that Bixler was putting together a feature article, possibly a book, about right-wing paramilitary groups. He had learned about the Legion of Odin and heard rumors that they had done something awful during the recent logging protest. He wanted to know more. He wondered if Owen could help.

Owen thought for a long time before answering. Bixler had his notebook and pen ready, but waited with resigned patience. "Well, Bix, it turns out that I do know more. A lot more." And Owen told him the truth. He told him the story of the protest, start to finish, including the death of Garth and the role of the Legion of Odin in that death. He also mentioned that he believed Garth's body was still in the woods, concealed by the Legion, though he was careful to avoid saying why he thought that. Bixler paid close attention to Owen's narration, taking notes throughout, and asking pertinent questions. He commented that the official story had the third tree-sitter fleeing into the woods and leaving the region for parts unknown.

"Bullshit." Owen observed.

"Could be," agreed Bixler. "Why do you believe Garth's body is in the woods?"

Owen sighed. It was the obvious question, impossible to avoid forever. "Just call it a hunch, I guess. We saw him killed and then the Legion forced us to leave the scene. They had the body. We tried to tell the police what happened, but they didn't listen. Then the story appeared that he'd run away. It doesn't take a degree in logic to think that the body never left the woods."

"Yeah. You've got a point. Well, thanks for your time. I think I have what I need but can I call you if I have more questions?"

"You could but I don't have a phone."

"What is this out here: the dark ages?"

Owen scribbled his email address on a scrap torn from an envelope and handed it to Bixler. "Dark in places, but not every corner. Use this instead."

After the interview was over and Bixler drove back through the trees, Owen had second thoughts about what he had done. There would be repercussions if even a fraction of that story made it into print. His uncle and the other psychopaths wouldn't like it, that was for sure. But what the hell, once he started talking, he couldn't stop himself. The story had been boiling inside and it needed to be released. He owed that much to Garth. Let the consequences come, he thought; if we can't live with the facts then what can we live with?

Two more weeks went by, then Dana showed up early one afternoon, honking the horn as she pulled to a stop in front of the house. Owen dropped his book and ran outside, grabbing her in a hug as soon as she stepped out of the van. She yielded to the hug for a moment, then stiffened, and Owen let go.

"Oh sorry, sorry... I didn't mean to... Damn." Owen's arms went limp and fell aside while his useless hands opened and closed.

Dana reached out and touched his shoulder. "It's okay; I should apologize to you! I'm so reactive. I wish I wasn't, but, you know... just the way it is inside my complicated head. Half the time I'm like the skin of a drum: tight, tight, tight, and don't touch me." She mimed the tightening of screws. "The other half I'm wild, enthusiastic, and flopping over everything, or so I'm told. Anyway, sorry, I'll try to calm down. I'm truly glad to see you. I've been looking forward to this ever since you left. Probably why I'm so keyed up. I promise we'll cuddle later; just give me time to adjust. Hey, you look pretty good in that scarf."

Owen blushed. He had, indeed, worn the scarf every day. He'd been tempted to wear it at night, too, but decided that would be too weird. When he finally removed it for the first time, he studied her knot and he'd been doing it the same way ever since.

She looked at him with puzzlement. "Has your hair really grown that much? It's definitely longer than it was when I saw you last."

He laughed and pulled it back as if to hide it away in a pony-tail, but it wasn't quite long enough for that. "Yeah, it grows fast. I got crazy hair genes."

"I didn't get those genes. My own shock of hair crawls out at a glacial pace. So be it, I'm keeping it short now, anyway. I suppose you'd prefer it long and flowing like those archetypal princesses in your mythic fables. Rhiannon of the Birds, right?" She did a pirouette with a flourish for emphasis and the extravagance reminded him of Dr. Chouinard.

Owen grinned nervously and shook his head. "No, no. Not at all. Rhiannon? Who knows what she looked like, really? Nowhere in the texts does it mention the length of her hair or even that she had any at all. She was full of magic and illusions, a shapeshifter, she could probably look like anything she wanted to. More than a princess, she was a goddess. Anyway, she's faded into the mist of time. But you – you're here! And I like your hair, it seems just right for you. Not that it matters, you're lovely any way... well, that's what I think...." Owen finished up with hesitation, aware that he was babbling and wondering if he had gone too far again.

Dana looked pleased at Owen's words, but she quickly averted her face, intently scanning the surroundings, taking in the house and barn, the snow-covered clearing, and the encircling wall of woods. She stared into the woods through a long silence, then turned back to Owen and took his hand. "Hey, you, don't I at least get a guided tour?"

Absorbed in trying to understand the tears in her eyes, the question surprised him. "You want a tour of the woods?"

She wiped her face, then laughed and poked him, "Not now, dummy. Later, I'll want to meet every tree. But for now, can we start with the house? I need a bathroom."

Owen melted at her revival of the word *dummy*. Holding her hand, he escorted her through the front door and pointed to the bathroom. He was glad that he had spent so much time cleaning the house.

"I'll put on some water for tea. Take your time, then I'll show you around."

He put two cups and a few biscuits on the table. When Dana finally emerged from the bathroom, she poured tea into a cup and stood next to the wood stove, warming her back and smiling at Owen. "Sir Owain, I find your dwelling altogether commodious," she said, holding the cup out to the side while she curtsied. Owen couldn't resist such silliness; laughing, he bowed in return.

She surveyed the exposed wood of the ceiling. "These beams are magnificent. Oak, right? And the house feels like you, Owen, warm and sheltering. I've been thinking about our meeting constantly. The emails have been a true delight. But that night we spent in the van was a revelation. I've never met a man who, once invited into my space, didn't make a move, no matter how noble they looked on the surface. I figured you'd be the same—we'd have crummy sex, then I'd never want to see you again."

Owen stared at her, afraid to breathe. Dana took a sip from the cup, then rubbed her free hand back and forth across the top of her head, ruffling the hair into random tufts. "I don't know why I keep putting myself in those situations. I'm an edge-walker, I guess. Sometimes it gets me into serious trouble. You'd think I would learn, but not really. Anyway, you didn't try to take advantage of me. Something's different about you. Something rich and deep and clean. I sensed it right away with your labyrinth and rhizome talk and that polite manner of yours. That's what led me here, to you and your murky, mysterious woods. Several times I wanted to cancel the rest of that damned tour and just drive straight here. But then I didn't want to seem too eager, too easy, you know? Which, of course, makes no sense after sleeping with you on the first date. Of course, it was just sleeping."

As Dana talked, Owen remembered what Dr. Chouinard had taught him about the connections between trauma and compulsive sex. It had helped him to understand his own desperate impulses. He wondered if Dana was struggling with something like that, but he wasn't going to bring it up now, not at this stage. He wanted to take her in his arms but that didn't seem quite right, either. There was an anxious, almost haunted look in her eyes that made his heart sore.

"Dana, look, I don't know how the sex thing is supposed to work, not really. I mean, it's not that I... well, I just don't know much about it." He blushed and realized that he might have lost all pretense at sophistication, admitting a lack of experience, but he plunged ahead. No reason to pretend that he was anything other than himself. He wasn't good at relationship games, and this seemed a poor time to put on an act. "Listen, I do understand something about intimacy. I've experienced profound connections to others. I know how important, and how rare, it is to find those connections, whether with a woman, a man, or... a tree. It's not something that can be faked or cheapened. When we spent that night together, I felt it with you. I felt connected to a truly *wondrous* being."

Owen studied Dana's face, seeing tears in her eyes again. She looked down and blew her nose on an old handkerchief. "Ah, Owen, you're pretty wondrous yourself...." Then she trailed off into an inaudible mutter. Before Owen could ask her to repeat it, she brightened and said, a little too cheerfully, "Hey, how about before we melt into sugar and slush that we have that tour of the estate? I really wouldn't mind a peek at your trees. I'm dying to see those famous Maine woods. You promised, right?" Hand on hip, she set her lips in a mock pout, sealing the vulnerability behind a pose.

First, he showed her the occupied parts of the house, noting that the rooms behind closed doors were "family museums, full of skeletons and ghosts." Donning boots and coats, they left the house by the back door. A drifted-over trail through the snowpack remained from Owen's regular visits to the woods. He made a habit of sharing blood every day, even if it meant he was saturating the vicinity. Couldn't hurt anything, he figured, and it made him feel like he was doing something.

When the trail ended at the edge of the woods, Dana said "ooooh" and waded off through the snow. She plowed back and forth among the trees, reaching out her hands and stroking the bark, and pressing her palm against the trunks. She would cock her head as if listening, and Owen wondered if she sensed the rich forest mind. He was going to ask her what she was doing when she came up to the white ash tree—the portal to the Thorn world.

"Is this a white ash? That's my namesake, you know."

"What do you mean?"

"Onnen—it's Welsh for white ash."

"It is?" Owen was speechless. He thought he knew all there was to know about these things. Obviously, he did not.

Dana walked around the trunk and saw the deep furrow in the bark. She reached out to touch it, then, before Owen could say anything, she pressed her fingers into the groove. The tips sank in the wood which was solid no longer and flowed out and around her knuckles. Owen reached toward her as she turned to look at him with a mixture of awe and fear. He grabbed her wrist and pulled. Reluctantly, the tree let go with a sucking sound, oozing quickly back to its original state.

Dana was flushed and breathing hard. "What the fucking hell was that?"

"Are you okay?"

Dana nodded curtly, impatient for an answer to her own question, glaring at Owen. He fussed over her, patting her and examining her fingers until she pulled away and looked straight into his eyes.

"I'm fine, really. Thanks for your concern. But right now, I need to know what just happened. You don't seem the slightest bit surprised. So, do tell."

Owen offered a reassuring smile that he suspected was closer to a grimace. Nervous, he launched into a rattling attempt to explain what happened, all the while cursing himself for allowing it. He didn't see how he could make any of this appear remotely normal. "No, no, there's nothing here in these woods that will hurt you. Well, aside from the usual kind of things like bears and ticks and such. Or a falling branch in a windstorm. But really, these woods are quite benign; they want to take care of you. This white ash right here," he reached out to pat the trunk, careful not to touch the furrow, "is a remarkable tree. It wasn't just glad to see you—although I'm sure it was, in its own way—but there was something else going on. It does things you would never imagine a tree could do. Never. And I have a completely outrageous story to go with it. Literally, you won't believe it. If I tell you, well, I'm afraid you'll think I'm a lunatic. It's a hell of a thing, something out of science fiction...." Owen started to run down, conscious that Dana still glared at him; she looked angry and frightened, and nothing he said changed that.

"But yes, you're right, you deserve to know. And I want you to know, even though it's something I've never told anyone about. However, it's a long story and rather than stand here in the woods and shiver through the telling, I suggest we go back to the house, throw some more wood on the stove, sit down with a fresh cup of tea and you can decide for yourself how crazy it all is. Okay?"

Dana's alarm softened to a milder form of worry as she peered into Owen's face, searching for what she hoped was there, something to trust. While she pondered, Owen wrestled with anxiety, wishing he knew how to provide reassurance. But nothing came to him. He looked at her, trying to let his eyes plead the case. She stared back at him while he watched the worry become a careful neutrality. Finally, she spoke. "No."

"No? Uh..."

"No. Tell me here. Now."

Owen saw that she would not be cajoled out of an explanation. His world of romance collapsed around him. He anticipated that if he told her the truth, he would end up sadly escorting her back to the van so she could drive away as fast as possible from the crazy Mainer and his crazy woods. But did he have any other choice? He wanted her to know everything; it was just happening faster than he had hoped. He shrugged and tried to smile despite the anxiety creeping up his spine. "Okay," he said. "Watch." Placing his own hand in the furrow on the tree, he maintained steady eye contact with Dana while the wood flowed around his fingers. He felt the tug of the ash but knowing what it was, he braced himself and arrested the suction. His left hand was buried in the tree to the wrist. Dana stared at him, aghast. He struggled to keep his voice in the vicinity of nonchalance. "This tree is a normal tree in most respects, but it has an additional property: it can morph cell structure. It does this at the quantum level by molding the plasticity of elementary particles. At human contact, it works on its own cells to open and stretch. Eventually it would start working on my cells as well, though it would require more than a hand to do much. By the way, the particles, like all elementary particles, are really strings, not little spheres of matter, and when they shift, they make music like any string that is bowed or plucked. Look, I know this sounds nutty, but it is physics, which is pretty nutty in general when you think about it." Owen remembered the lessons he had been taught by the Thorns, and with fondness in his heart for that connection, he felt some inspiration flow through him. Dana was still there, watching and listening, so he plunged ahead.

"Dana, I know you are sensitive, more so than most people. I want you to hear the music within the wood. Just take my hand, hold it tight, and let's see if comes to you through me." He offered her his open hand. She looked at it with child-like wariness.

"We're not gonna both get sucked in there? You promise me that?"

"There is a pull, yes. But you can see that I'm holding the position."

Shaking slightly, Dana placed her hand in Owen's. Their eyes locked. The music reverberating through the rhizome first came to him as a dull rhythm like the sound of a hundred faint, overlapping heartbeats. The sound grew louder, and the polyrhythms emerged in greater complexity, rippling on to the shore of his consciousness, filling every nook of his being. Underneath the rhythms he heard the tragic dirge as the forest grieved for its losses. Owen shuddered with the burden of grief. Dana watched him closely and saw the reactions coursing through his body. Her eyes widened when the wave of emotion crossed the boundary of flesh, hand to hand, and surged into her own awareness. Dana gasped and trembled, but she clung to Owen. He nodded at her and let the rhizome music flow into her for a while longer, then he slowly pulled his hand out of the tree, careful to maintain a grip on Dana.

"Oh my god!" She clutched his hand even tighter. "What was that? That, that was the sound of quantum strings, or whatever you called it? Tree music? Holy crap! I had no idea... What does it even mean?"

"The trees are sad. The forest sings about its grief, including its losses from the logging project down the road. And for the greater losses of the forest as humans destroy the equilibrium of the ecosystem."

"I heard that! I heard the sadness... oh, it was painful. But beautiful. God! Talk about wondrous!"

"Okay, so there's that. But there's more. A lot more. You heard the mind of the forest but not just the forest that stands in front of us. This amazing old ash tree is connected to another forest. A forest in another universe altogether. I know, I know. Just bear with me, even if it sounds insane. But it's not unthinkable, you know. Our physics theorizes that there could be alternate universes that exist in a parallel situation to our own. Well, it's more than theory; there really are such things. And the boundaries between these universes have been penetrated by the forest with its exploratory mycorrhizal networks, through the insistent probing for beneficial links with other beings. This ash tree is a direct connection. If you let it suck you in, it takes you to another world."

Dana crushed Owen's hand. Excitement leaped across her face. "This can't be true! Can it? You're shitting me, right? Right?!"

"Look. Take a breath, then I'm going to reconnect us to the tree. This time send your awareness directly into the tree, reach out to it, don't wait for it to grab you. And if you panic, no worries, pull back and you'll pop right out." Owen lifted their joined hands and pressed them into the furrow of the tree, which sucked them in, enveloping their grip. "Feel this, Dana. Does this feel like I'm shitting you?"

The rhizome washed through their nervous systems, a cascade of sound and sensation beyond anything Dana had imagined was possible. Her eyes were wide and dark. Her fear had mutated into the pure energy of curiosity. To Owen she resembled a child eager for her turn on the roller coaster, unable to contain the thrill as she vibrated in place. "Are we going through to the other world now?" She breathed the words in reverent awe.

"You want to?"

"Hell, yes! Are you kidding? This is like a dream come true!"

Owen pulled their hands out of the tree. "Yes," he said. "We can do that. But there are a few more things I need to tell you first. We would need to prepare for such an expedition. Can't just go popping in and out of the multiverse like Dr. Who. It's a bit more involved than that. Now can we go back to the house and I'll tell you the rest?"

Dana looked at Owen and sighed in disappointment. She turned her gaze to the tree and stroked its bark, careful to avoid the furrow. Then she leaned against the tree and kissed it. "Okay, fine. Let's go have a story."

Back in the warm house, Dana rushed through tea preparations while Owen dragged the couch across the dining room and placed it in front of the wood stove. As soon as the furniture was realigned, Dana thrust a steaming cup into his hands. She set her cup on the floor and plopped onto the couch, sitting at one end and stretching her legs along the length. She yanked off the socks and flexed her toes. "Okay, Owen Black, out with it. I want the whole story with no interruptions and every detail."

Owen chuckled at her regal manner and crammed more wood in the stove, before sitting at the other end of the couch. Dana lifted her feet so he could slide in under her legs, then placed her feet in his lap. She let him massage the wiggling toes while he talked. As he absently worked with his hands, he launched into the tale of his experiences: the depression after

Dr. Chouinard's death, the distorted fantasy about Ariadne's labyrinth, the decision to end his life, salvation on the tree, transportation to the alternate universe, the forest mind, all three of the Thorns, everything. Once he started talking, it all rolled out. Dana listened at first without expression, then with eyebrows raised, then her eyebrows danced this way and that, then finally she merely gaped at him. Almost an hour went by before he stopped, having also told her about the tree sit, Garth's death, his uncle, the intervention of the rhizome, the virus, and River.

Dana ran her fingers back and forth through her hair and scratched the top of her head. "A lot of people would hear your story and write it off as delusional. Even with an experience like I had out there, seeing the tree absorb my hand, hearing the music in the wood, most folks would devise some rational chain of explication, minimizing the testimony of their eyes and flesh. But I'm not going to do that. As a poet, I honor the vision, no matter how outlandish. I accept that there are powerful mysteries in life, things that are beyond our understanding but no less real for that. That old smarty-pants William Blake said: *in the universe, there are things that are known, and things that are unknown, and in between, there are doors.* And that's what I do, I look for those doors, especially the ones that can take me into communion with the forest. And, goddammit Owen, you have just shown me one, a real doozy. This is all quite strange, no doubt, and I'm a messed-up bundle, to be sure, but I'm not crazy, you're not crazy, and this is as real as it gets, right? Maybe more real than that – maybe a whole new level of reality. Thank you for telling me the story. Now I know that I was right; as I said before, you're not like other men."

Owen studied Dana as he stroked her feet, admiring her lanky beauty. He couldn't decide which pleased him more, her physical presence or her acceptance of his story. Put them together and he couldn't remember when he felt this joyful. Was it too soon to say that he loved her? He opened his mouth, but the words didn't come. He worried that if he went too far, she would reject him. Yes, it was definitely too soon for grand declarations, so he said nothing and tugged her toes, one by one. Purring, she let her eyes slide shut. Owen felt her muscles relax as he worked his way up her feet and along the ankles. Finally, in a sleepy voice, she said, "So when do we get to go to the other world?"

He thought about her request for a moment. "How about tomorrow?"

Her eyes snapped open and she stared at him with an unmistakable hunger. "Hell yes." She closed her eyes and drifted off again. He thought she was falling asleep, which was fine with him, he'd hold her like this all night, but then she spoke again, in a soft voice that he barely heard, "Falling in love, hmmm..."

[25]

Dana fell asleep on the couch, so Owen didn't move. It was peaceful to hold her feet and bask in the moment. Had anyone ever shown this much trust in him? No woman, certainly. In repose, the years slipped from her face and he saw the girl within, free of the scarred mask of the adult. He ached with a desire to protect her. At first, he congratulated himself on this noble impulse, but it wasn't long before memories conjured doubts. His own uncle had ordered the murder of a friend and followed that with the delivery of personal threats against Owen. Could he really protect Dana? He wondered if taking her into the Thorn world and getting her involved offered any safety or if he was putting her at risk. The risk seemed real. Perhaps it was selfish, but he still wanted her in his life. Surely there must be a way to do that. Eventually the wood burned low in the stove and Owen felt the expanding chill. He tried to slide out from under Dana's legs so he could tend the stove, but she woke as soon as he moved.

"Hey," she said.

"Oh sorry, just had to stoke the stove. Don't move; I'll get some blankets and I'm happy to keep the heat blazing all night."

"Nah," she countered. "It'd be more comfortable in your bed, don't you think? Together, so we can cuddle and keep each other warm. Am I being too forward?"

"No," he said. That's exactly what he wanted. Dana roused herself from the couch and they went upstairs, hand in hand.

Dana admired the bedroom décor, which resembled Dr. Chouinard's old office, with Indian blankets and baskets, prints of paintings by Carrington and Tanguy, and shelves and stacks of books. Dana remembered that she left her overnight bag in the van, so she ran downstairs and across the packed snow in bare feet, racing back in the door and up the stairs, squeaking like a mouse and hopping from foot to foot. When she ducked into the bathroom, Owen went downstairs and locked and bolted the front door. He wanted no surprise visits from uncles, Aryans, or even journalists. Dana emerged from the bathroom wearing Dr. Seuss flannel pajamas. Owen was certain she would look appealing in anything, but this outfit charmed him. He liked that she didn't try to edit who she was. She could be playful, she could be serious, but she was always intensely present. Dr. Chouinard had been like that.

Dana slipped under the comforter and snuggled close. She put her arms around Owen and wriggled to find the perfect fusion. Carefully, Owen returned the embrace. Holding together, they relished the contact and inhaled the animal warmth of each other. The feel of her body aroused him; he wondered if she noticed and if so, what she thought about that. The last thing he wanted was to become another one of those unpleasant men who seized an opportunity to have their way. Regardless of what might happen in the bed, he was certain that he shouldn't be the one to initiate anything sexual. He lay still, encouraging himself to relax, enjoy the intimacy of their embrace, and stop obsessing about what came next. His acceptance must have created a muscle signal, because Dana moved against him, kissing his lips and sliding her hands down his back, bringing his skin to full alertness with a long caress. He responded in kind, letting his hands trace her spine before fanning out to linger around her hips. She moaned and yielded to his touch. Then his curious fingers reached her inner thighs. Suddenly she gagged and tensed all her muscles. Their kiss fell apart, cracking into spasms of sobbing. He recognized the reaction, remembered his own breakdowns, and he quickly pulled his hands away.

"Oh, Dana... I'm sorry, I'm so sorry... don't worry, it's okay, it's okay." He didn't know what to say because he knew that it wasn't okay. So much for protecting her; first he would have to learn how to protect her from himself. With nothing meaningful to say, he held her gingerly while she cried.

The cries became sniffles and she wiped her tears on his shirt. He was glad for that gesture because it showed she was still connected to him. "I want to, Owen, I really do. More than anything. I mean, I've had a lot of sex, maybe too much. Of course, most of the time I would just turn off my head and let them do things to me. They get what they want, I guess. Never meant much to me except as a way to get it over with. But I don't want that with you. I don't want to be numb. I want to feel you, to really feel you. Seems like I'm not ready for that. Oh, maybe I'll never be ready! I'm sorry, this is terrible. I'm a total mess."

"Hush, you're not a mess at all. It's completely understandable. I've been there – or somewhere similar. It's the fallout from how we got hurt, that's all. I know you can't control it. Please don't have sex with me to *get it over with*. Whatever you need is what I want to give you. That includes time and space. Your trust is the most important thing to me because, well, because... I'm sure it's too early to say this, but I think I love you."

"You do?"

"Yes. I don't know what comes next; all I know is that I want to find out. Whatever that means. I've a hunch it's something worth waiting for. We'll get there, I believe that. There's no hurry, I'm here for you."

"Thank you, Owen... just... thank you. What did I do to deserve you? Great Danu is watching over me, I guess."

"Danu? The goddess?"

"That's the one. My other namesake."

"Talk about power names. Somebody gave you a mythic legacy."

"I think it was my father. Mom never talked much about him. Least not in a good way. And I never saw him since I was old enough to remember."

"That's a shame. I didn't know mine, either. What's with families, anyway? Is it really so hard to do the right thing?"

"Seems so."

Nothing was said for a while and Dana curled into Owen's shoulder. He felt her easing into sleep, but once again, he heard a whisper as she drifted off. "Night, Owen. Thanks." With the lightest of touch, he stroked her head.

Owen woke early and tip-toed down the stairs, hoping to pass the fourth step without activating the loud squeak. Despite his effort, the staircase protested his descent. At the bottom he listened but heard no stirrings from the bedroom. He added wood to the stove and opened the draft, then started making breakfast while he thought about their plan to go through the portal. He was eager to return to the Thorn world, anticipating the pleasure of reunion with the madcap crew of Thorns, if they were still around. He did remember them saying that it was a temporary form. Well, maybe they could be resurrected or rejuvenated or whatever they did to renew things. As soon as the thought emerged, he realized that a rejuvenation might be possible for Dana as well. The biochemical tinkering that Owen received from the Thorns had relieved most of his trauma-related effects. Would they be willing to do that for her?

When he looked up, Dana, still in pajamas, stood in the doorway, scratching her bottom. "Mmm, that smells good."

Owen almost gave her a hug, then remembered last night and settled for squeezing her shoulder. She reached up and placed a hand on top of his, then rotated into him, pulling his arm around her, ending up with her back pressed to his chest. "Good morning," she said.

Her maneuver suggested there was reason to hope for easier contact. Happy to touch her, he remembered his thought about getting relief in the Thorn world. "Hey, you still want to go through the portal today?"

She craned her head back so she could look at him. "Oh yeah. No time like the present, right?"

"Exactly." He reluctantly unwound from the hug so he could tend to the cooking. Glancing back at her, he tried to speak casually, not wanting to oversell his hope. "You remember the part of my story about getting neurochemical alterations in the Thorn world?" When she nodded, he continued, "It occurred to me that we might be able to get that for you, too. If you want it. Might help with some things. I mean, I feel better than I ever have. More even-keeled – definitely less reactive."

Dana eyed Owen pensively for a moment, then arched an eyebrow. "You want to get into my pants that bad?"

Owen blushed violently and started stammering. "No, I mean... only if you want to, of course... It's a good thing, though... in many ways, I think...." Then he collected his thoughts and decided to find a more honest way forward. "Look, Dana, I do want sex with you. I want us to be able to share that. I say that and I don't even know what I'm talking about, really. But it seems like such an important part of intimacy and relationship—and yes, I want it. If there's a way we can have it so it's not torture, then I'm all for it. But absolutely, it's your body and your choice."

Dana smiled at Owen. "Sorry, I shouldn't torment you like that. But, good answer. I also want all the options for us. Us—wow. Now I'm talking about *us*, like we're an item or something. A little early for that, right?"

"Yeah, I guess so," Owen said in a flat voice, thinking the opposite.

Dana raced through breakfast and then put on a display of nervous energy by darting back and forth to her van, bringing in various bags and armloads of clothes, throwing them all on the couch and standing back to assess the piles. Owen watched in fascination, peeking from the kitchen while he cleaned up.

Dana paused and rubbed her head, a gesture Owen now recognized as a habit. "I can't decide what to wear. Is it going to be cold?"

Owen finished with the dishes and sauntered into the dining room, taking a position next to her as they stared at the array on the couch. "That's just the thing. There's no reason to worry about what you're wearing because it won't go through the portal."

"What? Really?"

"I don't know how it works, exactly, but so far only living biological matter has made the translation. If you remember from the story, I ended up in the other world naked as a jay."

"Ohhh, right."

"Is that okay? I don't see why we can't get more fabric once we're there and make some clothes like I did."

"Nah, I don't mind. I've got nothing to hide."

"There's something else to consider. When I first went through a portal it left me knocked out for a while but the second time, when I came back, I was awake even before the transfer was complete. That may happen again, in which case you'll be unconscious while I'm awake. I'll watch over you, although there didn't seem to be any threats beyond the occasional bug bite. Don't worry, I'm an experienced bug swatter. But, you know, it means you have to trust me to take care of you while you're out."

Dana pursed and twisted her lips as she considered the situation. "That's interesting. Hmm... Call me crazy, but I do trust you. Besides, no way am I backing out of this. Adventure of a lifetime. To be honest, I've taken worse risks. Nope, I'm good to go." Dana started bouncing in place like a boxer warming up.

He suggested they wear old clothes and expendable boots since he anticipated that any fabrics would be consumed in the portal metamorphosis. Dana frowned but accepted his offer of sweatpants and a ragged pullover. She turned her back and shucked off the pajamas, slipping into the tattered clothes without hesitation. Owen politely looked away but still caught a glimpse of her bare back. Dana noticed his embarrassment and grinned.

They locked the house and Owen showed Dana where he hid the key. The mid-winter cold was piercing so they hurried toward the white ash tree. They talked about who should go first, then Owen suggested that the tree might take them both at the same time if they squeezed together. Dana liked that idea. Facing each other, chest to chest, they held hands and pushed into the furrow. The tree moved slowly at first, but then, as if sensing the bulk, quickly expanded the gap to accommodate them. Owen tasted Dana's breath as their arms were absorbed. He held her against the flow for a moment and asked how she was doing.

Her face was ecstatic. "I can hear it! Let's go, let's go!"

Owen relaxed his counter pressure and let the tree suck them in. The last thing he saw before being swallowed was the size of Dana's pupils, inches from his own.

He regained consciousness in a confusion of limbs. Tangled and topsy-turvy, they both emerged from a tree somewhere in the other world. Apparently, the translation process had flipped Dana over because her feet were wrapped around his head. As they slid out of the broad trunk, Owen tried to reach back to cushion her head when it emerged, but it was awkward, the skin was slimy, and she fell through his grasp on to the forest carpet. At least it was moss. He scrambled around to inspect her condition. She was unconscious but breathing, with a regular heartbeat, and appeared no worse for the transport. Relieved, he couldn't help but admire the form of her body, trim and strong. It didn't seem right to stare but his eyes lingered before looking away in guilt. She was a beautiful woman; there was nothing more to confirm about that.

He wanted to connect with the forest mind, through the Thorns, if possible, in order to help Dana. He arranged her into a more comfortable position with her head resting on a pillow of thick moss. Her face was relaxed, and Owen hoped that she would awake refreshed. He bent over and kissed her lightly on the lips, then stood to investigate the surroundings.

The forest floor featured open spaces between giant trees that rose into a distant over story, completely obscuring the sky. It resembled the place he'd landed in the first time he saw this world, although he recognized nothing specific, and he felt certain it wasn't the exact spot. Given what he knew, they could be a hundred yards or a hundred miles away from where he'd been. A barely perceptible breeze whispered through the forest, accentuating the silence. He saw no movement, large or small. The diffuse but strong light hinted that the sun soared high overhead, suggesting many hours left in the day. It was warmer than it had been before, a welcome change from the Maine winter. He turned in a full circle, scanning the trunks for the arcing shapes of the Thorns bounding down a tree. The impassive forest stared back. He closed his eyes and tried to open his thoughts to the rhizome mind. When he connected, he heard a rumble of a thousand threads of sound, like eavesdropping on the overlapping conversations of a vast city. Nothing was distinctive in the overwhelming roar, so he opened his eyes.

Well, he thought, I can always yell, maybe that'll work. He bellowed at the top of his lungs. "REDTHORN! BLACKTHORN! WHITETHORN?" Nothing moved. He repeated the call, feeling a bit silly. But he didn't know what else to do. He recognized that without a guide, this venture into the forest world might be more of a challenge than he had anticipated.

He heard a faint coughing sound and spun around, but he couldn't locate the source. "Hello?" he whispered.

The coughing repeated itself, a bit louder, and suddenly the largest dragonfly Owen had ever seen detached itself from the trunk of the portal tree and flew straight at him. Owen jerked back but the creature halted in a stationary hover, inches away from Owen's face. Its brown coloration had camouflaged it against the tree bark despite the ten-inch wingspan. Rather than the visage of an insect, it had a vaguely humanoid face. It scratched its nose with one of the forelegs and squeaked out a few words. "Redthorn! Bluethorn! Pinkthorn! What? Are you trying to wake the dead? Can't you see it's nap time?" The features of this whatever-it-was were human enough for it to muster an accusatory look.

The aggressive sarcasm took Owen off guard. "Oh, sorry. Just seeking old friends. Wasn't quite sure how to go about it. Have you seen them? Not sure they're still around. Marmoset sort of things, answer to names ending in Thorn – or at least that's what I call them."

The dragonfly sneered. "Oh, you and your Thorns. Good grief. You silly creature, have you learned nothing? It's all Thorn. Everything! All connected! We had hoped you might prove to be less dense. But enough chit chat: how is the progress with the virus transmission?"

"What?"

"Oh heavens, have we lost our wits, have we?" And the dragonfly used the tip of a foreleg to start beating itself in the head.

Dumbfounded, Owen sat down and put his hand on Dana's arm, an anchor to the familiar. Maybe it had been a mistake to return.

[26]

The dragonfly dropped from mid-air and landed on Dana's belly. Owen wanted to slap it away but decided against it. Probably no accident that the creature appeared on the portal tree. Obviously, no matter how unappealing, it was another representative of the forest. Owen took a deep breath and started over.

"Sorry to disturb nap time. A thousand apologies."

"Accepted," the dragonfly said with an exasperated look.

"Can you help me with my friend here? Please?"

"Oh, she's fine. She'll come to, eventually. So, did you have an answer to our question? The one about the virus? It hasn't slipped your mind?"

Owen struggled to sort the dragonfly's barrage. "Uh, yeah. I mean, no, it hasn't slipped my mind and I do have an answer. I'm just concerned about Dana, that's all. That's her name. Dana."

The dragonfly began to click together the tips of its forelegs, drumming a nervous rhythm. "Very nice. So glad that you have names. We'll add it to the to do list, naming the fifty billion aspects of mind. Hard to imagine how we've gotten along without it." The sneer was back.

Owen found the relentless sarcasm annoying. "Okay, okay, you're the wittiest thing in the universe. I'm impressed, I really am."

"Ho ho! It jabs back!" The dragonfly lifted off from Dana's belly and darted to Owen's right arm, the one with the rhizome tattoo. "Straighten the arm, straighten it out!" It demanded. Owen obliged and the dragonfly frenetically danced the lines of the tattoo, rotating around Owen's arm, tracing the knotwork with one of its forelegs, oblivious to Owen's irritation. Once again, he was tempted to smack it, but again he resisted the urge.

The dragonfly abruptly stopped its inspection and flew to a hover point in front of Owen's face. "Sort of a rhizome, is it? Vastly simplified, of course, barely scratching the surface of the concept, hardly engaging with the true complexities, but nonetheless, a distinct hint of a rhizome. Not bad, not bad. So, what was your report?"

Owen blinked while he mulled over the possibility that he had just received a compliment. "Okay, the virus. Well, I've passed blood into a lot of trees. I have no way of measuring the impact at this point, but I don't see how I, personally, could have done more. So far, anyway. All in the New England region. I inoculated another human who travelled across the continent, spreading the virus. He's now on the West Coast of North America continuing the work. Or so I believe."

"That's it? Just the two of you?"

Owen felt a twinge of guilt. "Well, yeah. It's not that easy, you know. Like I told the Thorns, it might take time to get this thing going. Humans are shy about exposure to blood, so it requires a damn good pretext to get them inoculated with the virus. A scheme is needed – a scheme I don't have yet. Meanwhile, I'm sure Dana would help. She's a creative thinker and she'll generate useful ideas. However, she suffers with underlying emotional damage—the same as I did. I was hoping that she could get a neurochemical enhancement like mine. It's been no end of helpful in keeping my shit together. Listen, our world over there is an unholy mess. One of my friends, a wonderful man, died while trying to defend the forests. He was killed right in front of me. Frankly, it feels like war. I've needed the neuro-enhancements just to stay functional. I don't want to think what it would be like without them. But I need allies, and Dana is an ally. So, if the Thorns are available, I'd very much like to have something similar done for her. If that's possible."

The dragonfly hung in place with a blank expression while Owen spoke. Then it puckered its lips, turned its head, and spat some unsavory looking juice, just missing Owen's leg. "Two things. One, you're an idiot. But then, you've suspected that all along, haven't you? You don't need someone else to perform the enhancements; you can do it yourself. Two, what you call the Thorns were a manifestation of the forest mind, a node in the network. This form, too," it pointed at itself, "is a node in that network. It's also a Thorn, because, as you've been told: it's – all – connected. At this point, sad to say, even you are a Thorn. Your terminology may have outpaced its limits of utility. Unless you want to just name everything Thorn. Knock yourself out."

"Wait. What did you say? I can do the enhancements myself? How?"

"Oh, please. Look at your fingers."

Owen held up his right hand and looked at the fingers. Blunt with short nails, they looked like his fingers always did. But as he stared, he noticed that the seam under the nails was wider than usual. He brought them closer to his eyes and saw, wriggling in the seam, tiny tendrils like the ones he had seen on the Thorns' fingers. His stomach lurched and he felt a moment of panic. When did this happen?

He waved the fingers at the dragonfly, who had backed away a bit when Owen started flapping in agitation. "What *is* this? What's going on?"

The dragonfly began to pick its tiny teeth with a foreleg. "You were trending that way anyway, but the second transfer through the portal gave you a boost. No doubt you'll find them quite useful, if you can calm down long enough to learn a few things."

"God." Owen stared at his fingers, horrified. The tendrils probed into the space beyond the fingertips, like the tongues of snakes, extending to double the length of his digits. Paralyzed by the Medusa of his hand, he wanted to scream but he couldn't draw a breath. Blood surged in his veins with a pounding rhythm, one that he had heard before in the forest mind. Now it was inside and part of his body.

The dragonfly continued to pick its teeth, looking bored. It landed again on Dana's belly. "Just for laughs, try inserting your fingers in the dirt."

Owen followed the recommendation, or command, or whatever it was. As his fingers pushed into the moss, the tendrils plunged ahead down through the layers of soil. When they reached the mycorrhizae, each tendril wrapped around a filament of the network. Contact with the rhizome hyphae produced a moist sensation, like touching a rotting stick. He ignored squeamish associations and let his mind fill with awareness of the rhizome. This awareness activated his visual nerves and he could actually see a three-dimensional representation of the rhizome, much like it had appeared when the Thorns facilitated his link to the gravity nexus in the stone circle. He heard more than rhythms and music, there were also voices and fragments of phrases accompanied by images emerging from peripheral mist and dancing through the network before fading from view. Submerged in the sensory onslaught, he maneuvered his attention to focus on one thing at a time. By all rights the unfiltered input should have left him overwhelmed and disoriented. Instead, he had dropped into the fabled infinite library, a realm of unlimited promise and discovery. He recalled the words of Borges, "*The universe (which others call the Library) is composed of an indefinite, perhaps infinite number of hexagonal galleries.*" At the time he had thought it an amusing fantasy; now he was in it, or something like it if you replaced the hexagons with a chaotic geometry.

"Well?" he heard the dragonfly speak. "Do you get it yet?"

Reluctantly, Owen withdrew his fingers from the earth and watched as the tendrils retracted into his fingers. He turned his hand over and inspected it; it looked normal.

"Get what? The library?"

The dragonfly stopped fidgeting. "That's what you saw? A library?"

"Yeah. Kind of."

"Interesting. It is a library, in a way. It's much more than that, of course, but it is at least that. If you want to heal your companion, search the *library* for the information you need. Once you find it, use your fledgling tendrils: just probe into the Dana-thing and make a bridge between the relevant node and her need. Really, it's so simple even a human could do it. Though, to be fair, it's apparent that you're not entirely human anymore. In case you hadn't noticed."

"Not human anymore..." The implications stunned Owen. It had occurred to him that he was changing, but the changes had been less obvious than shoots growing from his fingers. Other than fussing with his hair, he had avoided thinking about it. "Why? What does that mean?"

"Ah, at last the mind starts to work! Congratulations! On the downside, haven't we gone over this stuff before?" The dragonfly took off from Dana's belly and landed on Owen's head, where it began scratching through his hair. He stifled the impulse to protest. After a moment, he relaxed and allowed himself to enjoy the gentle massage.

"What are you finding? Anything useful?"

"A tasty mite here and there." Owen heard a brief crunching sound. "Okay, do try to pay attention now; it may improve your feeble comprehension of Very Important Things. As you may or may not know, evolution moves through several mechanisms. One is natural selection, where the urge to survive sorts out those who can adapt from those who can't. Another is mutation, when the recombination of genetic union can result in a new type of being. The most radical mechanism, though, is symbiogenesis, when entities join into mutual associations that configure an entirely new life-form. This was how life began in most universes. The forest mind is a product of symbiogenesis, where a multiplicity of beings is linked into a vast holobiont that becomes another type of being."

"Holobiont?"

"Yes. Humans get lost in the contemplation of species, but, in truth, there are no species, at least, not in the sense that humans use that word: beings utterly distinct from others. No, there are only assemblies of beings, which are called holobionts. You, yourself are an assembly of beings; in fact, it's been your biological reality since birth."

"How so?"

"Consider the thousand different life-forms that live in your digestive system, for example, without which you would have been dead long ago. Many systems of your body require symbiotic associations with other creatures, especially bacteria. Thus, you're not a discrete little package of humanity—more like a small world masquerading as an individual. A holobiont. When we address 'you,' we speak to the multitude."

Owen scratched his beard and tried to absorb the data. "Okay, as one holobiont to another, tell me: am I going to see the old Thorns, you know, the trio that I was with before?"

"Doubtful."

"So… does that mean that you're the only guide this time?"

"Whoa, kid, don't kill yourself with gratitude. This isn't exactly a plum assignment, you know. Escort the dim-wits; make sure they get back to where they belong. Beings aren't lining up for the privilege—but that probably never occurred to you."

Owen felt a twinge of guilt, but the dragonfly's melodrama made him burst out laughing. The creature sprang into the air with an offended look and returned to Dana's belly.

"Sorry to startle you. But, you know, your charm—I guess we could call it that—is kind of growing on me."

"Not required. The Odonata form, or dragonfly in your parlance, has been generated for the benefit of you and your companion while you're here. The forest mind maintains a certain fondness for you, although don't let it go to your head—the sum of that fondness doesn't average evenly across the rhizome."

"What does that mean?"

"This was explained before, but given the porous nature of your brain, let's review. The forest mind is a totality in the form of a multiplicity, not a unity. The total system occupies geographical space and its processes ebb and flow unevenly. Although energy is distributed across the system somewhat equitably, many things are not. Different nodes present different characteristics. The system is everywhere linked, but it is not everywhere the same."

"I get a headache trying to encompass that multiplicity stuff."

"Well, poor you—you can't function beyond the wiring of your brain. Trying to conceptualize a collectivity from the perspective of an individual is like trying to imagine four dimensions in a world of three. You're tethered to your limitations—we'll give you that. Though that should change, too. Anyway, the Odonata form has been generated because the forest mind is trying to express the fluid and multiple nature of being. But as was said before, it's all Thorns, if you care to open your eyes."

Owen massaged his cheeks, tired from the effort of thinking. He couldn't, on command, stretch his single-minded human brain into an ecological topology. The struggle reminded him of his efforts to understand string theory and the eleventh dimension, an endeavor that absorbed a lot of his time, without much success, after returning from the first trip.

"Okay, then. So, you're still a Thorn. Look, I'm trying to wrap myself around these complexities, even if it is the task of Sisyphus. However, in the spirit of common ground, I'll call you Thorn, too, even though you're not at all like the first Thorns."

"Whatever floats your boat." The dragonfly looked miffed and flew from Dana's belly to the tree, where it blended with the bark so well that Owen strained his eyes to make out its form. He thought about apologizing, though for what he wasn't sure. The temperamental creature looked dormant, and for now, Owen saw no reason to risk further offense.

He turned his attention to Dana and what he could do for her. It was weird to learn that his body had changed so much that he didn't need anyone else to alter her neurochemistry. Who was he becoming, anyway? He felt detached from the old familiarity of self, but he wasn't upset. Might as well embrace it, he thought.

What had Dana said at their first meeting about him seeming to be "not quite human?" Well, he had never wanted to belong to the species. Better to be a tree or rock far off in the wilderness, or an eagle soaring into the sun. Anything to separate himself from the cruelty and evil of humans. Now it was too late to wish for anything else.

He plunged his fingers into the moss alongside Dana's torso, both hands this time, and felt the tendrils whip out, drive through the soil, and grab fast to the rhizome. This time he used the meditation techniques Dr. Chouinard had taught him, focusing the breath, straightening his spine, relaxing muscles and nerves to welcome the full tide of energy as it flooded his body. As before, the information flow dazzled him at first, but the techniques helped establish a balance. Like paddling a kayak on confused seas, he shifted his center of gravity in rhythm with the pulls and pushes of current, riding steadily through the chaos. The more relaxed his body, the easier it was. And then vast sections of the rhizome resolved into focus: the images formed a tapestry, the rhythms a music, and he coursed along the pathways of the network like he belonged there.

Despite a clearer vision of the rhizome, much of the array and contents remained obscure. It might be an infinite library, but one without an index. He only needed one book, though, the one with information to heal Dana. Finding that book could be worse than hunting a needle in a haystack; he lacked a search method, something other than aimless wandering through the network. However, even one book might be too much. He thought about Eco's notion of what he called the Maximal Encyclopedia: the compendium that contains everything, even the material that has been deleted. Contemplating such a resource could bring on Vertigo of the Labyrinth—also Eco's language—the dizziness that follows an attempt to comprehend the infinite. To prevent this vertigo, you had to ignore the seduction of the totality and accept that it was okay for most of the contents to remain latent within the whole. Just learn how to retrieve what was needed without wading through everything all at once. If only he could decipher the catalog code of the rhizome. Unfortunately, he didn't know what he needed to know, a troubling paradox. Well, he could only start from where he was, namely wallowing in the random presentation of the system. But it wasn't random, not really, it still had a topology; it occupied space and his location was specific. He perceived the strands that connected to the portal tree, the tree only a few feet from his seated form and Dana's supine body. He followed these strands with his mind's eye, into the tree and up its trunk, sensing the new Thorn on the bark, and continued to rise through the network of arboreal cells. As he passed Thorn, he realized that the dragonfly echoed the essence of the tree itself; it was the same thing. Well, that's what they had said all along. He let his consciousness ascend the tree, surging through each branch to the crown and tip, where he burst into the realm of photosynthesis. He devoured sunlight for a glorious instant like a fish at the apex of its leap from the water. Then he dove back into the tree, sliding down to the pool of roots and the mycorrhizal network.

Exhilarated, he devised another experiment: the location of edible mushrooms. Holding this task at the front of his mind like a mantra, he saw the rhizome, in response, coalesce into a three-dimensional circuit diagram receding to a foggy distance. In the foreground scattered lights blinked on, pulsing green and blue. Sending his attention along the network to the lights brought him to mushrooms in every case. He had asked for information and it was delivered. As soon as he understood this, he saw that the rhizome was a map as well as a library. He could navigate this resource through the focus of his thoughts. No need to crack a code: all he had to do was generate a question and feed it into the rhizome. In response, the map would unfold.

A healing menu was not a simple request, however, and required thoughtful construction. He cleared his mind and identified the psychological elements necessary to heal from trauma, applying the analysis taught him by Dr. Chouinard. He assigned each element an approximate semiotic representation. He separated these signs, holding them within a discreet mental space, and ordered them into a structure like a molecule, a structure that formed an icon of his more complex message. He reviewed the elements and experimented with the order within the structure, seeking a graphic harmony that best captured his requirements. The work was both analytical and aesthetic. He surprised himself with his facility for the task, but it was an extension of his previous work with images, symbols, and myths, a new use for his obscure knowledge. After many trial assemblies, he settled on one; imperfect like all signs, but as close to a distilled version of his message as he could achieve. He moved through the icon to inspect the handiwork, painting the bonds with love for a finishing touch. With a gentle release, he let it slip out of his mind and into the rhizome. The icon blended into the information flow, dissolving into micro-replications of itself, and dispersed throughout the network.

Owen watched the pulsing rhizome, waiting to see how it handled his request. His assembled icon was no longer distinguishable from the background flow. Trusting that things were happening in the tangled system he synchronized his breath with the rhizome and drifted into meditation. Time passed, then far off in the network he noticed a new pulse, a bright golden node. As he watched, it slowly moved his way, meandering through the rhizome like a slow train in the night. It came to rest at the tip of one of his tendrils. He extended awareness into it, easing through the membrane of light that formed the node's boundary. Within the node he encountered a micro-labyrinth of signs and icons woven into a pattern that reminded him of a Persian rug. This was the healing array for Dana, formatted to guide her recovery.

Excited, he surfaced from the rhizome, breaching back into the forest, blowing out the excess like a whale while swallowing mouthfuls of air. Then he heard the sarcasm. "Hark. What manner of beast is this? And there's another nap gone to hell."

Owen snorted at the dragonfly's humor, which he admitted was funny if you didn't mind the sarcasm. "Wow. That was radical! How long was I out?"

"Out? Or in? Either way, we've had two days of blessed silence around here."

"Two days?" Owen looked down at Dana before swiveling his head to scan the timeless forest. It was daylight of an uncertain hour. His gaze returned to Dana. He admired her for a moment, noting that she looked blissful and unchanged, until he detected some movement in her pubic hair. He bent closer and saw ants crawling in and out of the curly thatch and along the genitals of the woman he was supposed to be protecting. "What the hell?"

He was about to start brushing them off when Thorn said, sternly, "We wouldn't do that if we were you."

Owen's hand stopped in mid-swipe. "What? Why not?"

"The ants are working on contract to keep your subject clean. They did the same for you, by the way, when you were unconscious. Waste production hardly stops with consciousness, it seems. Unless you want her to wake up mired in her own offal, it would be better to let them perform their service." Thorn flew from the tree to land on Dana's belly and peered down into her crotch, picking its teeth again. "Ah, they're doing a stellar job. Unless you'd rather tend to this duty yourself?"

Owen sat back and shrugged. "No, I guess not. Not really. Did you actually use the word *stellar*?"

"Anything wrong with that? Your language is pretty grim stuff, frankly. We're just trying to spruce it up as best we can."

"No, it's fine. Dana uses that word. I like it."

"Well, score one for her, then."


[27]

Thorn lifted off from Dana's belly and flew to the top of Owen's head. "Are you satisfied with what you found in the rhizome?"

"You know, it's fucking fantastic in there!"

"Yes, as a matter of fact, we do know, since it is in fact us." Owen watched another arc of brown juice fly over his nose, just missing his feet.

"What is that stuff you keep spitting?"

"Waste products. Highly nutritious to some life-forms. Would you care for some?"

"I'll pass, thanks. Surprisingly, I'm not very hungry. I mean, we've been here for a couple of days already and I haven't eaten a thing."

"When you're tapped into the rhizome, it feeds you. It is, primarily, an energy web, and your tendrils allow you to pull sugars and other nutrients out of the network. But more to the point, you have an annoying habit of not answering questions. Did you find what you were looking for in the rhizome? To work on the Dana form?" Thorn resumed scratching Owen's scalp in search of mites.

"Yes, I think so. I'm learning how to interact with the network. It's not unlike our internet system, only the physics are elegant and you don't need a hardware interface."

"Thou art that."

Owen recognized the phrase translated from Vedantic scripture but wasn't sure if Thorn used it to annoy him, show off, or as a teaching moment. He chose to ignore it. "Anyway, pretty sure I have what I need. Might as well get to it, then. I'm eager to bring her back."

"Don't mind us."

"Any idea how long this process will take?"

"Depends. There are too many variables for precise estimation. The only thing to be said with certainty is that it takes as long as it takes. *Tat tvam asi.* You'll be conscious during the process so you can monitor the passage of time if that's important to you. We'll be around to keep an eye on things. Don't worry – despite your usual bumbling, you remain a valuable commodity." Thorn crunched a mite and flew back to the trunk of the tree, where it again blended out of sight.

Owen found the repetition of the phrase pompous, this time in the original Sanskrit, and though he was tempted to craft a rejoinder, he forced himself to stay focused. "Where on Dana's body is the best place for this... operation? I guess that's as good a word as any."

"X marks the spot." Thorn turned its head to unleash another stream of juice that flew over Dana's chest to splash down as a viscous puddle in the center of her belly, just above her navel.

"Gross, man. What did you do that for?"

"You'll find that it makes an exceptional lubricant." Thorn vibrated its wings rapidly, then stilled and faded into the bark. Careful study was required to detect even the faintest outline of the dragonfly shape. Owen shrugged his shoulders, dipped a finger in the Thorn juice on Dana's abdomen, and brought it to his nose. Almost odorless, its texture reminded him of olive oil. He sighed in resignation. It was time to get to work. He looked forward to having a less demanding conversational companion.

Owen crossed his legs and scooted close to Dana. He placed his right hand carefully on the center of her smooth belly. He liked the feel of her skin and he allowed himself a moment to stare. He wanted her; there was no question about that. Closing his eyes to clear the distraction, he put his left hand on the ground and willed the tendrils to seek the rhizome. Effort was hardly necessary as the thin white strands slipped out of his fingers and into the dirt. He wondered how much of his being was still his own and how much was dispersed into a multiplicity beyond comprehension. Whatever the answer, it didn't change his resolve. Linked to the rhizome, he saw that the golden healing node had drifted slightly away from where he had left it. He gathered it up and pulled it back, close to the surface, and anchored it by weaving it into a mycorrhizal cage. He then guided his tendrils to penetrate into the node and initiate an outward flow of data. Starting slowly, the flow accelerated as a rising tide of energy, bringing with it vibrating harmonics that filled his being. He stirred the fingers of his right hand in the slick juice on Dana's belly. When the tendrils slid out and penetrated her skin, it happened so easily that he wondered if there was a cellular hunger for the connection.

Dana's internal landscape consisted of tightly woven muscle and nerve cells instead of the looser vegetable or fungoid tissue he navigated in the rhizome. The progress of his awareness through her system was slow. Finally, his tendrils found the nexus of nerves within her digestive system and attached to it. The flow of data from the healing node coursed its way through Owen and into Dana like a downhill rush. Membranes opened to welcome the flood of information. Owen was the bridge. This produced a pleasant sensation in his body, like laying in a creek bed on a sunny day and feeling the clear, cool water pass over the skin.

Wallowing in the data stream mesmerized him, but once he adjusted to the passive role, his awareness expanded to the surroundings, just as Thorn predicted. There wasn't much to see, though, outside the passage of the sun's light and the occasional insect, several of which bit him. A few times he saw Thorn dive from the tree trunk and pluck out of midair a mosquito homing in on Dana's face. Time flattened into a moment or an eternity, Owen couldn't tell the difference. None of it mattered, only the healing flow. He absorbed the interwoven beauty of the forest, perceived through his senses above and below ground, and he savored the complexities like a multi-course feast.

Days went by in a trance-like progression of sunlight and darkness before Dana showed signs of reviving. Attuned to her presence, he sensed an uptick of energy in her nerves. Her muscles twitched and flexed, barely perceptible to sight. Then, with no other warning, her eyes opened, and she looked at him. He smiled broadly and tried to adopt a cheery tone while wondering how she would be. "Hello, Dana. Welcome to a new world."

At first, she stared at him blankly, finally adding a thin smile. Glancing down her body, Owen's fingers buried two knuckles deep within her midriff caught her attention and she frowned. Clearing her throat, she looked at his face and asked in a weak voice, "Is this some new type of intercourse?"

Well, Owen thought, she wasn't screaming at him or thrashing in panic. Had the healing worked? Owen remembered how easily it had been for him to accept the experience of waking up with someone's digits in your body; despite how weird it was, he had accepted it as the most natural thing in the world. Owen retracted his fingers and tendrils from Dana and the ground, carefully wiping the greasy residue on the moss. She watched with curiosity. As soon as he was done, he bent and kissed her forehead.

"Sorry to take liberties. I'll explain more, but first: how do you feel?"

"I feel like a proper kiss would be a better way to greet a woman emerging from a coma, not a chaste peck on the head. Especially since you've apparently had your way with me. How long was I out?"

Owen needed no further encouragement; he covered her mouth with his. She returned the kiss, reaching her arms up and around his neck. A cramp in her elbow produced a grunt and they released the kiss in laughter. "Help me up, would you?"

Owen assisted and she leaned back against the trunk of the tree. She lifted one leg then the other, stretched her arms over her head, tilted head and torso, and shook her limbs to bring the blood back into her muscles. Owen watched every move, then answered her question. "Five days. You were out for five days, about. I might have missed one."

"You might have missed one? I thought you were gonna be the big protector. What happened to that?" Owen opened his mouth to offer an explanation, but he didn't get further than "Uhh..." before she put a finger on his lips. "Just kiss me again. I'll entertain your excuses later."

As they embraced and kissed, Owen felt a wild rush of excitement from the raw contact. He felt her acceptance of his touch and with his hands he suggested other things they might do, but she gently pushed him away. "I feel good, Owen. Really good. Better than I've ever felt, like I could run up and down this tree in an instant. And it's delightful to be in your arms, enjoying the closeness, and I don't feel the slightest bit jumpy about it. And... look, I don't mean to frustrate you, but I just got here, right? I want to know more about where we are, what happened, what we're doing, everything. Everything! Tell me, Owen. Please. And is there anything to drink? I feel like I could drink a bucket. Later we can play." She smiled again. He couldn't resist; he would give her anything she wanted.

He stood up and offered a hand, although she seemed fully re-covered. She accepted and bounced upright, leaning against him for a moment. With a firm grip on his shoulder, she scanned the forest. Owen studied the geography during his rhizome explo-rations and had learned that they weren't far from the first portal tree, which meant that it wasn't far to the stream that ran down from the ridge. He pointed through the woods.

"Stream's not far."

Dana craned her neck to peer into the forest canopy, then bent her knees and leaned back so she could sustain the perspec-tive. Awe was in her face as she gauged the scale. While she turned slowly in a circle, inspecting the surroundings, Owen again ad-mired her, barely able to corral his runaway thoughts. Entranced, Dana kept circling like a lighthouse beacon trying to penetrate the splendor of the forest.

"Owen, this is amazing! These trees are so huge! I've never seen anything like them! They even dwarf the giant sequoia, and that's saying something. We really are in another world, right? I can't believe it, yet I can see that we're definitely not in Kansas anymore... Wow, I don't even know where to begin. I want to see it all and do everything at once! But I'm damned thirsty. I sup-pose water is as good a place as any to start. Which way, again?"

Owen pointed and they started in that direction, then he stopped and called over his shoulder. "Thorn! You coming?"

Dana spun around to see where he was aiming his words. "The Thorns are here?"

The dragonfly barely looked up from its somnolent perch on the tree. "Neither one of you seems to have the slightest idea of how nap time works. Probably a waste of time to explain it. But briefly, it goes like this: we go to sleep, then we wake up... when we're ready. Being yanked out of sleep by an off-key marching band isn't the same thing as waking up when ready. Not to belabor the obvious."

Dana saw Thorn hanging upside down on the bark of the tree and she rushed over to get a closer look. "Oh god, isn't it adorable?" As if to provide a rejoinder, Thorn ejected a quick jet of brown juice. This didn't faze Dana in the least, even though some of it splashed on her toes. She looked in Thorn's face and commented, "You're not even remotely a marmoset."

"Neither are you."

Dana smiled at Thorn. "If you think you're gonna intimidate me with that smartass mouth, well, save your breath. Been there, done that."

Thorn stared back at Dana for an uncomfortable spell. Finally, it spoke. "Run along, children, and play. If you need help, you know where to find it." It went still, and as it stopped talking, it blended into the bark and became almost invisible.

Owen had watched the exchange with amusement. When Dana turned back to him, brow arched, Owen shrugged. "So, this time, instead of three cute marmosets for guides, we get this guy. I've been assured that it's all the same mind, though, for what that's worth. I guess we don't have a choice. Anyway, let's go find some water and food."

"Suits me."

"Hey, speaking of suits, if we want clothes, we should probably prevail on Thorn to get us some fabric, even though it does appear to be nap time for Mr. Cranky."

"I'm kind of digging this *au naturel* thing, believe it or not. The air here is delicious; I love the feel of it on my skin. It's kind of mythic, don't you think, like we're in the Garden of Eden? Besides, something tells me you don't really mind, right?" Dana looked slyly at Owen out of the corner of her eye.

Owen blushed and nodded slightly, glad to walk rather than fidget. Dana kept halting to look around, taking in the majesty of the forest as if she wanted to consume it. Owen rekindled his own awe of this world through hers, aware that the vicarious pleasure was another manifestation of his deepening affection for her. He felt lucky.

"So, Owen, what's the story with Thorn? Aside from the fact that he's definitely not a marmoset, he's also not quite as charming as you described. Kind of a pain in the ass, actually, though I wasn't going to give him the satisfaction of showing my annoyance."

"Yeah, I know what you mean. Though this Thorn is kind of growing on me, to be honest. It's fairly witty, if you don't mind the nastiness. It's not really a *him* because it doesn't have sex or gender, so I just call it an *it*, although there's so much personality with these nodes that it's hard not to think of them as distinct characters. As far as I can tell, these Thorn things aren't separate entities. The forest manifests them for specific purposes, such as guiding us, but they're temporary manifestations. The three Thorns I met before compared themselves to tree leaves or seeds that are produced, do a job, then fade away. This Thorn is different in appearance and temperament because, I assume, it represents another node of the forest mind's multiplicity. I'm still trying to comprehend the implications. At first, I was overwhelmed, but as I've developed more skills of interaction within the rhizome, I've come to appreciate how a complex system can function without becoming a unity. It's kind of an anarchistic thing, you could say."

As they strolled, Owen explained what happened after they came through the portal, what he had learned in his explorations of the rhizome, and how he had worked on Dana. She listened while they wandered around the great boles of the trees, sometimes grunting or nodding in response, and waited until he finished to comment. "Thank you, Owen, for everything. I have to say the whole thing is so bizarre it's hard to imagine talking about it with anyone back home. I can see why you kept so much to yourself. I feel honored that you shared it with me. Of course, when I stuck my hand in that tree back at your place, I didn't give you much choice." She paused to scrunch her face and rub the top of her head. "You know, for the first time in my life it seems that words are inadequate to express what I'm feeling. I'm like a new woman. Rambling amongst these trees, holding hands with a gorgeous naked man, talking to a dragonfly, it's like a dream of paradise. And I keep getting these odd inklings, like fragments of *déjà vu*, that make me think I have actually dreamed this, or imagined it in a vision, or a trance... There's a familiarity to it."

"Maybe because it's archetypal. When I was here before, I saw my old therapist in ephemeral visions, like she lived here. And the Thorns said some odd things, like maybe she *was* here. They even suggested that Carl Jung was part of the rhizome. I dunno. It's a strange place. The boundaries between the mind and physical reality aren't clear at all. No wonder, given that the whole forest is a mind. In our reality, right now, we walk around the elements of this mind as if it were a park. Linking directly to the rhizome, mind to mind, reveals it as it really is, not a metaphor or abstraction, but a thing that occupies space and matter as well as consciousness."

"The music that I heard when my hand was in the tree – was that the same kind of link?"

"Yes, only what you heard were snatches of the whole. Try to imagine what it's like to commune with the entire symphony. Then imagine being in a space where hundreds of symphonies are playing, creating layers of sound that are different, yet still work together."

"Oh, I want that!"

Owen thought for a moment. "Perhaps we should go back to the places I saw before. It seems like we're pretty much on our own, anyway. Then you could see the devastation of the bleached zone for yourself. And if we go there, it's not far to the stone circle and an unfiltered encounter with the mind. That jaunt was the Thorns' cram course, part of the recruiting pitch. No reason why you shouldn't do it, too, as long as you're up for it, of course. Involves a fair amount of walking, but I didn't need boots or anything. The seasons are reversed, I believe, so it's warm enough that I guess we don't need clothes for protection. Bugs aren't that bad."

"Definitely bearable. And yes to the itinerary. I want to see and experience what you did, as much as possible. Understanding how all this works is important to me."

They stopped at the stream, which carved a gentle course through the forest just as Owen had remembered it. The banks were lush with moss, lichen, and ferns. Without a word, they dropped to their knees and bent over to suck in gulps of clear water. They grinned at each other as water dripped from their chins. Owen took a few steps to a nearby trunk and broke off a couple of thin orange polypores. He chewed one and handed the other to Dana, who watched him work his jaws. She tasted the polypore cautiously, then with more determination as it became obvious that dainty nibbles would not suffice. A few bites later she announced, "Ritz crackers."

"Yeah, that's what I thought. More nourishing, though. You can practically live off this stuff."

"Mmfff." Dana chewed the fungus with vigor. Owen wandered a few steps upstream, thinking about the route to the bleached zone. He looked back to see Dana foraging a little way downstream. She seemed utterly at home in this world. He again thanked all the gods, spirits, and blind luck that helped to bring them together.

"Hey, Owen. Come see this." Dana stood still, pointing at something through the woods, so he jogged over. Following her outstretched arm, he saw what had drawn her attention: a hut.

[28]

Damn—a hut, Owen thought. On one level he was flabbergasted, but his reason told him he shouldn't be surprised. He knew that the primates in the overstory could probably make such a thing. Maybe there were other beings that he hadn't been told about. What he didn't know about this world could fill an infinite library. He had just assumed that the forest was all. Was it? When he'd been at this spot before, it had no dwelling. Where did it come from? And why here?

Dana stood close to him and sensed his agitation. She turned to study his face. "What does this mean, Owen? You never said anything about other people."

"I don't know what it means. Let's go find out." Taking her hand, they walked together along the creek, separating to leap over it as they approached the hut. Tucked between the protruding roots of a giant tree, the hut wasn't much larger than a camping tent, with vertical walls, a domed roof, and an exterior of bark shingles. The shingles resembled birch, a type of tree he had only seen high on the ridge; Owen thought that someone went to a lot of trouble for building materials. The hut appeared well-made, with the shingles lapped and joined in a way that would shed a rainstorm. A flap of heavy fabric hung over the entrance. Silent, they stood in front of the door and looked at each other. Owen called out "Hello?" twice. After no response to the second greeting, he bent down and pulled back the flap. Within the dappled light of the interior, Dr. Chouinard sat cross-legged on the dirt floor, clad in her familiar red cape pulled around her like a robe, head down, intent on craftwork. A parfleche of tools lay unfolded on her lap. It looked exactly like the pouch Owen had been given by the people in the trees.

He couldn't speak. Dana shouldered into the doorway next to him, and looked back and forth between the two. Kneeling, Owen put both hands on Dr. Chouinard's knees as tears rolled down his cheeks. "Dr. Chouinard! I can't believe you're here! I... I thought you were dead?" He hardly knew what to say; after all, he had been at her funeral a year ago. Despite his entreaty, the doctor did not respond and continued with her craft. "Dr. Chouinard, it's me! Owen!" He felt a disjointed panic, as if reality fractured, leaving him on the other side. Sitting back on his heels, he turned to Dana, the agony plain on his face. She knelt behind him and put her arms around his chest, pulling him to her. Owen fell into her embrace and let his head slump against her chest. At that moment Dr. Chouinard paused the work and raised her eyes to look directly at Dana. The doctor's focus drove through her to a distant point outside the hut, leaving Dana with a sensation of transparency. Time stopped for a moment, then the doctor bent back to her work.

"Owen, whatever is happening here, I think we've seen everything there is to see. Come, let's leave her to her work." Dana stood slowly, supporting Owen and dragging him backwards, a lifeguard move that required all her strength. She backed them out of the hut, reaching around Owen to close the flap over the door.

Owen blurted, "I don't even pretend to understand that."

Dana turned him until they faced away from the hut. "No, I can't imagine what that feels like. We have nothing in our experience to engage with that sort of phenomenon, unless you want to think of her as a ghost. But she seemed real to me. Maybe Thorn would know something about it."

Owen stood up straight and hugged her. "Thanks for pulling me out of there. Whatever that was, it's weird as hell. And yeah, might as well try our only resource. THORN!" He yelled across the creek in the general direction of the portal tree. Within a few minutes they saw the dragonfly darting this way and that through the trees, taking a wide zig-zag course that tested Owen's patience.

It landed on Owen's head and loosed a sigh. "Three moments from now would have been the start of nap time and you could have yelled until you were blue." It immediately set to picking through Owen's hair, stopping after a moment to make a crunching noise.

Dana watched Thorn closely. "Ewww, are you eating things from his hair?"

Thorn stopped pawing over Owen's scalp and turned to face Dana. "We're surprised you haven't gleaned all the tasty tidbits yourself. Sadly, your own hair is too short to support as many life-forms, though a few could be found, no doubt."

"They're just mites, Dana. Our bodies are covered with them. Too small for us to see. As annoying as it is to agree with Grand-master Odonata, I rather enjoy his scratching around. Feels good."

"If you say so. I think it's gross. But let's not get distracted."

Thorn spat a glob of juice. "Oh no, don't distract those brilliant brains – whatever would we do then?"

Owen turned around to face the hut. "What can you tell me about this structure and its inhabitant?"

"Oh, that. We were wondering if you were going to stumble across this little anomaly. Well, as you may have learned, it's Dr. Chouinard's hut."

"I think we figured out that much for ourselves – whatever it means to say that it's 'Dr. Chouinard's hut.' But I'm more interested in mechanical details, like how a person who died a year ago in my world ends up with some sort of life in this one. And if, indeed, what she has is life, why doesn't she interact with me?"

"Ah, so many angles of explanation. Where to begin?" And Thorn paused to pick its teeth.

Dana broke in. "Come on, buster. Out with it."

Thorn gave her a haughty glance. "All in good time, restless one. We're just trying to figure out how to provide an explanation that you might possibly grok."

"Grok? Did you say grok?"

"You heard us. Anyway, if there are no further interruptions..." Thorn leaned back on its rear legs and addressed the sky, as if it was delivering a lecture to an auditorium. "Even though the Dr. Chouinard that Owen knew did pass from her original biological form, it's important to keep two things in mind. One is that as a result of their relationship, she became a psychic introject in Owen's consciousness. He carries this introject as a functioning node within the rhizome of his own being. When Owen merged with the rhizome of this forest, a clone of the node was transplanted along with the other contents of Owen's mind. The clone is quite robust and has flourished here. Secondly, it's worth noting that the physical remains of Dr. Chouinard were converted to ashes and some of those ashes were scattered into the woods, by Owen's own hand, we understand. From that point, the ashes soaked down into the forest soil and were absorbed by the mycorrhizal network. The remains were transformed within the network into an essence of the original and transported to this world. This recycled essence reincorporated in our rhizome and eventually united with the previously downloaded psychic clone. The reunion of physical and psychological remnants then catalyzed the activation of a new material growth. Not surprisingly, this growth resembles the original form. The regeneration is a slow process and may never result in complete biological re-construction, but it's quite impressive so far." Thorn stopped and looked down on them as if expecting applause.

"My god," was all Owen could say.

"If you have a need to worship, go right ahead." Thorn preened itself.

Dana snorted. "He doesn't mean you, dummy."

Owen was excited with the implications of what he'd been told. "So, my memories of Dr. Chouinard have essentially been downloaded into the rhizome and reconstituted with her re-mains as a kind of autonomous being."

"Not precisely autonomous, but yes, something like that. The boundary of consciousness and physical matter is porous. In fact, those aren't really separate things. If you reduce these categories to an elementary level, as particles or strings or how-ever you want to envision them, they really are the same. It's use-ful to consider any so-called boundary as a porous membrane. Thought and matter are not different."

"Wow. That's cool. So, all those visions I've had of the doctor aren't just imaginary, they represent some kind of resonant vibra-tion within the rhizomatic systems."

"Watch out. Wouldn't want you to get a headache from too much thinking."

Owen ignored Thorn's taunt. "Will the doctor ever be able to interact with us?"

"Unknown. We'll just have to see. Each manifestation of this nature has its own arc of development."

Owen stepped toward the hut; Thorn sprang into the air and dropped on Dana's head. She flung her hand to swipe it away, caught herself and adjusted to scratch the back of her head as if that had been her intention. Owen stared at the doorway of the hut for a moment, then pulled back the flap and looked in. The apparition of Dr. Chouinard still sat in the same position, ignoring the intrusion.

He turned to Thorn, who closely inspected Dana's hair. "Please humor a metaphysical question, if it makes any sense. Is this the actual Dr. Chouinard, reconstituted from her original atoms, or something else as you implied—a clone or simulacrum derived from the recycled essence?"

"Yes. Some of each. Probably."

Dana, who had slumped her shoulders with relaxation under the scalp massage, opened her eyes. "Are we talking French philosophy again?"

Owen let the flap drop and stood up. "More like Philip K. Dick, I think."

"I've heard of him. Never did get into science fiction."

"An old passion of mine. I have to say it's been good preparation for traveling into alternate universes."

"I don't doubt that."

"So, to recap, Dr. Chouinard is here in some form, possibly to develop into more of herself as she was when she was alive. Well, I guess she's still alive, sort of. The upshot is that none of us, including the almighty forest mind, knows how it's gonna play out."

Thorn stopped foraging on Dana's head and looked up. "Was there a question?"

"No, I guess not. Doesn't seem to be much we can do about it, one way or the other. Anyway, I was thinking that it might be helpful for Dana to see the bleached zone and the stone circle, just to further her education, or training, or whatever you want to call it."

Thorn, intent on its grooming of Dana's head, kept at the scratching while answering Owen's query. "A generally acceptable agenda. Unfortunately, the bleached zone expanded and over-ran the nexus circle. The old stump of the circle was bio-terminated, and its multiple world links were severed. We have serious concerns that the toxin may have spread into the worlds connected through that link, though we've not been able to confirm that."

"What? You didn't say anything about this! That's an enormous loss."

"We think so. It's a link that has been sustained for a hundred thousand years."

Dana whispered to Thorn. "Stop scratching, you're putting me to sleep." Thorn obliged and returned to Owen's head. Dana rubbed the back of her neck and continued. "Owen told me about his experience at this circle, the nexus, as you call it. It sounded wondrous: a living connection between multiple universes. It's difficult enough to imagine one other universe, but several... and all linked at one place! That would be precious beyond value. And now it's dead?"

"Very." Thorn expressed another stream of brown juice that splattered on the ground in front of Owen's feet. "The bleached zone is easy enough to find. As you may or may not remember, depending on your sharpness of recall, following the stream uphill will take you there. You won't have to go far because the boundary is well below the ridge top. Regarding communion with the rhizome, that's another thing you can do yourself. If you recall how it was done for you at the stone circle, you may be able to connect the dots and devise a method. Put on the old thinking cap, eh?"

Dana stood on her toes and leaned on Owen's shoulder, putting her face up to Thorn's. "Hey, be nice to him. That's my boyfriend you're talking to."

Thorn stared back at her, picking its teeth. "So you say." The two glared at each other for a moment before Dana crumpled in laughter. Owen didn't mind, all he heard was the word "boyfriend."

They stuffed themselves with mushrooms and drank as much water as they could before their journey to the ridge. Thorn perched on the top of the hut and watched them but said nothing. Before leaving, Owen lifted the door flap for one more look at Dr. Chouinard. On the dirt floor in front of her lay a finished product, a small satchel with a shoulder strap. Owen bent to his knees and looked at the doctor's face, still hoping for recognition. She was impassive, absorbed in her work. He picked up the satchel and thought that, at least, here was a sign of response. He wanted to believe that it was a gift for him. Plus, it was something they could really use. "Thank you," he said, then closed the flap.

"Whether she's entirely alive or not, her handiwork seems real enough," he said, waving the bag as he walked to a tree and began to harvest polypores.

Dana grinned and jumped to help fill the satchel. "That is so cool!"

With a portable supply of food and knowing water would be available along the way, they set off up the stream. Thorn flew to

Dana's head for the ride. As they wandered over the soft soil and moss carpets along the stream, Owen and Dana held hands when the going was easy, dropping their grip and shifting to single file when there were roots to climb over or massive trunks to circumvent. Owen led with a steady pace until Dana darted ahead, letting him catch up when she paused to admire the surroundings. Her movements were often quick and abrupt, causing Thorn to lift off, chase after her and land on her head as soon as she slowed down. Owen laughed at this, especially when Dana made a game out of it.

The ground angled upward as they followed the stream. Daylight waned and Owen proposed that they stop and spend the night. Sagging into a clump of moss next to the stream, they opened the satchel of mushrooms. Thorn muttered something about an overdue nap and flew off to the nearest tree, perching on the trunk and resuming its camouflage.

As they crunched the fungus, Dana turned one over and over in her hand, inspecting it like a rare gem. "You know, these things look like shit, but they aren't bad at all."

Owen snorted. "Yeah. Maybe not gourmet but definitely tolerable. And filling."

Dana chewed in agreement. By the time they finished eating and drinking the shadows of dusk occupied the forest. Snuggling between tree roots, they arranged themselves like rabbits in a burrow. Owen put his arm around Dana's shoulder and pulled her close. With her head on his chest, he used his free hand to ruffle and smooth her hair. Dana let him pet her into drowsiness until he spoke. "That was so weird, that stuff with Dr. Chouinard, or whatever that apparition was that we saw today. I'm not fully convinced that it really was her or even something derived from her. Of course, I want to believe it."

"Yeah, I could tell that was hard. Bittersweet at best. I know she meant a lot to you and to have her back, but not really back, must, in some ways, be more frustrating than not to have her at all." Dana wrapped her arm around his torso, hugging him tightly.

"Well, it brings up a lot of stuff. The basic theme of my life is loss, and losing the doctor was a serious blow. Made me crazy with grief. What Thorn said about her being an introject is interesting, though. I hadn't really looked at it like that, that a memory can develop a kind of autonomous reality inside your mind. But it makes sense. I feel like she has continued to guide me, even after death. Though I suppose a cynic could say that an introject has no autonomy, it's all just a coincidence of imagination and memory."

"Well, that's a rather impoverished way to look at things. Reality is often more magical than our literal dreary brains want to pretend, right? I think Thorn spoke the truth: the doctor took on a life within you, a life that you transferred to the mind of the rhizome."

"A sort of immortality, then, eh? I'm sure that would tickle the doctor's fancy."

Dana threw her leg over Owen's hips and he responded by sliding his hand down her back. "Hey, Owen, wanna hear a poem?"

"You bet."

"I wrote this a few years ago about women who go to the woods, looking for sanctuary. You might find it relevant. I'm not saying it explains anything about Dr. Chouinard or her presence here, but, then again, maybe it does. At any rate, I've been thinking about it ever since we left the hut."

"Okay! Let's hear it."

Dana recited the poem in a quiet voice, just loud enough for Owen to hear:

"The sisters dream to be in the woods, lost among the dark trees. They make a bed on the thick carpet of the forest. The blanket of leaves softens the echo of the outside world. The tall pines, sighing in the wind, stand guard as they always have, ancient fathers. This is a secret grove. People who are unkind, men who talk out of the side of their mouths, and women who laugh with empty eyes are forbidden. The long cool mornings, the sun that streams pale and then warm, and the pure river waters are for the sisters alone. The silence is liquid; the hours are longer than in the old life. There is time to write a poem. There is time to make a shadow puppet. There is time to begin again. There is no need to hide. The sisters dream."

When the poem ended, Owen realized that he'd been holding his breath. "That's amazing, Dana. Made the hairs stand on my neck. It's as if you've tapped into Dr. Chouinard—the spirit that retreated to the great forest to, as you say, 'begin again.' It's beautiful."

"A retreat to the forest of *your* mind, Owen. A place where she can make a new life."

"Well, thank you for the poem... and thank you for that thought."

Done with words, they cuddled together. The forest was heavy in silence and as the last light evaporated, they made love, slowly and carefully, taking immaculate time with the possibilities of touch. They explored each other with delight, finding their way toward exaltation, then exhaustion. When they finally lay still, they slept without dreams.

[29]

In the morning, Owen peered through heavy lids to look straight into Dana's gaze. He smiled and she twined her fingers in the waves of his hair. Winding a lock around her index finger, uncurling it with a stroke, she fiddled her way through his mane. Such adoration was a luxury for Owen, and he wanted to stay in the moment forever. "I love you," he whispered.

Dana smiled broadly. "I love you, too."

They savored the moment and made no moves to rise from their mossy bed until Thorn landed on the side of Dana's head, coming in heavier than usual and making a squishing noise as he touched down. "Such devotion! Such rapture! The dialogue is a little repetitive, but it's the thought that counts! Meanwhile, trees are dying, life forms fall into extinction, and suns go nova. We should get going as soon as possible. Nap time is over."

Dana peered at Thorn out of the corner of her eye and snarled. "Oh, look, it's the buzzkill bug. We should adopt it, dear, so we can send it to finishing school. It may be educated but its manners leave something to be desired."

Owen laughed as he scrambled up and helped Dana to her feet. Thorn crawled around her head to stay on top but left when she bent down to the stream to splash her face. They munched mushrooms from the satchel while Thorn darted around them, hovering in front of one face, then the other, back and forth in an aerial ballet of impatience.

They ignored the dragonfly as best they could, until finally Owen asked it to explain the agitation. "What happened to the patience and pace of the vegetable mind? The eternal moment and the timeless perspective? *Tat tvam asi*, as someone once told me."

"Bah, change and transformation happen at every possible rate and usually beyond the control of actors in the system. While you two were getting drunk on each other, a critical threshold was breached. Uphill the transformation is proceeding at an alarming pace. In fact, we don't recommend that you drink any more water from this stream."

"What? Why not?"

Dana grabbed Owen's shoulder. "Owen, look!"

They turned to the stream and saw that the water, only moments ago so clear that it resembled liquid glass, now ran milky, as if stirred with sediment. While they watched, the translucent white color gradually turned opaque gray. "Oh my god," Owen said, and they stared in paralyzed fascination as the water continued to darken until it ran a glossy black.

Dana broke the stasis. "What's going on, Thorn?"

Thorn abandoned its airborne position between them and flew across the stream. It zoomed back and forth over the water like a ping-pong ball, pausing to hover a few inches above the surface, then shooting twenty feet up in the air and plunging back down abruptly. Trying to follow its course was difficult. Finally, it returned and landed on Dana's head. "Listen up. We're witnessing another level of the disaster. The bleached zone has now overcome the source of the stream. You may remember that place from your previous visit; you remarked on it at the time, where the water emerges into a rocky pool. Well, it's pristine no longer. And worse, we've learned that the toxin is more than just an inert chemical compound: it behaves like a virus or cancer that's capable of self-replication and colonization of ecosystems. In this case it's expanded from the rhizome into the hydraulic system and is propagating itself with increased efficiency. Soon the shores of the stream will die the white death before spreading the toxin laterally into the forest. We may be approaching an avalanche point of consequences."

"What about Dr. Chouinard? She's just downstream!" Owen said.

"Don't worry, we're already taking care of her, moving her along to a safer area. Meanwhile, we've secured a contract with the ant guilds to divert and dam the flow."

"Ants?" Owen challenged.

"You'd be surprised how much work gets done when a million ants bear down on a problem, especially earth moving, a passion of theirs. Right now, it's our best chance to slow things down. If the trend continues, if this cascading transformation of metastasis finds its way to the ocean, it could mean the death of the entire world."

Dana paced to and fro, flinging her arms and stomping her feet. Thorn fled to the nearest tree for a perch. Owen stared at her with open mouth until she brought her war dance to a sudden halt. "Owen, we've got to go back! If there's anything we can do to stop this, let's get to it! I can't stand the idea of doing nothing."

Owen hadn't seen this side of her before, but he liked it. She was fierce and a spur to action. She'd be good in a jam, he could tell.

"Yes. You're right. I don't think you need to see more to be convinced of the importance of intervention. Thorn, can you take us to a portal tree, or should we just go back to the one we came through?"

"We agree with the Dana. We can likely slow down this new toxic surge, but we still don't know how to neutralize it. It becomes increasingly important to arrest the contamination from your world and cut it off at the source. That is something you must do. Our only other option is to sever the rhizome links to your world but we're not desperate enough to do that. Not yet."

Dana scratched her head. "Hey, what about trying to contain the bleached zone by creating your own neutral zone around it, like a firebreak? It may buy more time or even stop it completely. Like what they do to cancer tumors: remove them from the body. In this case you'd be taking the body away from the tumor."

Dana settled into a thoughtful stance and Thorn returned to its perch on her head. "That idea was considered when the toxin first intruded. We should have done it then. Now the sacrifice would be much greater. Can you understand that to do such a thing is a desperate self-mutilation? It would be like chopping off your hand because it was infected. We've held out hope for a better solution, one that keeps us integrated instead of fragmented. We wanted humans to correct their own mistakes."

Owen hung his head, feeling inadequate and ashamed. As his eyes grew wet, he looked up at Thorn and said, "I don't know what else I could have done."

Thorn flew back to Owen's head. "Don't take it all on yourself. You didn't create this problem. But we do need you to succeed. For us, everything's at stake. Meanwhile, we've just made the decision to pursue the radical surgery for containment. That operation is starting now: we're going to encircle the bleached zone by killing ourselves in a wide swath, severing all mycorrhizal links, all surface links, all ecological interaction to the best of our ability. As we stand here, roots are shriveling, and arbors are being drained of life. The impact on this region is uncertain, so let's make haste back to the portal tree that brought you through the brane. Should you come back here again, chances are it won't be to this place; it's a lost cause."

As they marched back to the tree, Owen felt the grief welling up from the ground. It sang to him through the bottoms of his feet. He thought of what it had been like in his own world to feel the ravages of logging from the rhizome perspective. Then he had shared the agony; it had been almost unbearable. This was worse. This was the mass suicide of every rooted life-form within a broad sector. Beyond a soulful grief, it proclaimed a holocaust, a torrent of sharp-edged pain. Owen sobbed as he walked. Dana took his hand for comfort and stiffened in shock, feeling the contagion of suffering flowing through Owen. Thorn, riding on Dana's head, registered the reaction of her body and abandoned the perch.

Owen stumbled and fell to the ground. "Fuck! This is too much!" He clutched at Dana.

She kneeled to cradle him and stroked his forehead. "Owen, darling, don't try to carry this alone. Can you share the burden with me? Let me help."

"You don't know what you're asking!" He wailed.

"Yes, I do. I want to feel what's going on. If I can't handle this, how am I going to understand?"

Owen couldn't dispute her reasoning. Gritting his teeth, he forced his body into order. After three slow, deep breaths, he asked her to lay down. When she was in position, he drove his left-hand fingers into the ground while pressing the right fingers to her abdomen. She put both hands over Owen's right, holding firm his connection to her. Tendrils slithered out of his fingers into her skin and linked Dana's nervous system to the rhizome. She cried with the impact of the tide of grief as it roared through her. Tears leaked out between her crimped lids. Perched on the nearest tree, Thorn watched the communion. Dana and Owen rocked together, giving themselves over to the waves of pain and stabilizing each other in the roiling current.

The link was momentary, but it seemed eternal. Enough, Owen decided, and withdrew the tendrils, prompting Dana to gasp and sit upright, still gripping his hand.

Grief distorted her face and she sat with muscles tensed. Gradually, she relaxed. Shaking her head, she muttered, "...beneath us was nothing now to be seen but a black tempest."

Owen looked at her, puzzled. "What?"

"Give me a minute while I activate my shields."

"I'm not sure I get that, either."

Dana rubbed her head with her palms and took several slow breaths. "Sorry, when my boundaries are down, I regurgitate allusions like a schizophrenic. Anyway, the first thing was Blake. From *The Marriage of Heaven and Hell*. Fucking Blake. That guy knew things, strange things. It's unnerving what you find in his work. You know, the preamble to that passage is kind of prophetic, at least in relation to us: *'So I remaind with him sitting in the twisted root of an oak. He was suspended in a fungus with the head downward into the deep...'* But then Blake was all about prophecy and mystery." Dana jumped up and gave Owen a hand. "Anyway. We've got work to do."

"When did Blake write that stuff?"

"Seventeen nineties sometime. I'm not very good with dates."

"Impressive. Seems like these intuitive types, like Blake and Jung and the others, had some kind of awareness of the rhizome all along."

"Looks that way, doesn't it?"

Thorn zipped down from its tree, lighting on Dana's head. "If you're done with the poetry colloquium, we might get on with the business of saving the world. If it's not a bother, that is."

They trooped the rest of the way to the portal tree. Owen still had the satchel made by Dr. Chouinard. He was reluctant to part with it, but since it wouldn't go through the portal, he hung it on the branch of a nearby bush. Thorn flew to perch high on the bark of the portal tree, well out of reach. Owen gave it a salute. "Thorn, thanks for the guidance. The insults have been insulting, but not really that bad, so thanks for them, too. I hope we can make a difference."

Dana blew a kiss to Thorn. "Bye, sweetheart. It's been real."

Thorn was silent; its insect shape faded away until they saw nothing at all. It seemed to be gone, and perhaps it was. "Thorn?" Owen called out quietly but there was no response. "Strange dude. Alright, my dear, are you ready?"

Dana nodded and they pressed themselves together, then leaned against the tree. It had no obvious furrow like the ash tree in Owen's woods, but its bark parted readily, exposing the sapwood, yielding like wet clay, opening for them, and pulling them into an engulfing embrace. Within seconds they were gone.


[30]

The tree pushed them out onto the snowy ground of their world, naked and alert. They scrambled upright and ran toward the house. Dana sprinted past Owen, but she couldn't remember where the keys were hidden and checked behind the wrong shutters. He grabbed both keys and raced around the corner. Shivering and anxious to get inside, he still drew up short on the front steps. A crude sign scrawled on a paper plate was taped to the door. It said, "LEAVE NOW OR DIE LATER FAGGOT." Underneath the child-like block printing was a rough caricature of Owen with a bullet going through his head. He snarled and ripped it down while Dana exclaimed "What the fuck?" But it was too cold for a discussion. They burst through the door and donned the clothes left on the couch. Owen did a quick tour of the house, looking for signs of intrusion but nothing seemed amiss. He turned up the thermostat on the central heat, then shoved paper scraps, including the death note, into the wood stove with some kindling and a lit wooden match.

"What was that about?" Dana demanded.

"The evil uncle, no doubt, or his minions. I'm sorry to expose you to this. Pretty good chance it'll get worse, too, I'm afraid. We need to be careful." Owen studied Dana's expression to gauge the impact of his words, worried again that he had dragged her into something beyond his control.

Dana looked determined. "I know the type, all too well. I'm not going anywhere, Owen. You may have gotten me into something, but it's important and I'm not running away. This bullshit needs to stop."

"I absolutely love how fierce you are."

She smiled at him. "That's just because it's not directed at you. Hey, any chance of a shower?"

"Go for it. I'll make us some food. Without mushrooms."

After Dana went upstairs, Owen stoked the stove, force feeding it to a roar. Satisfied, he moved into the kitchen to busy himself with meal preparations. Gratitude for Dana's presence filled his heart. His feelings were so strong that it made him ache to think that something bad could happen to her. But what could he do? It was like love during war time: intense, passionate, uncertain.

Hot food waited under a lid when Dana came down the stairs. Wrapped in a large towel, she went directly to the wood stove and leaned over it to soak up the radiance. He watched silently from the kitchen entrance until she turned her head and smiled at him. "Hey," she said.

He didn't hesitate. He charged in from the kitchen and took her in his arms, kissing her ears, neck, and cheeks before settling in on the lips. His restless hands explored her back, lifting the towel to find the bare skin of her bottom.

"Mmm," she said, "I like the way you touch me." She nuzzled for a moment and pulled back to see his face. "I can't believe I'm not leaping out of my skin! The old me would have clocked you by now. I'm feeling good, it's a turn-on, and there's no panic! Whatever you did to me in the other world, or the rhizome did, or whoever, it worked. I can't believe it! I know I said it before, but I feel like a new person. A woman, not a mouse!" She leaned forward and reattached her lips to his.

He resumed his exploration of her nether regions. The towel dropped to the floor. "Whatever you do, don't stop now," she murmured. He didn't. They made love on the couch in front of the stove while the food cooled in the kitchen.

The next morning, over breakfast, in between the loopy smiles and contented looks, Dana brought them back to earth. "I have an idea."

"Uh oh. Should I applaud or flee?"

"I said an idea, not a penal sentence. But it seems like we need some way to activate this virus on a bigger scale, right?" Owen nodded. "Obviously going door-to-door isn't going to get us very far. We need to accelerate our range of contact, and that means popular media. Which means the internet: the fastest distribution format ever devised."

"You mean we should sell the virus on Amazon or eBay?"

"Shut up. No, this is more than an idea, it's an inspiration! Now you said that I was inoculated with the virus along with all the other neurochemical tinkering, right?" Owen nodded again, deciding to follow her advice and listen. "And I remember you telling me about your crazy notion of starting a cult or something to get people involved. Well, I think you were right about that. That's exactly what we should do: start a cult."

He looked at her curiously. "How? It has to be a little more complicated than registering as an LLC."

Dana talked rapidly. "Hush. Now, I've got some friends down in Cambridge, a radical film-making collective. They call themselves the Artemis Pod—lesbians, right? Far out in a lot of ways, but really good people. Their philosophy is environmental, feminist, activist, and pagan. Believe me, they would comprehend the rhizome concept without a problem, in fact, you could say that they already believe in something like that. They try to embody collectivity in ways beyond the norm. I mean, they do *everything* together. I'll spare you the details because it's embarrassing. Anyway, one time we worked together on a project. It was a blast and the film was incredible: compelling, transcendent, and with a kick. They know their shit. So here's the idea: we enlist them to help us make a short video, something in the forest, something that presents the sharing of blood as a kind of ritual catharsis, something that appeals to the hunger that's out there in the world for magic and meaning. With a thunderous poetic soundtrack that puts it in perspective and drives it home! Blake, maybe, Anne Waldman, or one of those other ranters – no shortage in the poetic world. And then we post it on the internet: bingo, we have a social media profile."

Owen put down his cup of tea. "You know, that might actually work! That's... brilliant!" He darted around the table to give her an embrace and kisses on top of her head. She basked in the approval, smiling to herself, still deep in her schemes.

Dana sent an email to the Artemis Pod and made a pitch. A day later she received an enthusiastic response. Owen read the email over Dana's shoulder, and from the tone of the writing, which bounced back and forth in styles and voices, it was obvious they would jump at the chance to do something with Dana. It gave Owen another perspective on who she was in the world, clearly someone who generated respect. He thought about asking how intimate she had been with these women, but he decided that was a conversation with poor prospects. It wasn't really his business and he wasn't sure he wanted to know, anyway.

The email from the collective stated that they would get back to Dana as soon as they worked out a few fundamentals. The next day brought another lively message with specific proposals. They wanted to shoot the film in the Walden Pond woods; it had been a light winter in eastern Massachusetts and the ground was free of snow. The leafless trees offered dramatic contrast in their skeletal phase and winter conditions reduced the possibility of random walkers intruding on the set. They recommended the Emerson's Cliff area, a previous stage for some of their pagan rituals. All they needed was a script, which they expected Dana to provide. Owen liked the location; Dr. Chouinard had urged him to read Thoreau's masterpiece when he was still in high school and it had affirmed many of his outsider suspicions, not only about society, but about humanity at large. He liked to think that if Thoreau had a choice, he would want to be in the rhizome himself, and given what had happened to Dr. Chouinard, maybe he was. Dana dismissed Thoreau, whom she thought priggish, but if the collective recommended the pond as a site, she was all for it.

She plunged into work on the video. They agreed that it should be short, no more than five minutes, to accommodate the modern attention span. Saturated with mysticism, the video aimed for New Age appeal. Both Owen and Dana had a degree of guilt about the cynicism of this choice, but they both thought that, in this case, the end justified the means. If viewers suspended enough rational thinking to open up to an intuitive or induced state of communion, the message could be absorbed. Appealing to the science of their problem would complicate the task, requiring them to prove many things (such as the existence of alternate universes) that were beyond simple proof. And these days people were impatient with the plodding pace of scientific inquiry; they preferred instant explanations and magical reasoning. Besides, there was no need to convince everyone, they only required enough people to accept and spread the virus. Perhaps even a few hundred would be enough, surely not an impossible achievement. Dana had been to New Age events, and Owen had inspected the health supplements in local markets; there seemed to be no end to gullible consumers. One night they argued about the ethics of what they were doing, but the argument was half-hearted and petered out when they realized that the price of their deception was a price they were willing to pay. All it took was the memory of the stream in Thorn's world running black amidst the cries of a dying rhizome. And, in the end, their actions would harm no one, unless opening the doors of perception could be considered harmful.

When they got to that stage of the discussion, Dana quoted the famous line from Blake: *"If the doors of perception were cleansed every thing would appear to man as it is, Infinite."* As soon as the words came out of her mouth, she dashed outside to her van. A moment later she jogged back waving a book. It proved to be a well-worn copy of the complete works of William Blake. "I've got it! We're going to use a monologue from Blake; it's perfect!" She started reading to Owen from *The Marriage of Heaven and Hell*, donning her bardic persona, performing as much as reading, lunging and twirling and shifting her posture in accordance with the words. Impressed with her energy, Owen remembered when he first saw her, how powerful she was, how the audience had fallen under her spell.

She stopped with a flourish and Owen clapped. "You should be the focus of this video, my dear. The star, the center, the point from which it all radiates. And that's the stuff to read, that right there."

Dana smiled at him, pleased that he was pleased, but a wave of insecurity left her looking down at the floor. "Oh, I don't know about that...."

"I do. It's incredible. *You're* incredible. This will work." Owen reinforced his words with a shower of kisses.

They collaborated on their ideas, shaping an outline while exchanging multiple emails with the collective. The Artemis Pod had costumes they could use, handmade robes from their pagan ceremonies. They concurred that Dana should be the focus, but they wanted to play roles in the film as well as work behind the scenes. No one expressed reluctance to share Dana's blood, not at all. That act could be shown in the film alongside giving blood to the trees. Staging a wild ritual that enfolded old taboos was nothing unusual for a collective with experience in flouting social norms.

Other than planning for the video, there was little to do at the Maine farm. The doldrums of late winter obscured the promise of spring. Nothing further had been heard of Caleb Black, nor had there been any sign of threats or vandalism. Owen received a note from John Bixler about the piece he wrote for *The New Yorker* and he sent a segment of the article that covered the interview with Owen, asking for approval of the text. It was accurate and Owen said so. Bixler said it should come out soon and he'd forward Owen a copy of the magazine when it was available.

After two weeks of preparation they were ready to shoot the film. Dana and Owen drove to Massachusetts in her van, listening to African music and chanting nonsense accompaniment. A park and ride area just off I-95 offered a place to halt for the night once they crossed over the state line. Dana was an old hand at this kind of camping, and they spent a comfortable evening drinking tea and reading to each other, followed by making love under a down-filled comforter.

They made it to Walden Pond shortly after dawn to find all seven members of the collective bustling around their own van, drinking coffee, chatting in high spirits, and packing gear for the one-mile hike to the top of Emerson's Cliff. Enthusiastic to see Dana, they clustered around her, hugging, kissing, and rubbing the top of her bristly head, acting like animals welcoming the return of a pack member. This enthusiasm included Owen as well, and though he was shy at first and sensitive to his gender, they joked with him and pestered him until he relaxed. He enjoyed their easy camaraderie and he wondered what it would be like to have a sister.

The sun rose and brought enough warmth to work outside. The collective went into action, demonstrating their skill and experience. They understood the requirements of the script and seemed to know what to do at every juncture. By early afternoon they had finished the shooting. Dana and Owen were invited to accompany the collective back to Cambridge to share a meal and spend the night. They gladly agreed, reluctant to part from the congenial company. Around the large communal table, they continued their lively interactions and overlapping dialogues. The hum and flow of talk and laughter reminded Owen of the rhythms of the rhizome. The next morning, the collective promised that they would prioritize the editing and the special effects and would email the video to them within a few days. Content to have accomplished something, even though they weren't quite sure what, Dana and Owen left after breakfast and drove back to Maine.

[31]

Four days later, the video arrived in Dana's email. She yelled at Owen and he ran from the kitchen, grabbing the nearest chair. With the eagerness of children at a matinee, they sat side-by-side to peer at the computer screen.

**[Fade in to a tight close-up of the furrowed trunk of a large oak tree. There is a low, rumbling background sound, difficult to identify, but resembling the arco tones of a contrabass. The abstract music continues as the film unfolds. A title emerges in the center of the screen, in a baroque font: A VISION OF ETERNITY. The camera pulls back and Dana strides into the frame, leans toward the tree and kisses it,**

then turns to face the camera. She is wearing a long wiccan robe of royal purple. It both clings to her body yet floats around it, alternately concealing and revealing her form. The large hood is pulled over her head, but her face is visible. As she stares into the camera, her eyes turn a solid black, then return to the original color. With a slight reverb to her voice, she begins a chant of lyrics, moving with gesture and dance to enhance the phrasing.]

*The nameless shadowy female rose from out the breast of the land: her snaky hair whipping in the winds; and thus her voice arose.*

*For the cherub with his flaming sword is commanded to leave his guard at the tree of life, and when he does, the whole creation will be consumed, and appear infinite.*

[Camera pulls back from its focus on Dana and tree to present a wide-angle view of the forest.]

*This will come to pass through a sensual enjoyment, sitting in the twisted root of an oak, suspended in a fungus, hung with the head downward into the deep: behold the fury of a Spiritual Exis-tence.*

[At the words "sensual enjoyment," Dana pulls from within the robe an obsidian knife which she uses to cut across her left palm. As the blood wells from the cut, she makes a quick incision in the tree and presses her hand onto the wound. She holds it there for a moment as the sounds of the contrabass become more insistent. Then she sinks down to sit with her back to the tree, bowing her head.]

"Wait a minute," said Owen. "Is that the way Blake wrote it?"

Dana paused the video. "No, that's not the way Blake wrote it. I moved some things

around and did a few other things. Poetic license. Just watch!"

[The music subsides into the background. Dana stands, slowly lifting her head to face the camera, and resumes the incantation.]

*But first the notion that man has a body distinct from his soul, is to be expunged; this I shall do, melting apparent surfaces away, and displaying the infinite which was hid.*

[The camera dives to the ground at Dana's feet, then the image of the ground dissolves and reforms into a graphic depiction of the mycorrhizal network, a complex, glowing circulatory system of infinite expanse and terrible beauty. Dana's voice continues.]

*If the doors of perception were cleansed every thing would appear to man as it is: infinite.*

[Camera view backs out of the rhizome, out of the ground, and returns to Dana in front of the tree.]

*For man has closed himself up, till he sees all things thro' narrow chinks of his cavern.*

[Dana walks around to the back of the tree where she finds Owen, sitting between the roots of the oak, fingers buried in the dirt. He is bent over, intent on the ground at the base of the tree. He wears a brown robe, hood up, and his face cannot be seen but strands of his long hair dangle from the cowl.]

*A fool sees not the same tree that a wise man sees.*

[Dana strokes the back of Owen's head. As this happens, the tree changes colors, each hue blending into the next until it cycles through the full spectrum before returning to the original. Dana continues around the tree and back to the front where there are now four women laying on the ground in a cross formation with their heads at the center. The women appear to be asleep. Each woman wears a robe like Dana's except they are colored red, black, white, and yellow. Dana circles them and resumes speaking.]

*I see the Four-fold Woman. The Humanity in deadly sleep and its fallen Emanation. The Spectre & its cruel Shadow. I see the Past, Present & Future, existing all at once before me; o Divine Spirit sustain me on thy wings!*

*The Eternal Female groan'd! It was heard over all the Earth:*

[The women awake and stand. They form a line. Dana re-opens the cut on her palm and the women pull out their own knives and do the same to their palms. Dana walks down the line, pressing her hand into each palm, sharing the blood.]

*The eyes of fire, the nostrils of air, the mouth of water, the beard of earth.*

*Where woman is not, nature is barren.*

[The women disperse to nearby trees and repeat the ritual of cutting into the tree and pressing a cut hand to the incision. As each completes the ritual, she sinks to sit at the base of the tree. Dana dances a slow, fluid dance as she watches the women perform their parts. When they are finished, she spins around and stops, staring into the camera as it moves in to a close-up of her face. As she speaks, the music ends.]

*Energy is the only life, and is from the Body; and Reason is the bound or outward circumference of Energy;*

*Energy is Eternal Delight.*

*For everything that lives is Holy.*

**[Camera pans slowly up Dana's face, almost caressing her as it ascends, finally coming to rest with a view of the tree-tops, the blue sky, and the rays of illuminating sunlight. The film ends with this image.]**

"Wow. That was impressively weird. Dana, you were fantastic! You should be an actress. Or maybe just a goddess, you know?"

"Yes, well, I'm not sure how I'd do with constant adulation, even from you. But did you dig the black eyes? Some killer special effects, right?"

"Oh yeah. Everything about it made me want to fuck you."

"Aren't you the little goddess groupie. Be a good supplicant and I'm sure we can work something out." They shared a kiss, then separated with shy, excited grins.

"Dana, will this really work? I mean, it's pretty cool and all, but I'm so biased I'd watch anything with you in it and think it's divine. No doubt it touched on some classic mythic and ritual themes. But, you know, it was kind of corny."

"I know, it was. But, get this, I think that's necessary to resonate with mass psychology. If you look at the celebrities and gurus and politicians who wield their charm in public, no matter how intelligent, they all truck mostly in clichés. It's the insistence of belief they put on it, the rhetoric, really, that pulls people in. And that's the reason for the Blake; I was shooting for some visionary depth along with the bombast. I hope that comes across."

"I think so. Those Artemis women know their stuff; you were right about that. The film was eerie, moody, and, this isn't a criticism, but the images seem to be rivetted into my skull. In fact, I'm having a hard time shaking it off like it's still playing."

"Yeah, me too. What is that? Could the rhizome be in it somehow? You were tapped in to the network the whole time, right?"

"Yep. I was trying to draw it in, at least to imbue the proceedings with mystery. Maybe too much came through and now the images carry some kind of memory-searing property. I know the Artemisians were feeling something: remember when they said at dinner how they felt the presence of a spirit during the work?"

"True. But can a film be a mystical experience?"

"Sure, why not? If a book can be the word of god, then why not a film? Plus, remember what the Thorns said about Dr. Chouinard: the boundary between consciousness and the physical realm is a thin membrane. If that's so, then it's not unthinkable that the rhizome inserted itself into the film. Don't forget that the rhizome has expertise at wrangling human data streams. Hopefully the whole thing isn't permanently lodged in our heads."

"Yeah, I can be vain but that'd be a bit much."

Dana sent a reply to the Artemis Pod approving the video and asking that it be released as soon as possible. The collective had their own means of distribution, primarily via social media channels. By the end of the day, "A Vision of Eternity" was available on the internet with invitations to share it freely. It didn't take long for a public response. Initial comments from fans who followed the collective tended to be favorable, although many were puzzled. Regardless, it quickly passed into the internet wilderness. Reactions tumbled out in an avalanche as the video went viral. Critics offered a variety of responses, ranging from "clear as mud" to "clearly demented," while for some it seemed a little creepy, or too apocalyptic, and "what was with the guy behind the tree?" Others were enthusiastic, claiming that it presented a new vision of inter-species relations and ecospirituality. They wanted to know about the "priestess" and was she available for public courses, seminars, or rituals? Was there a name for what they were doing? With every wave of enthusiasm came a parallel wave of condemnation. As it spread through the internet, the skeptics and trolls came out in force. When the attacks got sharper and nastier, the defenders became more avid. To take advantage of the notoriety before it dissipated, they needed to move fast.

After consulting the collective, Dana decided to host a seminar. It would be free, but prospective attendees had to apply for the limited slots. The Artemis Pod had previous experience managing group rituals and warned that throwing the event wide open to the public could result in unwanted participants or disruptors, given the climate of controversy around the video. Some evangelicals denounced it as satanic and heretical. Public health advocates condemned it due to the flagrant disregard for blood-handling protocols and accused the film-makers of irresponsibility and endangerment to the populace. Cynics dismissed it as juvenile. In the circumstances, safety precautions seemed prudent, so they set up a screening procedure. Interested people would have to apply for the seminar in writing, identify themselves, and provide a statement of why they wanted to attend. By doing this and keeping the total number under thirty, they hoped to establish a controlled environment.

Despite the variety of negative reactions, they received over two hundred applications. Some were obviously insincere or foolish and these were discarded. But even after screening, they were left with a hundred credible candidates. They decided to host one event and invite thirty-three of the hundred. If that went well, they could do more.

The first seminar took place in the woods of Dogtown Common on Cape Ann, Massachusetts, a large stretch of untended forest. After gathering at a parking area, the group, mostly women, followed Dana into a quiet section of the woods. She arranged them in a standing circle facing inward and roamed around while she talked, looking intently at the face of each participant. Meanwhile, Owen and three of the Artemis women monitored the proceedings from the periphery. Dana spoke of the blood practice in mythology and mysticism, buttressing her points with lyrical quotations. She asked for volunteers to share blood with her. No one would be shamed if they refrained, she promised. Everyone wanted her blood. Dana walked along the circle, nicking palms with razor blades and clasping hands. After each blade was used, it was given to the applicant with the instruction to find a tree in the surrounding woods to adopt and share their blood with that tree. As the group dispersed to perform this rite, they were encouraged to open their hearts to the tree, seek a communion, and carry that tree forever in their thoughts.

The group responded with reverence, moving in silence, taking their time to approach trees and pick one. It took almost an hour for everyone to complete this stage. At the closing circle, Dana asked people to go forth and continue the ritual on their own and bring others into it as they wished. There was no doctrine, no dogma, no leaders or priests. It was a ritual for people and trees to experience relationship, not a religion, she said.

Dana and Owen judged the first event to be a success, as were the following two. Participants reported that the simplicity of the rite inspired them. It was mystical, yes, but there were no requirements to shed beliefs or adopt them. The sharing of blood was less controversial than Owen had anticipated, at least among those who came to the events. Everyone seemed to have an intuitive understanding of the notion of "blood brothers and sisters." The underlying virus was never mentioned. Owen and Dana decided that since its presence was benign at worst and beneficial at best, bringing it into the conversation would only confuse matters. The ethics were murky, they didn't deny that, but the situation remained the same: the survival of a world was at stake. They talked the whole way home after the first seminar, neither one feeling comfortable with their deception. Still, they agreed that it seemed necessary. With the acceptance of mutual culpability, they reaffirmed their solidarity.

Dana started a website for the endeavor under the banner of "Arboreal Eternity." It featured announcements of new events, forums for participants, basic information about the practice, and, of course, the video. They didn't host many events; it was apparent from the enthusiasm in the forums that the work of spreading the virus into the forest was advancing at a surprising pace, at least in New England. However, a wider geographic dispersion was Owen's goal. Given the number of inquiries coming from other parts of the world, especially Germany, it seemed that it was time to launch a tour.

The Arboreal Eternity movement assumed a life of its own, with new activists going out to spread the ritual among like-minded folk. Owen thought there was something sad and disturbing about their success; they had clearly tapped into a hunger in the culture, a dissatisfaction with traditional mechanisms for connection and belonging. It was impressive how little it had taken to start the cult or whatever it was. No longer did he feel obligated to spread his own blood as the sole hope of the Thorn rhizome. Now, plenty of converts worked to that end. Although satisfying, it was also a bit overwhelming, and Owen found himself wanting to retreat from the consuming public matters into the more comfortable world of books and home. Dana, though, drew energy from the attention. She took on all the website duties, event planning, and fending off curiosity-seekers. She accepted Owen's withdrawal from the movement and, for the most part, left him to pursue his studies. He felt a twinge of missing out, but his primary response was a sigh of relief.

One evening, as Dana stared into her computer screen, Owen snuck up from behind and placed a book on top of her head, precariously balanced. Stifling an impulse to throw it at him, she guessed that he wanted her attention again. Keeping her head still, she reached up, snatching the book just before it fell. Annoyed, she turned to Owen, who grinned without shame. "What?" she said.

He pointed at the book. It was a paperback copy of *Finnegans Wake*. Dana looked at it with a puzzled expression, flipping pages without reading. "Yeah, so?"

"It's a rhizome. The book."

"How so? I haven't read it. I've heard it's pretty much unreadable."

"True, at least in the sense of how we usually read. You don't really read it like a novel, because it's not linear, it doesn't have a plot, characters are fluid, and it's not exactly written in English."

"Well, that sounds like fun."

"Sure, it is. Fun. Joyce was quite the wit and it's chock full of word play—the kind of stuff you love. It approaches language and culture like a rhizome, like a great, infinite bramble of connections. Best to read it in bits, taking the time with each phrase to untangle the thicket. More of a puzzle than a page-turner. But the stuff in it is amazing."

"Grudgingly, you're getting my interest."

He took the book from her and flipped it open to a bookmarked page. "Here, listen to this: *'For we are fed of its forest, clad in its wood, burqued by its bark and our lecture is its leave.'*"

"What? Read that again."

Owen read it again while Dana closed her eyes. "And check this out: *'...with all that's buried of sins insince insensed insides of me.'*"

"Whoa. I definitely need that one again." When Owen read it and showed her how it was written in the text, she took the book from him and started reading, turning the page. "Ho! Listen to this: *'Desire, for hire, would tire a shire, phone, phunkel, or wire.'* He's mad!"

Owen grabbed the book and opened to another mark. *"'As mad as brambles he is.'"* They both exploded in laughter.

After this interlude they played with the book for amusement, the "Finnegan Game"—trading it back and forth, finding quotes, dismantling them into components, sleuthing through the puns and portmanteaus as best they could, shrugging their shoulders and giving up when the references were too obscure, but overall enjoying the splendor of words shared between lovers. This kept them laughing and engaged with each other during the tenacious winter evenings.

Eventually, they sensed the advent of spring, heralded by longer days and a few bare spots in the thinning snowpack. They had settled into a balance of passion and companionship; neither of them wanted to remember what life was like before they met. One day Owen received a copy of *The New Yorker* in the mail. Not being a subscriber, he knew what that meant, and eagerly turned to the contents where he found Bixler's by-line under an article titled "Pledging Allegiance: Truth and Rhetoric of the Alt-Right." He skimmed the article until he found the section on the Legion of Odin. Pretty much everything he had told Bix was there, including his assertion that Garth's body was still in the woods. The article adopted a neutral tone, but it was hard to escape the underlying critique of the Legion and the other groups profiled. There was no need to editorialize, the facts spoke for themselves.

Seeing it in print brought back the intense pain of those events. Owen said nothing, just handed the magazine to Dana, folded open to the pages where he was quoted. She grabbed it and read, lips tight, a look of concern spreading across her face. Putting the magazine down, she embraced him. He nuzzled against her for a minute, then said, "That might have been a mistake."

"What do you mean?"

"The interview. Now that it's in print, I've got a bad feeling about this. We've got important work to do – this could be a distraction."

"Well, you told the truth. When is that wrong?"

"It's not wrong, but it may not be... tactical."

The next morning when they drove out for groceries, there was a large pile of garbage dumped in the driveway, right at the junction with the main road. They shoveled it into the back of Owen's truck as best they could, then took it to the town dump. The next day there was more trash in the same place. They cleaned this, too. Day three brought more of the same. The anonymity of the act was frustrating as well as frightening. Short of posting a guard, he wasn't sure what to do. He talked to the fellow who plowed snow out of the driveway and asked him to make a daily run to push the garbage to the side of the road. It was unsightly, but made quick work of the chore. Several days into this routine, large appliances started to appear, including a refrigerator. Everything got plowed to the new piles on either side of the drive.

At the end of the first week after the article was published, Owen received a letter in the mail. Printed by hand in crude letters, it looked like the paper plate message they had found after returning from the Thorn world. The letter said, in entirety: "YOUR DAYS ARE NUMBERED FAGGOT" and the bottom of the page featured several runes. He waved it at Dana, cursing. She looked at it and frowned at Owen.

"The Legion of Odin, no doubt," was all he said.

He noticed that some of the people in town looked at him with odd expressions. Nothing was said, friendly or hostile, but he knew it had something to do with the Bixler report. A week later, he picked up a copy of the Bangor Daily News and found an article, "Local Investigation Re-opened Into Tree-Sitter's Death." The state police initiated a new search of the woods, checking for Garth's body. They found their way to Owen's farm as well. Aggressive with their questions at first, as if Owen was a suspect, they changed their tone as he told his story, took notes, and left in a hurry. Two days later the newspaper carried a bold-face headline: "Tree-Sitter's Body Found in Cutler Woods."

[32]

Owen thought that after the discovery of Garth's body the Legion of Odin might draw some heat. Maybe that would send them into the shadows, though he knew that wasn't their style. The opposite seemed more likely, that they would want revenge. The trash dumping continued in the driveway, as well as threats in the mail, and although no one had come to the house, Owen thought it was only a matter of time. He urged Dana to put together some overseas events to get them out of town. She liked the idea and dived into the task. Owen still had enough savings to cover travel costs, so they purchased plane tickets to London.

They arranged to leave Dana's van with the Artemis collective in Cambridge. Owen certainly didn't want it sitting in his drive-way as a target for vandalism. The day before they left, as they packed up the last of their luggage and tidied the house, he heard a vehicle approaching. When he looked out the window, he saw his uncle's truck.

"Oh shit." He ran for the door, blurting at Dana, "stay in the house."

He struggled with his mood as he walked down the steps to confront his uncle. He didn't want him any closer to the house than necessary. Caleb climbed out of the cab and Owen found his harshest voice. "Far enough. Get the fuck out of here."

"Now, is that any way to greet your kin?"

"You heard me."

Owen noticed that Caleb left the truck running and stayed close to the open door. His uneasy posture suggested that he had not forgotten the last visit.

"Well, boy, I know you don't like me much. But we are kin, and because of that, and that only, I'm suggesting you might want to be very careful these days. There's an ugly wind blowin' and it's got your name on it. Probably you shouldn't have gone blabbin' to that fancy writer. If things'd been left to lie as they were, so to speak, this all might have blown over. But that don't seem possible anymore. You're a smart boy, I'm sure that don't come as no surprise." Caleb paused and spit on the ground. "By the way, when did you get into the garbage business? That's a nasty pile down the way. Your momma wouldn't have liked that one bit."

"You got nothing to say about my mother, you scum. If you've said your piece, you can leave. Even if you haven't, you can still leave."

"Yeah, well, you may not think so but I'm lookin' out for you, boy. But it looks like that's at an end. So...." Caleb stopped talking, narrowed his eyes, and looked past Owen toward the house. Owen turned and saw that Dana was standing in the open door, hands on her hips, glowering at Caleb. Owen felt instant dismay. "Hey hey, who's that charmer? Looks like you traded in your hippie boyfriend on a cleaner-cut model. But wait, don't tell me, why, that's a girl! You workin' both sides of the fence, now? Trust you to pick a girl that looks like a boy, though. Some things don't change, do they?"

Owen had heard enough and charged at Caleb. Thirty feet separated them and as soon as Owen moved, Caleb jumped in the idling truck, slammed the door and backed out of the drive in a spray of gravel. Yelling at the vehicle, Owen punched the air with his fist.

He marched back to the house and looked at Dana with exasperation. "Dana...!"

"I know, I know, you told me to stay in. I'm sorry, I had to do it. I'm not letting you face that creep by yourself. Ever again, you understand? I know you're strong, and clearly he's scared to death of you, but now I'm part of this, too. And I'm going to play my part. I know you're trying to protect me, and I appreciate that. But whatever happens, happens to both of us. That's the way it has to be."

Owen walked up the steps and threw his arms around her. "What did I do to deserve you?"

She kissed him and they went into the house. As soon as the door was shut behind them, Dana said, "Let's get out of here. Our flight is tomorrow but we can stay in the van tonight. I don't like this. I'm afraid, Owen."

Owen studied her concerned face and nodded. "You're right. Why wait? Caleb is a twisted man, but he probably thinks he's doing the right thing – in some way he's always been able to justify his bullshit—the rapes, the violence, everything. No doubt he sees himself as virtuous. He came out here, despite his reluctance, to offer a warning. I'm guessing there's good reason for that. So, yeah, we're mostly packed anyway – let's throw the rest of it together and get the hell out of here."

They rushed around the house, packing the remainder of the items they would need, and were on the road within an hour.

As soon as they were in the air and flying across the Atlantic, their tension dissolved into the excitement of travel. Dana had been to Paris before, right after graduating from high school, but the rest of the continent remained a novelty. Owen had never left the country except for a few trips to Canada. Traveling as light as possible, they each brought a medium-sized backpack. Dana had her laptop, journal, and a basic wardrobe. Owen found room for his copy of *Finnegans Wake* so they could play the game. Unburdened of the momentum of their life in Maine, they felt fresh. The idea of the trip rekindled their affections, and they nuzzled and cuddled in the cramped seats, giggling until they drew looks from other passengers, which only increased the hilarity.

Still patching together an agenda, they stopped first in Caernarvon, Wales, to meet a small pagan group. The Golden Bough, as they called themselves, contacted Dana soon after she opened the website. Passionate about their ritual practice, they claimed to represent an authentic Druid tradition passed along for thousands of years. Owen had studied enough Celtic myth and folklore as well as related archaeology and anthropology to be skeptical of these claims, but he and Dana decided that it was more important to spread the virus than critique the rationality of their participants. It didn't come easy, but they were learning the importance of strategic compromise.

After a brief stay in Caernarvon, where they introduced The Golden Bough to the blood ritual, they took the train to Harlech, a small town on the Welsh coast. Owen bubbled with excitement the whole way, lecturing Dana about how important this location was to the story cycle of *The Mabinogion*. She reminded him that she had read the stories, at his recommendation, she remembered them quite well, and did not need his recap. Nevertheless, his enthusiasm got the better of him and he launched into a retelling of the complete tale of Rhiannon and her birds, former residents of Harlech, until Dana glared at him so pointedly that he blushed and trailed off into muttering. Evidently, he thought, she had learned how to channel the independent Rhiannon for her own purposes. However, when they arrived, it was thrilling to hear the echo of lyrical birdsong everywhere while they explored the town's byways, as if the myth lived on.

The next event took place in the Vézère Valley in France, near Les Eyzies. This bucolic valley had been inhabited by humans for several hundred thousand years. Many of the world's most famous ice age painted caves could be found nearby, and they were eager to see these relics for themselves. As they explored the country, they met a variety of people in love with the past, or in love with their own notions of the past, and it helped them to understand that for many, it was necessary to imagine a human tradition more glorious than the historical reality. It seemed that people wanted to see themselves in the best light and the hard truths of human behavior were difficult to swallow. This led to convoluted explanations about prehistoric cultures based on a selective use of facts. The wiccans, druids, and other New Age celebrants hoped to find meaning in a past that, for the most part, never really existed. Owen agreed that this was harmless enough, as Dana pointed out, but he failed to see how it helped humanity to heal itself. The flaws at the core remained, as history demonstrated, and all the mystique and mummery wouldn't change that. Still, this was their target audience, whether Owen liked it or not. He wondered if humanity would ever be ready for reality.

From folks in the Vézère Valley, they received a tip about a group in the Liguria region of Italy, just over the border in the foothills of the maritime Alps. They went there, and from there to Munich, then Poland, Slovenia, and Corsica, finally ending up in Braga, Portugal, a medieval town near the interior mountains. The people from Braga took them along a trail in the nearby national park until they arrived at a thick grove enclosing an ancient circle of stones. It had the same worn, organic appearance as the stone circle in the Thorn world. While Dana led the ritual, Owen sat behind the proceedings and sent his tendrils into the rhizome. Connected, he listened to the murmur of the place, drawing in a mosaic of complex rhythms and songs. As always, he heard the grief.

Owen liked the Portuguese ritualists. They took their craft seriously, but never abandoned humor and perspective. On the drive back to Braga, Owen asked one of the participants about this maturity, and in excellent English, he was told that many people in Portugal were confronting their colonial past, and had accepted that, for centuries, their culture served as a conduit for terrifying deeds, including slavery. They wanted to look squarely at that past and do something about it. Ambitious, the group sought to create a fresh cultural context, one that defined a different way of being human.

They spent a few days in Braga and enjoyed the company. It helped to dispel some of Owen's cynicism. While they were there, Dana received an invitation to Japan. Reluctantly, they left behind their new friends and flew to Asia. In Japan, Dana received the treatment of a celebrity. It was overwhelming, but they facilitated a dozen ritual events. Although they knew the time in Japan was productive, the attention wore them down. Six weeks had passed since they left Maine and they were exhausted. They wanted to go home, no matter what awaited them.

They couldn't assess the situation in Maine at a distance. As far as they could tell, the news about Garth's body had fallen off the front page. Apparently, the investigation continued, but no charges had been filed nor was there any indication that charges would ever be filed. Whatever was going on, Owen felt compelled to see for himself. Dana worried about the dangers but understood that Owen didn't want to give up on his land. They decided that if things in Maine didn't feel right, they would take off in Dana's van and travel the continent. Spring was on the land and they could go to Canada, one of the great arboreal repositories.

[33]

It was late afternoon when they followed the driveway through the trees to Owen's house, past the decaying mounds of garbage. At least the piles hadn't grown. Despite the cool air, the ground was free of snow and bursting with growth as grasses, weeds, and wildflowers celebrated the return of spring. Dana pulled the van to a stop in front of the house and Owen leaped out. The door hung open, dangling from a single hinge. He raced into the house, yelling, with Dana right behind.

She gasped at the threshold. Furniture was turned over, books ripped apart and scattered, pictures broken, food hurled against the walls and on the floors amidst shredded blankets, pillows, and clothes—nothing appeared to have escaped the rampage. An intense odor permeated the house and it didn't take long to understand that whoever had done this had urinated and defecated with abandon.

Owen looked at Dana, his face twisted with emotion. He shook uncontrollably. She offered the comfort of words, saying she was sorry, so sorry, but then halted with a sudden choking sound. Words were useless. Instead, she stepped to him and held him tight, saying nothing. He leaned into her, glad for the contact with a loving body.

The embrace calmed Owen, allowing a cold anger to surface. "No fucking question in my mind who's behind this. Has to be the Legion of Odin, with or without my uncle. As fucked up as he is, it's hard to believe he'd do this to his sister's home, the place where he grew up. But who knows? Maybe he had a score to settle from his own childhood. There's definitely a sickness in the family. Whatever, I'm beyond guessing about this bullshit. All I know for sure is that it's not safe here. Not now, anyway. Let's see if there's anything to salvage, then I think we should hit the road."

"But Owen, this is your home, do we really just abandon it to those creeps? Are the cops really of no value here?"

"It doesn't feel like a home at this point, Dana, it feels more like a trap. I'll be damned if we just sit here and wait for the next invasion. I saw them kill a friend in cold blood. No reason why they wouldn't do that again. And, frankly, I don't trust the cops. At all. I think they're in on it."

"My heart doesn't want to admit it, but you're probably right. How can I help?"

"Check the kitchen and tool shed to see if there's anything we can use for the van. I'll see if I can dig out any clothes that haven't been ruined and sort through the books. But I'm not going to take long – I'd like to get on the road before dark."

Dana found several items that would be useful and ferried them to the van. Owen retrieved a few things that survived the onslaught. They concentrated on their sorting, eager to be away, and failed to notice the band of camouflaged men sneaking out of the woods toward the back of the house. Owen returned from the van when he heard a scream in the kitchen. He ran out to find half a dozen Legionnaires, some of whose faces he recognized from the logging protest, with assault rifles and automatic weapons. The muzzle of a pistol rested against the side of Dana's head. Then six more Legionnaires stormed in from the front.

A Legionnaire with a shaved head growled in his beard. Owen knew who he was; it was the same guy who threw Garth to his death. "You think we forgot about you? Not hardly, you fuck. You're done. And your little boyfriend here as well."

Owen looked at Dana. Her face was white. His heart broke with the implications of their predicament. This had been his worst fear. Every atom of his being wanted to find a way out of this, but he couldn't think, it was happening too fast.

"Look," he pleaded, knowing no other course, "your beef is with me. Okay, so be it. Just let her go – she's got nothing to do with any of it."

The big guy pretended surprise, then leaned back and looked Dana over. "She? Well, what do you know?" He waved aside the Legionnaire with the pistol while he continued to leer at Dana, then stepped toward her and grabbed one of her breasts. "Oh yeah, definitely a tittie in there." Dana hit him in the face as hard as she could, which was hard enough to rock him back. He jumped at her and threw her into the kitchen wall, hand to her throat, pressing her flat with his enormous bulk. Meanwhile, two Legionnaires grabbed Owen by the arms and pinioned him. He thrashed helplessly in their grip. The big guy motioned to two others to secure Dana against the wall while he unsheathed a large combat knife and sliced open her sweatshirt. She spat in his face. He slapped her twice, viciously. She moaned and kept still. The big guy cut and pulled off her upper garments until she was bare from the waist up. Owen yelled and threatened, resulting in a punch to his gut that left him doubled over and wheezing.

The big guy stared at Dana and pronounced, "Not bad. I've seen better. Definitely not a boy. You could've fooled me at first." This produced a round of laughter from the Legionnaires.

One of the men holding Dana leered at her and turned to the big guy. "Hey, chief, what do you say we have some fun with this one? She's a lively one but I bet we can work that right out." Approving grins showed that others in the group had the same thought.

Owen reclaimed his voice. "Come on, let her go. She did nothing. Do your worst to me but *let her go.*" He tried to muster authority in his voice, but it came out in a hoarse croak.

"Too late for that, I'd say. Take them out to the woods. Strip them and tie them to a tree. Bare asses out so we can do them both. We'll plant some of Odin's seeds in 'em, what do you say?" That drew a cheer from the Legionnaires. The big guy continued, "Meanwhile, you, go get the gas cans."

Four of the Legionnaires hustled Dana and Owen out the back door while two others accompanied them, guns ready. Owen threw an agonized look at Dana, but she replied by mouthing "I love you." Owen wondered where his uncle was, but perhaps he would never know. He tried to link with the rhizome as he was being jerked and dragged across the field, but he ended up getting clubbed over the back of the head and knocked senseless.

When he came to, he was naked and lashed face first to an old hemlock tree at the edge of the woods. Tied to the other side of the tree was Dana. Their arms overlapped enough so they could grip each other's forearms. By craning his head, he saw the rest of her arm and shoulder on one side. Standing a few feet away, the Legionnaires looked across the field at the house. "Dana?" he whispered.

"Yes, Owen." She whispered back.

"I'm sorry."

"Don't be."

"Did they do anything to you?"

"Just words so far."

"I love you, whatever happens. Don't give up."

The house exploded with stunning force and the rest of the Legionnaires came running toward the woods. They stood in a clump, laughing and slapping each other in rough glee, watching the house blaze into a massive bonfire. Even a hundred yards away, Owen felt a touch of the heat on his bare skin.

There was only one chance for them. Owen opened the tips of his fingers, letting the tendrils slide out and force their way into the tree bark. At the same time, he encouraged the sensitivity on the pads of his feet, feeling the ground and opening another contact with the rhizome. When the tendrils from his fingers burrowed through the bark and touched the sapwood, Owen felt a surge of power.

The rhizome responded without direction from Owen. Once linked to his mental state, it set its own course of action. Without warning, roots erupted from the ground and snared the legs of all the Legionnaires. Before they understood the nature of the trap, neurochemicals poured out of the roots, burnt through clothing and skin, and froze them into cataleptic trance. To Owen they appeared as statues of agony and struggle silhouetted against the bright pyre of his home. Next the hemlock came alive, waving its lowest branches like tentacles, reaching down and yanking each Legionnaire out of the grip of the roots. As if the bodies weighed nothing, the tree flung them one by one across the hundred yards of open space and into the inferno of the flaming house. Within minutes they were gone.

As the house blazed, other roots snaked up the hemlock trunk and tore off the ropes that held Dana and Owen. They fell into each other's arms, sobbing in relief. Holding on, not wanting to let go, they watched the fire devour the house.

"Oh my god!" Dana cried.

"Are you okay? Are you okay?" Owen kept asking as he kissed her head in nervous exhaustion. A chaotic mixture of thoughts flooded through his mind as the adrenalin ran down. By this time, it was night and they could only see by the flames of the house, which cast long, flickering shadows. Twelve men were dead, but he only cared that he and Dana were alive.

"Dana, let's leave this place. Now."

"I don't know, Owen, I think they burned the van, too."

"I don't mean that. I mean this whole fucked-up world."

"You mean back to the Thorn world?"

"Why not? There's nothing here. I think we've done what we can. If this virus thing is going to work, it can work without us."

"Wow. That's... drastic. But hell, why not indeed? At this point, I can't think of a single reason to stay and a lot of reasons to get as far away as possible."

"Exactly. Come on, the portal tree isn't far. Let's go before we freeze."

4

# INCORPORATION

*I always knew that if I turned up pregnant, I wanted the being in my womb to be a member of another species...*
Donna Haraway, *The Companion Species Manifesto*

[34]

It was morning when they slithered headfirst out of the tree into the Thorn world, still embraced, replaying the after images of their brutal experience. The full measure of what happened roiled in Dana's stomach. It made her nauseous: the violence, the loss of control, the defilement – these things always left scars. At least she knew how to carry scars. As for Owen, his inability to protect Dana or his home reduced him to dust. Was he worth anything, really? Maybe. After all, he had invoked the rhizome and its merciless retribution saved them from a horrible fate. Owen shed no tears for the twelve Legionnaires. Even though he played a part in the deaths, he didn't give a damn: the assholes had to die if he and Dana were going to live. Such horrors grew hard knots in the soul, but he would adapt.

They stood and looked at the woods, then gravity pulled them together. After a long embrace, Owen leaned back to see her face. He wiped tears from her cheeks without realizing that he cried, too. "Well, shit," he said.

She barked a laugh and licked the tears on his face. Owen shivered in delight at this weird intimacy. She smiled and said, "It's nice and warm here, isn't it?"

The normalcy of this comment settled into Owen's bones and he sighed, understanding that the horror was behind them and they would go on. "Warm and beautiful," he replied.

"Yeah, I'd forgotten how beautiful it was. But this looks different, it's not like where we were before."

"No, it isn't, is it?" Although surrounded by forest, they couldn't see much of it because of the density. Instead of giant conifers and open spaces, it resembled the deciduous woods of Maine—a mosaic of maple, oak, birch, and ash. The trees were closer together than in the conifer groves of this world, but there was still enough space between them for small, grassy clearings. It reminded Owen of a cultivated arboretum. Even in the denser sections, the trees didn't block all the sunlight, which streamed through the canopy in dappled patterns. It was a soft forest, not exactly majestic, but welcoming and comfortable. Dana sighed and relaxed into Owen's embrace.

"Um, recommend procession of movement around big boulder. Over there, sunward." They heard the squeaky voice and swiveled their heads back and forth. "Down here," it said. At their feet was a palm-size brown toad staring up at them. It blinked one eye, then the other, then both in unison.

"Are you a Thorn?" Owen asked.

"Sure, why not? Worked before, yes, names? Nothing wrong with consistency, not at all, nothing. Up to you, of course, up to you." The toad opened its mouth and shot out an impressive tongue, snatching an ant off Owen's big toe. "Shouldn't eat those, no. Still under contract, they are. But oh, so tasty. Occupational hazard for them, presumably covered… under terms of the deal." The toad performed its triad of blinks again.

Owen and Dana exchanged glances. She crouched to stroke the toad's back. "Pleased to meet you, Mr. Toad. I mean Mr. Thorn. Sorry, Mr. Toad was a character in one of my favorite books. I loved Mr. Toad! But he was a bit of a rascal and I'm guessing you're not like that at all. I'm guessing you're going to be very kind and helpful." The toad arched its back, responding to Dana's touch as if it were a cat. Dana grinned at Owen. "Seems like an upgrade so far."

Owen grunted in agreement. "So, what were you saying about the boulder?"

"Yes, instructions for refugees, very important. Request for your presence on other side of boulder, that's the gist of it."

"Refugees? You know what happened to us, then? And why we're here?"

"Oh, certainly, we know, we know. There was powerful resonance in rhizome, strings were singing, whiplash of action recoiled right through the brane, our knowing was infused with rugosities of your being. Suffering was much, assemblage was caustic, and lines of flight led directly here. And so, you came. Of which, you are welcome to your presence, space of occupation is available, sanctuary offered." This was followed by three blinks.

Dana offered her outstretched palm to the Thorn, who hopped on with dainty deliberation. She stood, transferring the toad to her shoulder. "Well then, would you be kind enough to accompany us to the other side of the boulder?"

"An honor, certainly."

The boulder stood alone like a glacial erratic a couple of hundred yards away up a gentle slope. As they walked, the Thorn resumed its curious speech. "We experience wide-ranging satisfaction at task accomplishment within your world boundaries. Virus levels have risen, yes they have, enough so we can monitor ecology of transformation. Pheromones are releasing, atmospheres charging, even as we speak, oh yes. Congratulations to your endeavor along with condolences for suffering experienced. Much sadness within souls of your kind, a surfeit of tragedy. Muchness is acute."

Dana glanced at Owen. "This iteration of Thorn doesn't quite grasp English, it seems."

Owen smiled. "I just assumed it had absorbed too much French philosophy. The 'lines of flight' phrase is a dead giveaway."

The Thorn burped out an unusual sound, halfway between a toadish croak and a snort of laughter. "Hey hey don't blow a fuse/If you don't grok Deleuze/Just kick off those shoes/And settle for a snooze..."

Dana, straight-faced, replied, "We may have to re-evaluate the upgrade classification."

Owen laughed. "This one seems to have incorporated Whitethorn's zest for doggerel. Harmless enough. One hopes. We can reserve judgment."

By the time the banter was exhausted they arrived at the boulder. "Now what?" Owen asked.

"Circumnavigate, circumnavigate!" The Thorn flexed its body up and down on Dana's shoulder as if homing in on a target.

They walked around the boulder and stopped. A diverse assembly of creatures arrayed under the boughs of an oak looked at them for a moment, then returned to their preoccupations. Beyond the tree stretched an open swath of grass encircling a rocky pond. A stab of light reflected off the surface of the pond and blinded Owen, leaving him unprepared for the three marmoset-like creatures bounding from the tree. They leaped at him, falling short of his shoulders and clutched onto arms and torso before scrambling to their same old positions. "Whitethorn, Redthorn, and Blackthorn?" Owen was pleased; he had not expected to see them again.

Whitethorn declaimed a greeting, "No matter where or when you roam/Here you'll never lack a home."

Dana bent double, hand cupped over her mouth, stifling laughter while the toad clung to her shoulder. A dragonfly zipped over from a tree branch and landed on her head. "Hmpf. Your loud-mouthed boyfriend hasn't changed. 'This Thorn! That Thorn!' Like something from a trashy romance. We fail to understand what you see in him. For example, why he leaves all these delicious edibles untouched remains utterly perplexing." The next thing Dana heard was a crunching sound as the dragonfly picked a mite from her scalp.

Owen appraised the remaining menagerie under the tree. Two crow-like birds bounced around, picking at things in the dirt. As one of them found something, it nudged the other to pick it up. With delicacy, it would do so, offering the morsel to the finder. As Owen watched, they went back and forth with this behavior, repeatedly collaborating, never acting individually. Against the trunk lounged a plump raccoon, sprawled out and scratching its matted fur; it looked like a slob watching television. A yellow snake coiled around an outstretched leg of the raccoon, who lifted the limb and gave a vigorous shake, forcing the snake to drop to the ground. Assorted blue-green rabbits foraged in the grass, hopping in aimless patterns between grazing spots. It could have been a bucolic scene from one of Owen's children's books except that the creatures were the wrong size, the wrong color, or just acting weird. Owen's inventory ended at a solitary mouse standing upright on one of the exposed roots of the oak, cleaning its whiskers. It wore a tiny backpack.

"Wow." Dana said, trying to take it all in.

"So, what's going on? These aren't real animals, are they? I mean, these are rhizome manifestations, right? Has the multiplicity come out to play?"

Redthorn cleared its throat. "In a manner of speaking, yes, that's exactly what's going on. We'll leave aside, for the moment, the question of biological identities. Are they really animals or something else? Does it matter? It's a welcoming committee. We know that humans relate better to animals than plants. We thought you might appreciate a milieu with characters, and various nodes were eager to explore their own expressions. Creative theater, if you will. You fled your world in fear, leaving everything behind. It's good that you escaped, and we're offering you a new home."

Blackthorn interrupted with loud coughing noises, then launched into its own speech. "We've contained the toxin expansion into our world, at least for now. More importantly, we sense that our plans are taking effect. At this point, we believe that the implemented changes will achieve the desired results in your world, or something very similar. The cascade of transformation starts slowly but builds momentum. Soon, there will be a crossing of the critical threshold; we feel it coming."

Owen thought about what he heard. "Well, we did the best we could. I never anticipated the kind of resistance that came at us."

Blackthorn continued. "Systems oppose change in various ways; that's one of the elements of their complexity. Rigid systems defy all changes without understanding that change is necessary. Whole-scale containment of change is not a strategy for survival, it's a drain that spirals inward to termination. For example, consider our containment of the bleached zone. Effective for now, yes, but a hole in our world, a void of pain that, if not healed, will eventually suck the life out of us. The only way forward is to integrate and resolve, to find the correct assemblage, to suffer the awkwardness of new multiplicities until a revised homeostasis can be achieved. This is the way of open systems: they must remain open or they will die."

The dragonfly snarled at Blackthorn. "Go on, it's like speaking to children; they struggle to comprehend the simplest things. Say 'open system' and they think about leaky faucets."

Dana admonished the dragonfly. "Pipe down with the insults or I'll evict you from your paradise of mites, you ingrate."

The toad stuck out its tongue at the dragonfly and croaked. "Oh, get it they do, they do. First, they must circle every wagon, oh yes, circle and circle."

Dana looked at the marmosets perched on Owen. "So, you did this for us? Companion critters and all?"

The marmosets stared back at her in silence. It was the toad who answered. "All this and more. A bounty of more. We are mechanics of your desire."

The dragonfly left Dana's head and hovered in front of her. "Bring on the ants, then. Let's get it over with before we're all curdled into a saccharine goo." It zipped off to the other side of the tree.

Owen spoke to the group draped around his head and shoulders. "I thought I'd never see you guys again. I know you're not really a 'you,' but what the hell. We humans need our 'yous' and 'theys.' Names and identities, that's the way we work. Besides, contemplation of the whole thing makes us dizzy—vertigo of the labyrinth and all that—so we pull out fragments and pretend they represent the whole. It's just the way we cope, you know. Anyway, what I'm trying to say is that even though it's part of the Thorn mind, I'm especially fond of these emissaries." He reached up to pat the trio, who purred at his touch.

Dana leaned against Owen, one arm encircling his waist while the other reached up to join the petting of the creatures. "Well said. It's true, we only interact with a fraction of each other, just the parts we can see. The bulk of our selves stays below the surface, like an iceberg. I hope we, I mean you and me, Owen my dear, can learn to appreciate more of each other, go deeper, towards a complete way of relating. I want to see those hidden parts. And no wisecracks, buster."

Owen opened his mouth to respond with the anticipated wisecrack but only managed a distracted "What...?" when he noticed a large bundle emerge from behind the oak tree. It floated inches above the ground with no visible support or propulsion, moving toward them at a slow pace. The dragonfly buzzed back and forth in front of the bundle as if directing its progress. The procession skirted the raccoon, who hissed and withdrew its legs.

When the bundle arrived at Dana and Owen's feet, a crowd of ants surged backward from underneath and dispersed, leaving it flush on the ground. It was a large, folded bolt of brown fabric.

"Wow, thanks. Stuff to make clothes."

"Oh, more than that," boasted the toad, "muchly much more. Unroll and you will see." The toad flexed its body up and down while blinking rapidly. As Dana bent over the bundle, the toad jumped to the ground and zapped a stray ant with its tongue.

"Shall I?" Dana looked back at Owen, who gestured for her to continue. Within the folds, exposed at each turn, were clothes made from plant fabric, well-crafted and decorated with small beads sewn in geometric designs, predominantly spirals. "Wow!" Dana held up a tunic and pants that seemed to be her size.

As Dana continued to unfold the bundle, Owen entertained suspicions about the source of the items, especially when he recognized the presence of carrying bags and a parfleche that he hoped contained tools. "Okay, where did all this come from?"

The dragonfly repeatedly landed on Dana's head and took off every time she moved. When it finally perched on nearby rock, it answered Owen's question. "Dr. Chouinard, you could presume. She's gotten very crafty these days."

"How did she know our sizes so well?" Dana had already slipped into the set made for her. It provided an excellent fit and she turned back and forth to model it for Owen.

"Dr. Chouinard! Where is she, anyway? Is she more, you know… herself?" Owen wanted to try on the clothes for him, but curiosity was stronger, and he waited for an answer.

The dragonfly returned to Dana's head and preened. "If by 'herself' you mean able to act like you, hmmm, blessedly the answer is no, not really. However, she has become more mobile and purposeful, and she wanders far and wide. She roamed off to the east a while ago, just after making these items. It seems she anticipated your return."

Owen, satisfied for the moment, removed Whitethorn, Blackthorn, and Redthorn so he could put on his outfit. It, too, was perfect. Dana looked at him and grinned. "We look like Indians."

"Might as well," he replied, "we're going to have to live like them."

"Yes," the dragonfly said, "there's a large piece of fabric you may use for a shelter cover, and plenty of additional scraps and tools to make things you need. Assuming, of course, that you can muster the patience to complete such tasks."

The toad butted in. "Here for real is where you commence and continue your being-in-the-world. Under tree, next to pond, amidst frolic and play of life-forms. Good as it gets!"

[35]

Owen rigged the fabric tarp under the branches of the oak tree, and they called it home. Retaining a section of material, they covered the moss with a ground cloth and added another piece for a bedcover, even though it wasn't cold enough for it, at least not yet. The hint of chill in the pre-dawn hour reminded Owen that winter, whatever it might be like, would be upon them soon enough. He was glad for the clothes. And when it rained, the tarp provided decent shelter. The water in the pond bubbled from an underground spring and it was fresh and clean. In truth, they lacked for nothing essential. They foraged for mushrooms and other fungi and learned about additional plant foods scattered throughout the forest: berries, tubers, and fruit or nut trees. The diet was repetitive but nutritious. Despite occasional cravings for ice cream, chocolate, or bacon, they ate what they had and were satisfied.

Shelter and food eased their survival. Instead of struggle, the days filled with the details of the new world and their love for each other. The circumstances of the flight from Owen's home became blurry, a welcome forgetting. Being in the present consumed all their attention, whether it was a long moment gazing across the pond to the trees on the other shore while absorbing the warm sun on the skin, or feeling the wind brush through the woods, tickling the hairs and setting the leaves dancing. The oak tree served as a fulcrum of relationship, and Owen set aside time each day to submerge his tendrils in the soil, communing with the local rhizome, learning more about the complexities of the system. When he disappeared into these trances, Dana leaned against him, partaking in the exchange, letting it distill through his body and into hers. This sharing brought them closer and they delved into areas of union neither one had imagined possible. Several weeks into their new life, Dana discovered that she, too, had tendrils sprouting from her fingers. With that development, they adapted their communion, using the tendrils to form a continuous loop with each other and the rhizome.

The original trio of Redthorn, Blackthorn, and Whitethorn stayed with Dana and Owen for a little while, then drifted off into the forest to be recycled as bio-matter. One day the dragonfly was gone as well. These departures involved no acknowledgment or farewell but passed like leaves falling from a tree. The toad, however, stayed close and served as their primary guide. Other creatures present at the welcoming also stuck around, roaming the clearing, typically going about their own business. Owen befriended one of the rabbits, and it often hopped under the tarp to snuggle with them. The raccoon rarely budged from the place where they'd first seen it, lounging against the trunk. Occasionally, it wandered off into the woods and would be gone for an hour or two, then, without fanfare, it would waddle back to resume its lazy posture. Owen talked to it, even inviting it to join them under the tarp when it rained, but beady eye contact was the only response. It watched them closely but never spoke. After a while, they just pretended it wasn't there. Sometimes when they made love, one of them would look up to notice the raccoon studying them.

The whole world seemed to hold its breath and watch during their intercourse. At first, they were shy about the exposure, but they learned to ignore the multiple attentions of the forest. Enamored with each other and with no distractions, they let desire have its way. Dana brought up the question of birth control, noting the obvious: they didn't have any. Neither of them wanted to curtail their amorous pursuits, so they talked about what it would be like to have a child. The burdens and the joys were discussed, and sometimes quibbled over, but they couldn't figure out how to decide, if there was even a decision to be made. Ultimately, they elected to follow Dana's rhythms, though she entertained little hope for the method. They accepted the risks. For both, it was a gift to have sex without the onus of trauma distorting every gesture or contact. Physical intimacy, instead of a tightrope walk through minefields of tension, became a fluid dream, an abandonment where they could experience unhindered delight.

As they explored the woods, surrounded by the mingled forms of arboreal life, they reacted to the Eros of the world, intoxicated by sensuous groves and lush meadows. Under the trees, on the ground, they lost themselves in each other. The rhizome responded to their passions by sending thread-like hyphae out of the soil to slip into their flesh, linking with their intercourse. Through these links came a steady flow of biochemical commerce, driving Owen and Dana into orgasms of brilliant intensity and forging yet another level of communion.

One warm afternoon, Dana sprawled on a rock by the side of the pond, sun-bathing. Motionless in the shallows and partly concealed by reeds, the toad sat and shared the silence. Oblivious to the peace and humming loudly, Owen returned from a foray into the woods, dumping a full satchel of polypores under the tarp. He looked for Dana and when he saw her lounging by the water, his thoughts turned to naiads and desire. Shedding his clothes, he sauntered over, still humming and eager for his lover's response.

When he bent down, blocking the light of the sun, her eyes flew open. She quickly appraised his condition. "Not now, darling, please. Later, you bet. I'm trying to compose a poem."

Owen sat on the rock with a sigh. "Well, poetry, that's good."

"Yes. But I'm having trouble keeping it straight. Usually I take notes and write it down as I go. Now I have to keep it all in my head. In fact, it'd probably be better if you didn't talk to me, either. I'll make it up to you, I promise." She smiled and closed her eyes, returning to a private realm of concentration.

Owen touched her arm lightly, then scooped up Thorn from the reeds and walked along the edge of the pond until they were out of earshot. He placed the toad in the water and sat on a log, stretching his bare feet to soak. "You heard her. Can't we cook up some kind of writing technology? I'm surprised she hasn't tried already. There was a poem of hers that talked about writing with charcoal on bark."

Thorn rotated in the water and faced Owen. "Expressions of needful requirements precipitate fulfillment, most typically. Ask not, have not. Charcoal and bark, yes, yes, possibilities. More delicate lines achieved with feathery pens and ink forged from alchemy of oak galls and iron, a production of hands preceded by quest of legs."

Owen was never sure he understood the toad's oblique syntax. After a pause, he replied. "So, let me get this straight: you're saying it would be possible to manufacture ink from... from oak galls and iron?"

"Precision of response keeps edges keen."

"Okay, okay. Oak galls shouldn't be that hard to find. In fact, I think there are some on our shelter tree, and certainly more could be collected in the woods. But iron?"

"Hence necessity of legs. Northwards, a journey afoot, a mountain of iron. Powdered galls ferried on high, mixed with rich mineral springs fleeing mountain's ferrous clutch, a mashing, a storage, a transportation. A brew devised to capture creativity. How noble! What alchemy!"

"God, you're weird. But I get it. I think. And perhaps one of those crows could donate a feather or two for quills?"

"Detach, derive, donate, deconstruct the corvid."

"Sure. So how do we find this iron mountain?"

"Crows are restless; crows can go."

"They wouldn't mind showing the way?"

"Expressions of needful requirements precipitate fulfillment."

"So you said. They've never talked to me before. Well, not in English, anyway."

"Language preference, hardly fluency."

As Thorn spoke, Owen heard the crows squawking in the woods. They were somewhere on the far side of the camp near the portal tree. Owen looked down at Thorn. "You okay here? I'm going to express some needful requirements to those crows."

"Stasis acceptable, gratitude for inquiry."

Owen wanted to tell Dana the news, but she lay still, absorbed in her poetics. He would talk to the crows first, if indeed they were willing to talk to him. Then he could present her with the project as a surprise.

At the tarp, he slipped into his clothes. They wore at least a minimal garment most of the time, for protection from the occasional insect or sharp branch or the coolness of the shade. Their feet were tough, but they used moccasins on rough ground, including journeys of any distance. For the occasion of asking the crows for a favor, Owen decided that clothes made the proceedings more dignified. A silly notion, no doubt, based on old habits; no matter how much he changed, his past remained the same.

He wandered off in the direction of the last crow calls. It had sounded like they were near the portal tree, but, of course, they could have flown away. Whatever they were up to, now they were doing it in silence. As Thorn said, they were restless, in constant movement, sometimes cruising over the pond, sometimes jumping around on the ground, other times flapping off into the woods, vocal at length, then quiet for spells, but never appearing to do the same thing twice.

When he arrived at the portal tree, he rotated slowly, looking deep into the woods in all directions. No crows. Owen stopped moving and listened, trying to sense them. He let his awareness descend into the rhizome and there he found the information, filtering back through the trees and along the mycorrhizal pathways of the network. They weren't far away.

He trotted through the woods to their perch. A flutter in the branches and a crow swept out of one tree and into another, disappearing behind the foliage. Owen stopped, took a deep breath, and having no better way to address them, called out, "Thorn!" It seemed strange, but now that was the name for everything. He still hadn't gotten used to it, even though it was his idea.

The treetops rustled and a crow swooped down to light on a branch just above Owen's head. It peered at him for a while, then croaked and said, "Are you talking…"

"…to us?" The sentence was finished by the other crow who dove in from a different angle and perched next to its companion.

Owen regarded the two crows. There was nothing to distinguish one from the other. "Yes, please. Thank you for your attention. I have a request."

As before, one crow initiated a response to be completed by the other. "Manners…"

"…are good."

"Regale us…"

"…with your request."

Owen sighed. Another permutation of the multiplicity, he supposed. They're all Thorn but they're all different. Then again, they shared knowledge and memories, he understood that, but the nodal expressions certainly demonstrated stylistic variety. And the content wasn't uniform; specific areas of the rhizome contained specialized data—all organized in a scheme too subtle for his comprehension. A mind, he was beginning to realize, was far more complex and sophisticated than a library, no matter how infinite the library. And an ecology that was also a mind… he pulled himself short before he fell into the vertigo.

Meanwhile, the crows groomed each other. Owen said, "I've been told that away to the north is a mountain of iron. I'd like to go there and Thorn, well, the toad, suggested that you two may be willing to guide me."

"Is there…"

"...a question?"

Owen looked dumbly at the crows. Literalists, he determined. "Will you be so kind as to guide me to this iron mountain?"

"Just..."

"...you?"

"Dana, too, if she wants to come and my guess is that she'll want to come."

"We will..."

"...do this deed."

"In addition..."

"...we will donate feathers."

"And we can help..."

"...harvest galls..."

"...high in the trees."

Owen was surprised at how fast the information had spread through the rhizome. The idea of the oak gall ink had only been discussed with the toad less than an hour before. "Thank you. When would you be willing to go?"

"Galls need..."

"...to be collected..."

"...to be crushed..."

"...and dried to a powder."

"We will start..."

"...gathering now."

"We gather..."

"...you smash and dry."

"Also worth noting..."

"...acorns work..."

"...as well as galls."

"Probably more acorns…"

"…this time of year."

"Okay, thank you! I'll go back to the camp and talk to Dana. Can you deliver galls and acorns there?"

"We…"

"…can…"

"…and will."

Owen saluted the crows and marched back to the pond. It was exhausting listening to them complete each other's statements. He didn't know why it should be so tiring, but it was. Perhaps another manifestation of the human mind's inadequate wiring for multiplicity.

When he returned to the campsite, Dana sat under the oak, parked with her back against the trunk next to the lounging raccoon. She waved at Owen with a mischievous expression that he knew well. Feigning absorption in the task of picking through polypore chunks, she exaggerated the required motions, occasionally elbowing the raccoon in the shoulder or dropping pieces of fungus on its head, then burping out an "oops!" or "oh my!" Owen laughed at her antics, none of which seemed to perturb the beast.

He dropped down beside her. "I've got a mission for us."

Dana looked at him with curiosity. "What, no queries for the bard? No 'did you complete your lyric, my dear'? No kiss? You just show up and we're off on a mission?"

He leaned toward her and kissed her ear. "An oversight, another one. Please forgive me, my liege. And how went your session with the muse?"

"Hmm. Inconclusive. I need to take notes."

"Well, you know, speaking of that... Remember your poem 'The Invention of Poetry'?"

Dana stared at Owen for a moment, then understood his reference. "Of course! Charcoal on bark! Duh! But wait a minute. We don't have the means to start a fire. Or do we? Is that why you're looking so smug?"

"Well, no, we don't at the moment, though I imagine we could figure that out. And if it gets much colder, we're going to need to. Not to mention a better shelter than the tarp. In one of his more lucid moments, my uncle taught me survival skills, and I do remember how to make a fire from a bow drill. So, yeah, we could do that. But—and this is the real news—I think I've figured out a way for you to write."

"What? Details, please."

"Have you ever heard of oak gall ink?"

"Sort of. At least I remember reading something about it once upon a time. It's what they used in medieval days, right?"

"Exactly. I talked about this with Thorn while you were composing. The ink is pretty simple to make, just a mixture of crushed oak galls and acorns fermented in a mash. Add ferrous sulfate and water and *voila*! Ink. A quill pen and bark fabric and you can write a book for the ages."

"Ferrous sulfate?"

"Iron, basically. According to Thorn, north of here is a mountain rich with iron. Some of the springs that flow from the mountain are heavy enough with the mineral that all we need to do is mix it with the gall mash, bottle, and store."

"Wow. Aren't you the clever subject? I may have to keep you around, after all."

"Thank you. I also had a conversation with those two crows. Yes, they talk! A little crazy, but I guess we're getting used to that…. Anyway, they can guide us to the iron mountain. In fact, they're scouring the woods as we speak, gathering galls for us. They also promised to supply you with feathers for pens."

The gleam in Dana's eye gratified Owen, but when she reached over and gave him a hug, planting kisses on his face, he recalled his earlier desire. She anticipated this ardor. "Hey there, hero, maybe it's time for your reward."

They rolled around to the other side of the tree and made love, ignoring the raccoon and the thump of oak galls and acorns being delivered, several at a time. Afterward, they gathered up the oak products and took them to a flat rock in the sun. Dana found a smooth, cylindrical stone in the pond's outlet stream, hefty enough for grinding but small enough to fit the hand. They took turns crushing the galls and acorns, then spreading the results across the broad surface of the rock to dry.

While the crushed remnants baked in the sun, they sat under the tarp and sewed containers. They would need one for the mash, likely to be gooey, one to collect iron water, and a third one to combine the two ingredients. Dana selected samples of the finest bark fabric to bring along for pen-on-paper tests. Owen hoped to find iron deposits along the flow of the springs, which might yield enough concentrate to bring home and manufacture ink without the travel. It took another day of crafting to make the containers and other gear needed for the journey, including two rucksacks to carry the bags, food, water for drinking, and other tools. By that time the galls and acorn fragments were dry enough to crush into a powder. Blended with water from the pond, the resulting goo filled a small pouch. Preparations complete, they packed and planned to leave the next morning.

[36]

At sunrise, the two crows stood on the sun-bathing rock next to the pond. There was a slight chill in the air, so Dana and Owen dressed quickly, shouldered their packs, and walked down to the water.

"Okay, corvus and corvus, which way to the fabulous riches?" Owen asked.

"Just..."

"...follow us." They launched into the air, did a few circles, and flapped off to the north.

Dana looked at Owen and laughed. "I see what you mean about them."

Rounding the pond and entering the woods, they wondered how to follow the birds, now out of sight. Stopping to consider their options, a caw echoed through the trees, followed by wing sounds as the two crows flew over their heads, turned without a word, and cruised back in the direction they came from, cawing loudly. Owen and Dana walked, tracking the noisy duo. The trees provided consistent cover but were not so dense as to deceive them into circles. Whenever they felt unsure about the way to go, the crows resumed their racket, leaving no doubt about the course.

They hiked steadily through the woods, enjoying the terrain. The land rolled up and down with no overall change in elevation and the forest offered an endless mix of hardwoods. Every so often they emerged into a small clearing where the sky and sun tempted them to linger, but the crows, perched on the opposite side, flew off as soon as the humans came into view, beckoning them on with their caws. They stopped every hour or so to drink water and munch a few polypores and dried berries from their packs. When they did, the crows returned, strutting back and forth in front of them with obvious disapproval.

While they journeyed, Owen and Dana chatted at times but mostly they moved in silence, focused on a walking trance. Occasionally Dana recited one of her poems, or lyrics she remembered from the poems of others. Another time Owen shared a version of the Welsh myth of Gwion Bach, accompanied by his own interpretations. They savored the act of travelling together on foot; there was a peace in the rhythm of movement and breath, and pleasure in the grace of being with each other.

The day wore on, the sky clouded over, and there were no longer shafts of raw sun filtering through the woods. The light became monochromatic, and they heard the wind increase in the tops of the trees. A hint of rain was in the air and they contemplated the consequences of bringing no shelter except the clothes they wore and the two blankets they used for a bed.

When they caught up to the crows, Owen called out. "Hey, you guys, wait up!"

The crows flew back and landed on the ground in front of them, standing with still feet but bending their heads and looking at the humans from different angles. "Yes..."

"...you called?"

Owen stated the obvious. "It feels like a storm is coming."

"You would be..."

"...entirely correct."

Owen and Dana looked at the crows expectantly and the crows looked back, continuing to twist and bend their heads but saying nothing.

"So... how far are we from the iron mountain?"

"For us..."

"...a few hours."

"For you..."

"...another day."

Dana giggled at the call and response. She contained herself enough to ask, "We wondered if you might, in your aerial wisdom, know of any shelter nearby that would serve to keep us dry. A cave, an overhang, anything of the sort."

"We welcome..."

"...your recognition..."

"...of our sagacity and yes..."

"...we know of something..."

"...that will serve..."

"...perfectly."

Owen nodded in appreciation. "Lead on, then, because it'd be nice to settle in before dark and rain. Not far, I hope?"

"Not..."

"...far."

The wind increased, strumming and twisting the upper boughs of the trees so that the forest rolled above them like a turbulent sea. Stepping out of the trees and onto an open expanse of grass earned brought respite from the churning woods. A stream ran through the meadow and Owen thought that in calm weather, this place would be an idyllic interlude from the continuous overstory. Now it left them exposed to the winds, reddening their faces. Large drops splattered from a darkening sky. The crows crossed the clearing, flapping hard to stay on course toward a point where the stream emerged from the far edge of the woods. The crows landed on what looked like a tipi. Owen pointed it out to Dana, but she was already staring at it. Eager, they picked up the pace.

It was a tipi. As they approached, they slowed and came to a halt several yards away. Owen called out, "Hello, anybody home?"

The crows were perched on the poles projecting above the peak. "Save your voice..."

"...there's no one home."

"Well, where did this come from? Whose is it?"

"We're pretty sure..."

"...that it's yours..."

"...now."

"What?"

"It was built..."

"...by that Chouinard..."

"...before she journeyed..."

"...off to the east..."

"...in quest of..."

"...something..."

"... but she didn't say..."

"...what."

"Unfuckingreal," Owen said. Dana studied the design painted over the door flaps, a double spiral, each of seven windings, with the tails joined in a continuous line. Emerging from the crotch where the two spirals met was a smaller, third spiral.

"Owen, did you see this? I wonder what it means?"

"She..."

"...didn't say."

The rainstorm unleashed its arsenal, with drops coming faster, harder, and closer together. Owen opened the flap and crawled into the tipi, closely followed by Dana. A stone-lined fire pit sat in the center, filled with kindling and small sticks ready for ignition. Next to the fire pit was a stack of dead branches, a bow drill, and a spark board. A packet contained strands of cedar bark. Owen looked at Dana and said, "Really now. The doctor's ghost, or whatever she is, is awfully considerate." Owen grabbed the fire-making materials. As he fumbled with the tools, his memory for the technique returned, and before long he had a smoldering spark in the board's trough, which he placed under the kindling. As it caught flame, he remembered that the smoke flaps were closed. Dana took over tending the fire while Owen dashed outside to spread the flaps with the two poles for that purpose. Despite the now driving rain, he paused long enough to admire the glow of fire within the tipi and Dana's silhouette outlined on the walls.

Owen ducked inside and shook off the bigger drops. He untied his ponytail to dry his hair in the fast-warming interior. When he looked at Dana, she was sitting on the other side of the fire with a puzzled look. "Check this out," she said.

He crawled around and sat next to her. In her lap was a neatly folded bundle about three feet long and two feet wide. "Go ahead, open it."

She placed it carefully on the ground and unfolded the cover. Inside were three other bundles, two large and one small. She unwrapped one of the large bundles to find a hooded parka. The exterior of the parka was made from a tough looking oilcloth. It was lined with a softer, cotton-like material. Dana fingered the rim of the hood, which looked like fur. "My god, it's some kind of shredded bark, I think."

She held up the parka to see that it was large for her, so she handed it to Owen and unrolled the next bundle. It contained another parka that looked more fitting and she slipped it over her head. "This is wonderful, Owen!" Her eyes gleamed. Owen tried on his parka. A perfect fit. With trembling hands, Dana picked up the last bundle and unrolled it to find a tiny, one-piece suit made in a similar fashion. She held it in the air as tears dripped from her eyes.

"You know, Owen, whatever Dr. Chouinard has become, she's pretty fucking magical."

Owen said nothing as feelings choked off all the words. He snuggled next to Dana, put his arm around her shoulder and squeezed. She hugged the baby suit to her chest and curled into his lap. He heard her say, in a muffled voice, "My period is late."

"What?"

"I didn't want to say anything, cause, you know, there could be a lot of reasons for that. But, maybe I'm pregnant."

Owen felt the blood drain from his head. He stroked Dana's hair, speaking softly. "I hope you are."

She rolled over so she could look up into his face. "But can we really make it work? I mean, we don't have any idea about the future or what kind of life we can provide or any of that. I always thought I would have a child in the right circumstances, but, you know, when I imagined circumstances, I never thought of any-thing like this."

"Me neither. Well, I never thought I'd have a kid, actually. It seemed hard enough to imagine having a girlfriend. But, if you think about it, and given the state of the world, I mean, worlds, are there any better circumstances?"

"I know what you mean. Do you suppose that lazy raccoon would babysit?"

Owen laughed and pulled Dana upright, crushing the baby suit between them as they embraced. The embrace became a long kiss, broken only to unroll their bedding and stoke the fire before making love in the flickering light.

[37]

The next day dawned with a chill in the air. It had rained through the night, pelting the skin of the tipi in steady drum-rolls, finally slacking by first light. When Owen emerged, he saw the crows, limp and draggled, as if they hadn't budged from the tipi poles.

"I'm sorry!" he called up to them. "We should have invited you inside."

"We do not care..."

"...for such confinement."

"Well, okay. Thanks for leading us here. An excellent shelter!"

"The good doctor..."

"...takes good care..."

"...of you and yours."

"By any chance do you know where she is or what she's do-ing?"

"We only know…"

"…that she's gone far…"

"…to the east…"

"and has no further need…"

"…of this shelter."

"When we return…"

"…from the mountain…"

"…you could take it…"

"…back to the pond…"

"…if you like."

Owen liked the idea of taking the tipi home with them, despite the weight and awkward bulk. But it would solve the need for better shelter. Dana stuck a disheveled head through the door flaps, "What's with all the cawing and jawing? Did I miss morning tea?"

"Afraid so. As did we all, since we have no tea. But now that we have a way to start fires, we might consider brewing some. There's gotta be caffeine in this ecosystem." Dana crawled out of the tipi and sauntered to Owen, giving him a hug and kiss. He responded in kind and continued with his line of thought. "You know, we've been content to live here and take things as they come, but I'm beginning to wonder if we're being too passive. Look what Dr. Chouinard has been up to: making huts, tipis, clothes, tools, and who knows what else? Admittedly, she's more integrated into this world and may have a better understanding of the potential, but if this is our new home, we should apply some imagination. I mean, you wanted to write and now we're assembling the materials to do that. We come from a world where things are provided in retail arenas and you exchange money to get them, but here, the only economy is the one we devise in living off the land."

"True enough, my ambitious mate. This is a bountiful place. But we need to be careful and consider the impact of resource extraction. It's not something we can do heedlessly, with no thought to consequences or the ultimate cost of the extraction. Here, our economy is the ecosystem itself. We need to think sustenance, not just advantage. Otherwise we'll just be replicating the fucked-up bullshit humans have done to the environment in our world, right?"

Owen stared across the open field and thought about what she said. "You're right on the money... so to speak." Dana groaned but Owen rushed on. "And thank you for saying that. Our job isn't just to live but to evolve a new culture. We can't allow ourselves to carry over the crap we grew up with. With fire comes power and we have to be careful with power. Sure, now we can burn things, but the things we burn are also our friends, our family, our whole fucking matrix of life. Are we going to start chopping down trees, splitting out lumber, building houses, banks, whatever? Is that the life we want for our... child?"

The crows interrupted. "Is someone..."

"...having a baby?" And followed this with raucous squawks.

Owen blushed and looked down while Dana spoke. "We don't know for sure, but, yeah, maybe."

The crows responded with an astounding variety of calls, bobbing their heads and stretching their necks while emitting an unprecedented racket.

When the noise subsided, Owen continued. "I'm glad you brought it up, Dana, it's something we need to work out. I think there are several ways we can orient ourselves to using resources. So far, we've mostly taken what's been given, but the ink idea came from a request. As Thorn said, in its toadish way, 'expressions of needful requirements precipitate fulfillment.'"

Dana giggled. "You do that well."

"Channeling the inner pedant, that's all. Anyway, if we approach needs with requests, either to our sterling representatives," and here Owen waved at the crows and bowed, "or directly into the rhizome when we're linked, we can learn how to use what's available. And we could do something like the Native Americans; they developed rituals of thanks and appreciation as a token of exchange for resources. Nothing was taken without an offering of prayers, tobacco, or even their own flesh."

"I like that. Though I can do without the self-mutilation part, thanks. But we can certainly develop our own rituals of gratitude."

"Yes! Maybe you could compose a poem for our prayer of thanks."

"Hmm. Interesting idea... let me think about that. You're right, though—there are things we could use that we've done without. Maybe we don't really have to abstain. For example, you could use a hairbrush or possibly it's too late for that, in which case you need scissors."

Owen tried to run his fingers through his long, matted hair but it was impossibly knotted. Dana scratched her own head. "And mine is starting to get shaggy. Time for a haircut. But you could probably just shave my head with one of those stone knives."

"Shave your head?"

"Sure, why not? Easier than trying to clip it down with stone tools. I've shaved it before, just to blow people's minds. Reinforces my egghead reputation. And it's wicked easy to take care of."

"Whatever you want. But I think the crows are getting restless. We should pack up and head for the mountain." Owen was right; the crows jumped from the tip of one tipi pole to another in a deliberate fashion, touching on all thirteen of the lodge poles before starting over. Dana and Owen watched with amusement.

Dana said, "I love this tipi. I wish we could keep it."

"Guess what? It seems we can. The crow twins suggested we bundle it up on the way back and take it to the pond."

"Great! Maybe we can roll it like a log. Hell, I'll drag it if we have to."

Owen scratched his beard, struck by a new thought. "Hey, Thorns, how did Dr. Chouinard get these lodge poles? Did she cut down live trees or where did they come from?"

The crows stopped jumping. "The poles..."

"...were gathered one by one..."

"...with love and affection..."

"...from the sacrifice area..."

"...surrounding the cancer..."

"...you call..."

"...the bleached zone."

"Ah, okay, that makes sense. Is there other dead wood in that area that we could use? Assuming we could transport it, of course."

"We don't see..."

"...why not."

Dana and Owen stuffed their bedding and extra items into the packs, refilled the water bottles from the stream, and resumed the journey northward to the iron mountain. As the sun rose, warmer air sifted through the trees and the effort of walking uphill forced them to soon shed their parkas. The trees got smaller and denser as Owen and Dana climbed and despite the tough fabric of their clothes, they acquired scratches and wounds from the sharp branches.

After a period of silence, Owen shared a thought that he'd been carrying for miles. "I really miss having some books. After we get the ink, I suppose we could write our own. But that doesn't seem quite the same."

"Me too. And no, it's not the same. I don't even count reading my own stuff as reading. At least not for pleasure."

When they caught up to the crows again, Owen voiced his wish. "Hey, before you two fly ahead, I have a question! Is there any possibility of accessing human literature in readable form? Probably sounds crazy – but I was told to think of the rhizome as a library. So, I wonder: any way we can check out some books?"

The crows sat together on a branch and looked at Owen with their obsidian eyes. Owen stared back at them and Dana watched all three. Finally, the crows spoke. "Do you have..."

"...a library card?" And they exploded in caws.

Owen looked miffed but Dana giggled. "They told a joke; that's awesome! Come on, lighten up." And she punched Owen in the shoulder.

"Some human culture..."

"...is stored..."

"...and is accessible."

"However…"

"…we can't offer…"

"…books as you know them."

Owen chewed his lip. "What can you offer?"

"What…"

"…do you want?"

"Well, can you get us a copy, I mean, a simulacrum or whatever it is you're offering, of, say… *Finnegans Wake*?"

Dana laughed. "Great, then we could resume our game! And, without a doubt, that's a book we could get a lot of mileage out of."

The crows went silent and seemed to be in conference, presumably with the rhizome mind. Finally, they turned to the humans and delivered their judgment. "Maybe…"

"…but it's not going to…"

"…resemble anything…"

"…you might expect."

Owen was impressed. "Really? You can produce a copy of *Finnegans Wake*? That's truly amazing. So how do we get it?"

"It will be…"

"…at the pond…"

"…waiting for your return."

"Warning…"

"…it will be…"

"…a bit unwieldy."

Dana and Owen traded glances, wondering what this meant, but the crows offered no further information. "Okay, well, thanks! I look forward to seeing it."

And the crows flapped off to the north.

They slowed their pace as the terrain steepened. During the last hour of travel, they'd caught glimpses of the mountain through the woods as they ascended. Crossing the tree limit, they stepped out of the forest to find themselves at the base of a massive monolith of rock, a round dome a half mile in diameter, gleaming with schists and silica in bands of contrasting colors. The crows cawed from a hundred yards away along the tree line. Owen and Dana scrambled through rocks and heather toward them, stumbling whenever they tried to gawk and move at the same time. As far as they could see there was forest, endless to the horizon.

The crows had perched on a small outcrop. At the base of the rock water bubbled from the face into an eroded trough. The resulting stream ran down the exposed ledge and into the grass and trees below. Along the sides of the trough the rock was stained a brownish red.

"There is…"

"…your iron…"

"…more than enough…"

"…in the water…"

"…and crystallized…"

"…on the rock."

"Great!" said Owen, "But it looks like the sun's going down and maybe it's a bit late to perform feats of metallurgy. I think we should go down into the woods for shelter and do this in the morning."

"Good thinking," said Dana, "and from the feel of it, it's going to be a cold night."

"Suit yourselves…"

"...but whatever you do..."

"...don't drink this water..."

"...or you won't shit..."

"...for a month." The crows, pleased with their latest joke, made a fabulous racket and flew off to the summit of the mountain, leaving the humans to digest the humor with pained expressions. On reflex, Owen checked the amount of water in his pouch. It was low, but they hadn't used any of Dana's, so there would be enough for the night. After a survey of the countryside in the declining light, they watched the sun drop past the edge of the world.

It was time to make camp. Unwilling to sacrifice elevation, they found a ledge just below tree limit. Hardly flat, at least it spanned enough for two bodies. They had no padding to go underneath and they weren't going to harvest the boughs of live trees for cushions, so they used what they had: thin blankets. Hunched in their parkas, they chewed rations and sipped water, careful not to use too much of either. With the last light draining from the sky, they crawled under a single blanket and snuggled as close as they could get, feeding off the mutual warmth. They said prayers to Dr. Chouinard for the parkas, which made the difference between merely being cold and experiencing hypothermia. Still, it was a long night.

## [38]

Spells of shivering pursued them through the night, forcing deeper embraces in which they preserved barely enough heat to get through the dark hours. The bark fabric of the blanket retained some body heat, the parkas even more, but never enough to relax. Yet the worst part of the night wasn't the temperature, it was the hardness of the rock. The blanket they used as a pad didn't soften anything, so after a few hours they put it on top with the other one and lay directly on the rough stone. The cold and the unforgiving density of the rock defined the night and seemed to last forever.

At the first peek of light from the east, Owen lifted his head and saw that Dana was wide awake, staring at him and trying to pull him closer, but there was no closer to get. Seeing that he was awake, she laughed, one of those staccato woodpecker laughs. Owen grinned, and soon they were kissing, hungry for the warmth inside each other's mouth.

"That was not the most fun way to sleep with my girlfriend, but I do thank you for your body heat."

"And I, you."

"Funny to hear myself calling you 'girlfriend,' you seem like so much more than that to me."

"Yes, I know what you mean. We're pretty well-mated at this point, you and I."

"Mate is the right term. Which makes me wonder, especially if we have a child: should we marry?"

"Hah! I can see the crows performing the ceremony, right?"

Owen chuckled at the thought. "Well, we could do it any way we wanted. By ourselves, with them, whatever. I mean, if you want to."

"Are you asking me to marry you?"

Owen took a breath and looked into Dana's brown eyes, admiring them, feeling an intensity of affection for her that seemed boundless. "Yeah, I am."

Dana laughed in delight. "You bet, buster. Let's do it. Well, maybe not right this instant."

"Right. When we get back."

"When we get back."

Their decision was sealed with a long kiss. After, Owen said, "Hey, this may sound a little batty but what about hiking up to the top of this rock before we start working on the ink? It would warm us up and I'd like to see the view. We've spent so much time beneath the canopy of trees and under the ground that it's really something to see the forest from above."

"Great idea! I'll race you."

Dana threw off the blankets, grabbed her pack, and chugged uphill, quickly bursting past the tree limit and onto the open rock. Owen chuckled and rolled out of the bedding. It took a few minutes to stuff the blankets into his pack and move off in leisurely pursuit. No way he would beat her to the top, anyway. She was too strong, too fast, and too competitive. He didn't care; he looked forward to the inevitable teasing.

He dumped the pack at the stream, but still huffed as he climbed the slope. It was steep, but not steep enough for hand-holds, so he compromised with a simian crouch, scrambling over the rock, using his hands when he could. From a distance, the dome appeared smooth, but up close it consisted of deep clefts and exfoliated slabs. Ledges and lower-angle sections were lit-tered with pebbles, gravel, and boulders. The footing required constant attention, not easy when his calves screamed for a break. It was light enough to see the country below, but every time he stole a glance, he stumbled. He gained renewed appreciation for Dana's strength and agility. By the time he grunted on to the summit, she sat on a bench-like formation of rock like she'd been there for days, kicking her feet in the air and popping mushrooms into her mouth.

"Look who's here," she said. grinning.

"Sensational appearance of the tortoise," he gasped, sagging onto the rock. She handed him the water pouch and the packet of food. The sun had breached the horizon and cast long shadows, painting the forest with layers of ocean: dark strands under the surface of the light-sparkled crowns. Dana pointed to the west and Owen followed her arm to see, on a distant ridge, the glaring white desert of the bleached zone. The rest of the world below their gaze spread out in waves of arboreal life, but the bleached zone presented a stark anomaly. Around it was the containment area, the circle of sacrificed trees cut off from the life of the rhizome, standing barren like charred stems after a forest fire. In that zone were places of beauty and importance – places Owen would never forget. Now they lived only in his memory.

"I guess if we need to remember what the last few months have been all about, there's that." Owen gestured to the distant ridge.

"Yeah. There's that. And an interesting few months it's been, I have to say."

"Are you sorry you got involved in this? With me?"

Dana frowned and shook her head. "Don't get all insecure on me. Of course not. This is life, my darling. You don't choose it or chart it, you navigate it. I think we're doing a fine job of that, all things considered."

"Sorry, old habits peeking through. No regrets here. I mean, I've lost a house and been a witness to mayhem, destruction and death, but what else can you expect during wartime? And I think that's what's going on. Humanity versus the universe. Or like that dumb tv show: Man v. Wild. Except it really ought to be man v. life. I guess that makes us traitors to man." As he talked, Owen lost his anxiety. "If we have to take sides, I'm on the side of life. And I'm on your side. Or by your side, as it happens." He nudged her shoulder.

"I wouldn't call it treason, what we're doing. Far from it. We're doing what we have to do to preserve life for the whole system, not just one stupid species. Life is too important to cast aside for undeserved loyalties, right?"

"Well put, o master of words. No wonder I brought you along."

Dana smiled. "Speaking of words, let's go make some ink."

They descended the dome to find the crows sitting on the outcrop at the stream, flaring their ruffs and bobbing heads in the style of true corvids.

"Good morning, Thorns, how goes the world?" Owen called out.

"Is this..."

"...a metaphysical inquiry..."

"...or human banter..."

"...absent of meaning?"

Dana snorted but Owen stopped and put his hands on his hips. "Now, now, no need for sarcasm, especially this early in the morning. I was merely inquiring as to the state of your being, but knowing that the two of you are manifestations of the forest mind, which is tantamount to saying the world, I thought to encompass the whole enchilada, as we like to say back home."

Dana giggled and waited for the response. The crows hopped around on the rock, cawing, but provided no further comment.

Opening their packs, Owen and Dana retrieved the components of the project: a pouch full of oak gall and acorn mash, an empty pouch for scooping up the iron-rich water, and a stirring stick. As Dana bent over the stream to fill the water pouch, Owen picked at the rusty crystals accumulated on the rock along the water's edge. "We should try to scrape up some of this stuff. It looks like pure iron – at least it's got that color. Maybe we can gather this for future batches."

"Good idea. Maybe you can find a stone with a scraping edge. I'm going to try mixing a little bit of this mash with the water to see if it makes ink. Of course," and here she looked pointedly at the crows, "I will need some sort of a quill to actually try writing."

"First they make jokes..."

"...at our expense..."

"...then they want..."

"...feathery favors."

Dana continued staring at the two crows. Owen stopped his task to watch the interaction. "Please." Dana said. The crows hopped about a bit, ignoring her, then one of them reached into its wing with the claws of one foot and plucked out a primary feather, casually dropping it in the stream. It floated down to Dana, who picked it up carefully, shaking off the water. "Thank you," she said, nodding at the crows.

Taking advantage of a concave depression in the rock, she had lined it with a section of waterproof fabric, making a shallow mixing bowl. It was full of the test batch—a blackish fluid that shimmered with promise. She pulled a few swatches of bark fabric and a knife from her pack. Slicing off the tip of the feather, she sharpened it to a point. She inspected the feather, turning it in her hand with ritual precision. Dipping the quill in the fluid, she put it to a smooth piece of fabric, drawing a short, blobby line. "Hmmm," she said, and reached for the water pouch to add a few drops to the mixture. She stirred and tried again. This time a smooth line rolled out from the tip of the quill. "Ooooh," she said, before bending over the parchment to write a few words. She leaned back and handed the scrap to Owen. It said, in careful script, "I love you."

Owen blushed to see it in writing. "Thank you! If you're satisfied with the proportions, go ahead and mix up the whole batch. I'll continue the iron scraping. This is so cool. We've just invented literature!" This pronouncement drew staccato protests from the crows and Owen quickly amended his statement. "Thanks to our doughty corvids!"

It was late morning when they completed the task. They had a hefty pouch of ink, perhaps a quart, and a fist-sized bundle heavy with iron scrapings. Time to go home. They packed their things and took in one last view before donning loads and striding down into the forest, preceded by the crows. It was dark when they reached the tipi. Exhausted from the climb and a restless night, they had a quick fire, ate the last of their food stores, and huddled together to sleep in warmth and comfort.

Though tired, they rose early, anticipating a long day of travel. While Dana foraged in the woods for edible fungi, Owen dismantled the tipi. He pulled down the cover, stretched it flat on the ground and folded the fabric into a bundle the size of a corpse. The poles made a neat stack next to the cover. When Dana returned, they sat on the bundle, munching polypores, and contemplated how best to move the tipi. The crows hopped around the grass, pecking at things or grooming one other.

Between bouts of fungus chewing, Owen shared his thoughts. "I guess we could rig up a kind of travois."

Dana, mouth full, muttered, "Whassat?"

"Plains Indian transport system. Take two long poles and lash them together at a single point about a quarter of the length from an end. The juncture sits on the shoulders of a pack animal, usually a horse or dog, and the two tails fan out in a triangle. A couple of sticks are lashed across the triangle, stabilizing the angles and supporting the load. The beast of burden, in this case us, is yoked to the apex and walks along, dragging the poles. Definitely a system for four-legged beasts, but our measly two each will have to serve. Should work. It's surprising how much weight can be moved by lifting one end and dragging. I've done that to log out fence poles and big branches back on the farm."

"Can one person drag the whole thing, poles and all?"

"I doubt that. I'm thinking two travois rigs: one for the tipi skin and our packs, the other for the remaining poles. We can always start and if it doesn't work, we can try something else. Even if we don't get it all the way home in one go, every step closer is progress. Maybe it'll take us several days to get it all there, but in the end, it'll be worth it."

"Agreed with that. But it'd be really nice to get it there today, don't you think?"

"Yeah, I do. So, let's do it."

As they laid out and lashed together two travois rigs, Owen called to the crows. "Hey, Thorns, how the hell did Dr. Chouinard move these poles all the way from the bleached zone? Last I saw her she looked an awful lot like a little old woman."

The crows stopped their preening and pecking and looked at Owen. "Oh, the doctor..."

"...has a deal..."

"...with the ants..."

"...to do her heavy lifting."

"A deal? What kind of a deal?"

"We're not..."

"...entirely sure."

"She operates with..."

"...a curious autonomy..."

"...regarding the rhizome..."

"...and seems to..."

"...forge her own alliances."

"Wait a minute. You're telling me that Dr. Chouinard has evolved enough independence to function within and without the rhizome, developing her own network of relationships, and her own agenda, which is not clear to you? Is that what you're saying?"

"Something..."

"...like that."

Owen looked at Dana and shrugged. "Would sure like to run into her again. I have more than a few questions. And just maybe she'd be willing to develop an alliance with us."

Dana smiled at him. "Well, really, I think she already has." She swept her hand to indicate the disassembled tipi and their belongings.

"True. I'd love for you to meet her, though. Whatever she is at this point. I do miss her. I don't know why it should matter, but it does. I don't like to leave good things behind. There are so few of them in a lifetime, I think."

Dana gave him a hug. "I know what you mean. Luckily we have each other."

"Yeah, meeting you was the best thing that's happened to me. And being with you is more than I ever imagined. But I don't like loose ends."

"Well then, let's tie them up and get on the road."

The sun had cleared the tree-tops before they left the meadow. After a testy debate, they apportioned the travois loads into roughly equal shares. At first, Owen had pressed to take the heavier burden, but Dana refused the deference. She reminded him of who won the race to the top of the iron mountain. He relented, finally, recognizing that he was being foolish. Anyway, it was an argument he wasn't going to win; he understood that much.

With the crossed poles resting on their shoulders, they tied lines around their chests for harness. They started the trek, walking in single file, taking slow and deliberate steps. It required tedious focus before they worked out a rhythm of movement, but once they found the best posture, they made progress. The width of the travois forced them into the most open course through the woods. When the trees were too close together, branches could snag the poles, causing the delicate balance of body rhythm to jar to a halt or slew to the side. These events summoned curses or screams, depending on their frustration. They welcomed opportunities to stop for food and water, though it was hard to get going again after the breaks. Once they learned how to haul the loads with relative grace, the two crows perched on the front of each projecting pole, riding like figureheads on the bow of a ship. Dana complained about favoritism when the crows rode with Owen, so they divided their attentions, one for each human. Their presence provided some amusement, though neither Dana nor Owen had the energy for talk. As each crow seemed able to offer only a quarter of a conversation, they travelled in silence.

The focused labor paid off and they made it back to their camp before dark. The travois rigs were dropped without ceremony and the crows fluttered into the air. Dana and Owen walked straight to the pond, stripped off their clothes, and waded in. It was good to be home.


[39]

A week went by before Owen and Dana, munching berries and fungi, sat under the oak tree and planned their wedding. "Should we recruit a Thorn to officiate the ceremony?" Owen asked.

"Nah. God knows what they'd make of it. Which one, anyway?" Dana scooped a handful of dried berries from a bag and filled her mouth.

"Yeah, I dunno."

"We…"

"…could do it," came the croaks from an overhead branch.

Owen looked up, wondering how long the two crows had been perched there, spying. "NO," he and Dana said at the same time. They grinned at the synchronicity and slapped a high five.

"We want to create our own ceremony, one that reflects our values," Owen said, and Dana nodded. "I can think of a few problems if we hand the ceremony over to the Thorns. Black, Red, and Whitethorn would squabble at the worst time, pushing and shoving, oozing sarcasm—all that stuff. At best, we'd have to endure pedantic lectures and bad rhymes. Lovable as they are, it'd be like having our wedding done by the Marx Brothers."

"True," Dana replied. "And the dragonfly is an asshole, so no way for that one. Can you imagine saying vows while it's picking mites off your scalp? Yuck. I kind of like the toad, but given the time required to interpret its word salad, it'd take forever and probably wouldn't make sense. When it comes right down to it, these Thorns are a distracting bunch, right?"

"What about meeee?" A squeaky voice from overhead drew their attention and they saw the mouse, suspended from a large maple leaf and gliding out of the tree toward their conference. It sailed past their heads, caught an updraft, and whirled out of control to crash into the head of a grazing rabbit. Spooked, the rabbit leaped in the air and dashed across the meadow, disappearing into a burrow.

Dana and Owen exchanged looks and laughed until they clung to each other, crying. Owen sniffed and said, "I think we'd better just do it ourselves, you know?"

"I do," she replied.

A few days later, they married by the pond, witnessed by the rabbits and the mouse, who ran up a boulder to watch the proceedings. The raccoon didn't budge from under the oak and the crows were nowhere to be seen. The couple drank water from the same pouch and anointed each other. Owen traced circles of moisture with his fingertip on Dana's scalp. She did the same along the windings of his tattoos. Laughing, Dana picked up one of the rabbits and handed it to Owen, who cuddled it, put it down, then picked up a different one to hand to her. They declared their love with improvised words, making brief statements of the heart. Bracelets fashioned from tough spruce roots were used instead of rings. Dana tied one on to Owen's left wrist, then he did the same to her. The root bracelets seemed a perfect symbol for their love, entwined as it was with the forest world. They kissed and then, arm in arm, strolled up to the tipi to consummate the union.

Missing her period had warned Dana about a possible pregnancy, but the advent of tender breasts and fatigue confirmed it. Sitting in front of the fire one evening, she told Owen of her certainty. The weather had grown cold and rainy, so they spent more time inside the tipi, burning wood to stay warm. When Dana made her announcement, he caught his breath, and slid closer to her, embracing and, between kisses, speaking of his love for her and the child to be. Dana soaked it up, letting Owen's generous spirit fill the empty spaces etched by anxiety.

Within minutes of Dana's revelation, they heard scratching at the door flap. At first, they were stunned; this had never happened. Left alone by the various mobile manifestations of Thorn, they kept their own company. The crows spent their time perched in the trees or off conducting aerial surveys and were rarely seen. The rabbits ran back and forth across the meadow, diligent with their digging projects, and allowed themselves to be picked up and patted whenever one of the humans wanted contact, but otherwise tended to their own affairs. Meanwhile, the raccoon maintained its truculent station under the oak, non-responsive to their attempts at interaction. Recently, Owen had noticed the mouse inside the tipi, crouched quietly next to the storage pile. The Thorns they had met earlier—the marmosets, dragonfly, and toad—had disappeared. Dana and Owen weren't lonely, though, lost as they were in the exploration of their coupled intimacy. And usually once a day they linked with the rhizome, absorbing the consciousness of the forest mind. Still, the isolation of their peculiar situation increased the value of their interactions with the animals, even if they weren't actual animals. When the scratching was heard on the flap, they perked up, welcoming the possibility of company.

"Come on in! Do you need help with the door?" Owen crawled over to the entry and was bowled over when the raccoon pushed through the flap and shouldered him aside. It lumbered directly to Dana, who sat on the other side of the fire, and put its paw on her belly.

"Time for the midwife," the raccoon said in a hoarse voice of indeterminate gender. Dana stared at it with an amused look while the raccoon shut its eyes in concentration and stroked her belly with gentle caresses. "We've known for some time that you're pregnant. We've been waiting for you to figure it out for yourself before starting medical care. But now that you know, we're here. And here we shall remain until the birth."

Dana's eyebrows arched. "You're... a midwife? How does that even work? Got a lot of experience with human childbirth, have you?"

"Tut, tut, my dear, no need for that kind of talk." And the raccoon wagged one of its fingers at her. "The forest mind chose this form as suitable for all the needs of the situation. Your needs and the needs of the child. Have no fear, you'll both be cared for." The raccoon removed its paw from her belly and sat back on its haunches, assuming the usual slouch.

Owen watched this exchange in astonishment, still parked on his butt where the raccoon had pushed him. He crawled around the fire to sit next to Dana. "This might be a good thing, dear, you know, having some kind of medical presence. I watched animals birthed on the farm, but I know nothing about human labor. Could be useful to have another resource." He patted her hand for comfort, keenly aware of her skeptical expression.

"Fine, I'm not opposed to that. But what did it mean by 'here we will remain'? Is this lounge lizard going to be living in our home?" She turned to the raccoon. "You are housebroken, I trust?"

"Now, now, pet, let's not get off on the wrong foot. This birth is very important to us. We believe it represents an evolutionary crossroads: symbiogenesis in all its glory, dear humans. We know not what will come with this child, but it's bound to be interesting."

Owen shook his head. "I hadn't thought about that, but it's right. Our genetic codes have been altered by passing between worlds, contact with the rhizome, and from the virus. So... raccoon, I mean, hell, might as well add you to the list: Thorn, to be specific, are you saying that our child will be... what? Not really human? And what does that mean? Should we be worried?"

"Let's not jump to conclusions. Our sense is that your child is healthy. Exceptionally healthy, in fact. However, it will be different. You've changed, both of you, developed into something more than human, you have, and the child is likely to be more so. Hard to predict just how, but probability of change is high. But good change, good change. Please do not fret. This is a moment for excitement!" Despite its talk of excitement, the raccoon looked so relaxed that it sank into a slump. It looked at Owen with a pleading expression. "Be a darling and fix up a backrest for an old midwife."

Owen burst into laughter. He rose to fetch an empty rucksack from their stores, noticed the mouse huddled in the corner, grabbed a couple of longer sticks from the woodpile next to the door, and walked around behind the raccoon. He used a rock as a hammer stone and drove the two sticks into the ground, then slid the empty pack over the sticks.

Dana watched Owen for a few minutes. When she understood what he was doing, she objected. "You're not going to encourage this mangy thing from parking in our space, are you?"

"I'm not sure we're being offered a choice." He turned to the raccoon. "Are we?"

"No, the stakes are too high."

Owen looked at Dana and shrugged, waving to Thorn to try the backrest. The raccoon scooted back until it met resistance, then slowly leaned its weight into the support. One of the sticks broke and the raccoon fell over. Dana erupted in laughter while the raccoon huffed and whimpered as it struggled to sit up.

Owen looked sheepish. "Well, this might require further refinements. Meanwhile you could just sit over there against the supplies for now."

The raccoon muttered while ambling around the fire to the pile of stores. It tentatively leaned back against the stack, relaxed when it realized that it wouldn't give way, then promptly fell asleep, snoring lightly.

Dana grimaced. "Owen! Do we really have to put up with that thing? It's been ogling us for ages. Bad enough when we were outside, under the tarp, but frankly I've enjoyed the privacy of our own space. Now we have to share? Really?"

"Well, that does seem to be the gist of it. Not sure why. Maybe it's negotiable. Meanwhile we can rig up a curtain around our bed, okay?"

Dana grunted but remained grumpy. "Whose side are you on, anyway?"

Owen felt anxious when he realized that Dana wasn't joking. "I'm on your side, always. But are you really opposed to having nearby medical assistance, or what passes for it in these parts?"

"Nearby is fine, as long as that means Not-In-My-Space. Sorry to be an ingrate, but I'm not on display. Actually, I'm not sorry. My body, my space. Is that really so hard to understand?"

Owen scratched his beard, searching for the right words. "No, it's not hard to understand. You're right. However, it sounds like Thorn sees something important in this birth. I bet the rhizome knows more than is being said, and certainly more than we know. I don't get why it's being so overprotective, though. Or why 'the stakes are too high.' Anyway, the coon is sound asleep. I don't want to chuck it out the door into the rain. Can we let it sleep for now and first thing in the morning, let's work out the ground rules? The coon can stay under the tree—it's only seconds away—I'll support you on that. I'll build it a hutch if it wants. Maybe the mouse can play a role as messenger or something."

"The mouse with the backpack? Yeah, I've seen it, too. It's kind of cute—reminds me of Kokopelli. At least it knows how to stay out of the way. I could live with that, I suppose."

"Okay, then, that's what we'll propose. I admit to being more than a little curious about the child. Thorn is talking it up like it's the second coming of Jesus or something. I understand that the genetics are exciting, but, you know, it's still just going to be our little one, our offspring. I'm not keen on getting grandiose about the biology."

"I know what you mean. It's a little scary, actually, hearing Thorn start in about mutations and so forth. I don't know what to think about that. That's part of what made me mad. It's my baby—our baby—and does not belong to the all-powerful rhizome of Oz."

"Hear, hear." Owen said. Dana started to cry and Owen went to her, sitting close and putting his arm around her shoulder. "Hey," he said, trying to cheer her, "how about a reading from *Finnegans Wake*?"

She looked at him. "Totally transparent attempt to change the subject."

Owen flushed. "Well, yeah, I suppose. Sorry. Just wanted to see you laugh."

Dana poked him in the ribs. "You're a funny guy, Owen Black. That makes me laugh. But sure, why not? I haven't finished any poems lately, so we might as well go back to the old standard."

Owen kissed her and went to the pile of stores, carefully stepping over the snoring raccoon. He picked out a bundle the size of a small duffel bag and gave it to Dana while he threw more sticks on the fire. Outside, the rain increased its tempo and they were glad for the snug shelter of the tipi. Dana unrolled the bundle to reveal an intricate assemblage of horsehair lichen, an interwoven wad of strands dislodged as a unit from a tree. After their journey to the iron mountain and return to camp, they had discovered an enormous clump of lichen tucked in under the tarp. Owen had pointed to it and asked the crows, "What the hell is that?"

"*Finnegans...*"

"...*Wake,*" had been the answer and the crows cawed and jeered as they flew off into the trees, leaving Owen and Dana to figure it out. He recalled his disbelief as he bent to look at the lichen and realized that the strands of the horsehair maze were covered with words in tiny print that ran back and forth along the lines and across the connections, flowing over and around the tangled lichenous mat. At the base, or root of the growth, one of the primary threads showed the opening: "*riverrun, past Eve and Adam's...*" with the text following out from there into the labyrinth of strands. Winding around to the base on the opposite side was a tiny branch that ended with: "*A way a lone a last a loved a long the.*" It was outlandish, a true rhizome of a book, and perfectly suited to Joyce's text.

"See what the rhizome grew for us," was all he had said as he handed it to Dana.

"My fucking god," had been her response.

Since then, they had played with the "book," picking through it, reading to each other fragments and sections, enjoying the word-play and the ensuing puzzles of interpretation, at least until their eyes grew tired from the strain of peering at the tiny print. Now, next to the fire, while the raccoon snoozed on their supplies, Owen nodded at Dana. "Your turn," he said.

She peered into it, pulling and reshaping the mass until something surfaced that caught her eye. Then she read. '...*every person, place and thing in the chaosmos of Alle anyway connected with the gobblydumped turkery was moving and changing every part of the time...*' How cool is that?"

"Very cool. What was that word, 'all-uh'?"

"*Alle*. German for 'all.'"

"*Alle* anyway connected – Joyce seemed to understand the nature of rhizomes, didn't he?"

"No shit. Hey, you know, maybe this could be our prayer of thanks when we harvest a resource from the land: '*Thanks to every person, place and thing in the chaosmos of Alle anyway connected.*' Not bad. I kinda like it."

"Me too. I'm still holding out for you to write one that's perfect, but that's damn good. I love that word 'chaosmos.'"

"Enough already. I'm zonked like you wouldn't believe. I think it's the new life, sucking all my juice. Let's go to bed."


[40]

They insisted on privacy regarding the raccoon's station, and after debate, everyone agreed that the mouse could stay in the tipi as an observer, ready to run for the raccoon in an emergency. As part of the deal, Dana agreed to weekly inspections by the midwife, letting it probe her abdomen and assess the health of mother and developing child. Owen offered to build a hutch for the raccoon, but the offer was declined. Instead, it sulked under the tree, regardless of weather, and even Dana felt twinges of regret when they left the cozy tipi and saw the bedraggled appearance of the creature. However, as the pregnancy advanced, Dana felt more protective of her space, not less, and refused to relent. The mouse was easier to tolerate. Most of the time she didn't see it, though she knew it lurked in the shadows, twitching its nose and watching.

If Dana and Owen left the camp and went into the woods, whether to forage or saunter, the raccoon insisted on accompanying them, lumbering along in its own way, sluggish and distracted, but never far behind. Despite its bulk and melodramatic sloth, it was remarkably agile when it needed to be. It handled Dana gently during the weekly examinations, cooing and clucking over her like a hyperactive parent. She came to appreciate and even enjoy these ministrations, though she was careful not to show it.

The winter was cold and wet. Between the rain and drizzle were frequent days of crisp sun, near-frost on the grass in the mornings, Sometimes the afternoons warmed to suggestions of spring. During one of the dry spells, and before Dana's belly started to distend, they took a journey from the uplands down to the giant forest where they had first transported into Thorn's world. They had learned through the rhizome data flow that the people who lived in the tree canopy were interested in the ink they made. Using the rhizome for communication, they arranged to meet and trade ink for fabric.

They often walked in silence to better feel the subtle rhythms of the forest, speaking only when a thought demanded expression. On the second day of their journey, after hiking for a couple of hours, Dana, who had been falling behind, lost in rumination, ran to catch up to Owen and took his hand. "You know, I've been mulling over what you mentioned."

"Ah yes. What I mentioned. When was that?"

"Ha ha, Mr. Funny. You know, back when we were talking about Native Americans and their rituals of gratitude. As we've been strolling along to our rendezvous, bringing our harvest of ink to trade for stuff someone else has harvested, it reminded me of the whole idea of harvest fairs. That association jiggled my memory about something my mother told me. Sure, she was a destructive parent and a wreck of a human being, but she was literate... when she wasn't stoned out of her head, of course. Anyway, she often repeated a line from Robert Louis Stevenson: *'Don't judge each day by the harvest you reap but by the seeds that you plant.'* Not that she ever lived by those words; she was all about taking as much as she could with little thought for tomorrow."

Dana paused, lost in the unwound threads of memory. Owen squeezed her hand and prompted her. "Okay, I'm all ears."

"I love your ears."

"Don't change the subject."

Dana grinned. "It's my prerogative as a woman, especially a pregnant one. But never mind, tell me what you think about this: *We give thanks for all the earth has given. We honor those that came before, and those who follow. We reap our share and return the seeds into the earth—a gift of hope for lasting life and beauty.*"

Owen softly spoke the words of the blessing, trying them out as best as he could remember. When he reached an impasse, he turned to Dana for help. After a few tries, he still stumbled over the words.

"Gee, it's kind of long."

"Look, you're the one that kept whining about wanting a poem of gratitude. So, I give you a poem and this is the gratitude I get: it's kind of long?"

Owen juggled his embarrassment while desperately trying to remember the words of the poem. "No, no, it's great, really. I just need some practice with it, that's all."

Dana shook her head. "Men," she said.

He stopped and hugged her, announcing, "I kiss the bard in gratitude for her gift."

"Oh, alright," she conceded. The embrace turned into fondling and stroking, and despite the cool air, they crumpled to the ground and used their bodies for mutual delight. The raccoon, tagging along as always, snorted and leaned up against a tree to watch. When they resumed their journey, they held hands and marched, chanting the words of the blessing.

Eventually the regal silence of the forest sapped their impulse for noisemaking and they walked in whispers. When they arrived at the old portal tree, a peaceful stillness pervaded the world. There was no sign of anyone waiting for a rendezvous. At the base of the massive trunk, Owen leaned back and yelled into the heights. Soon a figure appeared on the lowest branch, about seventy feet off the ground. Owen's first sight of these enigmatic people revealed an individual covered in short fur, like a gibbon or a lean chimpanzee. It waved to Owen but said nothing and lowered a rope with a basket on the end. When the basket touched ground, Dana placed a fat pouch of ink in it and gave a thumbs-up signal. The basket ascended without further communication. Within a few minutes the rope returned with a bundle on the end. Owen untied the bundle and the rope was hauled back. Owen caught a last glimpse of the figure as it disappeared into the canopy. Grinning, he yelled into the branches, "We give thanks for all the earth has given us!"

Dana unrolled the bundle to inspect the results of the trade. It contained a variety of fabrics: some thick and rugged-looking, others thin and delicate. Several swatches contained plant fibers new to Owen that formed a fabric like silk, smooth to the touch. The assembled material would keep them in clothing and containers for a long time. Before they could discuss the logistics of carrying the heavy bundle, Owen rolled it up and threw it over his shoulder, dropping the pack with their travelling gear for Dana. She protested, but he maintained a stone face and stared at her. She frowned at his mulish determination and he could see the arguments forming on her lips, but then she laughed, put on the pack, and they started on the two-day hike back home.

Dana's body changed throughout the winter and early spring. She insisted that Owen shave her head to a stubble whenever it threatened to need a comb. Otherwise her breasts and belly grew plump while her face filled out with a creamy roundness. Owen was enchanted with these changes, but Dana complained about feeling fat and nauseous and looked at him with skepticism when he praised her appearance. His love expanded with every swell in her body and he took pride in fussing over her, sometimes to her consternation, sometimes to her delight.

Along with the raccoon, the mouse, and the other expressions of the rhizome, it seemed that the whole world anticipated the birth of their child. When they tapped into the underground network, they heard a new music. Filled with subtle harmonies, it echoed the soothing sounds of tree life: slow, methodical, and rhythmic. Often this music put them to sleep and even if they slumbered for only a few minutes, they woke up refreshed and energetic. Owen figured out that the rhizome fed them, especially Dana, a nutrient-rich concoction. Whatever the nature of the potion, it functioned to ensure wellness and tranquility.

The heavy rains dwindled to occasional showers, the air warmed, insects ventured out into the world, and the humans no longer needed a steady fire in the tipi. They spent more time outside, sitting under the tree with the raccoon or sun-bathing at the pond. Dana's belly grew taut and she struggled to get up or lift things. Owen took over most of the camp labor, a specialization that annoyed Dana. She accepted it although never without complaint. She was slower than she wanted to be, but not incapacitated, and they still went on long strolls through the woods. These outings remained a touchstone of their relationship, openly entangled with the forest. They recognized each tree as a personality, a link in the community evoked by their position in the woods both above and below ground. Every tree was an instrument in the symphony of the rhizome and Owen and Dana celebrated them as they walked, touching them one by one, stroking the bark or fingering a leaf with delicate appreciation.

When summer arrived, Dana struggled to venture from camp. She insisted on movement, though, and Owen was happy to be with her regardless of how far they went or what they did.

As with other couples anticipating a birth, the circle of their lives narrowed to focus on the coming child. This being-in-formation kicked and squirmed in Dana's womb, an event that always conjured wonder in Owen. Few things pleased Dana more than his desire to caress and feel the child's movements in her belly. The raccoon declared every week that the health of the baby was excellent. When it started to mention the gender of the child, Dana quickly said she didn't want to be told. "I know it's a girl, but I don't want to hear about it," she said. The raccoon looked at her and squinted but said nothing.

Dana went into labor on a warm midsummer night. Her water broke long before dawn and the mouse scurried off to the oak tree to fetch the raccoon. Owen kindled the fire for light, but the moon was full and there was little to be done at this point except monitor and wait. Owen bounced around trying to think of things to do until Thorn told him to sit down, hold Dana's head in his lap, and use his tendrils to forge a connection between Dana and the rhizome. Owen sunk the fingers of one hand into the ground, feeling the tendrils connect through the dirt floor of the tipi, while with the other he attached to her recently shorn scalp. He accepted the role of go-between, bridging the flow of energy and health from the rhizome into his mate.

As the sun climbed toward zenith on the following day, with fierce grunts and yells, Dana gave birth to a girl. Owen stopped holding his breath and said "*We give thanks for all the earth has given us...*" He didn't know whether to laugh or cry and thus did both. Dana sighed when the child attached to her breast with a powerful suction. The two parents lay next to each other, exhausted, their attention focused on their amazing child. Despite the forecasts regarding mutation, she looked like every other baby girl they had seen, with one exception: she was their child and therefore more glorious than any others. During long debates throughout the winter and spring, they had settled on naming her Hawthorn, in honor of the world where she was born. A few hawthorn-like trees grew nearby, mixed in with the deciduous woods of the uplands. Just as those trees bore sweet fruits known as haws, the conjunction of forest and human had worked to produce their own little *Haw*.

They wanted to honor the relationships of culture and nature that gave meaning to their lives. A mythology of symbiosis took shape within their daily existence and they recognized the importance of passing that on. What better way than the name of their firstborn? So, while Dana and Owen welcomed their sweet Haw, incorporating her into their cultural project, the raccoon cleaned up, taking the afterbirth to the nearest hawthorn tree and burying it under the roots.

Haw grew like a weed. She flourished in the care of her parents as well as the constant attentions of the raccoon and the other varieties of Thorn that came out of the woods. Old forms, such as the marmosets and the dragonfly, returned to see the baby, doting on her and praising the parents before fading back into the forest. The magnetic appeal of their child reinforced the sense that Dana and Owen were part of a large, loving family. It didn't matter that the members of the family were complex, mutable life-forms—intelligence and personality were involved, and, overall, a vast compassion that conveyed its own justification for belonging. It was an odd family, but with enough love to satisfy any definition.

After the baby's arrival, life fell into a dream haze of interruptions and shifting schedules as Haw's needs filled their days and nights. Meanwhile, the seasons passed in the Thorn world, no longer a strange place but truly their home. Memories remained from their birth world, the beauty and pleasures, the complications, the losses, and the suffering. The link to their origins was forged from these powerful memories, yet they felt no compulsion to return.

Once Haw's neck could support her head, they made a pack to carry her on explorations of the world. Even the tree people were enticed to the ground to see her, and she became the center of attention as dozens of hairy folks descended from the canopies to touch the little one.

Dana, glowing like a goddess and showing no sign of the bleary fatigue common to mothers, wrote poem after poem, storing them in a waterproof satchel, a cultural legacy for her daughter. When a poem achieved her requirements of craft, she read it aloud, in the tipi or under the tree, depending on weather, and the local forest characters gathered for the event. The rabbits always lined up in front and listened with deep concentration, never saying a thing, and when Dana's last word hung in the air, they hopped briskly away. The crows seemed to anticipate these events, flying in to perch in the tree or stand at the back of the audience, making soft corvid sounds throughout. And the raccoon propped itself up dutifully but usually fell asleep before the end. Owen loved these occasions, not only because they were affirmations of family, but also because of the depth of pride he felt for his wife.

Owen found his own use for the ink and parchment. He started a map-making project, drafting an overview of the region and their pedestrian explorations, as well as additional detail maps of the local forest. He drew a schematic of the camp environs that named every tree. Once that was finished, he drew a companion map featuring an outline of the main mycorrhizal connections. The map-making was important to him, his own contribution to the culture they assembled. It seemed a natural extension of his early work with Dr. Chouinard, and he remembered that she introduced him to the labyrinth as a symbolic map of the unconscious. His own embellishments, the tattoos that adorned his arms, were a manifestation of that mapping urge, the semiotic compulsion to translate a complex, three-dimensional world into two-dimensional imagery. Owen's fascination with mythology transformed the landscape into a geographic mythos as every feature encoded character and narrative. Within the rhizome, there might be no need of names, but in human culture, names became agents of significance. Part of being human required an engagement with the compulsion to make and codify meaning. Rather than disdain such effort, Owen decided to make it his own, to shape it in such a way that he worked toward a culture that prioritized relationships over the independent self. On Owen's maps, trees were characters, and everything was connected.

As part of the mapping, Owen traced the steps of Dr. Chouinard across the Thorn world. Echoes of her presence rippled through the forest, but little was left behind to fix her locations besides the few shelters or items left for Owen and Dana. It seemed as if she appeared out of the ground, made some things, then dissolved back into the earth. Owen harassed the crows to search for her, and though they ventured off on long exploratory flights, they never brought back anything other than rumors or vague clues. He delved into the rhizome, reaching far beyond his previous linkages, looking for leads. Again, he found only shadows and reverberations. She influenced the world, but she remained a phantom or mythic being. Frustrated at first, in time he realized that it made perfect sense. The doctor would be pleased, he was sure. If she had any volition at this point, and it seemed that she did, then she made the choice to exist in this manner, a vanguard pushing into the unknown. The Thorns were also puzzled by the phenomenon of the doctor and were unable to explain the nature of her existence. They recognized that she derived energy and substance from the rhizome and used it for her own ends, but somehow, she did so without leaving a trail or surrendering autonomy. Every Thorn, when pressed, would offer its version of a shrug. Owen finally accepted her status as a living myth, letting go of any need to make her into something to serve his own needs.

Haw proved to be a precocious child. Before she was a year old, she toddled around the camp with accomplished balance. At first, they worried about the pond, but when she ventured toward the water, even before Owen or Dana could react, the rabbits appeared and herded her gently away. There was one part of the pond, very shallow and sandy, where Owen built a fenced enclosure so that Haw could wade and splash without danger. She loved to sit in the shallows and scoop wet sand from the bottom, dribbling it over her body and flinging it in all directions while shrieking with laughter.

As far as her parents could tell, Haw seemed like a healthy human child. Her skin had a faint greenish tinge, but they were used to living in a world where shades of green were predominant, so they didn't worry about it. An active and happy child, she learned rapidly, and the parents were satisfied. Then one day, Dana noticed Haw standing in the meadow, completely still, eyes closed, face to the sun, soaking up the light with a blissful expression.

The intensity of the posture alerted Dana. "Haw, honey, what are you doing?"

Haw didn't answer. Alarmed, Dana trotted over, sat down, and touched her daughter, but again, there was no response. Dana yelled for Owen. He looked up from his map work and ran over to join them.

"She won't respond! What's wrong? Owen!"

Owen crouched and put his hand on Haw's shoulder. Instinctively, tendrils slid out of his fingers and slipped into Haw's skin. Owen closed his eyes for a moment, then his body stiffened, and he sat back on the ground. "My god," he said.

"What? Tell me!"

"She's okay. No need to worry. But here, let's look at her feet." Owen carefully separated the grass from around Haw's toes and pointed at what he found. An array of thread-like tendrils protruded from under each toenail and extended into the ground. "She's linked."

Dana stroked the top of her daughter's feet. "Incredible," she said.

"Yes. She appears to have a more complex set of tendrils than we do. I guess this is what the Thorns were talking about."

"Sure. But what's she doing?"

"I think she's photosynthesizing – or something like that."

"What?"

"That greenish tint to her skin may mean that she has chlorophyll in her cells. If she does, then she can convert sunlight into sugar. Let's link to the rhizome and see if we can experience it from underneath. You could let your daughter feed you for a change."

[41]

Haw's first word was "da," which seemed to indicate either Dana or Owen. Her second word sounded like "thorn." By the age of one she called them "Mommy" and "Daddy", talked in sentences, listened carefully to Dana's poems, and studied Owen's maps. Her progress with speech was so rapid that every day brought new grammar and vocabulary. One day, Owen heard her mutter the word "riverrun." He asked her to repeat it and she said it again, clearly. Adopting a careful neutrality, he asked for the meaning of the word. Haw said, "Like 'riverrun, past Mommy and Daddy's'. Like that." Dana laughed, proclaiming that the chickens came home to roost. Owen just patted Haw on the head and praised her.

Sometimes their daughter behaved like an animal, sometimes like a plant. It took them a while to get used to the episodes of immobility. She rooted in one spot for hours or even the entire day, assuming a passive trance that made it difficult to intrude. When the sun went down, she disconnected from the rhizome, shook herself like a wet dog, and toddled back for a snuggle in the arms of the closest parent. If there was a schedule to these episodes, Dana and Owen couldn't figure it out. A developmental surge always followed a root session, involving physical and mental growth, which they assumed resulted from the rhizome link. Although it was strange to see their daughter stationary, swaying slightly in the breeze, Owen and Dana understood the logic of Haw's biology. A new kind of being, she embodied the evolutionary mechanism of symbiogenesis. Parenting such a child carried intimidating responsibilities and they had to adjust expectations, but that was true of most parents, regardless of a child's nature. They were proud of Haw and welcomed the challenge. A beautiful child, she loved the world, and her sensitivity to all life forms embodied an ethos they had long wished to see in their kind.

In the winter, when Haw reached one and a half, they thought about returning to the other world. An idle notion, they didn't really want to go back. They imagined that the chaos and malignancy of human society continued, and they were content to be out of it. They felt little inclination to uproot Haw, clearly a product of the Thorn world, especially to go where she would be a freak.

The rains of winter continued, confining them to the tipi for long spells. One evening as they sat around the fire, they heard scratching at the door. Owen quickly opened the flap, thinking it was the raccoon. The three marmosets stood in a huddle with their fur sleeked flat by the rain. Owen grinned and the Thorns exploded into the tipi like a gymnastics troupe. Redthorn somersaulted to Owen's shoulder, Blackthorn twirled pirouettes along Dana's arm and onto her head, and Whitethorn cannonballed into Haw's lap.

"The return of the Thorny triumvirate! Welcome!" Owen sat next to his family and patted each of the Thorns in turn.

"Looking well, everyone, especially little Haw," observed Redthorn.

"I'm not so little anymore," she contended, scratching Whitethorn's belly.

"No, in many ways you're not. Indeed, you're everything we hoped for, Haw. And more."

"We think so, too," said Dana, removing Blackthorn from the top of her head and placing it firmly in her lap.

After the greetings and chatter subsided, and a contented silence filled the tipi, Redthorn slid down from Owen's shoulder and faced the family, warming its back against the fire. "We do have some information."

"Ah," Owen said. "I wondered..."

"Yes. It's important. It seems that our project, the virus propagation, achieved critical mass. Great changes have come about."

"What! Did it work? What kind of changes?"

Blackthorn squirmed out of Dana's grip and jumped at Redthorn, knocking it off balance. Redthorn staggered to the side to avoid falling in the fire and Blackthorn seized the moment. "Oh, it worked, alright. Magnificent! The virus spread into the forests around the world thanks to the work of your human recruits. Inoculating even one tree resulted in virus propagation throughout an entire grove or forest system. As predicted, the infected trees released steady quantities of pheromones into the atmosphere, altering its composition. Slow at first, the build-up accelerated in geometric progression, also as predicted. Once it crossed the critical threshold, humans were inundated with unavoidable awareness of ecological relationships—the enlightenment. As you imagined, the initial response involved confusion and disruption."

"Oh god," said Owen, "I didn't want to be right about that."

Redthorn glared at Blackthorn throughout its entire speech and now took advantage of Owen's comment to regain a speaking role. "Well, it didn't take long before a new equilibrium formed in societies. However, due to atmospheric conditions, winds and storms, for example, not everyone was exposed at the same time. The impact of the enlightenment was uneven at first, though atmospheric saturation finally covered the entire globe."

Dana chimed in, "So what's it like there now? Are the maniacs finally chilled out?"

Redthorn licked its lips. "No... not exactly."

Whitethorn offered a lyrical perspective: "First you take a left/Then you take a right/But even with a map/You still need a light."

Blackthorn frowned at Whitethorn and opened its mouth but Redthorn spoke first. "Well, it's not that simple to turn off an entire cultural ethos and reset it. It seems that disorder from social confusion resulted in a few ill-advised military actions."

"What!?" Owen and Dana blurted simultaneously.

"Yes, well, people less affected by the pheromones tried to take advantage of others, incorrectly perceiving the enlightened ones as helpless. They should have tried to get along instead. Being less affected is not the same as being unaffected. They didn't anticipate that emotional feedback loops in the social system would rebound on them. Empathy overload crashed their egos and reduced them to jibbering dysfunction, which served to halt further aggressions. Things settled down. It looked as if, in time, it would all even out."

"What do you mean, 'as if'?"

Redthorn paused, offering no objection when Blackthorn edged forward and reclaimed the speaker role. "It may be in vain, but we do hope that you remember our conversations about emergence. Especially since that principle has directly affected your own bodies."

"Uh oh. So now we're getting to the punch line."

"No need for negativity. As your people say, it's all good. Anyway, once the atmospheric levels of the pheromones reached a saturation point and changes were activated in human perception and behavior, then something else happened. Something we didn't predict. The pheromones were absorbed back into the mycorrhizal systems where they catalyzed a different reaction. Namely, the fungal networks released a new variety of spore—massively. These spores have a mutated chemistry unknown to your world. Like most fungal spores, the new type floats in the atmosphere along with dust and other tiny substances, just like the pheromones. The air you breathe is filled with this stuff. However, when this particular spore is inhaled by humans, it immediately attacks cell structure, breaking it down and colonizing the biomass, converting the basic structures into... plant cells."

"You have got to be shitting me."

"No, that we are not."

"So, what are you saying? What does it mean, 'converting the biomass into plant cells'?'

Whitethorn broke in from its snug position in Haw's arms. "Kiss goodbye to the same old past/they've got a brand new biomass." Then it clapped its hand over its mouth and giggled.

Blackthorn shook its head back and forth before answering Owen's question. "What it means is that we have an extreme emergent effect: the conversion of an entire species population into an alternative species. Though, really, it's more accurate to say that one holobiont type reshuffled its components to form a new holobiont. Same building blocks of life, just a new structure. Anyway, it works like a cancer, colonizing and converting cells, but at a pace more rapid and robust than any known cancer. The complete transformation only takes a day or so. Within minutes of absorbing the spores the affected humans feel sluggish. After a few hours they are unable to move. Between ingestion and stasis, they experience a profound compulsion to seek fresh air and soil, leaving their dwellings and shedding their clothes in the process. When a suitable place is found, they scoop up dirt with their bare hands and pile it on their feet. A muscular rigor takes over as they stand upright and reach to the sky while the lower extremities harden into roots. The transformation flows steadily upward from the roots as mammalian flesh and bone convert to plant fibers. The individuals go through these changes in a focused trance; there's no overt resistance once the spores are inhaled. The outcome is a small tree of a species that reflects the substrate types where the spore originated, so, for example, spores from maple groves tend to beget maple trees."

Dana looked at Blackthorn with her mouth open; Owen stared down at the ground, trying to comprehend. "Okay, okay.

You're saying that humans are now trees? What the fuck! That's what you're saying?"

"Yes, and we're most sorry not to have foreseen the possibility. This wasn't the intent of the procedure. We had hoped to expand human consciousness; instead, it seems that we've also created a mutation. The humans in your world took the form of plants and now stand rooted in place."

Haw spoke, surprising everyone. "You mean like me?"

The Thorns admired Haw as she showed off the tendrils of her toes and fingers. Redthorn looked proud. "Haw, you're more human than plant, though you have the characteristics of both. You bridge those worlds in harmony, combining the best of two types to become your unique, beautiful self."

Owen shook his head. "So, we're the last humans. I've destroyed my entire species."

Redthorn patted Owen's knee with its hand. "No, no, you haven't destroyed anything. It was our work; you were a vessel. But remember that nothing is destroyed, only changed. We appreciate your despair, but even you yourself can no longer be considered entirely human. We urge you to consider that the change is something other than apocalyptic; it may even be an evolutionary improvement."

Dana snarled, "Easy for you to say."

Owen continued to shake his head. "I can't believe it. I can't fucking believe it."

"There is more. The humans, like yourself, that were inoculated with the virus demonstrate immunity to the spores, or at least they have so far. So, no, you are not the last humans. The virus does promote the development of rhizome characteristics, such as your tendrils, and a deep affinity for plant forms, but virus-infected humans remain primarily mammalian."

Owen lifted his head, a desperate hope on his face. Dana took his hand and said, "Well, this is a bit much to take in, right? We've been adjusting to life here for the last two and a half years, and I think we've done well. We're now a family, we feel a sense of belonging, and the fears and worries that we left behind in our old world have become pretty distant. We truly love this place. So now you've just dropped a bomb on our idyll. I understand that these changes were part of what we worked for, part of the mission we took on, but it's all a bit drastic, you know?"

"No shit," Owen agreed, while Haw looked from one parent to the other. She extended her toes into the tipi's dirt floor and quietly connected to the rhizome.

Redthorn sympathized. "We do appreciate the complexity of your feelings. We never assumed that our message would be received with a simple cheer. In fact, you're handling it rather well."

Blackthorn subtly edged in front of Redthorn and took over. "However, please consider the situation: the destructive civilization of humanity has been stopped. There are no toxins leaching into our world anymore. There is still the problem of residual deposits in your world, but no new toxins are being churned into the environment there, either. A small population of humans remain, enlightened, open to the intimacy of ecological relationships. There is now a possibility to rebuild and evolve in a way that promotes the health of systems. The price paid for this chance to start over is that a majority of humans are now required to experience life within the same forms they exploited so thoughtlessly for generations. Those forms are the same as the forms within which we live, which we hardly find objectionable. An improvement, really. Certainly, from our perspective it's not a punishment, or, if one wants to see it that way, it does carry an element of ironic justice. We didn't plan for things to happen like this, but it's not exactly a catastrophe, either. This is how evolution works, sometimes slowly and steadily, sometimes by fits and starts."

"Sure thing, professor, I get it. Humans get to live the rhizome life. Yay. But don't expect me to rejoice. This is an extreme outcome and not one that I ever considered."

"But we know that you've experienced much pain and suffering from your fellow humans and you have great bitterness about that. Such things as were done to you cannot happen any longer. Surely that's a change you can value."

"It's just not that simple. For better or worse, we humans have a dedicated notion of loyalty. I can't explain it, but that loyalty extends even to those who've hurt us. As much as I've hated my uncle, I'm not sure I ever wanted him to be turned into a chunk of wood."

Dana squeezed his hand. "You know, Owen, I think we need to hear this news and sit with it without trying to generate a final assessment. There's a lot to absorb. Regardless, it's done. We've got our family and our future. And, it sounds like, we still have friends in the other world, friends who are probably living a life akin to ours now: hunting, gathering, starting over."

Owen brought Dana's hand to his face and rubbed it against his cheek. "Yes. But you know, I think we should go back."

[42]

The wood crackled in the fire, the only sound in the tipi after Owen's pronouncement. Dana frowned and rubbed her hand across the short hairs on her head, causing them to stand up in disarray. "Are you sure, Owen? This is what I mean by letting the news soak in before we make any decisions. What's it really like back there? Can it possibly be better than what we have here? Sure, I'm encouraged to know that the Artemis women are probably the rulers of Cambridge now, but are the remains of human civilization the kind of environment we want for Haw? Here, we have a forest, beautiful, benign, and nurturing. There, we'd be living within a ragged shell of industrial debris."

Owen studied Dana's tense face and softened. He remembered why he loved her so much, with her wit and determination. "Yes, dear. As always, you're right. We'll chew it over."

Redthorn reminded them, "The portal remains open. You may come and go at will. You've certainly earned that privilege."

Whitethorn levered itself to a seated pose, its back leaning against Haw's chest. "The portal is ajar/Just do not go too far."

Owen nodded, lost in thought, until Haw broke in. "Can I go, Daddy? I want to see another world."

Dana scooted close to Haw and stroked her head and back while Owen stared. His daughter amazed him every day, always with perspective beyond her years. Unperturbed, she sat between them, her fingers in the dirt as she maintained a link to the rhizome while its mobile representative sat respectfully on her lap. A new species of creature, she radiated a peace that seemed correct in every way. Little Haw represented the future and a new way of life, one that could bridge differences. Perhaps there really was nothing to fear from all these changes, thought Owen. We live within the circle of nature and whatever happens, for better or worse, is an expression of nature. As always, nature works things out, but without a final purpose. Except to live, and that they were doing.

The Thorns spent the night and the six of them curled together in a snug pile. When Owen woke up the next morning, the Thorns were gone. In the gray light, the rain resumed. He ducked out to bring in more wood from the tarp while Dana kindled a fire and heated the stones to make hot water. By placing glowing rocks in a water-filled wooden bowl, they could heat enough for washing, eating, or drinking. They learned from the rhizome how to brew the leaves of a low bush that grew on the far side of the pond. It provided a stimulant as well as a complex, earthy flavor that now defined their mornings.

Haw crawled out of bed, took off her clothes and went outside to stand in the rain. They knew she would dig into the earth and let the plant nature take over. She preferred to do this in the sunshine, yet there were days when she welcomed the rain. She tried and couldn't explain it to Dana and Owen. It was through their links to the rhizome that they learned she enjoyed the feeling of absorbing rainwater fresh from the topsoil—the plant equivalent of going for a refreshing swim. Haw said, "it tickles."

While Haw was outside, Owen and Dana drank their tea and mulled over the situation. Dana closed her eyes and scrunched her face, an expression Owen recognized as a prelude to speech. He waited. "Owen, I think you're right about going back. Why not? We have a door that goes both ways, so it's hardly a final decision. Curiosity alone is probably reason enough to go, but also, we may be able to help the survivors. I'm guessing there's confusion and uncertainty about what's going on, about the future, about their own role at this point. They face the challenge of rebuilding a culture nearly from the beginning. We can help steer that, maybe. I mean, we must be the only ones who know what really happened. We can be guides, or teachers, promoting a culture based on love and respect. All that remains of society are the leftovers of a corrupt civilization. Eventually those relics will erode, but we want people to make conscious decisions about their relationships to those things. Otherwise I fear they'll recreate that consumer stupidity, based on an assumption that all that material stuff is essential, or just desirable. You know what I mean, right?"

"I do. I know exactly what you mean."

"And, I've been thinking..."

"I can tell," Owen said, flashing a grin.

"...you know, it might be a good thing for Haw. It's part of her heritage. Maybe it's important for her to learn about it first-hand."

Owen put down his cup and leaned over to kiss Dana. "Quite a turn around. I could quibble with your points if I wanted to be contrary. But I don't. I think we should go. We can always come back."

Five days later, on a sunny day, warmer than usual, they took off their clothes, stacking them into a neat pile in the tipi. The raccoon, who by this time seemed to be a permanent fixture of their camp, agreed to watch over their belongings, although it noted that it was unlikely that any life-form would want them since they smelled like humans. They explained the process of transportation across the brane boundary to Haw over and over, trying to keep it at her level, as best they understood what that was, and were consistently surprised at how much she already knew. They prepared her so relentlessly that she finally complained, "Can't we just go now?"

With no reason to delay, they walked away from the tipi, stepping lightly through the woods, Haw between her parents, holding hands until they arrived at the portal tree. Unused for two and a half years, it looked the same. Memories returned of their flight from the house, the fear of rape and death, the carnage of flames as the Legion of Odin burned with all of Owen and Dana's belongings. In remembrance of the terror, they paused at the tree. Who knows what they would find on the other side? The Thorns had provided an overview, but a lot of questions remained. They hoped that at least some clothes could be scrounged, if not from the ruins of the farm, then from the nearest neighbors, half a mile away and presumably no longer in need of such things. It would be early summer and warm enough to avoid serious discomfort. Of course, there could still be black flies and the ubiquitous mosquitoes, but they didn't plan on perishing from bug bites.

Owen started to explain the transfer again to Haw, but Dana interrupted, noting that "Really, Owen, it's too cold to linger and she's heard it before." Haw smiled at her mother, nodding. Owen sighed and gathered Haw up in his arms. Dana embraced him and Haw was sandwiched in between. They leaned into the tree. As soon as they touched the bark, it began to flow, opening to the inner layers of the wood, stretching wide to accommodate the three of them, pulling them inside the darkness that led to the next world.

[43]

On the other side of the portal, they slid out of the tree together, pushed in one smooth motion across the pebbles and sticks that littered the ground. Haw remained wide awake, which surprised them, like many other things about her. She pounced on the discrepancy.

"Daddy, you said I'd be asleep."

Owen patted her head and stood up, helping Dana with his free arm while he cradled Haw in the other. "Well, honey, you'll learn that your parents don't know everything."

"Speak for yourself," Dana said, raising an eyebrow.

They surveyed their surroundings. Through the trees Owen saw the desolate spot where his house had stood. Only the foundation walls remained, blackened from the burn. Otherwise, there didn't seem to be much left. He stared at the ruins, hardly responding to Haw's wiggling as she looked over his shoulder into the depths of the forest. "Mommy, what's that?"

"Owen," Dana said softly. He tore his gaze away from the remnants and turned. She pointed into the woods toward a small clearing in the trees. In the clearing was a domed hut. As soon as Owen saw the hut, a chill ran up his spine. Without a word, they moved toward the structure.

Resembling a Passamaquoddy wigwam, the structure formed an ovoid about seven feet high, fifteen feet long, and ten feet wide, completely covered in birch bark shingles. The curved roof had an opening for a smoke hole and the end of the hut provided an entrance covered with a large slab of bark. As they approached, Owen called out a greeting, once, then twice, but there was no answer. He handed Haw to Dana and removed the door cover. Inside it was neat and ready for occupation: a packed and swept dirt floor, a slightly used fire pit, and a small stack of dry branches and twigs tucked against the wall. Owen also noticed two bundles suspended from the arched framing poles.

He turned his head to Dana, standing in the doorway and trying to hang on to Haw while she squirmed. Finally, Dana gave up and put her down, and Haw dashed into the hut and began to explore. Owen, working to keep a neutral expression, said, "I've got a funny feeling about this."

"I know. Are you thinking this is more of the doctor's work?"

He nodded. "Strange, huh? She sure gets around for a dead person. Well, let's find out." He untied the smaller hanging bundle, placed it on the ground, and unwrapped it. Inside were three sets of clothes fashioned from plant fibers; each set included shirt, pants, and moccasins. As he held them up, he knew they would fit. The doctor's characteristic symbol, the classic labyrinth, was embroidered on the shirtsleeves. He called for Haw and helped her get dressed. When he offered her the little moccasins, she shook her head and pointed at her toes. Tendril tips sprouted from under the nails, reaching out, eager to taste the earth of a new world. He didn't want to frustrate her natural inclinations, but caution suggested that he didn't yet know what disturbances might lurk in the rhizome. "No, honey," he said to Haw, "wait a little while. Daddy needs to check something out."

Dana, wearing her new outfit, looked at Owen with curiosity. "What do you mean?"

"I was thinking about what happened here, the metamorphosis of humans into plants, and wondering what effect that's had on the rhizome. Could be benign or it could be a tempest of condensed suffering. Maybe it's fine but I want to link to it first before Haw dives in. Just to make sure."

"Well, at least above ground, the forest seems peaceful enough. All except for the damn mosquitoes, which didn't take long to find us. But I know what you mean." She sat next to Haw and pulled her onto her lap. "Let Daddy go first." Haw curled against her mother and stuck her thumb in her mouth.

Owen tugged on his clothes and sat cross-legged. He flattened both hands against the dirt floor, digging slightly into the hard surface with the tips of his fingers. The tendrils drove into the earth, finding and latching onto mycorrhizal filaments. Awareness of the forest slammed into him. The intensity alarmed him until he understood that the onslaught was the forest mind's equivalent of a welcoming hug. He accepted the embrace and the energy subsided, parting like drapes to reveal pathways into the network. As he advanced into the rhizome, he encountered an overall tone of contentment throughout the interlocking systems. The music rippled with a steady rhythm of work, the song of elements shifting materials within the ecology. As sunlight synthesized into glucose, the trees hummed, engaged with the task. Here and there Owen sensed faint grumbling as trees adapted to branches broken during the last storm, or as caterpillars chewed their way through foliage, or as trees conjured any number of the other adaptations required of a living forest. Further away he felt the panic of a hemlock besieged by wooly adelgids. The panic distressed Owen until he encountered the comforting waves from neighboring trees as they re-apportioned additional nutrients to the afflicted hemlock.

Owen pushed on through the rhizome, hearing the song of new growth from the grasses around his former house, grasses that survived the fire and repopulated the abandoned site. He found no trace of the dozen men who had perished in that fire; they were obliterated. He narrowed his focus, seeking any remnants of humanity. Reaching far into the network, he eventually found what he was looking for, and the reverberations set him on edge. Irregular in modulation, faint at first, then emerging in stronger pulses as he moved closer, the dissonance grated against the normal rhythms of the network. He wondered if the rhizome filtered this input, the expressions of the transformed humans, letting it into the larger network in constricted doses while holding most of it at bay. As Owen moved through the filtering layers, he understood why. The expressions were erratic, undisciplined, as individualistic and self-centered as they had ever been in their original forms. Apparently, the pacification of the enlightenment pheromones, if it had worked on humans as animals, had not carried over consistently when the humans became plants. The layers of the rhizome in proximity to the human plants roiled and seethed like a sea-surge on the rocks.

As Owen picked his way through the cacophony, he noticed that not all the transformed humans screeched in protest; many had adapted, accepting the rhizome, and even produced a music of their own. Less filtered and better connected to the network, these plants participated in the network economy. But dismay overcame him as he surveyed the remnants of his species and realized that a majority writhed in an agony of resistance, lashing at the network with their unwillingness to root in the reality of their new lives. Restrictions quarantined the worst entities from free access to the network community, instead providing a one-way stream of enriched carbon to encourage the growth of plant cells within their structures. In time, Owen saw that the memories of their human existence would fall away like autumn leaves, but for now, they represented a damaged segment of the rhizome consciousness.

He rewound his consciousness like Ariadne's thread, spooling backwards along the path of exploration, bundling his wide-angle perceptions into a focus and returning to his body. Withdrawing the tendrils from the ground, he shook his head and looked up to see the expression of concern on Dana's face.

"Wow. You were out for a while."

"Sorry. Took longer than I thought."

"And...?"

"Well, as far as I can tell the forest system is in working order. I don't see major problems for Haw; she'll feel welcome. Just stay close, honey, okay? Don't reach beyond a hundred trees—at most." Haw scrambled out of Dana's lap and plunged her toes into the dirt, closing her eyes and standing still while she connected to the rhizome. A smile spread over her face as she closed off her connection to the human world.

Owen watched Haw fall into a trance, then turned to Dana and frowned. "But the transformed humans... that's another story."

"Tell me, Owen. No delaying tactics."

"Well, the change seems to have eradicated the benefits of enlightenment, if they really ever experienced that state of unified consciousness. We only have the Thorns' interpretation for that."

"Are you doubting them?"

"No... well, yeah, maybe. I'm still not sure what to think about some of the ethics along the way. The Thorns saved my life and improved my metabolic functioning, all in the name of brotherly love or something. But didn't that turn out to be convenient for the ultimate purpose, namely finding a human agent for spreading their virus? Why didn't they just pump the virus back through the mycorrhizal links? Why use a human at all, unless it was to alleviate the blame?"

"Wow, Owen, where's this coming from? You sound bitter."

"Sensing the pain of the transformed humans was excruciating. Why didn't the so-called enlightenment open them to the possibilities of life, like it was supposed to, so that they embraced the metamorphosis? What went wrong? I'm not sure that a collective mind has the same relationship with interpersonal ethics as an individual. What it does have is a radically different perspective, one that probably promotes ends over means. I dunno, maybe I'm overreacting—but how do you tell?"

"You're over thinking it. Sometimes shit happens, and the emergent properties of systemic changes can't be foreseen—we've talked about that. Sure, there were risks; we didn't ignore the possibility. But we decided to go forward, anyway. Remember? Regardless, this is where we are. Or would you rather have us tied to the tree and raped by goons?"

Owen fell silent, staring at the ground, on the verge of tears. Dana slid over and put her arm around his shoulders. He looked up at her. "As usual, you're right. It's too complicated for simplistic moralizing. Maybe it's not such a great idea to be back here."

"Oh, I think it's the right thing to do. At least for now. But tell me more about what you sensed in the rhizome."

"Well, some transformed humans appear to be adapting to the metamorphosis, though even the best of them are a little confused. Many react as if they're being tortured and they broadcast nothing but anguish and suffering. The rhizome is containing them, sequestering their contact with the broader system while trying to feed them a nutrient cocktail to accelerate the growth of their plant consciousness. But those sections of the rhizome are pretty intense."

"'*Do not go gentle into that good night... Rage, rage, against the dying of the light.*'"

"What?"

"Dylan Thomas. Famous poem. About fighting against death, clinging to rage if that's all that's left. Not going out with a whimper. Typical macho stuff, really."

"Yeah, that fits. For now I think we should protect Haw from that discord. I'm not sure how it might affect her, especially given how much it's affected me. She'll be able to meld with the original forest with no problems, I think; the human agony is farther away from here."

"I agree that we should protect her. We don't really know how she's going to adapt, though from the looks of her right now, I'd say she's off to a good start. But, on a practical note, what are we going to eat?"

"Good question. I don't think the mushrooms of these woods offer the same level of sustenance as the ones in the Thorn world. Haw might be able to live off the land, literally, but our metabolisms probably require a certain amount of solid food. There are animals we could hunt, but we don't have weapons. Right now, we need food for today and the near future. There must be enormous stores of packaged food available for the taking. I mean, how many humans are left, anyway? Can't be too many. We could walk over to the neighbors' place and, assuming they no longer need it, round up some canned and dried items, along with utensils or anything else we need for a household. I suppose we could even take over their house."

"No thanks. That feels creepy. I'm used to the native way; we've been living it for two years. Let's stay right here. Besides, if we're truly going to rebuild culture, we're going to have to learn how to live off the land without relying on civilization's garbage, right?"

"Right. But at least scavenging takes care of our immediate needs until we can figure out a few things."

"Okay, but let's not forget to figure those things out."

"You bet. And as soon as possible, let's walk into town to see if there are any unchanged humans. I'm curious to talk to a survivor. I seem to remember a few locals came to your rituals."

"Not many. But yeah. I'm curious, too. Plus, if we find anyone, we can show off our daughter."


[44]

When Haw linked to the rhizome, her parents had no way of predicting how long she might stay in a trance. Usually, they left her alone, but hunger and the urge to explore prompted an interruption. Dana touched Haw's shoulder and let her own tendrils slip into her daughter's flesh. Opening her eyes, Haw smiled.

Owen stepped out of the wigwam and figured the sun had started its descent from zenith. Despite the length of the summer day, which meant that plenty of afternoon light remained, he wanted to get going. He paced back and forth in front of the wigwam, humming. Meanwhile, Dana tried to persuade Haw to put on her moccasins. Owen heard whimpering from the shelter before the two emerged fully clothed. He hoisted Haw to his shoulders, and she wrapped her arms around his head for comfort.

They walked out of the woods and into the clearing. Owen's steps slowed as he neared the old house site. "Haw, honey, this is where Daddy used to live. Once there was a house here."

"What's a house?"

"A house is like a tipi or wigwam, but bigger, and usually stays in one place. My house was made from pieces of wood. Lots of wood. But it burned down."

"Why'd it burn?"

"Well... some men burned it down. Bad men," he added.

"Daddy, what are bad men?"

Owen frowned as he struggled to explain. "Well, you know how sometimes trees get sick?"

"Yeah..."

"The things that cause the sickness are kind of like bad men. Uh... they're things that hurt other things – that's what they do."

"Why do they do that?"

Dana, concerned and amused, looked at Owen, her face flickering with mixed reactions. Owen flashed an appeal for help, but she shook her head. Haw, the product of a mutualistic ecosystem, had no vocabulary for willful malignancy. Left to fumble on, Owen tried to extricate himself. "Different reasons, honey. It's kind of hard to explain. But these men were tree killers, I guess you could say. They were mad at Daddy, so they burned down his house. When you get older, I'll tell you the whole story."

"How much older, Daddy?"

"Probably a lot older."

"Why a lot older?"

Dana snickered and Owen felt desperate. "Because," he said.

"Because what, Daddy?"

"Because... because Daddy can't figure out how to explain it right now."

"Oh."

As they passed the house site, Owen was surprised to see the basement cavity filled with dirt. It looked as if someone had bulldozed the burnt debris into the basement, then plowed over it until it was level. Two of the basement walls protruded above grade, but the other two were gone, probably pushed into the cavity with the other remains. Owen felt relief, glad that he didn't have to see the partially burned bones of the Legionnaires among the ruins of his house. Instead, grass repopulated the site. He wondered who had manicured the disaster. Certainly not the fire department—after extinguishing the smolders they would have gone home. Everything had been cleared away: not only the house, but the barn, his truck, Dana's van, everything. The site lay clean and fresh, almost inviting.

"This certainly isn't how we left it," Dana said.

"No, somebody cleaned it up. Looks like they just plowed it all under. I suppose that meant there wasn't much left to save, if anything. I'm glad, though. I'd rather look at the place as a new beginning than tarnished remains."

"Yes. Maybe we should move the wigwam up here. Fewer bugs out in the open."

"True. Let's think about it while we walk over to the neighbor's place."

"Lead on."

At the end of the driveway they joined the dirt road that ran past Owen's property. Someone had dozed the old garbage piles further into the brush. Since then, weeds and grasses had colonized the heaps, fostering the look of giant middens. Haw sang as she rode on Owen's shoulders, nonsense syllables at first until Dana chimed in and they improvised a song.

"B-b-b-bad men, b-b-b-bad men, bad men, bad men, bad men, BAD!" They chanted together, loud and strident, until the giggles made them stop.

After a mile of walking, they arrived at a two-acre clearing. A modular ranch-style home stood about thirty yards from the road's edge. The rest of the open space consisted of grass that hadn't been mowed for weeks. Two small maple trees grew in front of the house; he didn't remember them, but he had been gone for over two years and he never spent much time on this property. These were the same neighbors who had taken him snowmobiling when his mother hoped to set him up with their daughter. The incident had embarrassed him, and he started avoiding the neighbors. As he took over control of his mother's farm, he had more cause to interact with these folks. They were decent neighbors, helpful when needed, but like most people in this part of the country, they kept to themselves. Looking around now, Owen saw no signs that they were still living in the house.

"Dana, do you mind waiting while I check it out first?" She nodded, and he transferred Haw to her shoulders. Haw squirmed, wanting to get down, but Dana made a definitive hushing sound that subdued her.

Owen approached the house. Struck by a thought, he detoured through the grass to one of the trees and put his hand on the trunk. He immediately recoiled and looked back at Dana. "It's them," he said. He replaced his hand and withdrew it again after a few moments. "Could be worse. They're confused but connected to the rhizome. They're not really fighting it." He shrugged and went up the steps of the house. The door was unlocked. After a few minutes he popped back out and waved them in.

Owen located some canvas bags and started to fill them with canned food from the shelves. A foul odor leaked from the refrigerator and he didn't bother to open it. The pantry shelves featured one-gallon glass containers filled with rice, noodles, and other staples as well as quart jars of home-canned food and an assortment of commercial tins. He remembered that the neighbors had been survivalists, gardening with dedication and storing away supplies for the long-awaited political or religious apocalypse. Five-gallon jugs filled with water lined the bottom shelf; they'd definitely need to find a reliable source once this supply was gone. Although there was a brook further back in the woods on his own property, he wondered about driving a hand well near the house site. Maybe he could scavenge the pipe and a pump somewhere. When Dana came in, Owen stood in thought, scratching his beard. Wordlessly, he handed her a couple of bags and stepped back from the pantry so she could browse. Haw ran around the house, touching everything.

"Hey, I've got an idea," Owen said. "Just keep packing." He left the kitchen and went back to the front door. Before he could inspect the shelves next to the door, he heard Haw making noise down the hall and ran to find her in the bathroom, splashing in the toilet. He was glad that the water was clean. He picked her up, dried her hands on a towel, and carried her back to the kitchen, putting her alongside Dana. "The toilet, of course. Help your mother, honey, she has a lot of bags to fill."

Owen resumed his inspection of the shelves that held various household items: bills, coins, framed photos of the daughter, grown up and with her own family, ceramic trinkets, then finally found what he was looking for – the keys to the truck, no doubt parked in the garage. "Be right back!" He called over his shoulder as he went down the hall and through the breezeway into the over-sized garage. The pickup was there, a new model 4x4 with only a few dents and heavy, cleated tires. Hopping in the driver's seat, he turned the key. It started right away and the gas gauge registered nearly full. He turned it off and climbed out, muttering their prayer, *"we give thanks for all the earth has given us."* He hoisted the old-fashioned garage doors, metal squealing in protest. When he finished, Dana and Haw stared at him from the breezeway entrance.

Dana had her hands on her hips. "What are you doing?"

"I was thinking that it would be a lot of work to haul all this stuff to our place but then I realized, you know, we can just use their truck."

"Sure. So, just like that, you're going to resume burning fossil fuels in exchange for a little convenience? Isn't that how we fucked things up in the first place? Do you think this decision merits some discussion? Or do we just pick up the old ways because we can?"

Owen felt ashamed and dropped his eyes from Dana's accusations. "Oh god, you're right. I didn't even think about it. I just went straight for the utility. Wow."

Haw pranced down the steps and eagerly ran around the truck, touching the body, examining the undercarriage and shiny components with excitement. "What is this, Daddy?"

"Uh, it's a machine, sweetheart. Called a truck. It rolls along and carries people and things, all by itself. Sort of."

"Can we roll along in it, Daddy?"

"Well now, I don't know about that. Probably not. It's a can of many worms, Haw."

Dana interjected, "I didn't say *no*, I said we should talk about it. Look, I found some crackers and peanut butter and a bottle of apple juice. Why don't we sit on the deck, eat a bit, and consider what we're going to do with the booty."

Owen looked relieved. "Good idea."

They trooped back through the kitchen and sat around the picnic table on the deck overlooking the two-acre backyard. Owen found a thick, illustrated Bible along with a dictionary that he put under Haw as a booster. Even with that, her head barely cleared the table. While Dana and Owen reacquainted themselves with the taste of peanut butter, Haw nibbled at the gooey cracker in front of her.

"Aren't you hungry, dear?" asked Dana.

"I ate with the trees," Haw said. Her relationship with food had always been different than that of her parents. After she stopped nursing from Dana's breasts, she relied more on the nutrients accessible through the mycorrhizal network than on the above-ground food-stuffs used by Owen and Dana. Sometimes she would dine with them, perhaps more for the communal sharing than out of urgent need. She enjoyed snacking on polypores and was mad about the wild berries, but nothing eaten by mouth seemed essential for her survival. To please her mother, she took another bite of peanut butter cracker, then made a face. "Yuck," she said.

Owen laughed so hard he spit out cracker bits, which set off a chain reaction of giggles from Haw and Dana. They washed down the snack with apple juice and even Haw took a gulp.

"So," Owen began, "light of my life, let's consider our position towards society and its debris. I understand your concerns, I think, and I basically agree with them. After two years of living an indigenous, handmade lifestyle, we've landed in an abundance of complicated, devious technology that's freely available to use or avoid. I use the word *freely* with caution. We have some choices. But we need an ethos to sort through the stuff – there's just too much of it. And you're right, some of it is dangerous."

"I love it when you say I'm right. But yeah, it's tempting to pick up the remnants like we never left. It's all familiar to us; we grew up with it. It'd be piss-easy to get right back on the machine life. Given the amount of stuff, we could drive cars, run generators, and all that. At least until we ran out of gas."

"Even then, there are enormous tanks full of gas, practically everywhere. Hell, there are storage tanks down in Portland that must contain millions of gallons."

"Right. So, what are we building here? Something out of Mad Max?"

"Definitely not. And gasoline is only one aspect of the whole thing. I mean, some technology is good. Books. We introduced pen and ink technology in the Thorn world because we thought it had value. I guess it's going to come down to just that: value. And value means a lot of things, not just utility. Sustainability has to be part of it."

"And sustainability has to include doing no harm to the world around us. Donna Haraway came up with the term *flourishing*. She used it as a means of evaluating the health of the *natureculture* system. She pointed out that ethics play a key role in the multispecies encounter—if that encounter is mutually respectful and rewarding, then it contributes to the flourishing of nature and culture. Isn't that what we want?"

"Absolutely. Well said. Flourishing... I love it. It gives us a place to start—everything we do needs to pass a mutualism test. We have to calculate, to the best of our ability, the costs and benefits of our actions, and evaluate them from an ecosystem perspective, not an individual or a human-first perspective. Flourishing has to include all beings."

Haw rotated her head from parent to parent as they spoke, listening and watching with keen attention. Then she yawned, crawled down from her seat, walked around the table and pulled herself into Dana's lap, curling up and falling asleep. Dana looked at her fondly, stroking the scruffy curls of her hair, humming softly. When Haw relaxed into light snoring, Dana turned back to Owen, her face as peaceful as their child's.

"In a way, her needs will guide us. She lives in two worlds and represents a new type of being. She forces us to think across boundaries. What's best for her is probably going to be best for us and the world."

Owen reached across the table and took Dana's free hand, cupping it under his own. "You're a wise woman; you know that, don't you?"

They linked eyes while tendrils extended from their fingers and commingled in flesh, enacting the intimacy of their evolved condition.

Owen broke the silence. "Here's another angle, though. Deleuze and Guattari wrote about pragmatics, a discipline they called rhizomatics or the science of multiplicities. In order to make a rhizome, they said that you need to experiment, in other words, there is no set prescription for finding the path into a rhizomatic way of being. Sometimes you just need to try things. However, they also cautioned that it's important to utilize criteria for action, and to apply those criteria before acting, not as afterthoughts. So, according to their ideas, anyway, we're on the right track: we need to identify our criteria and we need to do it before we commit to a course of action. But, we also need to experiment as we find our way forward, at least cautiously, and to remain practical."

"Hmm. Heady stuff, right? But I take your point. So, what does that mean to you? Practically speaking."

"I'm not sure it means just one thing; it's more suggestive than definitive. But remember when we first met, at that poetry reading that now seems a hundred years ago?"

"Of course. It's been an interesting century, but I'll never forget that night."

Owen smiled. "Well, one thing you said was that the products of human activity, all our creations, are just as natural as anything else in the world. Our technology is part of how we express our nature."

Dana interrupted. "Yes, but I didn't say that means those creations are desirable. Even cancer is natural."

"Sure. However, though we might recoil at the use of a machine because we equate it with a destructive culture, our decision whether to use such machines should be based on a rational evaluation. A genuine cost/benefit analysis. It's hard to imagine, for example, that driving the truck back to our place will precipitate an ecological crisis."

"Oh Owen, you're blinded by logic. Where do we draw the line? I'm more concerned about our psychological investment in these machines. Do we have the discipline to drive the truck once and never again?"

Owen stroked his beard. "I get that, I really do. But I also feel like we need to experiment to find our way forward. There are so many things we don't know how to do. And if we can't develop the discipline to follow our own limits, how far are we going to get, anyway? A lot of indigenous cultures adopted machine technology without sabotaging their core values."

"Yes, but the technology is addictive, and you know how that goes. Need I remind you that many of those same people ended up strung out on sugar and alcohol? Not to mention how many bought into the capitalist ethos and started pillaging the land."

"I hope we're not naïve about the temptations. I understand that they exist. We have to do better, that's all."

"So, you're proposing that we use machines as long as they're helpful, but when we cross some vague line, we park them and let 'em rust? That's your proposal?"

"No, we need to be more stringent than that. We do need some rules."

"Precisely my point!"

"But consider the pragmatics: we've just arrived in this world. We have nothing, except for what Dr. Chouinard left us. Our skills in living off the land are oriented to Thorn's world, where, let's face it, things were made very easy. I'm sure we can learn how to live a low-impact lifestyle here, but it's going to take some time. Meanwhile, there's an abundance of stuff that could help us while we learn what we need to know. If we don't use this stuff, I'm worried that we're exposing ourselves to unnecessary hardship or even compromising our survival. The ecology of this world is not as benign as Thorn's world. What would you do if you encountered a cougar, for example? Rare, but not unknown. Or a pack of coyotes? There are predators, the winters are long, it's a tougher environment."

"Cougars? Really? That's not a pleasant thought." Dana shuddered.

"It's not."

"Okay, so what **are** you proposing?"

"Well, there are a couple of extra cans of gasoline in the garage and the tank in the truck is full. It's only a few miles to Machias, where there is, or was, a lumber-yard, sporting goods store, hardware, all that. I propose that we drive there, pick up tools for gardening, carpentry, that sort of thing: no generators or power tools, just hand tools so we can cultivate and forage. Then we could add some bows and arrows, perhaps even a gun, though I'm not sure about that. And, oh yeah, we should stop by the library... I'm thinking that if we get enough lumber, which may take more than one trip, we can build a small cabin, if not to live in then at least to store tools and food. When the truck runs out of gas, we park it."

Dana scrunched her face up as she contemplated Owen's program. "Can we get horses?"

"Great idea! And goats, too, I know a farm not too far away where they had both. If they're still alive."

"Goats, really? Okay, I'm sold. You can drive your truck, Haw gets her ride, and we trade all that in for the promised land."


[45]

Resuming the salvage work in the house, they found several plastic storage boxes stuffed with clothes; they stacked the clothes on a bed and filled the boxes with food and secured them with straps Owen found in the garage. Already they felt the pull of human technology and its ingenuous solutions to problems great and small. Despite their misgivings, they agreed that there was little point in bringing food to their place without protection from rodents and other pests.

On the bottom shelf of the daughter's former room, preserved as a memorial to childhood, perhaps, Haw found a stuffed rabbit. Despite its worn fabric and lumps, the ears stood with pride. Haw wanted to keep it. The request gave them pause, but they didn't have the heart to say no. Meanwhile, they had moved on from food to other items, such as kitchen utensils, pots and pans, knives, carpentry tools, axes, saws, and shovels. Owen was stacking this bounty in the truck when Dana walked into the garage holding up a giant package of toilet paper rolls and a questioning look on her face. They burst out laughing.

Haw, sitting in the front seat of the truck, clutched her bunny. "What's that, mommy?"

"Ground-up trees, sweetie. Ground up, pressed flat, and rolled into thin little sheaves. All to wipe your bottom with instead of leaves or moss."

"Mommy, do we have to use the ground-up trees?"

"Not at all, sweetheart." Dana tossed the package in the house.

Loaded up, they drove away, stopping to shut the garage door. Before getting back in the truck, Owen looked at the trees in front of the house and prayed, "We give thanks for all the earth has given us, we honor those that came before, those who will follow... we offer hope that life continues, in all its beauty...."

It was near dusk when they rolled to a halt in front of the old house site. They made a neat pile of what they had salvaged next to the truck and, after selecting two boxes, Owen covered the rest with a tarp. Dana grabbed a box and headed to the wigwam, followed by Owen carrying the other box along with a roll of window screen. Haw toddled behind, clutching her bunny. At the wigwam, Owen cut a section of screen to go over the smoke hole and another to place in front of the door. He considered how this separated them from the world. But his species wasn't the only one in the Maine woods to seek refuge from mosquitoes and flies. After two years in an environment with few gnawing insects, he was less than eager to renew his acquaintance.

The parents had a restless night and they talked quietly in bed about the loot they had taken from the neighbors. It felt weird and not quite right, rummaging through the house, no matter how pragmatic. After a long discussion, they agreed to make one run to town, then return the truck to the neighbors' garage. Instead of building a cabin to live in, they would stay in the wigwam. Any lumber they got would go toward a shed for storing the most important tools and extra food. They also decided to visit the sporting goods store for hunting weapons, including a rifle, and sleeping bags. Then they would get by... or they wouldn't. If things got desperate, they could return to the Thorn world.

Keyed up and curious, they drove into the town of Machias early in the morning. Excitement became a solemn awe as they saw no signs of human life on the streets or in the buildings. It was a ghost town. Birds darted and perched, singing the same old songs, and former pets, now skinny and feral, slunk into the shadows as they drove by. Everywhere they noticed saplings standing in unexpected places, waving in the breeze and bursting with the new growth of the season. Some had rooted in the gravel at the edge of the road, a few crowded together in the landscaped meridians of parking lots, but the majority sprang from the once-manicured lawns in front of houses and offices. All about eight feet high, maple, birch, oak, hemlock, and spruce: the evolved forms of the human race.

They entered the unlocked door of the sporting goods store with caution, overwhelmed by the aisles of abandoned commerce. Light beamed through the plate glass windows in front, but as they worked their way through the store, the shadows grew into an oppressive gloom. Dana and Haw searched for the camping department while Owen headed to the hunting section. He found the gun case broken open; many slots were empty. This surprised him, though he realized that it shouldn't. Of course, others would think of weapons. He hoped that whoever got here before him had the same modest aim and only wanted tools for gathering food. Owen tried to remember the basics he had learned from his uncle, who occasionally had something useful to teach. He selected a .308 caliber rifle for bigger game and a double-barrel 12-gauge shotgun. He was tempted to grab a handgun for self-defense and a .22 rifle, but he resisted the urge. Two firearms were probably more than enough. He picked up a daypack and threw in a few boxes of ammunition. He saw no reason to take too much; he wasn't going to war.

The archery section seemed more relevant to their philosophy. He inspected the compound bows, which resembled dungeon machines; he didn't like them and he knew Dana wouldn't either. Instead, he chose a couple of recurved long bows, a heavier one for himself and a slightly lighter one for Dana, then he put the light one back and selected another heavy bow. He knew she'd be pissed otherwise. When he contemplated the arrows, he figured that they'd need a bunch of them. His past attempts at archery had featured many lost and broken arrows. Though he supposed that they could make their own, in time, he wasn't quite sure when that time would be. If they were going to learn to hunt with bows, they would need a lot of arrows, he was sure of that.

"Daddy, Daddy, look!" Owen heard Haw running through the aisles and turned to catch her before she barreled into him. She was wearing a black balaclava pulled down over her face, giving her an appearance both sinister and silly.

"Oooh," he said, "who are you and what have you done with my daughter?"

"It's me, silly Daddy," Haw replied as she pulled off the mask, proud of her deception.

Dana came around a corner carrying two backpacks. Both were stuffed to the brim with sleeping bags, down coats, snow boots, socks and the other sheltering items they had discussed the night before. As she saw Owen with his hardware, she raised an eyebrow. "Armed to the teeth, are we?"

Owen felt sheepish. "Well, tell me if you think this is over the top. The bows are good—they represent a technology renewable in every way. It's harder to hunt and less useful for self-defense, but it certainly served our ancestors for thousands of years. The two guns just seemed kind of basic. The rifle for big game, the shotgun for birds or... well... self-defense."

"No, that's what we agreed on. I'm okay with it. At least for now. But let's do this and get going. It's eerie, this taking stuff for nothing. I feel like we're on a heist."

"Mommy, what's a *heist*?"

"Sweetheart, that's when you take something that doesn't belong to you."

"What's *belong to you* mean?"

"Uhhh… yeah, good question. We'll have to figure out an answer to that later, because I forgot, you don't know about property."

"What's *property*?"

"Tonight, after dinner, we'll try to explain it, okay? Although who knows if that's a good idea. Perhaps one of those notions best left out of our value system, right?" Dana turned to Owen and he grinned.

They drove from the sporting goods store and headed across town to the lumber-yard. As they turned back onto the main street, they were amazed to see a car cruising toward them. The car, a new model BMW, slowed gradually as it approached. They came to a stop side by side. Owen rolled down the truck window and looked at the man in the car and nodded. "Hey," he said.

"Hey yourself. You must be new to these parts. Name's Derek. I'd offer to shake your hand, but I don't think I can reach that high. Hell, it's not like there's any traffic. Might as well meet all proper and like." Derek shut off the car and stepped out, motioning to his two companions to join him. From the back seat emerged two women, both with long blonde hair. They leaned against the car and waited for Owen to step down from the cab. The man was middle-aged with slightly graying hair while the women looked at least ten years younger. The second woman was pregnant.

Owen stuck out his hand and shook with Derek. "I'm Owen." He walked down the line and met Sara and Stephanie, who introduced themselves as sisters. By the time Owen finished greeting everyone, Dana emerged from the truck carrying Haw, walking down the line and joining the greetings.

Sara stared at Dana for a minute, before exclaiming, "Wait, wait, I know you! I went to one of your workshops, you know, about that tree and blood ritual."

Derek joined in, "Oh yeah, you're the one in the video! Wow! Where did you guys come from? Have you been hiding out somewhere? You look like you've been living in the bush." He pointed at the clothes they wore, their Dr. Chouinard tribal gear.

Stephanie, the pregnant one, was cooing over Haw, petting her and making faces, which Haw soaked up like sunshine, beaming back at her. "Oh, she's such a beautiful child!" Stephanie said to Dana. "I'm due in two months. Although it can't come soon enough!"

Dana laughed. "I understand. Do you have someone to help you with the birth?"

"My sister is a doctor."

"Yeah, sis, but I'm only an osteopath. Hardly an expert in obstetrics."

"Still, a doctor. Better than no doctor."

"Luckily, we have a complete hospital just down the road," Sara waved. "Abandoned, sure, but we figured out how to activate the back-up generator so if anyone needs emergency care, well, at least we have the facility."

Dana and Owen watched the sisters banter, clearly a fond habit. Derek returned to his first thought, "So where have you guys been? Do you understand what happened? Things really got fucked-up, huh? There's not a lot of survivors. We sort of wondered if that blood ritual might have something to do with it, because everyone we've met that lived through The Change also did that ritual. But I don't know, none of it makes any sense."

Owen scratched his beard, hardly knowing how to answer these questions. "Well, yeah, we've been in other parts, living off the land for a while. I grew up nearby, down the road, so when we got back, yeah, things were different. Nobody around, for one thing. We borrowed this truck and came down for supplies."

"Borrowed! That's rich!" Derek guffawed. "From a living human? No, I didn't think so. No need to tiptoe around it; most people are gone, and it doesn't look like they're coming back! They sure don't need their stuff no more. So, when we want a ride, we just take a car, drive it until it runs out of gas, then go 'borrow' another one. There's no shortage!"

Owen exchanged glances with Dana. "True... Anyway, I'm not real sure what happened, but I guess you might be right about the ritual. It probably did protect you against the... what did you call it... The Change?"

Sara interjected in an earnest, almost anxious tone, "But do you know what actually happened? It's hard to believe that people just turned into trees. That goes against everything I know about biology. But I saw—we all saw, with our own eyes—people stumble out of their houses, dig their feet into the ground and... and just transform! It was a nightmare!"

"Hell yes, man, it was fucking biblical. Excuse my language, miss." Derek bowed to Haw.

Sara, Stephanie, and Derek seemed like nice enough people, but Owen was reluctant to reveal his knowledge of what had happened. He could see from Dana's expression that she shared his reluctance. Best to pretend ignorance for now. There would be plenty of time to present the truth when they had a better sense of who they were dealing with and how to talk about it.

"So, Derek, you implied there are others around who didn't change? Nearby?"

"Well, not many. We're the only ones right in town. We're living in a house down on Fremont Street, just across from the University. It's a nice big house, I'm sure you could move in with us. Right, girls?" Derek turned to Sara and Stephanie and they nodded. "Or if you wanted, you could use the house next door, or across the street. Plenty to choose from! Come on, we can take you over there now and you can check it out."

Owen felt an urgency to slow down Derek's momentum. "That's a very kind offer. We would certainly like to visit and check it out, but we're living on my family land out in Cutler and I think we'll stay there for now."

Derek's face wrinkled in thought. "Wait a minute, that's not the place that burned down a few years back because of those fascist assholes, was it?"

"Yeah, that's the place." Owen scratched his beard again, worried about the exposure of small-town society.

"Well, shit, man, there can't be much left! You sure you don't want to stay with us, at least for a while?"

"No, really, that's very generous of you. We've got a good shelter there in the woods and we're going to start rebuilding. Actually, right now we're headed to the lumber-yard to get some materials."

"Oh yeah, there's still a lot there. Group down on the cove has been using it, but there's enough wood to build a whole town, I imagine. Hey, you might go talk to them. One of 'em is a carpenter, knows all kinds of things. We go down there every now and then and party. Real nice folks. From out West, kind of hippie types, but we don't mind."

An intuition crept up Owen's spine. "What group down on the cove? Which cove?"

Derek smiled. "Cove Road, right out of Cutler, the one that goes down toward Otter Point. Yeah, they've got a regular tribe going there, women, children, vans, school bus, all kinds of things. A busy bunch. You head down that way, you'll find 'em. Just ask for the guy named River. He's the builder."

"River, you say?"

"Yeah, funny name, huh? But you know those hippies. They all have names like that. Good folks, though."

Dana caught Owen's eye and with a glance told him that she was ready to move on. Owen nodded. "Well, Derek, Sara, Stephanie, we're going to get over to the lumber-yard so we can load what we want and get it back to our place. We've got a lot of work to do. But it's been very nice to meet you."

"Oh hey, you bet!" Derek said heartily, visibly forcing down his disappointment. "Sure you don't want to come over and have some lunch with us? We were heading down to the hospital to do another ultrasound on Stephanie, but we can do that later. Baby's healthy and all, but seems the last ultrasound was kind of weird, so we've been checking regular."

Sara looked at Derek with tight lips. "Derek," Sara said, "let these folks go about their chores. We have forever to get acquainted. And I don't think we should postpone the ultrasound."

Derek scuffed his feet and acted like a chastised child. "Okay, okay. Well, doctor knows best. But you folks come see us now. Can't miss it, right down Fremont Street."

"I know where that is. We'll be by, just as soon as we get squared away. Thanks for the invitation. And good luck with the ultrasound—hope things are okay."

They all shook hands, except that Stephanie gave Dana and Haw a hug. When they were back in the truck, heading to the lumber-yard, Dana let out a big sigh. "I don't know if I'm quite ready for socialization! That seemed really weird."

"Mommy, what's *socialization*?"

"Talking with other people, honey. Especially ones you don't know."

"Yeah, I know what you mean. Plus, I'm not so sure about that guy Derek."

"No shit! He was a bit of a yahoo, don't you think? Got on my nerves right away. Not sure what those women see in him, but I guess, given everything, maybe there isn't a lot of choice. But that guy he mentioned, River, any chance that's your old friend?"

"Mommy, what's a *yahoo*?"

"Oh dear, that's a word we never, ever use again. I hope. You know, Owen, we're going to have to watch our language. Especially now that we'll be seeing other people, right?"

"Definitely. And yes, I'm guessing that the River he mentioned is my old friend. I'm eager to go see. But let's get our wood and take all this stuff home. Tomorrow we can check it out. Sounds like he's not going anywhere."

[46]

The morning came with a wall of moist heat and dead air; they put water, food, and the stuffed bunny in a day pack and set off to find River and his tribe. Dana carried the pack and Owen carried Haw, that is, when she didn't insist on walking, which never lasted for long. Owen was impatient to see his friend, but he knew better than to force the rhythm of the family. Walking to Cove Road required two miles of strolling on level backroads; they would soon get there. No need to waste the gas or their values with the truck.

Yesterday, on the way back from the lumberyard, they took a detour to a farm where Owen thought they might find animals. When they got there, two horses stood in the pasture, munching grass. The barn door hung open to the field, allowing free access. As Owen, Dana, and Haw climbed out of the truck, the horses sauntered to the fence. Owen remembered goats at the farm, too, but he didn't see them. Run off, perhaps, or fallen prey to bears. Dana declared that it made sense to leave the horses where they were for now. Once settled and prepared, they could walk over and ride the horses back to their place. Meanwhile, the tack was stored out of the weather and the horses had plenty of grass. Owen thought that if they wanted to host animals, they should build at least a small barn and some fenced areas. Dana argued that the Indians didn't have barns for their horses and that ambitious building projects suggested more reliance on machines and civilization's leftovers. They resolved nothing, recognizing that the complex interplay of values and needs called for ongoing consideration rather than simplistic, impulsive decisions.

In the humid morning, as they walked along the road to the shore, Haw peppered them with questions about the horses. Their size and beauty captured her imagination and she couldn't stop talking about them. She wanted to ride a horse, just as she had wanted to ride in the truck. But the horses excited her in a way that the truck did not and her quest for details left Dana and Owen repeating what little they knew over and over.

Cove Road ended in weeds at the boundary of the state land reserve, the same one they had tried to save from logging. A hundred feet before the boundary marker, a gravel driveway sliced off into the woods. Parked on the shoulder they saw an old bulldozer and an equally battered fuel truck. A garish sign perched on top of a pole at the junction proclaimed, in a crude array of rainbow colors, "YEWTOPIA." Dana looked at Owen with an arched eyebrow and Owen shook his head, muttering, "Looks like River's work to me."

About two hundred yards down the gravel spur they found the encampment in a clearing overlooking the cove. The setting was typical for coastal Maine, a finger of saltwater stretching inland, held in check by granite ledges that formed their own fingers reaching into the sea. The water of the cove, clear to the gravel bottom, formed a greenish lens streaked with kelp and other strands of algae. An assortment of vehicles and small structures stood in line along the inland shoulder of the road. They spotted an old school bus with a stovepipe protruding from the roof. Weeds embraced the wheels, suggesting that it hadn't moved in a while, and painted on the side of the bus was a fading mural depicting a forest. Beyond the bus they saw a shed made from rough-cut lumber and two large step-vans, one painted with elaborate rainbows, unicorns, and stars whereas the other was covered with a colorful abstraction. Past that, Owen saw the incomplete frame of a barn.

Sitting in front of the bus in a folding chair, under the shade of an awning, was a woman reading a book to a child curled in her lap. She paused at the end of a page and looked calmly at Owen, Dana, and Haw, then put the child down and stood up.

Before any word of greeting, Haw squirmed powerfully on Owen's shoulders and broadcast directly in his ear. "Put me down put me down put me down." Owen obliged and Haw ran directly to the other child, who was slightly taller, and gave her a hug. The other child glanced at her mother, who nodded, then returned the hug. Haw stepped back and announced, "We're not yahoos." Owen and Dana grimaced with embarrassment, but the woman laughed.

"I'm sorry, she's not used to other people. Neither are we, much. I apologize for showing up unannounced, though I guess there isn't much choice about that these days. Anyway, I'm Owen, this is Dana, and that's our daughter, Haw. I was looking for a fellow named River, who I heard might live around here."

The woman wore dirty sweatpants and a torn long-sleeved hooded tee shirt but despite her worn clothes, she had a striking appearance with piercing blue eyes and black hair that hung to her waist. "You're not *the* Owen, are you? The guy we drove three thousand miles to see?"

Owen blushed. "Uh, could be, yeah. River said he'd come back, but he never said when. We lost touch. And then things got pretty crazy. We had to leave in a hurry. Just got back a few days ago."

The woman walked around the fire pit and gracefully gave Owen and Dana a warm embrace. "I'm Kris, River's partner. And that's our girl, Sage. She's three. Looks like she's made a new friend." Indeed, Sage and Haw were absorbed in each other, chattering and stacking up sticks and rocks as if embarked on a long-promised reunion project. Kris stepped back from Dana and inspected her. "I know who you are! You're the woman in that video. Glad to meet you; we must have watched it a dozen times, showing it to folks to spread the tree ritual. Anyway, welcome to our home. River went out fishing this morning, but he should be back soon. He'll be very excited to see you, Owen. After finding the remains of your house, we feared that you were dead."

"You saw that?"

"Oh yeah, that's the first place we went. We had a pretty tight commune out in Oregon and after River returned from Maine, he couldn't stop talking about the things that happened out here, both good and bad. He finally convinced us to make a pilgrimage, to find you, and to learn more about communion with the forest."

Owen nodded and smiled, happy to hear that River hadn't forgotten their time together. It occurred to him to resolve some lingering questions. "Is that your bulldozer up the way? Was it River that cleaned up the mess at my house, burying the debris?"

"No, that wasn't him. You mean graded flat with just the foundation sticking out? That's the way we found it. But we've only been here for a year or so."

"So, you guys were here when everything changed?"

"Yeah, River said that even if you weren't around that he loved this area and wanted to stay. Especially because it was so close to where his best friend had died. Garth, you know? Oh, of course you know, you were part of that. Anyway, it's so beautiful, it wasn't hard to persuade everyone. We found this land for sale. Too primitive for most folks, I guess. We pooled our money for a down payment and signed a contract for the rest. Looks like it's all ours now, whatever that means anymore."

"Yeah, a lot has changed."

"I love your outfits, they look Indian or something." She extended her hand toward Dana's sleeve, "May I?" Dana nodded and Kris rubbed the fabric between her fingers. "Oh, wow. What is this stuff?"

"Bark, mostly, with some other plant fibers. Not exactly sure. It was a gift."

"It's really cool. But come, sit and have tea while we wait for River. He and Quake, one of the other guys, went fishing for bass. Or, if you like, I could show you around the compound; you can meet the folks and see what we've done."

Dana and Owen wanted the tour, so the kids were extricated from their play and they followed Kris down the road, Sage holding Haw's hand as they did their best to keep up. At the barn construction site, a man and two women marked wooden beams in preparation for cutting. One of the women, tall and muscular, stepped forward and introduced herself as "Sunshine, Quake's partner." She waved to a boy of around ten years who sat in the corner, planing boards by hand, "That's our son, Superboy. Well, we just call him that 'cause he likes it. His real name is Fergus. He's got autism so he won't pay attention to you unless you get in his way." The other two adults were a pair, "Rufous with an 'o' and Brittany." Both Rufous and Brittany were short and plump, but like the others, they looked strong and tough.

They shook hands and Kris explained that Owen was *the* Owen. After some chat, the builders declared that they needed to return to their task if they were going to meet their goals for the day, but they promised to talk later.

As they walked back to the bus, Owen thanked Kris for the hospitality. "I admire your industry and fortitude. I mean, civilization as we know it just collapsed and you all pick up and keep going. That's a great attribute."

"Yes, it's wondrous," Dana added.

"Well," Kris replied, "we've always kind of lived outside the mainstream, anyway, so when things got weird, it wasn't a total crisis for us, you know? I mean, sure, we lost some family and friends, that was painful, but it didn't much change the way we lived. Back in Oregon, we were part of a community where people wanted to live outside of power grids, commerce networks, and the whole capitalist system, really. As much as we could. And now, well, that's the way it has to be, isn't it?"

"We met some folks back in town, in Machias, that didn't seem quite so convinced."

"Oh, you met Derek and his ladies? They're not so bad – good at heart, I think. Sara is a doctor, which is really nice to have around, you know? They keep claiming that we're wasting our time here, that there's plenty of stuff to live on and why build things? They're a little bit... fatalistic, maybe? Like it's the end of the world and there's no reason for anything but having a good time. But we don't see it that way. It's not the end of the world. Maybe it's the beginning of a new one."

Dana and Owen exchanged glances and smiled. This was the kind of thing they were hoping to hear. Back at the bus, Kris pulled out two more folding chairs and told them to sit while she made tea. Sage took Haw inside to see her nook, a small space for her bed and toys. While Haw was introduced to Sage's artifacts, the three adults continued their conversation as they stared at the water in the cove. Kris told them that they recently salvaged fifty solar power panels. They'd already had six, which they used for florescent lamps, a cd player, and a battery charger, but they wanted to expand their ability to generate power. She said they'd located a small hydro unit and one of the main projects for the summer was to install it on the property. A nearby creek rushed over an outcrop back in the woods and could be harnessed to generate electricity, not only for domestic purposes, but ultimately to power a full wood and metal shop so they could fabricate anything, including replacement parts for their machines.

Kris said that when The Change happened and all the power and communication grids went down, River freaked about the possibility of meltdowns in nuclear plants. One of the first things they had done was go to the library and research the location of nearby nukes. They debated moving further north, away from possible contamination, but eventually they learned that nuclear facilities had automatic shutdown systems that would probably prevent meltdowns and off-site contamination. These studies led to other subjects and they ended up taking all the books and journals they could find on sustainable, low-impact technologies. Given their situation, they agreed that information itself was their most valuable tool. Everyone spent some free time studying a technical specialty and once a week, they convened to pool their knowledge.

A hearty cry came over the water, interrupting further recitation of the communal deeds. A skiff rowed around the headland, powered by an enormous black man who handled the oars like they were toothpicks. As the craft skimmed across the water, River, sitting in the bow, hoisted a clutch of fat fish. Owen felt a rush of excitement and joy. Waving his arms, he ran down to the shore to greet his friend.

"Fuckin' A, Owen. Dude!" River stood and leaped off the boat, agile as always, as Quake brought it in to the small dock. Ignoring Quake's cries about securing the boat, River ran to Owen. They grabbed each other in a hug, rocking back and forth.

"Shit, man, I thought you were dead!"

"No, man," Owen replied, slipping into River's vernacular, "just travelling. Things got more than a little tense after you left. In fact, I've got an incredible fucking story to tell. I'm guessing you have one, too. But come meet my family, man."

"You've got a family? Of course, you do, I knew some woman would snatch you up—you just had to look up from the page once in a while."

The reunion brought a radiant warmth to everyone. Dana smiled to see Owen happy, and she laughed at the boyish banter percolating through his exchanges with River. Both she and Owen were mostly loners, but they still missed good company. Despite the relaxed hippie mode of the commune, Dana appreciated the organization and practicality. She sensed the commitment attained without sacrificing humor or perspective. The way

Kris was with Sage, and with River, showed Dana that she could trust her. As she watched Owen and River's joyous reunion, Dana remembered some of her past friendships with women and how important they had been. Perhaps it was possible to have that again. She came out of her introspection when Kris sat down next to her and took her hand, holding it gently in her own. While the men urged each other to laughter and exclamation, the women watched with amusement. When they finally started their own conversation, it was a weaving together from the tangled threads of their lives.

The entire commune gathered late in the afternoon for a fish dinner. High spirits prevailed as they ate and talked while the long summer evening lingered on the land. Dana recited a poem and the listeners begged for more, which she obliged, pleased at having a new audience that whooped and cheered her efforts. River set up a backpacking tent for them on the barn platform and they slept all night and through the dawn, exhausted from the intensity of social exchange.

When they woke, they were called to a group breakfast wherein everyone gathered at the front of the bus. Sunshine stood and in a solemn voice invited them to become members of the commune. This was seconded by hearty applause. Owen and Dana looked at each other, flattered and embarrassed. With the slightest flickering of facial muscles, they shared with each other what was in their hearts.

Dana nodded at Owen and he addressed the group. "We're humbled by your invitation. We already feel a love and friendship with you that's a true blessing. But I think we will decline your invitation. Not out of disinterest or rejection, because we hope to share our time and energy with you, build with you, celebrate with you, work with you to plant the seeds of a new human culture. But consider this: we're already your neighbors! It's hardly two miles through the woods to our farm. We want to rebuild there, to reclaim that place. Not as a way to separate from you, but as a way to expand the idea of community that you've started. So: no to living on the cove but yes to being together! I hope you understand."

River spoke. "Man, you always were an eloquent dude. Almost as eloquent as your wife, eh? Anyway, I get it. I think it's great. I know you've got a lot of history up there and it's a good thing to reclaim, make it your own all over again. Long time coming, my man, long time coming."

Kris smiled at them. "And I think it's safe to say that if you want help with anything, you should call on us. Like, if you need stuff built, or whatever, we're gonna be there."

Quake bellowed, "Oh YEAH!"

Full of good cheer and promises of another social feast as soon as possible, Owen, Dana, and Haw hugged, kissed, and said goodbye and walked back along the roads and paths to their place. It was agreed that in two days River and a few others would come up and help them put up their shed and consider plans for what else they might need. Owen relished the reconnection with his friend, yet he was even more thrilled to be part of founding a human network that resembled the rhizome, a cooperative biological link to sustain and nurture the spirit. They talked about that all the way home, feeling hopeful that a rebirth of human culture was not impossible. They also answered the endless questions from Haw about everything. Sage had given her a child-sized backpack, and Haw proudly marched along, when she wasn't tired, with the head and ears of her stuffed bunny protruding through the unzipped opening.

The next day, in preparation for the work crew from the commune, Owen walked the periphery of the clearing, mulling over where to locate things. He thought about putting a small barn over the old house site, but worried that horses might sense the restless ghosts buried underneath. No, they could put the barn on the other side of the driveway. Over the house there should be a tree, preferably a white ash tree to stand alone and mighty, a tree to reclaim the profane ground and make it hallowed. The work of time, time beyond his own lifespan, but good work, nonetheless.

He wandered into the woods and sat down, leaning against a sapling. He extended his tendrils into the soil and tuned in to the rhizome. With a shock he realized that the tree he leaned against was a spirit known to him. It was the transformed remainder of his uncle. It groaned in a steady rhythm of sorrow, rolling in slow earth tones, an outpouring of grief and regret. He knew, as he accessed the consciousness of this transformed being, that it had been his uncle who had buried the house site, who had done everything he could to cleanse and repair the land that was also part of his own family's legacy, however tainted it had become by his own deeds. Owen sensed that his uncle was living an atonement, accepting the embrace of the rhizome consciousness, letting go of his shallow ego, his narcissistic ways, his life of suffering that had tortured and twisted him. Owen observed this flow of grief and directed his own forgiveness into the rhizome pathways. Whatever had happened between them was over, long over, and would not come back. He was done with it. Be at peace, he thought, be at peace.

When he moved his awareness past the uncle tree, further into the rhizome, away to the other trees that had once been human, he encountered many souls relaxing into the peace of grief. However, far too many thrashed and resisted, filling the woods with the echoes of anguish. A lot of work was left to do.

# BIBLIOGRAPHY

I relied on a variety of sources to imagine the realm of this story. Legitimate science and philosophy are incorporated, although twisted through speculation to satisfy my own ends. For those interested in the concepts and quotes, here are the core texts:

Blake, William, *The Poetical Works of William Blake*, Oxford University Press, London 1938

Borges, Jorge Luis, "The Library of Babel," *Collected Fictions*, translated by Andrew Hurley, Penguin Books, New York 1998

Damasio, Antonio, *Self Comes to Mind: Constructing the Conscious Brain*, Vintage Books, London 2012

Davies, Sioned, translator, *The Mabinogion*, Oxford University Press, Oxford 2008

Deleuze, Gilles, and Guattari, Felix, *A Thousand Plateaus: Capitalism and Schizophrenia*, translated by Brian Massumi, University of Minnesota Press, Minneapolis 1987

Eco, Umberto, *From the Tree to the Labyrinth: Historical Studies on the Sign and Interpretation*, translated by Anthony Oldcorn, Harvard University Press, Cambridge 2014

Filotas, Elise, et. al. (2014), "Viewing forests through the lends of complex systems science," *Ecosphere*, volume 5(1)

Gilbert, Scott, and Epel, David, *Ecological Developmental Biology: Integrating Epigenetics, Medicine, and Evolution*, Sinauer Associates, Inc., Sunderland, Massachusetts 2009

Greene, Brian, *The Hidden Reality: Parallel Universes and the Deep Laws of the Cosmos*, Vintage Books, New York 2011

Haraway, Donna J., *When Species Meet*, University of Minnesota Press, Minneapolis 2008

*Manifestly Haraway*, University of Minnesota Press, Minneapolis 2016

Joyce, James, *Finnegans Wake*, Penguin Books, New York 1999

Jung, Carl G., *Man and His Symbols*, Doubleday, New York 1969

Kohn, Eduardo, *How Forests Think: Toward an Anthropology beyond the Human*, University of California Press, Berkeley 2013

Landry, Susan T., "The Invention of Poetry," *Balancing Act 2*, Littoral Books, Portland, Maine 2018

"The Sisters," unpublished

Marder, Michael (2012), "Plant intentionality and the phenomenological framework of plant intelligence," *Plant Signaling & Behavior*, 7:11, 1365-1372

Randall, Lisa, *Warped Passages: Unraveling the Mysteries of the Universe's Hidden Dimensions*, Harper Perennial, New York 2006

Simard, Suzanne, et. al. (2012), "Mycorrhizal networks: Mechanisms, ecology and modelling," *Fungal Biology Reviews 26*

Simard, Suzanne, and Durall, Daniel M. (2004), "Mycorrhizal Networks: a review of their extent, function, and importance," *Canadian Journal of Botany* 82

Solé, Ricard, and Goodwin, Brian, *Signs of Life: How Complexity Pervades Biology*, Basic Books, New York 2000

Tsing, Anna Lowenhaupt, *The Mushroom at the End of the World: On the Possibility of Life in Capitalist Ruins*, Princeton University Press, Princeton 2015

**James M. Wright** worked for many years as a psychotherapist and wilderness guide. Currently he lives on the Maine Coast where he reads, writes, walks in the woods, and builds skin-on-frame kayaks. He is the author of a novel, *The Gorge of Despair*, and a work of non-fiction, *Mirror of Beasts: Episodes of a Reflected Ecology*. He has published essays and reviews in various journals, including *Shaman's Drum, Orion*, and *Circles on the Mountain*.